Beyond Lies London

School Court

Ermine Tower

Court

Main Gate

School Yard

Sable Tower

Jackernapes Arena

THIS BOOK
BELONGS TO:

'With gorgeous story-telling and magical illustrations,
a new heroine has arrived on our bookshelves. I adore Jack Joliffe
and am sure kids will too – she's funny and feisty as hell!'
Mel Giedroyc

Praise for other novels by Henry Chancellor:

'A crackling, magical read'
Waterstone's Books Quarterly

'Gripping… highly readable and original'
Sunday Times

'An irresistible adventure in a world of dust,
magic potions, missing jewels and stuffed animals'
Publishing News

First published in Great Britain 2021 by One Line Books.

Typeset and designed by Come Hither Design.

Printed and bound in Great Britain by TJ Books Limited, Padstow, Cornwall.

Text and illustrations copyright @ Henry Chancellor 2021

A CIP catalogue record for this book is available from the British Library.

ISBN 978-1-8382813-0-4

MIX
Paper from
responsible sources
FSC® C013056

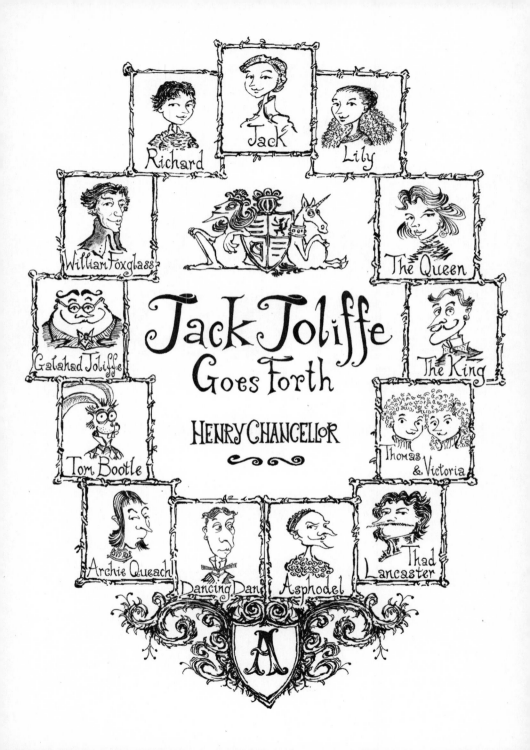

Richard

Jack

Lily

William Foxglass

The Queen

Galahad Joliffe

The King

Tom Bootle

Thomas & Victoria

Jack Joliffe
Goes Forth

HENRY CHANCELLOR

Archie Queach

Dancing Dan

Asphodel

Thad Lancaster

For Esme, who read this first. Sorry it took so long.

An Introduction

MY **NAME IS JACK** and let me tell you about myself. I'm twelve years old. Not short, neither am I tall, and I'm thin, sort of bony thin rather than starving thin. And I'm a girl. Why am I called Jack? I don't know. That is one of the many mysteries in my life. Another is that if you saw me, the first thing you'd notice is my lack of hair. For some reason my hair doesn't grow and it never has — at least not properly. It sort of sprouts in patches and gives up in others, looking scraggy and weird. Which is why I keep it shaved. That way it doesn't frighten people so much. And it's also the reason why I'm often mistaken for being a boy, along with my name.

The last thing you should know about me is that my parents died in a car crash when I was six months old. Ever since I've lived with a pair of elderly guardians, Oscar and Phil. Oscarina and Philomena are their full names, and they were friends for forty years. Oscar had once been a cook at St James's Palace, and she was a little bit like a mole. Round and lumpy, with large hands and terrible eyesight, she was forever fussing over things like ants in the kitchen and moths in the cupboards. Phil had also once worked at St James's Palace, doing what exactly I never knew. She claimed she'd once been a great beauty and danced with kings, though nowadays she wore long flowing dresses and didn't dance with anyone. I got the sense that she had been vaguely important in some way. She certainly had the attitude of someone important. She would lie around on the sofa all day wearing a hat, spouting poetry and saying things like:

'If you can't be bothered going to school, Jack, don't. You're far better off lying in the grass and counting the clouds. School will teach you nothing useful.'

'Actually school *will* teach you something useful,' said my headmistress, looking a little surprised when I told her this.

'But why wouldn't you want to do nothing? Cats do nothing. Dogs do nothing. *Frogs* do nothing. The only animal that ever went to school was a fish, and look where that got them!'

'Animals don't have to learn to read and write, as you well know,' replied my headmistress.

'Balderdash! Why is it the rule to go to school?'

'Because that is the law of the land,' said my headmistress sharply. 'Rules are made to help children, not hinder them.'

'Balderdash!' declared Phil again. (She really did use words like that.) 'Rules are made to keep children silent and afraid. Rules are for fools!'

You see what I mean? It was sort of hard not to agree with her. Only Phil didn't want me to agree with her either. I think she rather liked me asking questions. Answers were less important.

But there was one rule. Always be nice to Mr Foxglass.

Every year on my birthday we had a visitor and his name was William Foxglass. William Foxglass was tall and wide-shouldered, and always wore a long blue coat with a high collar and large brass buttons. He had thick black hair and thin leather gloves, which he never removed, and he carried a battered brown briefcase. I suppose you might call him interesting looking, though he was quite handsome, in a foxy sort of way.

'Hello Jack,' he said, shaking my hand formally. 'How are you?'

'Very well, thank you very much,' I replied, because it was true.

Mr Foxglass's hazel-coloured eyes glinted. He watched me carefully.

'So you're happy?'

'I am.'

'Certain?'

'Yes.'

'Excellent,' he said, and he smiled, or maybe he didn't, it was hard to tell, as William Foxglass had one of those mouths that sort of went up at one end and down at the other. 'Keep on smiling, Jack, and the world will smile back.'

I sensed that Mr Foxglass was very important. His approval was definitely important.

After lunch William Foxglass and Phil would sit beneath the apple tree at the end of the garden while Oscar and I washed up.

'What are they talking about?' I asked, watching them through the window.

'Oh, just the usual, I expect,' Oscar replied.

That meant palace business. Phil was always referring to palace business in a top-secret kind of way, and I guessed Mr Foxglass probably had something to do with all that.

'What did Phil actually do at the palace?'

Oscar smiled vaguely, and peered at me through her thick spectacles.

'My dear, I often ask myself the same question.'

'So she's never told you?'

'Oh she's told me all right. But as you and I both know, nothing's ever straightforward with Phil, is it? Sometimes I wonder if it's all balderdash,' she said with a wink. 'But you never heard me say that.'

I watched as William Foxglass and Phil went on talking until the evening shadows stretched across the grass and they were nothing more than a pair of silhouettes against the sky. Then Mr Foxglass would leave, always without his briefcase, and we would go out for a pizza to celebrate. I guessed the case must have been full of money, and quite a lot of it, because Oscar and Phil were always very cheerful after that.

So that was how the first twelve years of my life whizzed by. Whizzed is perhaps the wrong word, because it wasn't exactly exciting. But I wasn't bored. I grew up. I went to school sometimes. I probably had a bit of an attitude and I definitely used some peculiar words. But I was loved. That's all you need to know. We didn't have any enemies.

At least, that's what I thought.

⋰∿⋱ 2 ⋰∿⋱
Tragedy Strikes

('THERE, THERE, DEAR.'

The detective named Sandra handed me a tissue as I gulped down my tears. We watched in silence as the undertakers carefully lifted the two coffins off their shoulders and set them down in the centre of the church. There they were. Oscar and Phil, my beloved guardians. Gone. Just like that.

⤳ 3 ⤲
Abel Goodnight

'**S**O YOU HAVE NO REASON** to suspect anyone?'

I was sitting with Sandra the detective in the police station, directly after it had happened. I shrugged. For a start, I wasn't certain about the police. It was that 'rules are for fools' thing. The police liked rules, didn't they? Rules and uniforms… I suppose Phil's opinions had rubbed off a bit. Sandra smiled and tried again.

'Is there anyone you can think of who might've wished them harm?'

I made a show of thinking hard. Well, the milkman was always complaining he was never paid. Then the lady from the council said I should be going to school more. And then there was Mr

Boyne at the top of the lane, who was very angry to come home and find we had driven in circles all over his garden, smashing his gnomes and his dinosaur arrangement, which... There's no point describing it; whatever you're imagining is probably right. But it wasn't Phil's fault, because she wasn't driving – I was driving, and she was teaching me, except Philomena's idea of a driving lesson was to sit in the back reciting poems about riding to market on cock horses and piebald mares while I tried to work out which was the brake. She wasn't going to bother to tell me which pedal was which, or any other rules of the road... I had to find it all out for myself.

'Anyone at all?' repeated Sandra the detective.

There was one man. The man who came by one evening last week. An enormous man in an old brown overcoat with a greasy hat jammed on the back of his head. He had hands like baseball mitts and smelled strongly of bonfires. And there was something odd about his eyes. His pupils didn't seem to be quite the right shape.

'Bingo,' he muttered quietly to himself when he saw me coming to the front door.

'No, it's Jack,' I said.

The man grinned, the matchstick between his teeth sliding from one side to the other.

'You're a funny one, aren't ya, missy?'

'Am I?'

He climbed back into his large black truck.

'Bingo,' he repeated with a smirk.

'Someone said bingo once,' I said.

Sandra the detective stared at me like I was winding her up.

'*Bingo?*'

'Yes. Like "bingo, I've found it".'

The man who had said bingo was called Abel Goodnight (so he claimed). He supplied logs and charcoal, and lived in the forest over the way. He said he'd never been to our village before. That wasn't surprising. It was so well hidden in the deep lanes you might easily miss it. Most people did. Perhaps Abel Goodnight said bingo because he'd found it at last, but I had a feeling it wasn't that. Phil had shuddered when he'd pressed his grubby card into her hand. Abel Goodnight's thick lips had stretched into a grin. Yes, he seemed to be saying. Yes, that's right. It's me.

'And did your guardians have any reason to suspect that this

Abel Goodnight might be looking for them?' asked Sandra.

They most certainly did. That night there'd been a big argument, which was odd, because Oscar and Phil never normally argued about anything. I could hear it from my bedroom.

'But how can you be certain, Philomena?'

'His eyes, Oscar dear, his *eyes*. Couldn't you tell? And that *smell*.'

'Just because someone smells of bonfires doesn't mean—'

'It might mean everything. We mustn't panic. I shall call William in the morning.'

'And tell him what? I don't understand—'

'Of course you don't, Oscarina, because you never have. It's *her*. Don't you see?'

'What are you talking about?' I asked.

They looked up abruptly, shocked to see me standing in the doorway.

'Nothing,' Phil lied. 'I think you should go back to bed, dearest child, it's very late.'

'What's the problem with Abel Goodnight?'

They looked at each other.

'There's no problem with Abel Goodnight,' said Phil. 'Why d'you ask?'

'You sound worried about him.'

'We're not worried about him.'

'Then why are you talking about him?'

'We're not.'

This was a new experience for me. For the first time in my life I knew they were both lying. I didn't like it at all.

'Well?'

Sandra the detective stared at me across the table.

'I think perhaps they did,' I said, knowing that now I was lying too.

'What else can you remember?'

Everything, because there was no sleeping after that. Oscar and Phil kept on whispering and I couldn't really make out what they were saying. Eventually they stopped. It was almost two o'clock in the morning, and I was still wide awake. I remember going downstairs and taking a trifle out of the fridge that Oscar had made, and standing at the kitchen window eating it. I looked out onto the back garden, the meadow and river beyond. In the moonlight everything was a jumble of dark blue shadows. All was still. And yet as I stood there, I sensed I was being watched. I just had that feeling...

Then I heard something. The rattle of the letterbox. I walked through into the hall and looked at the front door. There it was, rattling. Someone was pushing it from the outside. Who was that? Obviously not the postman, it was the middle of the night... I stared at the rattling letterbox. This was a little frightening. And then I heard a voice. It was a gruff, growling sort of voice.

'Go round the back. There's bound to be a window open.'

I was scared now. I quietly went back into the kitchen and put down the trifle bowl. As I did so I heard scrabbling above me. Someone was on the roof! When I say someone, it was more like some *thing*, as it was definitely scrabbling, and it must have jumped up there somehow... Then I heard a window smash. That was my bedroom window, which was above the kitchen. Whatever it was was in my bedroom!

My heart was hammering now. I went to the back door, slipped out as silently as I could, then stood beside the wall, panting in terror. What could I do? Someone was at the front of the house.

Something else was upstairs in my bedroom. If I ran out onto the lane I'd be seen; if I ran away down the garden, I'd been seen too… I needed somewhere to hide, right now, and right here. And the only thing right here was a water butt. A big green water butt, with a wooden lid. So I lifted up the lid and climbed inside. And if that sounds like a crazy thing to do, it was, because the water was black and dirty and freezing cold… but I was glad I did, as the next second the side gate smashed open.

'She's still here, I smell it,' growled that low voice. Heavy footsteps approached. I sank down a little further into the black water, trembling in the darkness. The footsteps stopped right in front of me.

'Come out, little mouse, wherever you are. I know you're here.'

Trying very hard not to panic, again I did the only thing I could think of. Taking a deep breath, I slipped silently down into the black water, as deep as I could. My fingers brushed against a concrete block at the bottom and I held onto that. Suddenly I heard the lid of the water butt being lifted off, and I dared to look up. There was a wobbly silhouette against the moonlit sky. I wondered if I was dreaming, because the silhouette… well, it wasn't exactly; it was more like… It stared down into the black water. I stared back. Then something brushed the surface, bursting the silhouette into a thousand ripples. The lid thumped on again and the footsteps thundered away. I counted to five and could hold on no longer. I broke the surface, gasping, and listened. That growly voice was out in the road again.

'You prize noggin, what did you have to break the window for? Look at that! And that!'

I dared to lift the wooden lid and spotted the neighbours' lights coming on.

'Quick!'

A big engine started and a door slammed. I listened as it sped away.

I blinked again. Sandra the detective was still staring at me. I looked at the cup of water on the grey table. Was I supposed to tell her all that?

'I can't remember much,' I said. 'But I think… maybe some sort of wild animal did it.'

'A wild animal?'

I nodded. Whatever it was had scrambled onto the roof, smashed my bedroom window, and scared Oscar and Phil to death. Literally. They both had heart attacks and died on the spot. There was not a mark on them.

'And the man you saw. What did he look like?'

I hesitated. This was not going to be easy.

'I think he was wearing a mask.'

'What sort of mask?'

'He had sticking-up ears, a long nose and very large teeth.'

Sandra stared at me hard. A mask would be the obvious conclusion.

'And he had claws. Large hairy claws. As well.'

Sandra smiled sympathetically. I could tell what she was thinking. I was in a state of shock. I was going to need a lot of counselling. And with no money or relations, I needed to be put in a children's home as soon as possible.

ᔰᔰ 4 ᔰᔰ
Goodbye

W**E FOLLOWED THE COFFINS** out into the graveyard. Away from the main group of mourners I noticed some odd people standing to one side, keeping themselves to themselves. They were all wearing long coats of different colours like William Foxglass's. One of the women had dyed blue hair and a couple of men were wearing bowler hats. I supposed they must have been friends of Philomena's, for they all seemed a little like her.

'Ashes to ashes, dust to dust…'

The vicar smiled kindly at me. I looked down at the two coffins, side by side. One short and wide, the other long and thin. I picked up a handful of dirt in each hand.

'Goodbye Oscar,' I said to myself. 'You always told me you were very boring, but you weren't, and I loved you.' I threw a handful of earth down, then turned to the other. 'Goodbye Phil. Rules are for fools, you said. But there's one rule that applies to everyone. And now, I'm afraid, you're dead.' It was a terrible poem, but it was the best I could do in the circumstances. I threw the other handful of earth down. Bang it went on the wooden coffin lid.

'I loved you both. So much,' I said out loud.

'Oh!' Sandra dissolved into sniffles.

It was strange how numb I felt. Perhaps I should have shed a few more tears, but somehow I didn't feel like crying. I just felt... guilty. Because somehow I knew that whatever had happened to my beloved guardians was my fault. I should have been down there in a coffin. There should have been three coffins in that grave. I should have died too.

Except I hadn't.

~~~ 5 ~~~
A Strange Event

LATER, IN THE PUB, everyone was milling about eating sandwiches and drinking cups of tea.

'So Mr Loveday – the lovely man who runs the children's home – will come at three thirty to take you over and help you settle in,' said Sandra, gobbling cheese sandwiches like they were about to be taken away. She'd said this twice already. 'And I'll be on hand if you need anything else, Jack. We're all here to help.'

'I think I'll just wander about a bit,' I said, anxious to get away.

'You do that, love. Get some air. Good idea.'

I walked around the pub in a sort of daze. It was one of those old pubs with low sagging ceilings and lots of little rooms and dark corridors all jumbled together. Whenever anyone saw me, they smiled sadly and turned away. No one knew what to say. What could you say? Nothing, really. I wanted to find the odd–looking people I'd seen at the funeral in the colourful long coats, but they seemed to have already left. I stared out at the sunlit garden towards the wooded hills in the distance.

'Oh she's definitely still here.'

'Good.'

'I told her you'd be coming to pick her up. She definitely knows you're coming.'

'Good.'

I stopped in the corridor and listened to Sandra's voice. This was obviously Mr Loveday from the children's home. He was early. All I could see of him was a big shadow in the mirror. For some reason I didn't turn the corner, I just stood there, listening as Sandra went on.

'She's had a terrible time, poor little thing. Still in shock. It hasn't really sunk in yet I don't think.'

Sandra gave a nervous laugh. Mr Loveday grunted.

'Between you and me, Mr Loveday, she's not the easiest. Doesn't care much for authority.'

'Oh yes?'

'Her guardians were very alternative, you see. I don't want to speak ill of the dead, but I think she's hardly been to school. Maybe that's because of her other problem. You know.'

Mr Loveday didn't know, and neither did I.

'She's got no *hair*,' Sandra whispered loudly. 'That's why she wears that funny hat. You know how cruel kids can be.'

'Ah.'

'And she told me it was a wild animal that did it.'

'Did she now.'

'I know. I thought she was joking at first. Only way to make sense of it, I suppose. I just ignored it. If that's what she wants to believe, let her believe it, poor little love. I'd say nothing if I were you.'

Mr Loveday grunted again and rattled his keys loudly. Actually he had been rattling his keys all along.

'I'd like to come and help her settle in if you don't mind,' said Sandra.

'Best give it a couple of days, Detective.'

'The thing is, there's no other family. No one at all.'

'She's got me now, ain't she? I'm her new family.'

I don't know how I got there but I was already out in the garden and running down the path towards the trees. I wasn't going to be Mr Loveday's new family. I wasn't going to be passed around like an unwanted present. If no one wanted to look after me, then I'd... I didn't know what I was going to do, something–

'Jack! Jack, wait!'

I turned and saw a tall figure leap over the gate and chase down the path towards me, waving his arm aloft. My heart leapt. It was William Foxglass! I stopped. At long last, a friendly face. William Foxglass caught me up and stared at me breathlessly.

'Oh Jack, I'm so, so sorry. Are you okay? Of course you're not. Come here.'

I couldn't pretend any longer. Before he knew it I flung my arms around him, tears rolling down my cheeks. I just had to hug someone, and William Foxglass...

'What a business,' he said, gently patting me on the shoulder. 'Tell me what happened.'

Tell him what happened? That felt... I don't know... Anyway I did. We sat down on a bench beside the river and William Foxglass listened, sort of frowning and smiling in that wonky way of his.

'And how much of this did you tell the detective?' he asked when I'd finished.

'A bit,' I said, wiping my eyes. 'She didn't believe me.'

'I'm not surprised.'

'But you do, don't you?'

'Oh I believe you, Jack. Absolutely.'

That was a relief. I watched him a moment. He had a very foxy face, did William Foxglass. You didn't quite know what was going on behind those hazel eyes. He stared back at the pub.

'I think perhaps the time has come for me to tell you a few things,' he said quietly. 'But let's not talk here. Let's find somewhere a little safer.'

Safer? Were we in danger?

Already William Foxglass was marching back down the path. I ran to catch him up, nervous now, because I had no idea what he was talking about, except he was serious, and therefore I'd better stick by his side.

'Where is this Mr Loveday?' he asked.

'He's waiting for me inside. I'm *not* going into his home, Mr Foxglass. You can't make me.'

'Obviously not, Jack. But you can't run off and live in the woods either.'

'Why not? I could. Easily.'

'Well I'd much prefer it if you didn't. At least, not those woods,' he said, glancing across the valley.

I didn't understand. Mr Foxglass opened the back door of the pub and I followed his tall shape down the corridor towards the bar. Suddenly he stopped and pressed a gloved finger to his lips.

We listened. I recognised the voice around the corner, still talking to Sandra the detective.

'Maybe I should go and find her,' said Mr Loveday, still swinging his keys impatiently.

'You don't think she's run away, do you?' Sandra asked.

'It's happened before,' Mr Loveday grunted. 'Sometimes they get a bit...' Suddenly he stopped swinging his keys and listened. In the silence I heard him sniff the air. 'Spooked,' he said.

'Spooked?' repeated Sandra, confused.

I looked at Mr Foxglass. This, it seemed, was what he wanted to know.

'Quick. Follow me,' he whispered.

Moving at speed, we threaded through the gloomy corridors towards the front door.

'Oh!'

I couldn't help that. Through the window I caught a glimpse of a huge shape standing outside, waiting. Again I smelt that vague smell of bonfires, and saw a matchstick sliding between his lips... It was Abel Goodnight, no question. Mr Foxglass stared at the big man a moment.

'Right.'

Back we went through the dark corridors towards the garden...

'Oh!'

That was me again, I couldn't help it. Through the frosted glass there was another man, exactly like Abel Goodnight, now standing beside the back door... Mr Loveday?

'Precisely,' whispered William Foxglass. 'This is what I was worried about.'

We turned and retraced our steps, and hurrying around a corner saw a waitress push through a swing door carrying a plate of sandwiches. Mr Foxglass abruptly ducked into the kitchen, strode past the curious chefs and straight out the back. Skirting around a line of bins he trotted down the small path to the road.

'Have they come for me?' I asked, struggling to keep up.

'So it seems.'

'Why?'

'I'll tell you later, Jack,' he said, marching past the line of cars to the end, where a very old green van was parked. It looked like a small loaf of bread on wheels, and on the side was a smudge that might once have been a royal crest.

'Hop in,' he said, doing the same. The cab was ancient, full of maps and old switches and brass dials, and above our heads was a bookshelf crammed with worn leather volumes, all with the same title, '*Field Guide to the Creatures of Albion, Ancient and Modern, 3rd Edition*'.

'This is the collector's van,' said Mr Foxglass, by way of explanation, which obviously was no kind of explanation at all. Especially when he started the wheezy old engine and I was sure I heard a distant bleat from the back.

'Now let's hope they don't see us, because this cranky old thing doesn't exactly– whoops!'

No sooner had we lurched forward than Mr Foxglass slammed on the brakes. Out of the pub in front of us stormed Abel Goodnight and Mr Loveday, who together looked even more identical and enormous. Luckily they were far too busy arguing with each other to notice us.

'You prize noggin!' roared Abel Goodnight.

'She never came passed me, Abel, I swear it!'

'What about the kitchen?'

'You was watching the kitchen–'

'No, *you* was watching the kitchen–'

'But Abel you said–'

'Get round there, you great twassock, or I'll break your blinkin' neck! She ain't escaping again!'

Mr Foxglass let go of the brake, and slowly and silently we began to roll back down the hill, watching them running in different directions around the pub. We freewheeled all the way to the bottom, then William Foxglass dared to start the engine again.

'That was close, wasn't it?' he grinned as we rumbled away. 'Though perhaps we should make absolutely sure.'

He unbuttoned his blue coat and I stared in amazement; inside was a patchwork of pockets filled with spikes, wires, hammers, ropes, even a bridle… Drawing out a small lace handkerchief he handed it to me.

'Would you mind wiping your face, Jack,' he said.

Wiping my face?

'It's rather important.'

I did what I was told, then handed him back the handkerchief.

'Thanks,' he smiled, and promptly threw it out the window. 'Let them chase that. Save the hardware for when we find ourselves in a proper scrape.'

~~ 6 ~~
Mr Foxglass's Proposal

WILLIAM FOXGLASS pulled into the empty supermarket car park and five minutes later we sat facing each other across a pair of steaming cups. Black coffee for him, hot chocolate for me. I leant forward and let that sweet chocolate smell flood my senses. Mr Foxglass watched with that strange lopsided smile of his.

'I suppose you must have a lot of questions to ask,' he said at last.

I did. Far, far too many, because although I was only twelve, I wasn't so daft as to go gallivanting over the horizon in the company of a man as strange as William Foxglass without asking a few questions. (Philomena always used phrases like 'gallivanting over the horizon'.) I looked at Mr Foxglass. I looked out at that peculiar green van. Where to begin?

'Who is Abel Goodnight?'

'Abel Goodnight is a werewolf.'

I stared at him blankly.

'And so is his brother, Mr Loveday. Abel Goodnight's very well known. About fifteen years ago he led an escape from their vault, and now there's about sixty of them wandering around out here. Abel Goodnight's extremely dangerous and certainly not to be trusted.'

A werewolf. Werewolves. Now I wished he hadn't said that. I wanted William Foxglass to be a normal, sensible sort of person. Not the sort of person who said things like that.

'Werewolves don't exist,' I said.

William Foxglass smiled.

'Oh they do, Jack. And they can be very unpredictable. They bear deep grudges and can suddenly turn violent for no reason. I suspect Abel Goodnight sensed that you all had something to do with the palace, which provoked him into a fit of rage. I dare say old Sybil Lupercomb would've been able to tell us. She was their keeper, you see. But unfortunately they ate her when they escaped.'

I stared into William Foxglass's foxy face, trying to read that strange expression of his. Was he serious?

'But I don't have anything to do with the palace.'

'Yes you do, Jack.'

Mr Foxglass delved into his long coat then slid a photograph across the table. There was a small, fat, jolly-looking man with neatly oiled hair and little gold-rimmed glasses. He posed nonchalantly before the palace, beaming a smile so wide it was difficult not to smile back.

'That's your uncle. His name's Galahad Joliffe. He was Runnymede Pursuivant, Inspector of Badgewinkles, Condor Bisque, and for thirty years he was also Phasma Argent, which is the official title of the Royal Keeper of Ghosts.'

I stared at the photograph.

'My *uncle*?'

'Your mother's older brother. Did Phil never mention him?'

I stared at the fat little man. I'd never seen him before in my life.

'Galahad Joliffe's been providing for you all these years. After your parents died, he entrusted you to the care of his old friends Oscarina and Philomena. Every year I brought a briefcase of money from the palace which was his gift to you. He would've liked to come himself, but unfortunately the delicate nature of his work always seemed to prevent it. So you had to put up with me instead,' he smiled, reading my thoughts. 'You don't believe me, do you?'

Of course I didn't. Surely Oscar and Phil would have told me this. And I certainly would have remembered a name like Galahad. 'Who are you, really?'

'I do various things at St James's Palace. If I told you my official title, you'd probably be even more confused.'

This was not much of an answer. I stared at the photograph.
'How can he be the Royal Keeper of *Ghosts*?'

'At the palace there are keepers of everything that has ever been imagined. I mean giants, dragons, fairies, snarks, hobs, goblins, ghosts, you name it. They're all real, all true. People these days think they're myths and superstitions; the sorts of things you read about in poems or see carved around the doors of old churches. But they're not. They're alive, and as much a part of these islands as the trees and rivers and mud. Some belong to the old world before the people came, when there was plenty of wilderness and forest to roam in, others are much more recent. They can be large, small, harmless, totally terrifying, and I don't think any of them feel at home in the modern world any longer, which is why we have to keep them hidden away from prying eyes. At St James's Palace there's been a long tradition of keeping them. And that is what your uncle has done. And I'm sure he hoped that, as his only relation, one day, around your sixteenth birthday, you would take over.'

It was an explanation of sorts. And I suppose it was quite convincing. Sort of convincing...

'The Royal Keepers of Albion are a very ancient and secret society,' William Foxglass went on. 'We live at the back of the palace and most people have no idea we exist. Obviously from time to time we have to come out and collect something that's woken up after a long sleep, or quietly remove a local troublemaker. There's still a quite a few out here, terrifying people in the middle of the night,' he said, smiling that lopsided smile.

Again I nodded, as if this was the most normal thing in the world. I glanced out at the ancient green van. Above the faded royal crest I could just make out the words 'Palace Removals.

Specialist Collections & Deliveries' in old grey letters. How could this possibly be true?

'So were my parents also keepers?'

'No they weren't.'

'Did you know them?'

'I'm afraid not.'

That was a shame. Somehow I'd always assumed he'd known my parents and that one day he might tell me about them.

'So what happens now?' I asked.

William Foxglass drummed one gloved hand on the table.

'That's a good question, Jack,' he said. 'Because there's something else I haven't told you.'

Really? I wasn't surprised. Somehow there still seemed to be a lot William Foxglass hadn't told me...

'Your uncle has disappeared.'

'What d'you mean?'

'He was last seen four weeks ago. No one seems to know where he's gone or when he'll be back, if indeed he's coming back. Which is a problem, because the ghost vault is a very important vault, one of the oldest in the palace, and it's currently without its keeper.'

I looked down at the photograph of my beaming uncle. Galahad Joliffe.

'What d'you think has happened to him?'

William Foxglass shrugged.

'I don't know. Luckily he's much more devious than he looks. But it's so unexpected and out of character, I'm beginning to wonder if perhaps he's gone for good.'

William Foxglass clasped his gloved hands together and fixed me with his hazel eyes. I was beginning to understand what he was getting at. I stared at him uneasily.

'So... what are you saying? You want *me* to take over, as the Keeper of Ghosts?'

William Foxglass shrugged. I took that as a yes.

'When?'

'How about now?'

'Right now?'

'I'm not sure what the alternative is, Jack. Abel Goodnight is never going to give up chasing you. Not after what's just happened. Killing children is what he's known for, and you won't be the first, I'm afraid. If your uncle hadn't come back by next week, I'd have come to tell you all this anyway.'

I took a deep breath. To be honest, if William Foxglass had suddenly laughed and said 'Just kidding!' I would've believed him. But he didn't. He was completely serious, rather strange, yet sort of magnetic: powerful in some way. For some reason I was drawn to him...

'Couldn't I come back to the palace with you now, and *not* be the Keeper of Ghosts? Just sort of... be there?'

'Impossible.'

'Why not?'

'You cannot just be there, Jack. And besides, the Ghost Vault needs its keeper. Joliffes have held the post of Royal Keeper of Ghosts for over four hundred years. I'm sure your uncle would regard it as your destiny, what you were born to do.'

I didn't doubt it. Even so, this was all so... strange. I picked up the photograph of Galahad Joliffe again, beaming his jolly smile.

'Are you *sure* he's my uncle?'

'Positive. And he has no other living relations. You're not the first person to suddenly discover you have a connection with our world, Jack. You may not think it, but you're a very special person.'

I shook my head. That definitely wasn't true.

'Does it matter that I've never even seen a ghost?'

'Not a bit.'

'And I'm twelve?'

'So what?'

'But shouldn't I have some sort of special abilities? I mean, I don't even know if I *like* ghosts.'

William Foxglass laughed.

'If you were going to become a keeper of dragons, or basilisks, or even horn-headed hodmadods, I might be concerned. Ghosts are pussycats, Jack, you've got nothing to worry about.' William Foxglass's gloved fingers stopped drumming on the table. He fixed me with those watchful eyes.

'Well? What d'you think?'

'I don't really have a choice, do I?'

He smiled again. I thought not.

»» 7 ««
To the Palace

SO THAT WAS HOW it all began. If you're thinking it all sounds very strange, then just imagine how *I* felt. But Mr Foxglass was right; I didn't have a choice, and as it turned out, Abel Goodnight *was* very persistent indeed... But I'm rushing ahead. Down to London we went, extremely slowly, as the collector's van rattled along at about twenty-five miles an hour and Mr Foxglass seemed to prefer to take every back road he could find. After a couple of hours I heard groaning from the back, at which point he pulled off into the woods and got out. There was a shot, and moments later he returned with a rabbit dangling from his fingers. Without so much as a word, Mr Foxglass opened a hatch in the back of the van and flung the unfortunate creature in. There followed a low growl and a scraping sound.

'What's that?' I said.

'What's what?'

'In the back.'

There was a strange squawk and a sound of bones crunching.

'I'm not entirely sure myself,' said Mr Foxglass, pulling away. And that was the end of it.

As you might expect, soon enough we left the woods and fields and passed through villages and towns glittering orange in the darkness. As you might not expect, it being the beginning of May, the air definitely became colder the closer we got to the capital. I think I'd fallen asleep, because by the time we reached the city it was after midnight and thick snowflakes were drifting down, covering everything in a soft marshmallowy carpet. It was freezing. I remembered hearing about this on the news; Philomena was particularly interested in it. London was shrouded in a great freezing snow cloud, and nobody seemed to know why. Mr Foxglass didn't seem too bothered; he merely did up his coat and wiped the steamed–up windscreen occasionally. I thought of asking him about it, but I was nervous of appearing too stupid in front of William Foxglass. Don't forget, I'd barely been to school, or even left our village much. All this was completely new to me, and besides, I had something else on my mind… Ghosts. I was fairly certain I wasn't going to like them. The further we went through the snowy streets, the more anxious I became. I watched the thick snowflakes swirling past and began to wish I'd never said yes…

Somewhere near Piccadilly Circus we turned into a series of narrow alleys with tall black buildings on either side. This was an old part of the city, I supposed, as it was cobbled and dimly lit. At a corner we slowed to a crawl and turned down towards an enormous stone arch, blocked up by bricks and old bits of stone. In the middle of it was a tiny wooden door.

William Foxglass drew up and flashed his headlights three times. Out of the grubby office came a stooped figure in a top hat and cloak, torch in hand. He shone it into Mr Foxglass's face.

'Good to see you back, sir. Did you get it?'

'I did, Cyril.'

'Any bother?'

'A little. The usual.'

'Well done, sir.' The man called Cyril grinned and flashed his torch in my direction. I'd taken the precaution of wearing my large red beanie to avoid the inevitable reaction to my lack of hair. 'And who have we here?'

'This is Galahad Joliffe's *niece*,' William Foxglass replied, putting particular emphasis on that last word. 'I was in the neighbourhood so I thought I'd offer her a lift.'

Cyril shone his torch at me curiously.

'You'll be the new Keeper of Ghosts, I take it?'

'With everything to learn,' said Mr Foxglass sternly. I glanced at him. If you say so.

'Pleased to make your acquaintance, Miss Joliffe. Welcome to the palace.'

Cyril's nose twitched and he withdrew, satisfied with what he had seen. Mr Foxglass turned on the engine and we stared at the bricked-up archway ahead of us. You can probably imagine what I was thinking. There was no way we could squeeze through that narrow wooden door. So...

'It always takes a little bit of effort to go somewhere more interesting,' said Mr Foxglass, revving the engine unhelpfully. Just when I thought he really *was* going to attempt to drive the van straight through the wall, there was a loud clanking and we began to sink down below the level of the street.

'In our line of work, it's much better not to draw too much attention to ourselves,' he winked, smiling that topsy-turvy smile. 'Now d'you have a phone on you, or anything like that?'

Of course I did. I took it out of my pocket.

'Should I turn it off?'

'Erm… maybe put it there,' he said, pulling out a small tray next to the gear stick.

I did as I was told. I imagined that it might be some sort of security thing. Scanners or X-rays or something like that. This was a royal palace, after all. The lift slowed and we juddered to a halt at the bottom of a ramp. Ahead there was a small slope leading up into a cobbled alley, very like the one we'd just left. Mr Foxglass drove the rickety little van up into the moonlight and stopped at the end.

'And here we are. Welcome to St James's Palace, Jack.'

I got out and looked around. In front of us was a small half-timbered inn with shadows moving behind the fogged-up windows. The sign outside the door said 'The Black Coat Inn'. High above us was a forest of narrow towers and twisting chimneys, all silently puffing into the cold night air. The clock tower read quarter past two. It was like some ancient walled city, muffled and snuggling down in the bitter cold. William Foxglass was watching me take it all in.

'Not quite what you were expecting?'

I shook my head. He nodded, his breath steaming.

'I remember thinking the same thing when I first arrived. But we're perfectly safe inside here. Nothing can get in uninvited.'

I wasn't quite sure what he meant and he wasn't about to explain.

'How's your phone?'

How's my phone? That was a strange question, or it seemed to be, until I reached into the van to get it…

'Oh!'

I stared in horror at the melted screen. The glass had cracked in a thousand places, and there was a wisp of smoke coming out of the side.

'Yes, I was afraid that might happen,' said Mr Foxglass. 'Nothing electronic ever seems to work in here. Probably on account of...' He checked himself. 'This is the last part of the old country left, and in here there are many older forces at work. That's the way it has to be, I'm afraid. No signal, either. I'm sorry, Jack.'

I looked at the smoking phone with a twinge of sadness. All my memories of Oscar and Phil, all the stuff from my life... That was the moment I realised I'd really left it all behind. William Foxglass was smiling at me kindly. He didn't understand. There was yet another long moan from the back of the van.

'I've just realised what that is. Hear that?'

The moan sounded again, louder, like a pathetic foghorn.

'It's singing. Listen.'

I listened to the strange song. William Foxglass attempted to translate.

'Cheese and mice, oh, *ohhh*,

Are not as nice,

As mice,

On their *own*,

Own, oowwn...'

Mr Foxglass smiled. 'That's a Northumberland bluetail. I thought the last one died three hundred years ago. Ambrose Dunk will be amazed.'

I was mystified. And I think I was supposed to be. William Foxglass seemed excited.

'It's a jabberwock, Jack. Not a dragon at all.' He put his arm on my shoulder and smiled. 'Ready for this?'

～ 8 ～
Out of Sight

I WAS READY. Ready to join this strange and ancient society that by some accident of fate I was apparently a member of. Taking a deep breath, I followed Mr Foxglass through a small arched doorway and into a long corridor. Dim lanterns hung from the black bricks and there was a vague smell of cabbage.

'Obviously this is the back entrance,' he said, his breath steaming.

Obviously. It wasn't exactly like a palace. It felt more like a prison.

'Why is it so cold down here?' I asked.

'No idea,' he replied. 'Who can predict the weather these days? It's crazy, isn't it?'

Maybe, though I thought Mr Foxglass might have had a better answer than that.

'Is that why you always wear a pair of gloves?' I asked.

William Foxglass seemed surprised by the question.

'Oh no,' he breezed. 'I had an accident many years ago. Burnt my hand so badly I almost lost it.'

Asking any more might feel like prying, so I didn't. On we went into the labyrinth, up steps, down passages, navigating by the dim lamps. Strange carved animals guarded the doorways and stone knights stood in alcoves, heads bowed. Eventually we came out into a moonlit courtyard, bright with snow. In the centre stood a large fountain, frozen solid like everything else. All around, high buildings twinkled with lights.

'This is the Keepers' Courtyard,' said William Foxglass. 'My rooms are up there.' He pointed up to the narrowest tower on the far side, barely thicker than a finger. 'And yours are over there,' he said, pointing at another tower opposite.

'And what's that?' I asked, noticing a forlorn tree standing just beyond the fountain. Strangely enough, it was inside a cage. Even stranger in this snowy courtyard, the earth all around the base was black.

'That's the Isabella tree.'

I waited for an explanation.

'It's a long story, Jack. Everything in the palace has a story, and I've no doubt you'll hear them all soon enough. Plenty of people will tell you about Isabella Royle.'

Round the cloister we went, then up a circular staircase in the corner. Up and up and up…

'The Keeper of Ghosts' rooms are some of the best in the palace. And if there's one thing I know about your uncle, it's his knack of arranging everything just as he liked it.'

I thought of that little round man huffing and puffing all the way up to the sixth floor. Perhaps Galahad Joliffe hadn't arranged everything *quite* as he liked it… At last we reached the top, and stood before a wide door on which an elaborate crest had been painted in gold.

'The Joliffe coat of arms. Your uncle insisted on having that done,' nodded Mr Foxglass. Drawing out a ring of keys, he eventually found the right one and let us in.

It was a large round room, with a roaring fire and two wide armchairs set before it. The walls were filled with bookcases and deep green tapestries, and there were a lot of pictures of toads; there was even a family of brass ones squatting on the side table. Uncle Galahad obviously had a liking for them, perhaps because he was a little toad-like himself. Beyond was a grand bedroom with a huge four-poster bed, and a washstand, and another fireplace, and more pictures of toads. Everything was faded and soft and flowery.

'Not bad, is it?' said William Foxglass.

I looked around and smiled.

'I don't know what to say.'

'Then don't say anything.' He grinned in that curious way of his. 'It's very good to have you around, Jack. Yes it is.' He glanced across at the cupboard absently. 'Ah. I don't suppose you have any clothes?'

Obviously not. My bag containing everything I owned was still back in the pub waiting to be taken to the children's home. Already that seemed like a lifetime ago.

'Not to worry. I'll have Bootle attend to it. See you tomorrow, Jack.'

With a smile he left. I listened to his footsteps echo away down the stairs, then sat down on the bed. It was very soft and springy. I stared out at the snow-covered roofs of the palace. There were chimneys of every size and shape, all puffing away, and beyond – far beyond, it seemed, under the gently falling snow – I could just make out the black shadows of London. I looked at it all, and for the first time I thought this might actually be quite good. The Royal Keeper of Ghosts. That was me. Above the washstand there was another photograph of Uncle Galahad dressed in all the finery of his office. He was wearing some sort of black velvet doublet, a long fur-lined coat, and a huge hat with peacock feathers. The Royal Keeper of Ghosts. I still couldn't quite believe it...

Now this might seem like a good place to finish the chapter. Me, safely tucked up in this springy old bed, amazed at my good fortune – if that's what it was. But there is something else I should add. When I looked out of the window at that forest of chimneys, I was sure I saw a shadow flitting from one to another, dancing through the snowflakes. This shadow came back to me as I slept, and when I opened my eyes, I thought I saw a pale white face at the window, peering in through the wobbly glass... When I blinked again, it was gone...

～ 9 ～
Tom Bootle

THE FOLLOWING MORNING, I woke to find myself sunk so deep into the Joliffe four-poster bed it was as if I had fallen into a trench. Hauling myself up to the surface, I blinked to see the curtains already open and a neatly folded pile of clothes on the chair. Beside them hung a long green coat, high collared and double-breasted, with silver buttons all down the front. Apart from the colour, it was exactly the same shape and cut as William Foxglass's. On the corner of the collar, JJ was neatly stitched in gold thread. Pulling it on, I stood before the mirror and struck a pose. This coat made you want to do that, somehow. It fitted most precisely. Either I had been measured during the night, or someone had made a very good guess...

At the bottom of the pocket I felt something. A whistle. Obviously I blew it. Barely had I taken it from my lips when I noticed the jug on the washstand move.

'Hello?'

The jug did not reply.

'Hello?' I said again, a little louder.

'Tell you something. It's s'trordinarily snug in here. S'trordinarily snug.'

The small growly voice seemed to be coming from the jug.

'I do believe I'm going to be late now. Tardy on his very first day. That will never do.'

I watched the jug. The jug, I sensed, was watching me back.

'I'm not sure you are late,' I said.

'Bootle is most definitely late.'

'Well you'd better come out before you get any later.'

'If only I could. Trouble is, I've gone and got myself stuck. What a banana!'

Stuck? I peered into the jug and—

'Oh!'

There at the bottom was a fat black toad.

'You see? How am I ever going to get out? That wicked Princess chucked me in here and I can't get out.'

It couldn't have been the toad talking, but it seemed to be...

'Ta-dah!'

I gasped.

From behind the curtain a large white rabbit appeared. It was standing on its hind legs, wearing blue britches and an ancient chequered jacket that looked like it had been mended a thousand times.

'Tom Bootle, sir. Pleased to make your acquaintance,' said the white rabbit. He bowed elaborately and shook my hand. Not with his paw, but with his hand, because Tom Bootle had long pink fingers. So obviously he wasn't a *real* rabbit, he just happened to be a very small person who looked like a rabbit… or perhaps a very large rabbit that happened to talk like a person…

'Very old trick but it always works,' he said, winking mischievously. 'Might I enquire whether the clothes are a good fit?'

I nodded. I was still in shock.

'Fantabulous! You'll be quite the dazzle of the Palace. I've always been a dab hand with clobber though I say it myself. I'm your new servant, sir.'

'Hello,' I said.
'My name is Jack.'

'Yes, I was told.
The stitching on the lapel,
does Master like it?'

'It's very beautiful, thank you.'

'Beautiful. JJ. Yes, not bad.
Thank you, Master.'

'Actually I'm a girl.'

'Oh that's nice. Isn't that lovely!'

'So you needn't call me Master.'

'What you talkin' about?'

'You can call me something else
if you like.'

'But you are my Master.
That is…' Tom Bootle
smiled again. I wondered
whether he actually

understood. 'Oh look at that.' He beckoned me forward to window, then from behind my left ear he produced an egg.

'Ha-ha! What a strange thing to keep behind your ear! Now shall we see what's inside?'

He closed his pink fingers around the egg, and when he opened them, there was a white mouse. He winked.

'See? Still got me magical luppers! I ain't forgotten me tricks!'

I smiled again, though I'll admit I was already wondering if there would be this much fuss every morning.

'Once I was the court jester, you see. Magician and Fool, First Class. A very important person, I'll have you know.'

Except that now he seemed to have become a rabbit. Before I had a chance to ask why, the snowy silence was pierced by a bell, bright and sharp in the cold morning air. Somewhere in the palace a door opened and a clatter of footsteps rose up to my window.

'What's that?' I asked.

Tom Bootle hopped up onto the chair and looked out.

'I believe that to be the breakfast bell. Yes that will be it.'

I listened to the hum of voices. Children. They seemed to be coming from somewhere near the front of the palace.

'Is that a school, Mr Bootle?'

'Yes it is. That's the Royal School, that is. Over there.'

As you might have guessed, this was suddenly very interesting to me. We listened as the voices went inside and a heavy door shut behind them.

'Keepers and servants are never allowed over to the royal side, 'tis forbidden – most forbidden. You mustn't even *think* about it, and if you do, well *unthink* it, tooty de sweety.' Bootle smiled and hopped down from the window. 'Cold isn't it? Brrr. Bitter. *Heigh ho, the wind and the snow, Oh when will the Phoenix Child come…*'

he sang. 'Do you know that one? Old forest song, that one. Fairy song they say, hmm.'

'It is strange that it's so cold here,' I said.

'Isn't it just? They say it's a sign she's returned.'

'Who's returned?'

'*Heigh-ho, the wind and the snow, Heigh-ho, the wind and the snow,*' Tom Bootle sang, then rubbed his face violently. 'Custards and chicken, I ain't heard nothing about that! And even if I had – *which I hasn't* – but just supposing I *had*, I ain't cackling. Not a word. Oh no. I know what o' clock it is. Oh yes, I do indeed.'

I watched Tom Bootle scratching his ears and humming to himself. He was quite strange.

'Thursday is pancake day, Mastress. Yes, I shall call you Mastress. Left at the bottom of the stairs, then follow the passage all the way down to the Keepers' Hall. You'll find them all in there. Most particular about pancakes are the keepers. Best not keep them waiting,' he smiled.

Waiting? For me?

'You are to be introduced, Mastress.' Tom Bootle brushed fluff off my coat and ushered me to the door. 'Best not keep them waiting. Good luck.'

ᨠᨠ 10 ᨠᨠ
Welcome Stranger

I **STOOD NERVOUSLY** before the great door of the Keepers'
Hall. Despite Bootle's simple instructions it had taken me a
little while to find it, as the corridors were so dark and the
distances seemed far longer, and sometimes far shorter, than they
really were... but here I was. Taking a deep breath, I turned the
massive iron ring and stepped inside. It was a long high room, dark
panelled and lit with candles. Old portraits lined the walls, and
there seemed to be lots of gold writing everywhere in a language
I didn't recognise. Down each side ran two long tables, filled with
keepers in different coloured coats, and at the end was a high table,
in the centre of which sat an ancient man in a white coat, his

collar so high it almost obscured his face. William Foxglass sat to one side of him, and on the other side sat a short, cross-looking woman with a large clock hanging round her neck. Mr Foxglass spotted me and nodded kindly, indicating a gap between two very elderly keepers on the left-hand table. I closed the great door as quietly as possible and hurried over to my place.

'Ambrose Dunk, Keeper of Jabberwocks,' whispered the man on my left. He shook my hand very softly, then returned to the book he was reading.

'Norris Hebbedy, Keeper of Worms,' whispered the man on my right, again shaking my hand so limply I barely felt it. He gave me a vague smile then returned to the pamphlet he was reading. I stared up and down the long wooden table. There was no one here my age, or even close... just lines of peculiar old men and women, all in different coloured keepers' coats, carefully eating their pancakes. It was the same on the other table, except at the far end, where a rowdy group of blue-coated keepers were laughing loudly. Every one of them seemed to have suffered some kind of injury – fingers missing, eyes missing, broken teeth. They looked like pirates, which was quite good, I thought. Perhaps I could go and sit over there...

'That's where you've got to!'

A very short and wide man with hair like a porcupine and thick gold earrings smiled broadly and grabbed me by the hand.

'You must be Jack Joliffe! Delighted to make your acquaintance. Sam Yuell, Keeper of Royal Beasts. Absolutely delighted.'

Sam Yuell was wearing an old red coat, faded to pink at the shoulders, and he was so wide he took up at least two places. There was much grumbling as he swung himself onto the bench opposite and slapped a huge plate of pancakes down between us.

I felt something soft slide in past my feet—

'Ohh!' I yelped. I couldn't help it.

'Quiet there, Stinky!' hissed Sam Yuell out of the side of his mouth. 'Don't mind her, Jack,' he whispered, 'she's a bit moody this morning. Doesn't like this weather.'

It was some kind of a leopard, with yellow eyes and gold and red spots across its back. Stinky looked at me and growled again, sparks flying from her nose.

'Quiet there, Stinky!'

I might have smiled but I kept my eyes on Stinky under the table. Yes, those really were *sparks* flying from her nostrils, I could feel them...

'I suppose you know how dangerous it is, bringing a royal leopard in here, Mr Yuell?' whispered Ambrose Dunk. 'That's how palaces burn to the ground.'

'She's not well, Ambrose, she likes pancakes, and she's not bothering you,' Sam Yuell replied.

'The Wriggling Worm of Warrington Castle is not well either, but I don't bring it into the Keepers' Hall,' tutted Norris Hebbedy. 'The Master would take a very dim view if he knew.'

'But he's not going to know, because no one's going to tell him, are they?' said Sam, smiling at them. The two old keepers waggled their ears disapprovingly and went back to their reading. Sam Yuell winked at me, picked up a pancake, spread it thickly with honey then quietly slipped it under the table. 'Now William's asked me to fill you in, so you'd better get started on those or Stinky'll have the lot.'

I'd forgotten how hungry I was. As I began to guzzle, Sam Yuell told me all about St James's Palace. He spoke incredibly fast, and with such a strong accent that if I tried to write it all down there would be nothing but pages and pages of 'thees' and 'thars' and 'hecks' and 'credit-its'; I shall abbreviate. There were three hundred and forty-nine keepers, and they all lived in this hidden side of the palace. Each had a vault containing some curious creature or thing from Albion's legendary past, and each wore a different coloured coat. Most of the keepers had been here a very long time indeed, especially the Master, Valentine Oak, who was eighty-eight. William Foxglass was the Second Master, known as Black Zodiac, and that round woman on the other side wearing the clock was Ocelot Malodure, Keeper of Time and Enforcer of Rules. They were the three most important keepers.

'So we are always very nice to them, especially Valentine Oak, who was an absolute legend in his time, probably the most famous keeper that ever was,' said Sam, pointing out the portrait of the man in the long white coat hanging above the high table. 'For fifty years there's been peace and harmony and it's all been Valentine's doing. Absolute legend, Valentine.'

I looked from the heroic portrait down to the ancient man hunched in the great chair below. Valentine Oak didn't look like an absolute legend any more. He looked like a shrivelled old wasp. And that gang of blue-coated pirates on the far side?

'Dragon Keepers,' sighed Sam. 'Ruffians and scallywags the lot of them.'

A bell rang, and there was silence. William Foxglass stood up.

'Ladies and gentlemen, I don't want to keep you from your pancakes a moment longer than necessary, but I have a brief announcement to make. Today we welcome a new keeper to our ranks.'

Murmuring filled the hall. Keepers began looking around. I felt my heart beat faster.

'Due to the continuing and perhaps permanent absence of

Galahad Joliffe, we have decided to appoint a new Keeper of Ghosts to take on the role of Phasma Argent. Starting today.'

William Foxglass looked over at me and beckoned me forward. I felt my heart galloping as all eyes in the room turned towards me.

'Go on lass,' grinned Sam encouragingly.

I clambered off the bench and nervously walked down the centre of the hall towards the high table. Wizened old keepers whispered to each other as I passed.

'Is it a child?'

'No. It can't be. 'Tis a goblin.'

'A Joliffe goblin?'

'No. That's a sewer goblin, that is.'

Mr Foxglass smiled that lopsided smile and helped the Master to his feet. Valentine Oak shuffled forward. Picking up a narrow leather box he mumbled a few words in a language I'd never heard, then reverently handed it to me.

'This belongs to you and you only,' he said. With a nod he indicated that I should open it. Inside was a large and well-used key.

'We are keepers, Miss Joliffe. We keep, so that others may be safe. Control your vault; don't let it control you. That is the only really important rule we have in here.' He winked. I glanced at Ocelot Malodure to his left. I wasn't sure she agreed.

'Welcome to the palace, Jack Joliffe. Welcome.'

I picked up the key. It felt strangely heavy. And cold.

'Thank you.'

The Master nodded.

'Remember that rule, Miss Joliffe,' he said in his whispery voice. 'Control your vault; don't let it control you.' I nodded and smiled again. I couldn't think of what else to do.

Mr Foxglass indicated that I should turn and face the room. By now everyone was watching me very carefully. He said, 'May I present Jack Joliffe, Galahad Joliffe's *niece*. The eighteenth Joliffe to hold the title of Royal Keeper of Ghosts.'

There was silence.

'Jellybean's niece?' said someone.

'Yes,' William Foxglass replied. 'His *niece*.'

The Dragon Keepers began clapping and whistling, and the rest rather begrudgingly followed suit. I turned back to Mr Foxglass. The Master was still smiling at me in a sort of absent way. For some reason I seemed to interest him.

'Good luck, Miss Joliffe,' he whispered again.

'Is someone going to show me what to do?' I asked.

'Everything has been arranged, Jack,' said Mr Foxglass reassuringly. 'I'm sure your uncle has left the vault in fine shape. He was a very conscientious man.'

Ocelot Malodure let out a little snort. There were many other questions I should have liked to ask William Foxglass at that moment, but the Master gripped his arm and pulled him away.

I returned to my place, feeling nervous.

'Is it difficult being a keeper, Sam?'

'Oh no, lass. It's easy. And you're a Joliffe, so straight away the ghosts will know who you are and what they're dealing with.'

I glanced back at Mr Foxglass talking to the Master.

'So my uncle just sort of disappeared?'

'Apparently. Four weeks ago. Left in the middle of the night. There's a story there, I'm sure. Foxglass has been doing his nut ever since. Can't have a vault without a keeper. Lucky you were able to step into the breach, eh?'

I nodded. Maybe.

'Play your cards right and you could end up like William,' said

Sam, following my gaze. 'Him and me both started out here aged seven. I was apprentice to my father, who was then Keeper of Royal Beasts, and William was pushing barrows of scraps around to feed the jumblies. Palace boy-of-all-work he was, that low down the pecking order his job didn't even have a title. No family connections, nothing. But little by little he worked his way up. He became a Junior Under-Keeper of Dragons, then a full Keeper of Dragons, then the *Head* Keeper of Dragons, and now the Master has made him Black Zodiac, above us all. Chummy with the Queen, rubs shoulders with the government; William's a very important man. The Master relies on him for everything.'

I watched them talking. William Foxglass, tall, dark, with that peculiar lopsided expression. The Master, as pale as snow.

'Funny to be so important yet still wear that tatty old coat,' I said.

'Isn't it just? William's never been the type to enjoy privileges of position. Doesn't seem to bother him. He could fly falcons from the roof, ride a black horse down the corridors, wear all manner of chains and sashes... It annoys the hell out of some people that he doesn't,' murmured Sam. 'Makes them feel uncomfortable, y'know?'

'All rise!'

Everyone stopped eating and suddenly stood up.

Out went Valentine Oak in a formal procession, leaning on the arm of William Foxglass, followed by Ocelot Malodure, who looked at me sharply as they passed. I had a feeling, even then, that perhaps we weren't going to get on. Then the rest of the keepers followed suit.

'Right lass, I'll take her ladyship back to the vault for her nap, and then I'm to escort you to the library,' said Sam Yuell, gathering up his stick and hat. 'I expect you can't wait to find out what old Jellybean's let you in for, eh?'

✺✤ 11 ✤✺
Snowbound

OUT WE WENT through the heavy arched door into the snow-covered cloister. A savage blast of wind took my breath away.

'Not bad for May is it?'

With a grim laugh Sam Yuell wrapped his coat about him and stomped through the drifts.

'Does anyone know why it's so cold here?'

'No. Nobody does. Bin like this since Christmas. Like living under a great dollop of frozen fog. Permanent blinking winter! And it's only getting colder, that's what. And this blinking courtyard is the blinking coldest place of all!'

He hurried across to an archway on the far side and blew on his fingers.

I looked at the shadowy fountain, locked in ice. And on the far side, that strange dead-looking tree, encased in a cage. The earth all around it was still black, despite the snow, as if nothing would settle on it...

'Sam, who was Isabella Royle?' I asked.

'What's that?'

'Mr Foxglass told me that's called the Isabella tree.'

'Don't you go worrying yourself about Isabella Royle, Jack, that's ancient history. You don't want to be messing about with that.'

'Why doesn't the snow—'

Already Sam had ducked through a doorway and was crossing the next courtyard. I ran to catch up.

'And I tell you something else, Jack. We've a royal presentation in three weeks' time and half my beasts are still hibernating. The Brown Bear of Bothelswaite, he's that dopey I reckon I'll have ter—' Sam stopped suddenly and grabbed my arm. 'Look through there, lass. You'll not often see that.'

Through another archway we saw a cart loaded up with blankets rattling through a huge gate. Beyond it, on the other side of the palace, children were rushing around in the snow having a snowball fight. I watched them enviously. At the far side I spotted a thin, dark-haired boy in a heavy coat and hat, shivering in the corner. He was leaning on a stick and looked extremely cold.

'Prince Richard, our future king, God help us,' said Sam, giving a cheery wave. Richard raised a hand weakly. There were dark rings under his eyes and his skin was almost green. He coughed and stared at me curiously.

'What's the matter with him?' I whispered.

'What's *not* the matter with him, Jack. Royal blood's cursed, they say. Makes yer sick just to look at him, poor fella.'

A tall girl with golden hair and rosy cheeks came up to Richard and began talking to him and laughing. Richard said something and she turned to look at us also. She smiled then took his arm. Away they went, Richard glancing back at me as the gate closed.

'Why's there a school over there, Sam?'

'You bin livin' under a stone or something? Don't you remember the assassination?'

'The assassination?'

Sam snorted in amazement.

'Stephen? Don't you remember? Cracking lad he was—'

And then in a flash I did remember. There was never much on the news about the royal family, they weren't at all popular, but Oscar and Phil had been very upset about it. There'd been some big royal event a few years ago, and one moment Stephen was out there in the crowds, shaking hands and smiling, the next... I remembered the pictures... the coffin. It was gruesome. But I knew nothing about the rest of them.

'So after Stephen's death it was decided that the royal children should be educated inside the palace. Safe in here, see, 'specially after Valentine had dealt with what's-her-face.'

'What's-her-face?'

'That one.' He pointed with his chin towards the Isabella tree in the cage. 'Only the Queen didn't want them in here on their own, so she arranged for the school to come to them. 'Course there always used to be a royal school in the palace, I'm talking hundreds of years ago, back in Tudor times. Now there's quite a few of them over there. Sons of dukes, daughters of earls, a smattering of rich kids from around the world, and then a few lucky ones from the ballot, which you definitely won't have heard of, because that's secret,' he winked. 'Best place for 'em—'

'Sam, who *was* Isabella Royle?'

Sam Yuell stopped his prattling and paused before the library door. I think he realised he could no longer keep avoiding the question.

'What did the Master tell you when he gave you that key?'

I had to think for a second.

'He said the most important thing is to keep control of your vault. Never let your vault control you.'

'Right. Because that way darkness lies, and that's what Isabella Royle did. She was the Keeper of Fairies, and she staged a revolution, and held the palace to ransom. But she was caught and put to death, and now that tree is all that's left of her.'

I looked back at that strange black tree in its cage.

'Why doesn't anyone want to talk about her?'

'Because they can all remember. It was only fifteen years ago, and the wounds are still raw. And also...' Sam Yuell shook his head. 'There's far too much gossip in this place. Now come into the Keepers' Library, lass, before we catch our death.'

∞ 12 ∞
Family Tradition

THE KEEPERS' LIBRARY was a tall, fuggy, magnificent room with several floors of ancient leather-bound books stretching up to the ceiling. Here and there, stooped keepers went about their business by candlelight.

'I love this place,' whispered Sam, looking up at the book stacks. 'The sheer splendiferousness of it all. You can just smell the history, the learning.'

Down the central aisle we went, leaving a trail of soggy footprints behind. Sam Yuell pointed up at the gold letters above each section with his stick.

'Giants in there, Nursery Bogeys in there, Griffins, Snarks,

Fairies, Bandersnatches. Your uncle was very keen on this part of the job.'

'What do you mean "this part"?'

'Record-keeping.'

I followed Sam Yuell into the Ghost section. He climbed up the ladder leaning against the wall, returning with a book almost as long as his arm. Blowing the dust from the cover he thumped it down on the table.

'Take a peek.'

I opened it. The page was blank. And so was the next, and so was the next…

'Ahh, invisible ink,' snorted Sam Yuell. 'Must be a precaution. These are the nasty characters no one wants to read about.'

Down came another book, this one filled with handwritten pages, as neat as if they had been printed.

'Joliffes have kept their books in the same way for four hundred years. Such pride in their work. Real proper craftsmen, your lot,' said Sam.

I squinted at the immaculate looping letters, page after page of them. Not a single crossing out. Not a single mistake.

'So I have to write in this?'

'Oh yes, lass. In here there's a record of every ghost in the country. You have to keep it up to date.'

'*Every* ghost in the country?' I repeated. 'But isn't that thousands?'

'Might be, but as you're the Royal Keeper o' Ghosts, you have to know what they're up to, don't yer?'

I peered at the first entry and began to read.

'*Harry Titfer of Clopton. Pig rustler. First sighted at midnight, 12th November, 1732, stealing Missy and her twelve piglets from their sty. AJ–*'

'That will be Absolom Joliffe, a famous ancestor of yours,'

interrupted Sam.

'*Captured Titfer by phantasmiphication. Given… 150-year sentence?* Isn't that, quite long?' I asked.

'Not if you're a ghost it's not. What's time if you're dead already, eh?' said Sam with a merry snort.

Well I suppose so. I read on. Now the ink had changed colour, but the handwriting seemed exactly the same.

'*21ˢᵗ June, 1845. Released for good behaviour. New Year's Eve, 1936. F-J–*'

'That will be Felbrigg Joliffe.'

'*Called out to find Harry Titfer back to his old tricks. He let out a hundred piglets, and in the mayhem rode off on a prize boar named Bismark. F-J pursued by bicycle, almost netted him, but then Titfer galloped Bismark straight through a hedge and declared: "You'll not be capturing me again, toad-face! I'll see you in hell, so I will, so I will!" Ghost and pig never seen again. The next time Harry Titfer reappears, recommend immediate bottling followed by a very, very long sentence.*'

I closed the book. Somehow I couldn't quite believe that it was me who was being asked to do this. I was overwhelmed. And if I'm honest, not entirely thrilled.

'Is it difficult, catching ghosts?'

'No idea. Never tried it,' said Sam. 'But I suppose once you learn all 'em techniques… I shouldn't think it's too difficult.'

'I suppose my uncle was very good at it?'

'Oh yes, Jellybean was very very good. According to him, anyway. Funny bloke, your uncle. Sense of humour, y'know?'

'Is that why everyone calls him Jellybean?'

'He said his mother called him Jellybean because he was pink and round and liked jumping about. And he never got along with Galahad. Sounded like a Knight of the Round Table. And he didn't care for round tables at all,' Sam winked. 'As I said, funny bloke, your uncle.'

I looked up at the towering walls of books. I couldn't help feeling a little trapped. Trapped by all this history. Trapped by my destiny. I suppose my nervousness must have been clear as day.

'Don't worry, lass! Everything'll be fine!' laughed Sam, throwing a great hand over my shoulder. 'You're a Joliffe, don't you forget it. Every ghost'll immediately recognise and respect you for that. Which'll make it a heck of a lot easier, I'd a' thought.'

So he'd already told me.

'What about you, Sam? As Keeper of Royal Beasts do you have to keep records too?'

Sam Yuell rolled his shoulders.

'Not really. I'm more like a zookeeper, y'know? There's only a few royal beasts; I know them, they know me, I know their moods – they're me mates. You can't get that from a book. And like a lot of keepers in here, it's a family thing. My dad taught me the ropes, his mum taught him, her dad taught her... it's sort of second nature.'

I was envious already. To the left was a section that said 'Dragons'. Unlike all the other books in the library these weren't neatly arranged on the shelves, but scattered all over the place. Upside down, half open on the floor... and most of them seemed to have been burnt in some way.

'Keepers of Dragons are a law unto themselves,' tutted Sam. 'I don't suppose half of 'em can read at all.'

'Sam Yuell in the library? This is a rare surprise.'

We turned around to see a sharp-looking woman emerge from the 'Fairies' section. She was wearing a pale pink keeper's coat, fitted very tight at the waist, and a dainty pair of shoes.

'Good morning, Snowdrop.'

They bowed to each other like a pair of trees (quite a lot of bowing went on in this palace, as I was to discover). The lady called Snowdrop had straight black hair and wore wide glasses which magnified her eyes so much she looked a little like an insect. Those big eyes moved over to me.

'So you're Galahad's niece?'

'That's right.'

Snowdrop looked me up and down, struggling to find any family resemblance. She held out her hand.

'Snowdrop Scott, Keeper of Fairies. I suppose you find all this rather intimidating.'

'A bit.'

'You'll soon get used to it. I remember my first day. Absolute disaster. Yours, Sam?'

'Oh yes. Total disaster.'

'Never mind. Galahad was always going to be a hard act for anyone to follow. Don't panic, is my advice. And if you do panic, don't show it. That's the cardinal rule around here, Miss Joliffe. Give them a sniff of freedom and there will be mayhem.'

'That's what I've bin tellin' her, Snowdrop. Firm hand.'

'Firm hand indeed.' She smiled. 'But once you get settled, you'll find this palace an oasis from that harsh world out there. Welcome to our sceptred isle, Jack. This fortress built by nature against infection and the hand of war, this precious stone set in the silver sea. This is the very beating heart of Albion, Jack. A place many have dreamt of, but few will ever see.' Snowdrop Scott smiled and bowed, then wafted around a corner out of sight.

I stared after her in amazement.

'Don't be fooled by the fancy poetry, Jack,' said Sam quietly.

'Snowdrop Scott is hard as an anvil. For good reason.'

'Why?'

'Because fairies are the most dangerous creatures of the lot.'

I looked at him, confused. Sam Yuell nodded.

'Aye. They don't look it, buzzin' about like little hummingbirds, but believe me they are. The very worst. Don't you forget that.'

At the door appeared a tall, bored-looking boy, with a long bony face and black hair hanging like a tent around his shoulders. He was dressed in some sort of palace costume with yellow stockings, and he had a woolly scarf wound around his neck.

'Ah, here's young Archie Queach,' said Sam. 'Mr Foxglass especially asked that Archie show you down to the vault. Someone your own age to talk to at last.'

~ 13 ~
Guided Tour

I COULDN'T UNDERSTAND what William Foxglass was thinking. Unless this was his idea of a joke.

'*Jack?*'

The snigger that followed warned me what I was in for. First we went round the royal beast yard (I could hear roaring and whinnying coming from inside) and I made the mistake of asking what they were. Archie Queach went out of his way to describe the dangers of the Black Bull of Clarence, the Red Dragon of Wales, the three Golden Lions of England and the Silver Yale of Beaufort...

'You've probably never heard of a yale, I expect?' His voice was high and lispy. 'No, I didn't think so...'

On we went, down into a series of thickly vaulted chambers, with doorways and cages running off both sides. It was something like an ancient jail crossed with a zoo.

'Giants and ogres,' said Archie, extending a long thin finger to the left. We passed one huge snoring lump after another, most deliberately facing the back wall or playing with sticks like sad old gorillas in cages. 'Don't think you'll ever be allowed in there to talk to them, Joliffe. That's much too dangerous for children.'

Archie, by the way, was only fifteen himself. Down a floor and we arrived at what looked like the snake house.

'These are the ancient worms, Joliffe,' said Archie Queach, indicating the massive coils lurking in corners. Here was the Lambton Worm, the Trent Worm, the Wriggling Worm of Warrington Castle... all enormous, oily, and thankfully asleep.

'Don't think you'll ever be allowed to feed them, either. We can't let a *child* do that.'

Another floor down and we were amongst the phantom dogs.

'Black Shuck,' said Archie, pretending not to notice as the huge shaggy creature flung itself at the steel bars, barking wildly. 'Red Rokeby, the Beast of Shapwick, the Hound of the Baskervilles...'

Archie did his best to look bored as one after another the mad creatures slathered at their cage doors like they wanted to rip us apart. 'I suppose you find all this rather frightening.'

Yes I did, but I was determined not to show it.

'Where are the dragons?' I asked.

Archie Queach smirked and waved vaguely down a corridor.

'Under the next courtyard. But I hardly think you could cope with them.'

I was beginning not to care very much what Archie Queach thought.

'What are you keeper of, Archie?' I asked.

He sneered unpleasantly.

'None of your business.'

It turned out it was the Back Stairs. In twenty years' time, if he was lucky, it might be the Front Stairs.

At the end of the vaulted corridor was a large door above which was carved 'Faerie Kingdom'. Before Archie Queach could repeat his warning, I walked up to the door and slid back the inspection hatch. Beyond was a steel mesh with a locked door saying 'DO NOT ENTER'. There was not a fairy to be seen.

'What's so dangerous about fairies?' I asked.

Archie Queach curled his upper lip into his gum and made a sucking noise through his teeth. It was quite obvious what he was suggesting.

'Oh you mean they're like rabbits?'

Archie threw a despairing glance at the ceiling.

'No, Joliffe. Not rabbits. They're bloodsuckers. They drink your blood, like vampires.'

'I see.'

Archie gave up his impression and slammed the hatch shut.

'It will take you years to get an invitation in there. Miss Scott is very careful these days. For obvious reasons.'

'I suppose you've been into all the vaults, haven't you, Archie?'

Archie Queach pretended he hadn't heard that.

Down we went to the fourth floor, and stopped before a cage of witches squatting around a fire. These were not nice witches, you understand, more like the proper warty-nosed toothless old women you might see in pictures. For ten long minutes Archie made a great show of knowing them. It was all, 'How are your verrucas, Greymalkin? Has your toad had kittens? Oh I do like your lovely new broomstick'– la-di-dah… On he gossiped with these cackling old hags, every once in a while peering over his shoulder to give me a sneer… 'Yes it's a girl, a proper little urchin, Galahad Joliffe's *niece*, can you believe it? Oh I *know*…' Archie knew very well I was itching to get on, and so I might have, if I'd only known where to go…

Which turned out to be only as far as the end of the corridor, where there stood a thick arched door, with the words 'Ghosts, Phantoms, Wisps' carved in enormous letters above.

'I expect you might find the lock a bit difficult, it being so heavy and you being so small.'

'I think I can manage it.'

In went the huge key. There was a loud click and thankfully it turned. Archie Queach looked vaguely disappointed.

'After you,' he smirked.

✎ 14 ✎
The Ghost Vault

I **DON'T KNOW WHAT** you might expect to find if you went into a vault containing every troublesome ghost, phantom and wisp in the land, but it was certainly nothing like I was expecting. The room was wide and round, and in the centre a thick stone column rose up like a giant tree trunk. It was quiet. And it was dark.

'Will Miss Joliffe be requiring more light?'

I looked at Archie Queach. He definitely hadn't said that. He was clearly as mystified as I was, but somehow kept up that superior sneer.

'Yes. Please,' I added, though I wasn't sure about the please.

Were you supposed to be polite to ghosts? What did I know?

Lamps began switching on all around the vault, and I could see that the walls were lined with green glass jars in racks, each with a thick cork stopper. All the way round the central column hung portraits of the Royal Ghost Keepers, from Oberon Joliffe at the top in his doublet with yellow silk sleeves, right through to my uncle, Galahad Joliffe, in exactly the same costume four hundred years later. Eighteen Joliffes in a line, and every single one of them was a beaming, toad-faced man*. The family resemblance was uncanny. Shocking, in fact.

'This is the Ghost Keepers' manual, I expect. Oh how fascinating,' said Archie, attempting to yawn loudly as he opened a heavy black book on the table. Instantly the book slammed shut, sending a cloud of dust into the air. Archie Queach sniggered to conceal his nerves, then picked up the old walking stick resting beside the book.

'And this is the keeper's staff,' he said, looking it up and down knowledgeably.

'What's it for?'

'Keeping them under control,' he replied, twirling it about like a sword.

'Do I have to fight them?'

Archie rolled his eyes and tutted.

'You've got a lot to learn, Joliffe. A *lot* to learn.'

Archie carelessly dropped the staff onto the table. I picked it up. The head was, predictably, carved into the head of a toad. It felt light, strong, and looked very well used.

'Mr Queach will be leaving now,' said the same voice that had

---

* The line of toad-faced ancestors can be seen on page 306.

asked about the light: a deep, mournful voice. Archie made a point of ignoring it.

'Keeper of Ghosts is not a particularly high office, Joliffe,' he drawled, wandering around the vault poking this and that. 'Not like Head Keeper of Dragons, or Keeper of Time. No one likes ghosts much.'

'Why's that?'

'They're too slippery. And there are too many of them.'

'Mr Queach *will* be leaving now,' droned the voice again.

'*I* wouldn't take this job. Even if I had just inherited it.'

CRASH!

Archie jumped. He spun around to find a pair of cymbals floating in the air right in front of his face.

'Mr Queach *will* be leaving now.'

The cymbals advanced menacingly.

'As Under-Keeper of the Back Stairs, Mr Queach knows that he's not entitled to come in here.'

'I am, actually–'

'And he should keep his opinions about ghosts to himself. Otherwise Mr Queach can expect such a spooking–'

'All right mate, keep your hair on–'

'Good day to you, Mr Queach.'

'See what I mean?' said Archie, still attempting to be brave. 'Ghosts, huh–'

CRASH! CRASH! CRASH!

Archie squealed as the cymbals chased him out of the vault and down the corridor. Then the door closed of its own accord. There was silence. I too was feeling a little frightened now. But also quite pleased.

'Good morning, ma'am.'

'Good morning,' I replied, to nothing.

First a face, and then a body, arms and legs appeared in the air. The ghost was immaculately dressed in a long black coat, and there was a sad, thoughtful expression on his face. He looked like a butler who had just received some very bad news.

'My name is Dancing Dan Dravot. Mr Joliffe called me Dancing Dan,' said Dancing Dan. I noticed his shoes were polished like mirrors, and he didn't seem to be exactly touching the ground.

'I am here to keep everything in the vault in order.'

I smiled nervously. My first proper ghost.

'It is very orderly.'

Dancing Dan bowed.

'Mr Joliffe liked everything just so,' he said. 'I took the liberty of assuming you'd wish to continue the tradition.'

'All right. If you like.'

Dancing Dan nodded and danced his way towards a cupboard. There he took out a green and black chequered gown, a pair of dainty red slippers, and a small silver cap with a tassel.

'Mr Joliffe liked to wear these to work.'

'He did?'

'He said he found them very calming. And comfortable.'

I saw no choice in the matter. Taking off my keeper's coat and boots, I put them on. The slippers were far too small and the gown was enormous, but I don't suppose it mattered. Dancing Dan hung my coat in the cupboard.

'Mr Joliffe also considered it necessary to stop work at 11.26 each morning, eat a small beef sandwich, a slice of strawberry sponge cake, and take a cup of palace wine. Does Miss Joliffe wish to carry on in the footsteps of her ancestors?'

'Erm…' I wasn't sure about the wine, or the beef, but the cake sounded good. Dancing Dan hovered, waiting. I didn't want to upset him. Not on my first day.

'That sounds lovely,' I said.

The ghost bowed.

'Dancing Dan is here to serve and protect the order of the vault. If ma'am permits, I shall now be retiring until the aforementioned time, and I shall endeavour to in no way break the silence of the vault and disturb ma'am's concentration as she goes about her business. The Keepers of Ghosts have always believed that silence is the golden rule of the vault.'

I smiled nervously.

'Great.'

With yet another bow Dancing Dan took his leave, floating up into the rafters where he disappeared. Silence. Endless, utter silence. The golden rule of the vault.

I walked around the back of the column and found a small desk with a swivel chair and a lamp. On the desk lay a thick cream envelope. 'To My Worthy Successor!' it read, in large squiggly writing. I opened it. It was from Uncle Galahad.

Dear Joliffe Junior (whoever you may be),

Welcome to the Ghost Vault! How I wish I could be there in person to greet you and show you the ropes! Alas, alack, it is not to be! I still remember the letter my own Uncle Mostyn left me the day I arrived, like you, a newbee in short trousers over thirty years ago. How I clung to his words! Like a drowning man clings to a crate in a tempest! Never mind! Being a Joliffe, you will succeed, I know it!

We Joliffes are blessed with abilities others can only marvel at!
So, here are my tips for dealing with ghosts.
They are very simple, but they WORK!

I turned the page. This is what I found.

1. To catch a ghost, you must first charm it. Not with magic! (Doh! No such thing as magic! Well, not in the Ghost Vault anyway. Magic is for the fairies!) You must *charm*. Flatter. Be witty. Agree with them. Laugh at their jokes. Cry at their woes. Chat! *Charm* them.

2. Once charmed, a ghost goes blue and wobbly. Even the most ferocious beast will go wobbly eventually. They can't help it! Then you have a number of options before you. The Joliffes have invented many contraptions to capture spooks over the years, and they're all in the storeroom downstairs. Use or ignore, the choice is yours, but my own preferred method is the oldest, simplest, and I think, the best! All you need is a jolly old straw, and a jolly old catching bottle! Mine belonged to Oberon Joliffe, the famous ancestor above your head (!) and it is, I'll hazard a guess, a *jolly* old bottle indeed!

So this is what you do. Once the charmed spook starts turning blue and wobbly (or hazy — you will know it) simply approach, with *stealth*, and suck it up fast through your straw, taking care not to swallow, sneeze or inhale! (Never inhale!) Then, *blow* said spook into your catching bottle. Don't forget to stop it up quick! This takes *practice*, but it's beautifully simple and effective, and size is *not* a problem! A charmed ghost is extremely squishable! I've even performed this operation on a runaway stagecoach!

3. Remember that headless ghosts are *particularly* troublesome! They have no idea where they are going and are always bumping into things. Reunite heads and bodies as soon as possible!

4. Lastly, *Jellybean's Most Important Rule*. (If ever the Joliffes have had *one* family secret worth keeping, it's *this*.) Every ghost captured here is troublesome, but if you just so happen to *accidentally* release one into the vault (yes, it's happened to the best of us!) the ghost will not try to escape. Why not? Because generations of Joliffes have convinced them that the walls of the vault are so thick, and armed with so many cunning devices, it's quite impossible for any ghost to pass through. Should they try, they will evaporate! This is *The Royal Ghost Vault*, after all! They know this, so they don't try. On no account tell them the truth, which is... there are no cunning devices! There is nothing to stop them escaping at all! If they do — there will be chaos!

5. Direct all other questions about anything else to Dancing Dan Dravot. He is my right-hand ghost and knows everything. Dancing Dan will show you all the tricks of the trade, and also how to use the Ghost Keeper's staff, so you can command like the Joliffe that you are! None of Galahad's rules apply to him as he's far too sly, and tends to wander about the palace doing his own thing. Dancing Dan used to dance with dowagers on

cruise ships, then poison their afternoon tea. His first ten victims he threw overboard... the rest were never found!

Here endeth Uncle Galahad's rules. As Mostyn Joliffe said unto me, I say unto you, the Joliffe family motto: '*Lepos Vincit Omnia!*' (Charm Conquers All!)

Good luck!!!

I stared at the enormous squiggly signature. All those exclamation marks made me nervous. And when I turned the page there were more.

PS I forgot! There are a <u>*very*</u> small number of ghosts who know this vault cannot hold them. These are extremely dangerous and kept in the <u>*black-topped*</u> jars, well out of sight. On no account ever let them out! Mayhem! Chaos!

Oh and one last thing (<u>*the very last, I promise!?!*</u>). It's a little-known fact in the ghost business that <u>*you cannot communicate with your relations*</u>. You might see them, but they can't see you. So have no fears about any interfering ancestors telling you what to do! The vault is yours and yours alone!

Now to your left is the jolly old bottle and straw, and there's a little something to practise with in the jar in front of you. She's called Mabel, and she's an absolute poppet!

I peered into the jar. Mabel?

⋙ 15 ⋘
Charm Conquers All

THIS PART OF THE STORY I'd rather not be writing as it's frankly embarrassing. But I suppose you'll want to know. Unfortunately I admit that Mabel was not an axe-wielding zombie, which might have made what happened next more understandable. In fact Mabel was a duck – a headless duck. She still *had* her head; it was just that it tended to come off. A lot. But I didn't know that till I opened the lid of the jar.

There was a puff of mist, a clatter of wings and then somehow a ball of feathers became an angry white duck standing on the desk. She gave me a hard stare.

'Freedom!' she shouted. Breaking into a fast waddle, Mabel ran straight at me, and before I knew it she'd bounced off my back and taken off towards the ceiling.

'Mabel, come back!' I cried. Too late. Mabel smashed into the rafters and came down in a heap – two heaps to be precise. One was her head.

'Not again!' The head turned to me. 'Who are you?'

'Jack Joliffe. I'm the new–'

'You're no Joliffe!'

'I am.'

'Hogwash!'

'Excuse me?'

'If you're a Joliffe then I'm a cat!'

'But I am a Jol–'

'Bat droppings! Seagull filth! Slug turds!'

It's hard to describe the look Mabel was giving me. You can probably imagine it. Or maybe you can't.

'I'm going to let out every spook in this place,' she said. 'Every last one of them.'

'Please don't do that–'

'Are *you* going to stop me?'

'Mabel… Mabel!'

Mabel's body waddled straight through my legs and crashed into the wall behind. Panicking, she took off and began flying wildly around the vault, followed by her head, clanging from one side to the other. Jars trembled in their racks. One fell and I managed to catch it, then another tumbled down… then another… Smash! Smash! Strange brown slithering shapes began to swirl up from the floor…

'Mabel!'

The shapes became men, swarthy and armed, in long boots

and tricorn hats. They turned to each other.

'Why, if it isn't Harry Horseface Hobson–'

'Well, if it isn't George Jumblebum Jobson–'

'Stand and deliver, you rogue!'

'Deliver and stand to you too – ha-ha!'

Out came the swords. Snick! Snack! And after the next snick, Hobson's hand came clean off.

'Touché!'

Jobson's ear fell to the ground. Both Hobson and Jobson found this tremendously funny. The swords flashed again and again as the duellers chased around the central column.

'You think I'm afraid of you, you horsenosed halfwit?'

'You think I'm scared of you, you jumblebummed jackdaw? Take that, you greasy bird!'

Off came a finger, a boot, another ear. The racks of glass bottles trembled and shook as the phantom blades whizzed and clashed.

'Mabel you've got to help me!' I cried, watching them chase each other round and round.

The duck was still clanging about the rafters.

'I'm leaving!' she shouted. 'These walls shall hold me no more. I'm a duck; my place is the pond, the river, the open sky – skimming over the marshes at sunset...'

'But you'll never get out, you know that,' I said, quickly remembering Galahad's rule. 'The walls will never let you through.'

'But I'm a dreamer! I dare to dream ducky dreams.'

'And that!'

Down came another bottle. Somehow I managed to catch it. Then another. Diving, I caught that one too.

'I go where my wings take me. I fly... to the west – or maybe... to the east–'

Mabel flew straight at me, her head floating somewhere behind.

'STOP IT!' I shouted, as the duellers duelled and everything rattled and clinked. In desperation I grabbed the keeper's staff and banged it hard on the floor.

'STOP IT, STOP IT, STOP IT!'

Somehow my panic finally communicated itself. Or perhaps it was the staff, I don't know. Mabel crashed straight into the central pillar. The highwaymen stopped their duelling and stared at me, panting.

'What are you doing?' I said.

'Trying to chop off his head,' said Jobson.

'Trying to slice off his fingers,' said Hobson.

'Why?'

Hobson and Jobson looked at each other and shrugged.

'This is what we do, isn't it?'

'And you?'

Mabel, a little cross-eyed, hauled herself off the floor. Her body waddled over, picked up her head and tucked it under her wing. She stared at me sadly.

'All I want, more than anything, is to go home,' she sniffed. 'Home, to my pond. That is all I wish for.'

I remembered Uncle Galahad's first rule. Charm them.

'Then let me set you free,' I said.

Mabel stared up at me in wonder.

'Could you do that?'

I nodded.

'I could. For you, Mabel. Just for you.'

You might think I had a plan about this, but the truth was I had none at all. *Charm them.* Be charming. I picked up the bottle and the straw.

'I'm going to put you in here, then take you out of the palace and let you go.'

Mabel's attitude seemed to change. The suspicious glare in her eyes returned.

'Galahad Joliffe was always saying things like that. He was always trying to get me into that nasty bottle, but he'd never let me out again.'

'That's because... he didn't like ducks very much.'

'No he didn't! He was a toad man. Toady, through and through.'

'But I'm different.'

Mabel looked me up and down.

'Yes. You're very different from those mean old Joliffes. They all hated ducks. Particularly beautiful ducks like me.'

I smiled again. Charm them. Be charming.

'And how beautiful you are, Mabel. You are the most beautiful duck I've ever seen.'

'Exactly! Why, it's criminal that here I am, stuck... *What* did you say?'

'I said you're the most beautiful duck I've ever seen.'

Mabel's outline began to turn a little blue at the edges. She fluttered her eyelids.

'How nicely you talk. You are full of sense, Jack. Do carry on.'

'Your beauty is beyond description. I can't describe it.'

'You really think so?' If a duck can be said to smile, that is what Mabel did. 'Have a go,' she cooed.

'Erm... well, your... your white feathers sparkle like... like frost in the morning sun.'

'Very good.'

'And your back is as smooth as silver–'

'Not very original, but keep going.'

'And your eyes, they're like little golden...'

'Buttons?' she suggested, blurring a little more.

'Yes exactly. Little golden buttons. And your beautiful webbed feet are like...'

'Pancakes?'

'Pancakes—'

'Are they golden?'

'They are.'

'Do they match my eyes?'

'They match them perfectly.'

'Oh!' Mabel was becoming wobblier by the second.

'And what else?'

My mind went blank. Mabel sighed in contentment.

'You know something, Jack, I like you. You're a sensible girl.'

'Thank you.'

'Do you know why I'm in here? That toad-faced Joliffe up there said I was responsible for one hundred and twenty-nine car crashes. Me, a humble duck? How is that possible?'

'It's outrageous,' I nodded. Car crashes?

'That's exactly what it is. All I was doing was walking back to my pond. I never knew they were going to turn it into a motorway.'

'How could you know that?'

'Exactly! If in doubt, blame poor Mabel.'

'It's very unfair.'

'Ahh, it's so wonderful, to think that soon I will be free. Free, free; free as a bird.'

Mabel the duck was now sitting on the floor smiling. She had turned entirely blue, and trembled like a flame of gas. Perhaps this was the moment?

Carefully I placed the straw in my mouth and pointed the

end right in front of her bill. Mabel didn't seem to notice. She was sitting in a sort of dreamy daze. Trying to remember the instructions, I sucked hard. Suddenly my mouth felt full and lumpy and my cheeks puffed out like a hamster. Quacking came from somewhere inside, and I thought I was going to sneeze… I grabbed the bottle and blew hard, then quickly jammed down the stopper. I sneezed and coughed. That was very strange indeed… I peered through the glass. There was nothing there, nothing but a distant quack… What an awful trick I'd played. I felt genuinely sorry for Mabel. She was going to be very cross if I ever let her out again… I carefully carried the jar back to a shelf and placed it right at the back. Never let Mabel out again. Ever. Quack. Quack.

Needless to say, I somehow managed to pull the same trick on Hobson and Jobson, once they had finished hacking each other to pieces. They had been rivals in life and companions in death, having swung from the same gibbet, and being highwaymen, they turned out to be even more susceptible to flattery than Mabel. They liked nothing better than to boast of all the grand folk they had robbed, all the earls and duchesses they'd tied to trees… Soon they were both slapping their thighs in a merry trance and as wobbly as jellyfish. Blowing them back into their bottles was easy.

At 11.26 precisely, Dancing Dan waltzed in on his floating feet bearing a tray loaded with beef sandwiches, a slice of strawberry sponge cake and a small silver tankard of palace wine. I had never felt more like eating elevenses in all my life.

'How is Miss Jack finding her first day?'

'Not bad,' I said, pushing a piece of smashed glass under the desk with my toe.

Dancing Dan bowed approvingly.

'Continuing in the grand tradition of the Joliffes, then.'

'That's it.'

I munched on some sponge cake for a bit. Dancing Dan hovered behind a pillar.

'Erm… Dancing Dan?'

'Yes, ma'am?'

'Mabel the duck didn't seem to think I was a Joliffe.'

'Ah.'

'She seemed pretty convinced about it actually. Why would she think that? Can ghosts tell who you really are?'

'One shouldn't set too much store by the opinion of a troublesome duck, ma'am. And Mabel is a *very* troublesome duck.'

'But what do *you* think, Dancing Dan?'

Dancing Dan leaned in the air in that hovering way of his.

'Appearances can be very deceptive, ma'am. One shouldn't rush to conclusions simply because one doesn't resemble one's ancestors.'

That was true. Just because I didn't look like a toad didn't mean I wasn't one. A Joliffe, I mean.

'But you think I'm a Joliffe, don't you, Dancing Dan?'

'It is not my place to offer an opinion one way or another.'

'Even though I'm asking for your opinion?'

Dancing Dan smiled weakly.

'Whatever I think is not worth a bag of beans, ma'am. I'm almost certainly wrong about everything. Every day one is painfully aware of one's own limitations.'

He wasn't going to say. The question remained. How frustrating.

'Perhaps Miss Jack would consider perusing the pending files,' he said, changing the subject. Dancing Dan floated over to the large leather-bound ledger at the end of the desk. He opened it and the pages whirred past until the right one turned itself very slowly.

'Mr Joliffe was a stickler for lists. There are, I believe, thirteen ghosts that are due to be released this week, and a further three that have been causing trouble and require dealing with.'

'Dealing with?'

Dancing Dan pointed to the black pipe that descended from the ceiling. At the bottom were three silver capsules, a little like carrots, held in a rack.

'Mr Joliffe was an enthusiastic promoter of ghost-watching societies around the country. Whenever there was a report of some peculiar activity, he would encourage them to send him their information. The Royal Keeper of Ghosts would then set about identifying the spook by a process known as 'phantasmiphication', invented by Horatio Joliffe over two hundred years ago.'

'I see,' I said. Obviously I didn't have a clue what he meant. My blank look must have prompted Dancing Dan to continue. He promised many long, merry hours in the Keepers' Library; longer, merrier nights pouring over family trees and local maps; and whole weeks learning Clarence Joliffe's staff-wielding rules for beginners, techniques for extracting skeletons from their closets, the rudimentary principles of goosing a graveyard... Somehow I stifled my yawns and nodded, and as Dancing Dan droned on and on, my mind wandered up to the lines of toad-faced ancestors hanging above me. I could just imagine Uncle Galahad doing all this with a merry smile on his face. What a privilege it was, to be The Royal Ghost Keeper! Phasma Argent! An ancient post one could hold for the rest of one's life!

ᨆᨏ 16 ᨏᨆ
Night Visitors

I STARED UP AT THE CEILING of my four-poster bed that night and wondered. Life. *Life.* That sounded like a very long time. I wasn't at all sure that I wanted to spend the rest of my life goosing about in graveyards and extracting skeletons from closets. But maybe I was wrong. Maybe I should just accept my destiny. In time there'd be a portrait of me in the vault, dressed in the royal robes of my office, with a jumble of letters after my name: Inspector of Budgerigars, Fazzy Argent, or whatever it was. I'd grow fat and clever, and wear a green tweed suit like all my toady ancestors...

While I was thinking these none too pleasant thoughts, I had a sense I was being watched from the window again. I was sure there was not one, but two white faces staring at me through the narrow latticed window. This time I knew it wasn't a dream. I dared to turn and look straight at them. They didn't flinch. They just stared.

I got up and opened the window.

'Hello?'

'Oh hullo.'

'Hullo!' said the other, smiling.

There were two children, a boy and a girl, about seven years old and almost identical, balancing on the narrow window ledge. How they'd got there I don't know, but they didn't seem the least surprised to see me.

'Aren't you going to invite us in?' asked the boy.

'We're very cold,' said the girl.

Down they jumped and made straight for the fire. Both were wearing identical blue velvet jackets and gloves. Both had thick tumbles of blonde hair down to their shoulders. I stared at it enviously. You can't help it, when you're me.

'Not bad in here is it?' said the boy.

'Not bad,' agreed the girl.

'Do you have any brandy?' asked the boy.

'Brandy?'

'We always drink brandy when we're cold,' said the girl, and they seemed very disappointed that I hadn't got any.

'Chocolate cake?'

Ditto. Having inspected the room to check I wasn't hiding any brandy or chocolate cake, they decided instead to help themselves to Uncle Galahad's collection of golden toads, cramming their pockets with them.

'Oh it's all right, we can take these,' said the boy cheerfully. Pockets full, they looked me up and down.

'We've been wondering what you are,' said the boy. 'We're not sure.'

'We saw Mr Bootle fussing about in your room,' said the girl. 'He waved to us so we knew someone was coming to live here. But we can't work out *what* you are.'

'Because you're not very *usual* are you?' said the boy. 'Normal people don't shave their hair off, do they?'

'Not unless they want to look disgusting, or they're having like a head replacement or something,' said the girl, with a spiteful little giggle.

'So? Which is it?'

I explained my appearance, wondering quite why I was being so polite to this cocky little pair. All the while they stood in the middle of the room, staring at me.

'I'm Thomas,' said the boy, his legs planted firmly apart, his hands thrust deep in his pockets.

'I'm Victoria,' said Victoria, standing hand on hip. Both had a way of looking at you with their jaws jutting forward that seemed to say—

'We're royal, by the way,' they said together. I'd guessed as much.

'Our brother Richard is going to be King when Papa dies—'

'But he won't be King for very long.'

'Why not?' I asked.

'Because he's always so ill.'

'He's got all the bad blood, you see.'

'So when he dies we'll be the King and the Queen together.'

I nodded. They had a funny way of staring, these two. Just standing legs apart, hands in pockets, staring.

'Then you'll have to curtsey to us,' said Thomas. 'Bow would be better. 'Cos you're not really much of a girl, are you?'

'Perhaps you should burtsey,' giggled Victoria. 'You haven't burtseyed yet. BURTSEY!' she screamed suddenly.

'BURTSEY!' screamed Thomas.

I wasn't sure if they were joking. I didn't think they were.

''S'all right. We'll let you off this time,' grinned Thomas, rocking on his heels.

'So you're definitely a girl?'

'Yes.'

'And you're definitely called *Jack*?'

'Yes.'

'Weird.'

That, it seemed, was all they needed to know.

'By the way, people'll probably tell you that we're absolutely appalling, and we really *are* you know,' said Victoria, rather pleased. 'So don't be surprised if something truly shocking happens–'

'Because it nearly always does when you're as awful as us,' added Thomas with glee. 'We're completely and utterly dreadful. That's what Mama says. Goodbye, Jock.'

I watched as the twins climbed out of the window. I assumed they hadn't fallen because I soon heard them giggling and calling to each other amongst the forest of chimneys, then I spotted two small silhouettes walking along a high ridge beside the gatehouse. With a laugh they slid down into the school and out of sight. Well, that was strange. And more was to follow.

⚘ 17 ⚘
Bootle's Complaint

'GOOD MORNING, MASTRESS!'

It was dawn, and there was Tom Bootle standing at the end of the bed with a cup of tea. The snow outside the window was still a deep blue.

'Good morning, Bootle,' I groaned, fuzzy with sleep.

'And what a lovely morning it is. I do believe the palace is quite as frozen as it was yesterday, and the day before that, and the day before that.' Tom Bootle grinned.

'What time is it, Bootle?'

'Oh gosh it's early. I couldn't say by how much, but it's certainly early, oh yes, hmm.'

Wearily I hauled myself out of the trench of Uncle Galahad's bed and propped myself up amongst the pillows. Tom Bootle hopped onto the table beside the window and sat, legs crossed, waiting patiently. Was he going to wake me up this early every morning? I hoped not.

'Might I enquire how her ladyship is getting along in the vault?'

'Very well, thank you.'

Tom Bootle smiled to himself. I noticed that today he wore a large gold ring on his finger. Every so often he admired it.

'Takes me back all this. I can remember Mr Galahad Joliffe's first day. And Mr Mostyn Joliffe's first day. And Mr Felbrigg Joliffe's first day, and Mr Percy—'

'I am sure he can.'

'Got a long memory, see. There is not much I don't know in this palace, yes indeed.'

I listened to the school bell tolling outside.

'D'you know why Prince Richard is so sick, Bootle?'

Bootle cocked his head. He smiled.

'Royal blood is the worst, they say. He can't help the way he is.'

'I feel sorry for him,' I said, thinking about his younger brother and sister. Tom Bootle nodded. He looked out the window.

''Tis a mysterious thing, Richard's sickness. Some are saying it's not natural. Some are saying that a deep and dangerous evil has returned to the palace. Well I don't know about that, but there's definitely a funny atmosphere about. Most peculiar. But it cannot be who they think it is, can it? Because she's dead. Everyone saw what they did to her. Gruesome it was, gruesome. White as bone she went, white as the sky…'

I was wide awake now and listening as Bootle gossiped to himself, staring down into the Keepers' Courtyard.

'Course the stones are talking again. And the tapestries. I've heard them myself. So *bold* they are. No wonder the Master is worried. Heigh-ho, the wind and the sn… the sn… the sn…'

Tom Bootle's mouth opened and shut like a gasping fish. He cleared his throat and tried to speak. Again, nothing happened.

'Mr Bootle? What is the matter?'

He seemed to have no idea. Bootle took off his ring and placed it in the palm of his hand.

'There.'

He opened his hand and the ring was gone. In its place was a small white mouse, the same long-suffering white mouse he used for all his tricks.

'That's what comes of telling stories, Miss Jack. Don't I know it. That's a warning. She'll turn you. Yes she will.' He stroked the mouse and put it back in his waistcoat.

I stared at Tom Bootle a moment.

'Are you talking about–'

'Shan't speak of it. Can't. Must never speak of it.'

He looked at me, shaking his head. Okay. I changed the subject to something safer, or so I thought.

'I had a visit from the royal twins last night,' I said.

Bootle stiffened a little.

'They were sitting outside on the windowsill. They'd climbed across from the other side of the palace. They wanted to see who I was.'

'I'm not surprised.'

'Do they come over here a lot?'

Bootle shrugged. I took that as a yes.

'I suppose they do as they please, being who they are.'

Tom Bootle nodded again, then looked out of the window.

'The Keeper of Time has most particularly forbidden me to speak, wave, or even smile at the royal children,' he whispered. 'Terrible things will happen if I'm caught. Strict rules, Mastress.'

'Why's that?'

'This side of the palace is very dangerous for them. And I, apparently, aren't to be trusted.'

I looked at him, and Bootle shook his head. He wasn't about to say why.

'Well, I'm sure you've done nothing wrong–'

'No I haven't! I ain't luring them over rooftops for a chinwag! It's them that keeps oglin' at me from behind chimneys, laughin' and gigglin' as I goes about me business! They's the royal family, ain't they? What can I do?'

Tom Bootle suddenly jumped down to the floor and slunk away, his ears hanging flat.

'I shall be going along now. Mastress will be wanting to dress.'

'Bye.'

Tom Bootle shut the door without replying. I couldn't understand his reaction. It seemed a little ridiculous. I was beginning to realise that Tom Bootle was very sensitive about what he had become. And he also knew far more secrets about the palace than he'd care to admit...

ᕫᕬ 18 ᕬᕫ
A Sterner Test

I T WAS MY SECOND DAY in the Ghost Vault. There I stood, wearing the silk dressing gown and cap of the Joliffes, and there Dancing Dan stood – actually sort of floated in that way of his – pale and immaculate in his striped trousers and black swallowtail coat. He waited patiently as I looked around the walls lined with glass bottles. So much to learn. Where to start?

'Perhaps with something practical?' suggested Dancing Dan. I think he realised that his lectures on phantasmiphication were not exactly thrilling. He approached the long table where thirteen bottles stood waiting.

'As I mentioned, ma'am, these are due to be released this week.

Perhaps one might consider releasing one or two, then charming them back into their bottles using other methods?'

This sounded like a good idea.

'Yes I thought it might,' he said.

Dancing Dan had this slightly annoying habit of anticipating your thoughts. It took a little while to get used to.

'I'm afraid it does, ma'am. My apologies.'

I glanced at him sharply. His mouth twitched. I stood beside him and peered at the labels on the bottles.

'Lolo, Brigit and Trix, the Three Sad Sisters of Surbiton Station,' I read.

'They were run down by a train,' murmured Dancing Dan. 'It was their habit to sit quietly on a bench at the end of the platform, but after about thirty years they decided they would rather be playing hopscotch on the track. This scared so many train drivers out of their wits that Oswald Joliffe was summoned to take them away.'

I looked at the glass bottle. Three sad sisters. It couldn't be that difficult, could it? All they were going to do was play hopscotch.

'Exactly,' droned Dancing Dan. 'What method of charming would Miss Jack prefer? Straw and bottle again, or perhaps something more elaborate?'

'Perhaps I should see them first,' I said.

'Very wise. One never knows.'

I stood in the centre of the room and carefully pulled the cork stopper from the bottle. At first nothing happened, then there was a distant coughing, then voices all talking together… Something green puffed out of the bottle, and the next moment there were three girls, identically dressed in capes and pinafores. They looked at the vault, then at Dancing Dan, then at me.

'Where is the funny little man with the ermine collar and

spats?' said the tallest.

'The one who looked just like a toad,' said the middle one.

'He said we must sit still and be good while he fetched some candyfloss, but he still hasn't come back!' cried the smallest.

'I expect that was Mostyn Joliffe, ma'am,' murmured Dancing Dan.

The youngest looked at me suspiciously.

'Are you a porter at this station?'

'Yes I am.'

She didn't seem entirely convinced.

'Come on, Trix, let's play.'

And on they went with their game. Dancing Dan shimmered up to my side.

'They seem very docile, ma'am,' he whispered. 'May I suggest a basic miniaturisation?'

'Is that easy?'

'I shall bring the apparatus.'

A minute later I was holding a sort of bicycle pump with a trumpet at both ends which Dancing Dan said I should point at them.

'Don't I need to charm them first to make this work?' I whispered.

'In normal circumstances that would be so, but perhaps I should be allowed to take that part in the proceedings while ma'am masters the equipment?'

'If you like,' I shrugged.

Dancing Dan seemed extremely pleased. He slid out in front of the sisters and clasped his hands together.

'My dear girls, I wonder if I might be permitted to tell you a limerick or two to pass the time?'

They stared at him suspiciously. Dancing Dan cleared his throat.

'There was an old man from Dungannon,
Whose head was fired from a cannon,
When asked why this was,
He said it's because,
He wanted to see over the Shannon.'

This wasn't the greatest limerick, nor was it even vaguely funny, but for some reason the three sisters thought it was hilarious. They elbowed each other and giggled.

'Tell us another!' shouted the smallest.

Dancing Dan bowed.

'There once was a cat from Strathclyde,
Whose mouth was incredibly wide,
When asked why this was,
She said it's because,
I swallow up whales at low tide.'

'Swallow whales at low tide?' giggled the middle one. Again, for some mysterious reason, they thought this was the funniest thing they'd ever heard.

'Bravo!' cheered the tallest. 'More!'

Dancing Dan was beginning to enjoy this.

'I met an old horse from Penang,
Whose stable blew up with a bang!
When asked why this was,
He said it's because—'

'Another!'

'There was a tall tailor from Bude,
Whose parrot was incredibly rude,
When asked why this was,
He said it's because—'

'Another!'

'There was a young lady called Maud,

Who liked to tickle moles with a sword,

When asked why this was–'

She said it's because… I could go on but you've probably realised that Dancing Dan's limericks were basically all identical and not very funny at all, yet for some reason the three sisters from Surbiton were rolling around on the floor, choking with laughter.

'Stop!' they howled. 'Please… stop!'

Very soon the girls began to go blue around the edges and started to wobble. I took this as my cue and began to pump the pump…

'Whoops!'

I thought it would be like putting air into a bicycle tyre, but this was a far more delicate operation. One pump and they were twice the size; two, and their heads were touching the ceiling. Their giggling became deafening–

'STOP IT!' they boomed.

'Other way round, ma'am,' murmured Dancing Dan. 'Small end down. Gently does it.'

Ah. Yes. Quickly I turned the pump around and pumped again, slower and more carefully this time. With each stroke, the giant sisters shrank down and down and down, back to their normal size, then smaller and smaller, laughing at the terrible limericks all the while.

'Careful not to lose 'em, ma'am,' said Dancing Dan, as the three tiny sisters lay giggling in the centre of the floor. I knelt down and carefully placed the bottle neck over the top of them then stoppered it up.

'Well done, ma'am. Your first miniaturisation.'

I was feeling rather proud of myself. My first miniaturisation. But would it be possible to do this on my own, out in some haunted house perhaps?

'That is where the skill of the Keeper of Ghosts comes in,' droned Dancing Dan. 'To be able to charm while quietly selecting a method of capture and executing it at the same time. It's an art, ma'am.'

I looked up at the line of toad-faced ancestors with a new respect.

'Shall we try another, Dancing Dan?'

Dancing Dan bowed and floated over to the table. We looked at the labels on the bottles. Millicent Spratt of Beccles, the Hungerford Horseman, Narrow Nigel, Black Lowther–

'I think perhaps it would be wise not to release Black Lowther within the vault, ma'am.'

'Why not, Dancing Dan?'

'I do recall he finds steering very difficult.'

I held up the bottle and listened. There was a distant whinnying coming from inside.

'Black Lowther is a headless horseman who drives his coach and six headless horses at a full gallop. As headless horsemen go, Black Lowther certainly goes, ma'am.'

I stared at the bottle. More whinnying and jangling carriage noises.

'How does one charm a carriage and six galloping horses into a bottle anyway, Dancing Dan?'

'One has to be extremely charming, ma'am.'

'But... aren't they going too fast?'

'There are the ghost drogues, ma'am. Fired into the rear, they open up like parachutes.'

These sounded interesting.

'Or one could lay a shirk.'

'What's that?'

'It's a puddle, ma'am, comprised of spinning air. Brings them to an immediate standstill. The horses find themselves running on the spot.'

'So you sort of lay it on the ground like a carpet?'

'No no,' tittered Dancing Dan. 'Shirk is very flammable, ma'am. It has to be especially made.'

Of course, all this was far beyond me.

'I fear so, ma'am. Shirking takes considerable practice.'

Fine. I turned to the last bottle. Doctor Grimsditch…

'I believe Doctor Grimsditch's only crime was to fall asleep in chairs. After ten years, the other teachers in the staffroom got fed up of his snoring.'

A sleeping teacher. That didn't sound too difficult… did it?

'It's harder than it seems, ma'am. However charming one might be, dozing ghosts keep falling asleep. One has to grab their attention by other means. May I suggest using the staff for a simple net cast?'

Dancing Dan explained the basics then handed me the glass bottle. It seemed strangely warm, actually it was getting hotter, actually it was becoming very, very hot… so hot it was burning my fingers…

'Dancing Dan? What's going on?'

For the first time Dancing Dan looked as mystified as I did.

'I fear that might be anger, ma'am. Bottled rage–'

'But you said he was asleep!'

The bottle leapt from my hands, glowing like a furnace. Not even Dancing Dan Dravot was going to save this one. The glass smashed and a mass of grey forms swept up from the floor… Doctor Grimsditch?

'HA!' shouted a wild-looking man in a black gown and mortar board. He spun around and faced the vault, which had suddenly become a schoolroom with twenty pupils cowering at their desks.

'YOU!' he screamed at me. 'DID I ASK YOU TO STAND?'

'Me?'

'D'you know the answer? What is it then? Spit it out!'

Doctor Grimsditch advanced towards me, cane in hand, his eyeballs red with fury. I had to remind myself that he was actually a ghost...

'GIVE ME THE ANSWER!' he screamed. 'WHAT IS IT?!'

Trying not to panic, I walked carefully across to the table and picked up the staff.

'WELL?'

Dr Grimsditch seemed to be about to explode. I screwed up my eyes and said the words as Dancing Dan had instructed.

'Spirit of man, unquiet soul,

I capture you!'

I banged the ghost staff hard on the floor. Nothing happened. The class stared at me in horror.

'What was that?'

Doctor Grimsditch's manner suddenly changed. In an instant he went from being shouty and scary to sly and clever, which in a way was even scarier.

'Couldn't agree more, ma'am,' whispered Dancing Dan, hiding behind a pillar. 'I do believe we might have confused this Doctor Grimsditch with another–'

'I know who *you* are,' said the ghost, circling around me like some enormous bat. 'Your toady little predecessor decided to put me in a bottle. That's right! He said the pupils in my class were complaining about me behind my back. They didn't like my lessons.'

I shuddered as he wound himself around me then turned back to his class.

'I want to know *who* was complaining about me!' roared Doctor Grimsditch. '*Who* was complaining? I want to know.' He stalked between the desks, eyeing his terrified pupils. 'Was it you, Freddie Drake? Or you, Violet Nossington? Perhaps it was you, George Stiggles?'

Not one of them moved. Again I said the words and banged my staff on the floor. This time a small silvery net popped out of the toad's mouth and flopped to the ground uselessly.

'Keep going, ma'am,' said Dancing Dan from the shadows. I wondered how any Joliffe had ever managed to charm this fearful bully and his class into that bottle. It was surely impossible...

'I'm waiting,' he thundered. 'Five more seconds, or I'll thrash the lot of you!'

Silence.

Dr Grimsditch smashed his cane down on a desk.

'Nancy Plumb! Come to the front!'

A little blonde girl with ringlets did so.

'Hold out your hand.'

Shaking in terror, she obeyed. He raised his cane. This was too much. Tightening my fist around the staff, I really concentrated and tried again.

'Spirit of man! Unquiet soul!

I CAPTURE YOU!'

I banged down the staff, and this time, somehow, a long plume of gas shot out of the toad's mouth.

'Good cast, ma'am,' whispered Dancing Dan, watching it turn into a large slithering net.

'And what's *that* supposed to do?' barked Doctor Grimsditch, seeing the silver net float towards him like an enormous bubble. With a sneer, he slashed at it with his cane. 'HA HA!' he laughed.

'HA HA HA!' he roared. 'HA!' he screamed as he cut it to shreds. Smack! Down went the cane on poor Nancy Plumb's hand. She screamed and quickly walked away, sobbing.

Doctor Grimsditch was completely mad. What could I do? Charm, then. Charm it had to be.

'I don't know why you think everyone hates you, Dr Grim—'

'I am hated by everyone for good reason!' screeched the ghost. 'Stiggles!'

Little George Stiggles approached in terror.

'Put out your hand, boy!'

'But I'm sure someone must think you're lovely—'

'No one thinks I'm lovely! I'm not lovely! I'm not lovely at all!'

Smack!

'Violet Nossington!'

'Dancing Dan, any ideas?'

Dancing Dan wasn't there. He'd retreated up to the rafters in terror. By now the room was full of weeping and wailing. Doctor Grimsditch may have only been a ghost beating other ghosts, but... The register in the library! Surely that would help. I closed the door of the vault as quietly as I could, locked it, and then ran up and out through the icy courtyards...

There was a disapproving murmur as I burst in through the great library door and raced down to the Ghost section. Grimsditch... In a couple of minutes I had found the entry, as neat as those above and below.

Doctor Grimsditch
  An absent-minded history teacher
  who falls asleep in chairs.

What? That couldn't be right – and then I looked below.

Not to be confused with Doctor Grimswitch.

First sighting 18th May 1904 at All Saints School, Wakefield. Dr Grimswitch made his class stay on after school for some collective misdemeanour, when the building was struck by lightning. Dr Grimswitch refused to let his pupils go till they had finished their punishment, by which time the school was ablaze. All perished. S-J[*] spent five nights attempting every charming technique ancient and modern, in the end resorting to a suction bomb, bottling Grimswitch, his class, and the schoolroom as well.

Conclusion: Dr Grimswitch is an extremely dangerous character. Charm does not work on him. Recommend indefinite captivity.

Oh dear. It was too late now. A suction bomb? What was that?

'Suction bombs are very dangerous when used inside, ma'am,' whispered Dancing Dan. 'They suck everything down into them, including the roof and sometimes the floor. This is the Royal Vault, ma'am. There'd be nothing left.'

'But do we have any?'

'I believe there are two, down in the stores.'

I stared at Doctor Grimswitch stalking up and down his phantoms classroom, shouting at his petrified pupils.

'Is that ink on your hands, Frankie Nolan? Well, if it isn't ink, WHAT IS IT?'

---

[*] (Selwyn Joliffe I guessed)

Smack!

'Violet Nossington. You *again*, Violet Nossington?'

There was only one thing for it.

'DOCTOR GRIMSWITCH!' I shouted.

'SILENCE!' he roared.

'DOCTOR GRIMSWITCH!'

'I WILL HAVE SILENCE!'

'THEN SHUT UP AND LISTEN YOU STUPID OLD FOOL!'

The raging man turned to me, foam flying from his mouth. I swung open the great door of the vault.

'I am releasing you. You are free to go.'

Doctor Grimswitch stared at the open door. He stared at his class of terrified, sobbing children. He stared at me, suspecting some trick.

'Free? To *go*?'

'Yes. In fact, go now. I don't want to see you ever again.'

Dancing Dan shook his head, muttering something about 'a very bad idea' and 'coming back to haunt us'. Doctor Grimswitch's mouth split into a sneer. And off he went, out into the dark corridor and through a wall.

'Ma'am, that was foolish—'

'What else could I do, Dancing Dan?'

The class of ghosts stared at me in astonishment. Dancing Dan stared at me in astonishment. Actually I felt quite good. At last I had done something. It may have been completely the wrong thing to do, but at least I had done it.

'I don't suppose you can remember any more limericks?'

A vague smile crossed Dancing Dan's face.

'Maybe one or two, ma'am,' he said.

LEPOS VINCIT OMNIA

⧼⧽ 19 ⧼⧽
Learning the Ropes

A **ND SO MY ADVENTURE** as Keeper of Ghosts began. As the days of my first week went by, I learnt how to cast revealing dust, fire ghost drogues, lay shirks, and listen more patiently as Dancing Dan droned on and on about ghoulology and the basic rules of phantasmiphication. Did I get any better at it? I'd like to say yes, only what Mabel the duck had said about me not being a Joliffe seemed to have stuck somehow. It just didn't come naturally at all. But I was trying.

When I wasn't in the Ghost Vault I seemed to spend most of the time getting lost. St James's Palace was a great jumble of corridors, twisting staircases and whispering galleries that whispered...

Everything was old and dark and slightly strange. I found myself saying 'excuse me' to shadows, only to find they were statues of bowmen lurking in corners, and wondering at crows on ledges, only to find they were coats of arms.

Patrolling this shadowy world was a strange woman named Enid Cribbage. Enid Cribbage was the Keeper of the Night, and she would stalk the cloisters and galleries after dark in long felt slippers and a tall hat, carrying a wooden box of bats on her back. With a hiss and a shriek she would send them up chimneys or down staircases in search of anything that was out of its vault.

'Never seen daylight, ever,' said Sam Yuell. 'And she speaks bat.'

'How do you speak bat?'

'Exactly.'

Not surprisingly, I was a little nervous of Enid Cribbage. And I was also a little nervous of her boss, Ocelot Malodure, the Keeper of Time and Enforcer of Rules. She would sit beside the Master at high table looking rather stern, and spent a lot of time checking the collection of watches she wore up her sleeves, which all seemed to be set to different times.

'This Doctor Grimswitch – is he armed?'

'Erm... no, not *exactly* armed. He has a cane.'

I glanced at Archie Queach grinning at the end of the corridor. Of course Archie had told her everything as soon as he'd heard. Ocelot Malodure peered at me over her half-moon glasses. She was a large lady with small features and eyebrows drawn on with pencil.

'One mistake we can cope with. But no more, Miss Joliffe. These are extraordinary times, and the safety of the royal children is paramount. Nothing must be allowed to escape, and no one, repeat no one, can cross over to their side of the palace. There are *severe* penalties for those that do so. Do you understand?'

'Yes, Red Tempest.' (That was her proper title, and it had nothing to do with her coat, her temper, or the fact that she looked like she'd just stepped out of a wind tunnel.)

'Very well.' She turned on her heel and saw Archie gawping in the corridor. 'Catching flies, Queach?'

Archie gulped like a fish.

'Me? Erm, no erm...'

'Off you go.'

Away he scuttled with his brushes. Ocelot Malodure gave me a sour look.

'Jellybean's niece, eh?'

From then on Archie Queach was in heaven. He'd already decided that I didn't deserve to be where I was, and now he seemed determined to make my life as difficult as possible. He was always there to laugh when I got lost and to give me stupid answers to anything I asked him.

'It was such a scene, you should have seen it! Oh yes, big black mark.' There he was as usual, gossiping with the witches at the end of my corridor.

'Obviously has no talent at all. Far too young. I did tell them. Keeper of Ghosts at that age? That's not right. Oh I expect they'll send her back to whatever stone she crawled out from soon enough...'

I may have made an enemy in Archie Queach, but he was right about one thing. I did seem to be the youngest keeper here by about fifty years. Every day I walked into the Keepers' Hall, lines of ancient keepers would be slowly eating their soup; every time I went into the library, more ancient keepers would be snoring softly in corners, collapsed under books, dozing in armchairs... What did they do all day? Nothing, as far as I could see. Perhaps there was nothing *to* do. I walked down past the vault doors, reading the names and trying to imagine what they contained. Baggajags, Basilisks, Battleswine, Belagogs, Bettysnorts, Boggarts, Borogoves (Mimsy), and that was just B... Did these creatures actually exist? And what about the vaults containing Broken Promises, Wandering Reflections, Wild Rumours...

'I suppose you've never heard any wild rumours, have you, Joliffe?' sneered Archie Queach.

'Only the one about you, Archie.'

'Oh yeah?'

'You're about to be thrown into the palace sewer for leaving your mop outside Ocelot Malodure's vault.'

'No way! But that's not fair! But, but...'

Archie panicked, then remembered to sneer again.

'Oh, ha ha, Joliffe. I suppose you find that funny?'

'It's only a rumour, Archie.'

'Oh, well done.'

In fact there was one other keeper nearly my age. Patrick Pettifog was the new Keeper of Extraordinary Plants, and he'd only just taken over after the death of his father a few months ago. Patrick had never been to school, and whenever he'd left the palace it had been to go and capture some extraordinary plant that was causing trouble. (I know; how could a *plant* cause trouble? Believe me they did... a *lot* of trouble... but I mustn't get ahead of myself). Anyway, Patrick had just come back from some bog in Somerset, having captured an extremely rare and poisonous iris, and he was very pleased about it.

'It was only tiny, but it spat like a snake, and the venom was more poisonous than cyanide!' said Patrick with a nervous laugh. Patrick Pettifog laughed nervously a lot. He wore white dungarees under his keeper's coat and was often pushing odd-looking plants around in cages. Rambling roses (they all carried walking sticks), shrinking violets (they kept disappearing), climbing beans (they would suddenly leap out of his hair)… you get the idea. But most of Patrick's time was spent trying to cope with the ever-changing demands of his most famous plant of all – an enormous, ancient lily called Fleur de Lys. The first time I met Fleur was when Patrick pushed her into the Keepers' Hall in an old wheelchair, wrapped up in a shawl and several scarves like a very old lady.

'You are not understanding my feelings,' she bleated. 'Why is nobody listening to me? I am dying!'

Patrick Pettifog laughed nervously as he sat down next to me.

'You've caught a cold, Fleur. A little touch of frost in your roots. It's nothing to worry about.'

'A touch of frost in my roots! Écoutez-moi, rosbif! My soul is bleeding!'

'I think Fleur's being rather dramatic–'

'Oui! Je suis dramatique! Zis is zer end of Fleur de Lys! After one thousand years of life, I die, alone, in a foreign country! Congratulations, English pig, I 'ope you are proud of what you 'ave done!'

Fleur de Lys did indeed look very old, and very ill, but once she was apparently the most beautiful plant in the world. Fleur was a gift from the King of France, and in medieval battles her picture was on a thousand flags and coats of arms, knights rode out to defend her honour, and she was given pride of place at every banquet, every coronation… but now, like so much else in the palace, age seemed to have finally caught up with her. All that was left of the famous Fleur de Lys was a single pale trumpet flower on top of a blackened stalk.

Fleur sniffled forlornly and stared at me. She shook her head.

'Rot in 'ell, you rat-eating rosbifs. Voici la fin.'

'Soup?' said Patrick, stirring some vile-smelling liquid.

'Zoup? ZOUP! Adieu!' Fleur slumped dramatically onto the table.

Patrick Pettifog laughed nervously.

'I don't know what's got into her, Jack. Every day this week she's died. Now let's see if we can bring Fleur back to life, shall we?' And with that he carefully held the trumpet flower up like a cup and poured a little stinking liquid into it.

'FFFF!' The soup was spat back all over the table.

'If you don't let me feed you, Fleur, then you certainly won't be getting any better.'

'How can I eat when I am dead?' croaked Fleur.

'Okay. Tomorrow we'll try some proper English food. Soggy dumplings, mushy peas, boiled Brussel sprouts–'

'You 'ave no right to threaten me, rosbif!' she roared, suddenly rising up from the table. 'My soul is being devoured! Zis is treason! When zer King 'ears of zis 'e will chop off your head an' put it on a pole!'

Patrick Pettifog glanced at me and laughed nervously again.

'What can you do? I suppose you have some troublesome customers in your vault too, eh, Jack?'

I did. But luckily I didn't have to feed them red maggots, dogs' toenails, stillborn mice, scabs from underneath dragons… I'll stop there. It was disgusting what Patrick Pettifog kept on his shelves. And this is not a cookery book, after all…

ᵔ᷾ 20 ᷾ᵔ
The Sable Tower

'**H** OW ABOUT A CHANGE of scene this morning?'
Sam Yuell slid onto the bench opposite me and smiled.
It was Saturday, the Keepers' Hall was half empty, and
I suppose it must have been obvious I wasn't looking forward
to yet another thrilling instalment of Dancing Dan's A–Z of
ghoulology. We'd only got as far as C.

'What d'you mean, Sam?'

'I'm going over t'royal side. There's a lovely old fella over there
that wants feeding. Care to tag along?'

Care to? My smile must have answered his question.

'Thought so. You'll go mad in this place if you're not careful,' he winked, nodding over to Patrick Pettifog pushing a heavily wrapped Fleur de Lys around singing nursery rhymes. On the other side, Norris Hebbedy, the Keeper of Worms, was actually snoring into his porridge.

'Half an hour then?'

Half an hour later we were trudging through the snowy courtyards, Sam bearing a huge sack slung over his shoulder. He wouldn't say who it was for, or what it was, only that the creature was called Umballoo.

'The greatest of them all. Without Umballoo this place wouldn't exist, I tell yer,' he smiled mysteriously.

We approached the great gate that separated the two sides of the palace and the sentry came out of his box.

'Hey up, Tiny.'

Tiny Torquil (for that was his name) was completely massive and dressed in a red and black doublet and matching skirt. He wasn't exactly armed, but he did have a small dagger in his sock, and he looked extremely angry.

'Going to bring Umballoo his rations. She's taggin' along for the ride. That's okay, isn't it?'

Tiny Torquil stared down at me, then mumbled something and we were on our way into a warren of cloisters and courtyards. It was almost the same as our side – the fountains hung with icicles, statues white with frost, a deep silent chill gripping everything. Almost everything. On the other side of the wall we were walking along, I could hear shouts and bangs and loud whistles… it sounded like a game.

'What's that?' I asked.

'In there? Oh that's the Jackernapes.'

'Jackernapes?'

"S'one of them old royal games, y'know. With castles and nets and fog. The ball's someone's head, I think.'

'Someone's *head*?'

'Aye. Forget whose. The kids play it all the time. They love it. Mad game.'

I rather wanted to watch this Jackernapes game, but before I could ask any more we'd stepped through yet another archway, and there before us rose a large black tower topped with battlements. 'That is the Sable Tower, lass,' said Sam. 'The oldest and most closely guarded place in the whole palace.' I looked up at the arrow slits and the massive round walls. 'What's in it, the Crown Jewels?' 'Almost. That's where Umballoo lives.'

It had started to snow again as we crossed the small courtyard and went into a high hall hung with pikes and shields. Before the roaring fire stood a massive creature with a small castle on its back.

'Bet you weren't expecting *that*, eh?' winked Sam. 'Hey up, Umballoo, brought someone to meet yer.'

It's hard to know where to begin with Umballoo. But I know that if that cranky old palace possessed a noble heart that beat, a constant ally, a true defender in times of danger, it was Umballoo. So, what was he? Umballoo was an oliphant. Not an *elephant*, which is three times smaller and half as intelligent; Umballoo was an oliphant, six hundred and twelve years old, and his great age had turned his skin the colour of a well-polished conker. As he had once been a warrior oliphant, he had two massive corkscrew tusks that had been sawn off and capped with brass, and on his back he carried a small wooden castle, lined with velvet. But perhaps the strangest things about him were the enormous purple slippers that he wore on his feet.

'A couple of bags of candied vegetables a week, and once a month a long bath and a scrub, that's all you need, isn't it?' said Sam, setting down his sack and opening it. Umballoo helped himself, crunching a sugar-coated turnip loudly. 'Very low maintenance. If only they were all like you.' Sam Yuell gave Umballoo's trunk a friendly rub, and Umballoo returned it. 'Make a friend in Umballoo and you'll have no worries around this place, Jack.'

The trunk curled up and moved around my face, then removed my cap and investigated my shaven head. It was a strange sensation. He seemed to be inspecting me, but also greeting me. I looked up into the sad black eyes high above.

'Hi,' I said.

The trunk stroked my cheeks. It tickled and I giggled.

'See? Umballoo knows all about you now. I think you're going to get on famously.'

Umballoo picked up another carrot and went back to his newspaper.

'So what does Umballoo actually do?'

Sam Yuell gave the oliphant a friendly pat and drew me away.

'Umballoo is Keeper of the Sable Tower. Inside there is every present given to the royal family in the last seven hundred years. Six floors of them, everything from phoenix eggs to boxes of invisible chocolates, you name it. And these presents don't just sit there collecting dust. Every time some foreign dignitary comes to visit, they're expected to give the King a present, and he's expected to give them a present in return. This is where he gets them from.'

I understood. The tower was like a giant present cupboard. Everything was recycled. And Umballoo was in charge.

'Why do they trust him?'

'Because he's an oliphant. You may have heard that an elephant never forgets, but an oliphant? Different league entirely. He can remember exactly who gave what to whom, when that was, where he's put it, and what they were given in return. He's never once made a mistake. And I don't doubt that over the years Umballoo's been given all sorts of things to keep that aren't presents at all. Potions, poisons, love letters, mysterious disguises, probably even things that were never supposed to exist... They're all safe in the Sable Tower with Umballoo. They're like his herd, see. He'll defend them to the death.' Sam Yuell winked slyly. 'They say he knows that many secrets he could bring down the entire royal family if he wanted to. Which is probably why they're all so nice to him. Big daft old thing, aren't yer? Wouldn't hurt a flea.'

So Umballoo was the Keeper of Palace Secrets as well. The oliphant scratched his ear with a carrot and turned the page of his newspaper. It was not hard to see why Sam Yuell was so fond of the great creature.

Neither of us had noticed the voices till Umballoo indicated that we should turn around. I gulped, as walking towards us was a tall blonde man in a dark blue suit. I vaguely recognised him from a biscuit tin. Beside him was an equally well-dressed woman – very pretty, with pale blue eyes and perfect hair, and an expression that suggested no nonsense. Needless to say, I guessed who she was too. Sam Yuell instantly bowed and I did the same.

'Good morning, Sam,' said the Queen.

'Good morning, ma'am.'

'Beastly cold isn't it?'

'Shocking, ma'am.'

'How are your animals coping?'

'Sleeping mostly, ma'am.'

'Very wise. I suppose the last thing they'll want to do is get up for the big day. And how is Fleur de Lys?'

'Doing her very best, ma'am.'

'Nothing Mr Pettifog can't cope with I'm sure,' she smiled, and they moved over to me. The King looked at me with a sort of vacant curiosity. Maybe I should have been curtseying? Or perhaps even burtseying?

'May I introduce the new Keeper of Ghosts and Phantoms, Your Highness,' said Sam Yuell. 'Jack Joliffe, Mr Joliffe's niece.'

The King snorted.

'Jellybean's *niece*? Well I'll be damned. What did yer say yer name was again?'

'Jack Joliffe, Your Highness.'

The King attempted not to look puzzled. I noticed that the Queen was now looking at me very closely.

'And what's the story with the erm... thingy?' The King twizzled his finger in the direction of my shaved head. 'D'you have lice, or are you joining the army or something?'

'It doesn't grow properly, Your Highness. Never has.'

'Ah. How jolly inconvenient for you.'

'Yes it is, Your Highness.'

'Did anyone ever find out what happened to old Jellybean? Did he retire or disappear into thin air, or what?'

The Queen shot him a glance.

'Ah. Nobody knows. The plot thickens. Well, Jellybean was a most amusing fellow. I'm sure you have what it takes to follow in his footsteps, Jack, but probably not his suits – unless you're short of a tent, what?'

Somewhere beneath his moustache there was a honking sound.

'We should be getting along, sir,' said Sam.

'Snap!' said the King. 'Cheerio Yuell, Joliffe Junior.'

'Nice to meet you, Jack,' smiled the Queen kindly. 'I'm sure you'll settle in splendidly. Now Umballoo, what treats have you dug out for our visitors this week?'

We retreated to the door and watched the King and Queen's delight as he handed back the Queen's list, then set down a collection of presents from his velvet castle: a small silver aeroplane for the Queen of Denmark's nephew Ferdy (Umballoo remembered he was five and liked aeroplanes, and this one had a real engine), a two-hundred-year-old jar of Hungarian honey for the Japanese Emperor (Umballoo remembered he had a very sweet tooth and the bees that made it were now extinct), and a special spray that claimed to make your hands disappear temporarily. That was for the American Ambassador's wife, who took Halloween very seriously. Everything Umballoo had chosen was, as ever, perfect.

'What a wonderful creature you are, you are, what a wonderful creature you are,' honked the King. I think he was singing. 'Don't suppose you can find me something to give to ghastly politicians, like farting powder or something?'

'Not a good idea, darling,' smiled the Queen.

'Watch this,' said Sam, as Umballoo hoisted the sack of vegetables up into the castle on his back and ambled towards the great iron door at the end of the hall. Umballoo's trunk reached up and pulled back a bolt in the top corner, while his foot wedged under the bottom corner and sort of lifted and twisted at the same time. There was a creak as the door moved up a fraction, then swung open.

'That door weighs nine tons,' whispered Sam. 'Only an oliphant can do that. And there's another one behind it, just in case anyone tries to sneak in with him.'

The huge leathery oliphant sauntered into the gloom, then slowly turned around to close the door. Just before it shut, I was sure I saw something move up in that velvet castle. It was only for a second… two dark eyes and a mop of black hair–

'Come on lass.'

Sam Yuell was already walking away. When I turned to look again, it was gone…

~ 21 ~
Rumours

W E RETURNED to our side of the palace by a different route. Having met the King and Queen for the first time I was full of questions which Sam answered patiently, though I sensed he was keeping his true feelings to himself.

'We all know the King's not the sharpest tool in the box, Jack, but he's harmless enough. It's the Queen you've got to watch. She's really in charge around here. The Prime Minister says we'd be far better off without the lot of 'em, but where would that leave us keepers, and all the creatures in the vaults? At the mercy of politicians, and you know what they say about *them*. Better the devil y'know.'

It was snowing hard again. Sam Yuell withdrew his head deep into the collar of his coat like a tortoise.

'Truth is, they put a brave face on it, but they've never really got over the death of Stephen,' said Sam quietly. 'He was special, that lad. Born to be a king. Whereas Richard...' Sam Yuell shook his head. 'You look at him sometimes and wonder if he'll make it to nightfall.'

'Does anyone know what's the matter with him, Sam?'

'No. Though you've heard the rumours, I expect.'

'That royal blood is cursed, or something like that.'

'Aye, something like that.' Sam looked up and down the empty cloister and drew me close. 'Everyone knows Richard was never this ill before Stephen died. It's only since he's come to live in here that the lad's gone downhill so quick. Which suggests something, don't it?'

'But wasn't he brought in here for his own protection?'

'Aye, though protection's a funny thing, isn't it? You can have too much "protection", just like you can have too much of anything. Perhaps those protecting that lad don't exactly have his best interests at heart. But you never heard me say that.'

On round the Keepers' Courtyard we went. I glanced across at the Isabella tree in its cage. My mind was racing.

'Tom Bootle seemed to think the palace was under some sort of spell.'

'Did he now?'

'He seemed to think Isabella Royle might have something to do with it. The cold and the fog, and Richard being so sick.'

Sam Yuell rolled his massive shoulders and snorted.

'Listen, Jack, Tom Bootle is the biggest gossip in this palace.

He was the court jester before she turned him into a rabbit for all his interfering. Just can't keep his mouth shut, never has. Tom Bootle…' Sam shook his head, then carried on in a whisper. 'Isabella Royle was a very clever and dangerous young lady. She was Keeper of Fairies before Snowdrop Scott, and maybe she was the greatest keeper who ever lived, who knows, but here's the thing: she's *dead*. She was executed, right there; I saw it with my own eyes.' Sam nodded across at the blackened tree in its cage. 'But if I believed every shred of gossip flying around this palace, I'd think the heffalumps had taken to wearing pyjamas, the Hound of the Baskervilles was learning the saxophone, and Isabella Royle was riding a jabberwock down the corridors calling for another revolution. If you want my advice, Jack, don't pay any attention to anything Tom Bootle says. He means well, but he's an interfering menace.'

Sam stared at me hard. He meant it.

'So you really think she's got nothing to do with it?'

'It's the people that are *alive* that I worry about, Jack. Not them that aren't.'

And with that Sam Yuell trudged away across the courtyard, his bulky silhouette disappearing into the mist.

ᵈᵉ 22 ᵈᵉ
Kidnapped

I HAVE TO SAY, I found Sam Yuell's opinions quite surprising. Isabella Royle may have been dead, and Tom Bootle may have been a terrible gossip, but wasn't something strange going on in this palace? What did I know? I'd only been here a week. Maybe this was normal...

That evening I had another surprise. I opened the door to my room to find it dark and freezing cold. A biting wind was blowing hard through the open window. There was no fire, and no sign of Tom Bootle either.

'Hello?'

Silence.

'Hello?'

I shut the window and wandered into the bedroom. The bed was unmade, my clothes were strewn all over the place, the chairs were overturned… I'm not suggesting that already I had such airs and graces that this bothered me, but it did make me wonder where Tom Bootle was. He was always so pleased to see me when I came back from the vault, fussing and fidgeting: 'Can I take your coat, Miss Jack? Have a seat, have a seat, warm yourself in front of the fire. Oh this weather. Tea? Muffins? How about some magic…' He would pull that same old mouse from my pocket and turn it into that long-suffering toad. 'Have you seen this trick before, Mastress? No?' Of course the truth would offend him, but I couldn't help liking Tom Bootle, for all his faults. He seemed so desperate to please…

So where was he now? Kneeling before the fireplace, I scraped a few bits of wood and paper together, and then noticed some wobbly words scrawled in white chalk on the floorboards.

HULO JOK!
We av kidnapt the funnee litel Bootel person wot livs in yur room. Bootel is ower prisnor now. If yu wan to sea im agin yowd beter cum wiv a MILYUN POWN ransum TUNIYT. Or els we shal tortur him to DEF. Cos we will u no. No jokin!

No prizes for guessing who this was from. I stared at the message, thinking hard. The twins were only seven, they wouldn't really… would they? Something told me they might. Poor Tom Bootle… I looked across the snowy rooftops towards the Ermine Tower on the other side where they lived. It was a sheer drop down to the gutter below. The only way over there was to climb up and along the slippery ridges, all the way round to the gatehouse, slide down into the school half of the palace, and then follow the narrow battlements round the courtyards until somehow... just thinking about it was making it seem impossible... but Tom Bootle was my servant. Even though he was quite strange, and also slightly annoying, I couldn't leave him to the mercy of those two little monsters... could I?

With a thumping heart I climbed out of the window and began to edge along the slippery battlements. It was, of course, completely terrifying, and as I crept along I couldn't help peering down into the keepers' rooms below. There was Snowdrop Scott, sitting beside her fire, embroidering a tiny frock coat. There was Archie Queach, guzzling a cake; he glanced up guiltily as I passed. Enid Cribbage almost spotted me. Just as I reached the high wall separating the two sides of the palace, she appeared at the corner of a cloister with her lamp staff in her hand. Clinging to a thin lightning conductor, I ducked and slid down the snowy roof into the school. I saw a pillow fight in a dormitory, a group of girls sitting in a window seat talking, some children my age playing cards and laughing... I watched them all through the windows enviously. What was I doing out here? The last bit involved sliding down a steep snowy roof that would bring me to a window in the Ermine Tower. Whose window it was, I didn't know, but at least it was the right place. As I sat on the corner of a clock tower, wondering how to do this last bit, I saw a girl through the window below. She had curly blonde hair in a ponytail, and when she turned around, I recognised her from that first morning. She looked out at the snowy rooftops and spotted me, sitting up next to the clock. I waved, and she stared at me in surprise. She opened the window.

'Are you alright up there?' she asked.

'I'm fine,' I said, my teeth chattering. 'Can I come in?'

Another person came and stood beside her. It was Richard, his dark hair flopping down over his temples.

'What are you doing?' he said.

'She wants to come in, Cuz.'

'In here?' He looked up at me in amazement. 'Aren't you Jack, the new Keeper of Ghosts?'

'Yes.'

'Just get out of the way, Cuz. Let's make something for her to land on.'

A minute later the girl had moved the chairs and made a huge pile of cushions below the window.

'Slide down the roof and you'll be fine,' she said, waving me on.

I confess I was a little terrified; it was a long way down.

'Come on!' smiled the girl.

For the first time — but not the last — I put my faith in that rosy-cheeked girl with the ponytail. Letting go of the clock, I slid straight down the side of the roof, picking up speed alarmingly–

'Slow down!'

There was a crash, bang and a wallop, but I didn't see any of it. The next thing I knew I was in a huge heap of cushions in the centre of an octagonal room. There were suits of armour and tapestries and books strewn all about.

'So you really don't have any hair.'

I turned around to find Richard staring down at me curiously. There was something immediately familiar about the thin, pale boy with dark shadows under his eyes. I couldn't think what.

''Fraid not,' I replied, pulling myself to my feet gingerly. I must have seemed a little angry because he stopped staring at my shaved head and smiled.

'Sorry. I'm very rude,' he said, handing me my cap. 'I'm Richard.'

'I know.'

'Welcome,' he said, then coughed a surprisingly deep cough that seemed to shake his whole body.

'You're not quite what we were expecting,' said the girl. 'Apparently you smoke a pipe, the ghost of a parrot sits on your shoulder, and you're always drunk.'

The next question answered itself.

'Hi. I'm Lily Lancaster, Richard's cousin.'

'Hi.'

Lily was freckled, healthy, smiling; everything Richard was not. She looked at me a moment – curious and vaguely impressed.

'So you like roof-climbing as well?'

'Not exactly,' I said, and explained about the note.

'You came all the way over here to rescue Tom Bootle?' asked Richard. Clearly he thought that was a mad idea.

'Probably a good idea, Cuz,' said Lily. 'D'you remember what they did to that fairy? Last year Thomas and Victoria stole one of those fairies,' Lily explained. 'It was injured or sick or something, and Snowdrop Thingy was taking it to the vet. She only left it in a corridor for five seconds and they stole it, took it back to their room, smashed open its cage, pulled its wings off, put it on the fire and then they *ate* it! Caused such a fuss. Snowdrop complained and it went right up to Uncle Edward–'

'And my father thought it was terribly funny. Yes I do remember, Lily,' said Richard impatiently.

'But you've got to admit, Cuz, that was a pretty crazy thing to do. I mean, to actually *eat* it? Snowdrop Whatsit was gobsmacked.'

I wasn't surprised; so was I.

'I'm afraid my younger brother and sister are absolutely monstrous, Jack,' said Richard. 'I apologise in advance.'

'No but they really are, Jack, they *really* are,' agreed Lily. 'We should come down with you. If you go on your own, you'll never be able to rescue him. Honestly you won't.'

Lily was so insistent that I agreed, so down the spiral staircase we went to the floor below, Richard doing his best to hurry but still only taking one step at a time. Again and again he coughed that terrible cough.

'Enter!'

I opened the door and found the twins sitting at a table sharpening long sticks with penknives. All about them was a chaos of toys and games. They didn't seem the least surprised to see me.

'Oh hello, Jock,' smiled Victoria. 'I hope you've bought a million pounds with you.'

'Because if you *haven't—*' Thomas stopped when he saw Lily walk in, followed by Richard.

'Where's Tom Bootle? What have you done with him?' she demanded.

Thomas and Victoria looked at each other.

'Thank goodness you're here. The rabbit man is hiding in our bedroom and needs arresting immediately.'

'He should probably be killed, because he's on our side of the palace,' said Thomas. 'That's what the rules say, don't they?'

'He's only on this side of the palace because you kidnapped him,' I said.

'We didn't kidnap him, Jock. He wanted to come with us,' said Thomas.

'Did he indeed,' Richard murmured.

'He did, Richard. He said he wanted to do anything we wanted to do. So we put him in a sack and carried him back over the rooftops—'

'Which was jolly hard, because Bootle is fat,' added Thomas.

'But the trouble was, when we got him out of the bag, he just lay on the floor! "Oh I've been so bumped about! Oh I don't feel like playing any games any more."'

'So he had to have his toes stamped on,' said Thomas with a merry smile. 'That woke him up.'

'So then I put on his nappy and bonnet, and made him eat baby food—'

'Soggy paper and mashed up crayons, by any chance?' asked Richard.

'Maybe,' smirked Victoria. 'And after a bit he said, "This isn't very exciting. Why don't I do some tricks for you?"'

'Totally rubbish tricks,' said Thomas. 'The worst tricks I've ever seen in my life. All he had was a mouse and a toad—'

'"Not good enough, Bootle, we want some proper excitement," said Victoria. 'So we put him in a pram and raced him round and round, but stupid Bootle kept crashing into things and falling out! And after he'd smashed into the door for the millionth time he started moaning and saying, "Oh this is too much, I wish I could die, I wish I could die," over and over like that—'

'Which is why we threw him down the stairs,' smiled Thomas.

I stared at the little blonde boy, speechless.

'You did *what*?'

'We did *try* to kill him,' said Victoria primly. ' "I wish I could die, I wish I could die." He kept saying it, Jock. Trouble was, he bounced all the way down, and only went *properly* splat at the bottom.'

'That was a very cruel thing to do,' I said.

'No it wasn't. He deserved it,' said Thomas.

'You two are going to get in big trouble for this,' said Lily, crossing her arms and standing before them in a big-sisterly way.

'That's just what I told them,' said a scared-looking young woman in uniform poking her head around the door. 'They've been ever so naughty–'

'Oh shut up, Pinkerton. You're about to be fired,' sneered Thomas.

Nanny Pinkerton tried to speak.

'Well it was silly Pinkerton's fault, wasn't it?' said Victoria. 'She let us get completely out of control. If she hadn't let us get completely out of control, none of this would've happened. Isn't that true, Pinkerton?'

Nanny Pinkerton looked flustered.

'So predictable,' sighed Thomas. 'Just pack your bags, Pinkerton.'

'I–'

'YOU'RE USELESS!' screamed Victoria. 'GO AWAY!'

Amazingly Nanny Pinkerton burst into tears and then did exactly as she was told.

'Why are you so unpleasant?' said Richard. 'I can't believe I'm even related to you.'

'And I can't believe I'm even related to *you*,' said Thomas.

'Me neither,' added Victoria. 'Weedy Richard. We don't have to listen to you anyway, because you're about to die.'

'That is very unkind,' said Lily sternly.

'Richard's so ill he'll probably die tomorrow. Everyone says so–'

'Victoria–'

'Mummy says so. Even Daddy says so–'

'SHUT UP YOU TWO OR ELSE!' shouted Lily, marching forward, fists clenched. I think she was about to hit them. I didn't blame her.

'Or else what, Lily?'

'Yeah — or else what?'

Thomas and Victoria collapsed to the floor in a fit of giggles. Richard coughed painfully.

'Come on, Lily,' he said, pulling her away. 'These idiots aren't worth it.'

We left the twins rolling about on the floor in helpless laughter and pushed through into their bedroom. Predictably, everything here was in chaos too. Opposite their grand bunk bed stood an old oak cupboard on which 'PRISUN' had been scribbled in large letters. The twins had made holes in the sides and there were sticks and even spears lying about.

'Tom Bootle?'

I opened the door and knelt before it, peering into the darkness.

'Bootle, are you in there?'

From behind an upturned box in the far corner, a pair of wide, frightened eyes turned to stare at me.

'Mastress? Is that you?'

'Yes, Bootle, it's me, Jack. I've come to take you back.'

Tom Bootle's eyes opened even wider.

'Will you come back with me?' I asked.

'Back with you?'

'Yes. Come back with me, right now. Because if you stay here, I think they might eat you.'

Tom Bootle's wide eyes blinked.

'But they only said that to frighten me—'

'No, they said that because they meant it,' said Lily. 'They probably *are* going to eat you if you stay here. This is your last chance to escape.'

Bootle stared at us.

'Oh!'

At last he saw sense. Slowly, painfully, Tom Bootle crawled out from his hiding place at the back of the cupboard. Everything about him drooped and draggled. His jester's jacket was torn in many places and his long pink fingers were bruised and scratched. Half his tail had been pulled out.

'Are you sure you're okay?' I asked.

Bootle sniffed in confusion.

'So I was to be eaten as punishment, then?'

'I'm afraid my brother and sister are utterly vile,' said Richard. 'Please ignore everything they say.'

Tom Bootle cocked his head and stared in wonder at his future King.

'I didn't mean to talk to them, Your Highness; it's just that I… they said it was a Royal Command.'

'I bet they did.'

'I've seen men hanged for disobeying a Royal Command. And worse. There was one partic'lar jester, Dingo Skuppitt he was called–'

'No one will blame you for being over here, Mr Bootle. If you go back with Jack now, I'll make sure no one knows about it.'

'Well I… I thank you, Your Highness, I thank you. Thank you.'

Tom Bootle bowed low, then sank to one knee and bowed again. And again. And again. A little too much bowing, I thought. Still, I was glad they hadn't roasted him. He straightened his jacket and pulled the cobwebs from his ears and we all walked back past the twins. Thomas and Victoria stared at Tom Bootle like a pair of cross little teddy bears who had been told there was no tea party.

'Bye-bye Mr Bootle,' said Victoria, waving with cheerful spite. 'Next time we'll cook you proper.'

'Stick a prong right through you and turn you on a spit like a real rabbit,' Thomas giggled.

'BOOTLE'S GOING TO DIE!' screamed Victoria, flinging a shoe at the door with glee. Lily closed it just in time.

'Someone's going to have to do something about those two,' she huffed.

'Like what, Lily?' said Richard. 'Father thinks they're hilarious.'

We went back upstairs to Richard's room. Tom Bootle was so bashed about that he took even longer than Richard to climb the stairs, and he stubbornly refused any help.

'Aren't you very young to be a keeper, Jack?' asked Lily, as we waited beside the window. I told them the story of how I got there. I noticed they were listening intently.

'No one tells us much about your side of the palace at all,' said Richard. 'Only Archie Queach, spinning ridiculous stories about bandersnatches and jabberwocks. As if *that* were true,' he coughed.

'But it is true. There are.'

They stared at me.

'What, real ones?'

'Yes. There's seven floors under the palace. Ghosts are almost normal, because everyone's heard of ghosts.'

'Are you serious?' Richard really didn't know. I did my best to explain.

'Wow,' said Lily. 'We just thought Archie Queach was showing off.'

Richard was still staring at me intently. Now I realised why there was something familiar about him. It was his eyes; they were exactly the same colour as my own.

'Why don't you come to tea tomorrow and tell us more about it?' he asked suddenly.

'Would that be allowed?'

'Probably not. But if I sent you a proper invitation, I can't see that they could object. It's not as if you're going to kill me.' Richard smiled a sickly smile. 'Will you?'

My expression must have answered his question. Of course I wanted to come back over here. Why wouldn't I?

'Tea tomorrow then,' he grinned, flicking his mop of thick black hair out of his eyes. 'I'll send you a royal invitation.'

Tom Bootle appeared at the door, blowing hard.

'Just a little soreness about the toes, Your Highness, that's all.' Straightening his patchwork jacket, Tom Bootle limped across to the window with as much dignity as he could muster.

'Think you can make it back with Jack, Mr Bootle?' asked Lily.

Tom Bootle looked at the drop. He looked up at that clock tower. A mischievous glint returned to his eye.

'Now let me tell you a story. Old King George decided to hold a Halloween ball and he summoned his finest fool to his chamber. "Bootle," he said, "at midnight I want you to frighten the pants off my cousin, the King of Prussia." "Frighten the pants, Your Highness?" "Frighten the pants and the socks and the very garters off him, Bootle." "But how, Your Highness?" "I leave that up to you, Bootle, but you should know that the King of Prussia is very much afraid of owls – big brown owls, with big golden eyes. Oh! They have him puking into his pudding! That is what I would like to see, Bootle!" So I scratches me head and thinks. Hmm... What if I got some feathers, made myself a hat and wings, and the moment that clock strikes midnight I'll burst in through his window like this!'

And with that he leapt across onto the roof and climbed up, still gossiping away...

ᵔᵔ 23 ᵔᵔ
Snowdrop's Advice

RICHARD WAS AS GOOD as his word. The next morning as I sat in the Keepers' Hall, eating my pancakes as usual, I noticed that the silence all around me had grown particularly silent. I looked up and saw the reason: a white squirrel was running down the centre of the long table, and every keeper had stopped to watch. The grumpy-looking creature wore a short red jacket with silver buttons, and a black top hat. In a sack it carried an envelope. When the squirrel reached me it stopped and with a haughty snort slapped the letter down into my pancakes, before scampering away as fast as it could. It didn't seem remotely friendly, and neither did it want to hang around.

'That is the King's harbinger,' whispered Ambrose Dunk, staring after the white squirrel with a mixture of curiosity and disapproval. 'I can't remember the last time one of those dared to show its face in here.'

I looked at the thick cream envelope with my name on it. I realised everyone at the long table was waiting for me to open it. So I did.

Come to tea at 4pm this afternoon

R

'Be very careful consorting with the royal family, Miss Joliffe,' muttered Norris Hebbedy, reading the invitation beside me. 'They don't like us, and we don't like them.'

'Why don't we like them?'

The elderly keepers all glanced at each other and went back to their pancakes. I noticed Snowdrop Scott staring at me. When she'd finished, she came and tapped me on the shoulder.

'I think you should come down and see me this morning,' she said quietly, adding: 'You're interested in fairies, aren't you?' With a mysterious smile she hurried away.

Yes I was interested in fairies, particularly after what Sam Yuell had told me, but why was she asking me now? Ever since that first morning I'd seen very little of Snowdrop Scott. Sometimes I would spot her trotting around a cloister carrying a basket under her arm as if she was going somewhere, and once, as I was crossing the

Keepers' Courtyard, I happened to stop and stare at that mysterious Isabella tree in its cage and noticed Snowdrop Scott watching me from a window. The Keeper of Fairies kept herself very much to herself, which made her invitation almost as interesting as Richard's...

When I got back to my room, I handed the gold-rimmed card to Tom Bootle, who stared at it in awe.

'Do you think this will be enough to get me through the gate?' I asked.

'An official royal invitation, written in *green ink*? Why, this could get you to the moon, Mastress! Perhaps I should brush your coat, shine the buttons and buff the buckles?' he said.

'If you like,' I said, seeing that he was very keen to do so.

'Then it shall be done. We must zhoosh you up, Mastress! Sick of body he may be, but noble of mind, yes indeed; a most excellent Prince.'

Now that he was Richard's greatest fan, there wasn't much sense to be had out of Tom Bootle.

A couple of hours of revealing lessons passed before I made an excuse to Dancing Dan and found my way down to the Fairy Vault on the fourth floor. Not surprisingly, somewhere in the gloom I almost tripped over Archie Queach and his brushes.

'Lost again are you, Joliffe?'

'No.'

I walked up to the great door and knocked. Archie was outraged.

'Are you out of your tiny mind? You can't just walk in there!'

The door opened.

'Ah, Jack. How nice to see you.'

I couldn't resist giving scowling Archie a little wave as I stepped inside.

Snowdrop Scott led the way passed a couple of large fridges into a little workroom that might have belonged to a dolls' clothes maker. It was overflowing with boxes stuffed with delicate bits of material, half-completed jackets and hats, all sewn in amazing detail – and yet it was impossible not to stare out through the big caged window into the forest beyond. Because it *was* a forest. Huge ancient trees stretched out into the distance. In the shafts of golden light, I could just make out tiny glittering creatures dancing and dipping like butterflies.

'How can there be a forest under the palace?' I asked, genuinely amazed.

'Perhaps it's easier to think of it the other way round,' said Snowdrop Scott. 'The Enchanted Forest was always here. The palace happens to be built on top of it. This is the last enchanted forest in Albion. There used to be many others, with fairy lanes running between them, a long time ago.'

Snowdrop Scott sat down, and taking a large lump of cheese began cutting it into tiny squares with a sharp knife.

'It's not a crime to be interested in fairies, Jack,' she smiled, watching me watching them through the caged window. 'Fairies are by far the most complex and fascinating creatures in Albion. But then I would say that, wouldn't I?'

She began to tell me about them. I listened politely, wondering what this was all about. Maybe Snowdrop Scott was lonely, and if she was, I knew that feeling. Being a keeper could be a solitary business. And yet I sensed she had some other purpose in mind…

Snowdrop told me there were about four hundred fairies in the Enchanted Forest, and they all belonged to ancient families who regarded themselves as the first and only true inhabitants of Albion. They were forever bickering and feuding with each other,

and the only thing that united them was their intense hatred of humans and longing for the day when, according to their ancient lore, the Fairy Queen would return and their forest magic would once again flow through the land. Understanding fairy lore and their long history in Albion took years of study, and so did the twelve different fairy languages they spoke.

'I began learning them when I was six,' said Snowdrop. 'By the age of eleven I could speak three; by fourteen, eight. The last four are secret languages, and I'm not sure I'll ever master them. My mother tried. The only person who's ever been able to speak all twelve fluently was Isabella Royle.'

I looked at Snowdrop Scott. She smiled at me.

'The old knowledge has been passed down, you see, mother to daughter, down the years. I can't imagine how you even know where to begin, being pitchforked into it all.'

So I'd been told.

'That's very unusual then?'

Snowdrop peered at me over those large spectacles.

'My dear Jack, it's most peculiar. The handover between one

keeper and another usually takes months, sometimes years. I for one was very surprised when Galahad Joliffe mysteriously disappeared and suddenly there you were, somehow expected to know what to do. I suspect they've all got so old they've forgotten what it's like to begin at the very beginning.'

I felt heartened by this. Perhaps too much had been expected of me. Perhaps my job was actually impossible.

'I've made a lot of mistakes,' I admitted. 'I've already lost one ghost. He was so crazy I had to let him walk out the door.'

'I'm not surprised,' Snowdrop Scott smiled. 'I remember when I met my first fairy. Eglantine. A perfectly delightful creature, until I realised her true nature. And the rest of them are just the same. Fairies can be wonderful company when they feel like it, but at heart they're cold, scheming and vicious. There's only been one fairy that has escaped from this vault in six hundred years, and on that occasion the palace almost burnt to the ground. A single match was all it took.'

There was a hint of pride in Snowdrop's voice. She seemed rather pleased to be in charge of the most devious creatures.

'But it's Isabella Royle who you really want to know about, isn't it? Isabella Royle, the most brilliant and dangerous keeper that ever lived. I don't suppose anyone will tell you about her, because her power scared people, and keepers can be very superstitious – as if she's still alive somewhere, when she quite obviously isn't.'

'So you knew her well, then?'

Snowdrop Scott put her plate of cheese aside and started on another.

'Isabella Royle was like an older sister to me. The Master brought her here when she was eight. She'd been abandoned by her parents in some awful boarding school, and where she came from before that I'm not sure anyone knows. Isabella always said her father had been a great Russian wizard, and her mother an English countess, and they'd been famous jewellery thieves who'd robbed banks and were now on the run in South America. She always wanted people to think she was important, high-born, special. She needn't have bothered trying so hard, because she was immensely gifted. I remember watching her ask the water in the fountain to change direction, seeing her open and close flowers by stretching her fingers. It was instinct. When she was twelve my mother decided she was old enough to come into the vault, and Isabella learnt so fast it was frightening. In a matter of months, she could make fairy fire and walk out into the Enchanted Forest unprotected. If I were to do that now I'd be dead in minutes.'

I looked out into the trees at the brilliant creatures flitting about and remembered what Archie had told me.

'Why didn't they kill her?'

Snowdrop Scott shrugged.

'Isabella had mastered so much fairy magic she could control them. That is a very rare thing. No other fairy keeper has ever managed it. Fairies' fangs are full of ancient venoms from the forest, you see. Even if they like you, they still might bite you and you'll die. That's what happened to my mother,' she added matter-of-factly.

I stared at her.

'Out there. In the forest. Somehow she found herself locked inside. Isabella had just started as her under-keeper and she claimed she never heard her screams. I'm sure it wasn't an accident.'

I was shocked. Snowdrop Scott didn't seem particularly sad about it. She went out to one of the large fridges and returned with a couple of dark red plastic packets.

'This is what fairies like best,' she said. 'Good hard Lincolnshire Cheddar and fresh blood. Cheese, blood and the occasional mouse if I can catch one,' she said.

Snipping the corner off a packet, she began to carefully pour out the blood into little dishes. It was fascinating and disgusting at the same time.

'What happened after that?'

'Isabella Royle became the next Keeper of Fairies. Obviously in the natural scheme of things it would have been me, but no one could ignore Isabella's genius. Two years later she started a revolution. Isabella was a passionate and persuasive person. She believed that the ancient creatures of Albion shouldn't be kept in cages underground, oppressed and hidden away like guilty secrets. They should be set free and returned to their old hunting grounds, and Albion itself should go back to what it once was a long time ago – a living, breathing, wild place. Isabella said she would go out into the hills and call the sleeping spirits back to life, restore the ancient enchanted forests, and bring back the natural chaos of the land. The only law that would exist would be fairy law – the oldest law there is. And then she would rule it, as the Fairy Queen.'

That sounded amazing. Terrifying. Crazy.

'And could she really do that?'

'She believed she could.'

'What about everything that's already here?'

'It would have to go.'

'Go? Go where?'

Snowdrop Scott shrugged. Maybe if you'd spent your whole life inside the palace you wouldn't be interested in little things like that.

'Isabella Royle was barely seventeen, but she had this immense confidence – arrogance, perhaps – that she could do anything she wanted. Many keepers secretly supported her. Even the palace was on her side.'

Snowdrop Scott peered at me over those enormous glasses. She wasn't joking.

'On the night of her uprising, every door locked itself, every staircase became a thicket, every corridor a wood, stone arches fell in on themselves and water rose up through the wells. Isabella then marched on the Sable Tower, intending to hold the palace to ransom, but she never got inside.'

'Why not?'

'Umballoo wouldn't let her. He knew that there was something in there that she wanted, needed probably, for her revolution to succeed. Some powerful, magical fairy object from Albion's past, I suspect. He decided she wasn't having it. They had a great fight just outside the door, and eventually Isabella fell wounded and was captured.'

Wow. No wonder everyone was so nice to Umballoo.

'And is it true what happened next?' I asked.

Snowdrop snipped off the corner of another packet and carefully began pouring out more dark puddles of blood.

'I watched from an upstairs window and very much wish I hadn't. It was barbaric. Isabella was led out into the Keepers' Courtyard, and tied between two posts. Then Valentine Oak declared that Isabella must have been part fairy to do what she had done. Her powers were not human. Fairy blood was the cause of it, he said. Fairy blood had poisoned her body and infected her soul. So body and soul must be separated forever. Her blood must be returned to Albion's earth, and her soul released to the air. There was only one way to do that. Isabella was cut with a wizard's knife. Cut, and cut, a thousand tiny cuts, till there was no more blood left in her body.'

I shuddered. Even now, after everything that has happened, I still feel sick to think of it...

'When they took her down, Isabella was white as snow, and the earth all around black and sodden. The next day a small tree had grown in the place where she'd fallen. No amount of killing can get rid of that tree. They've chopped it, burnt it, poisoned it, but every morning it comes back. So it's been left there with a cage around it as a warning to her supporters – who were many, by the way, though they've never been identified. They've all just melted back into their vaults, hoping no one will remember.'

The tray between us was now all neatly arranged. Regiments of diced cheese on one side, dishes of blood on the other. Snowdrop Scott looked at me.

'Isabella Royle was a very powerful person, Jack. She had a dream and she died for it, and she's not been forgotten. And there are many who've never forgiven the Master for the manner of her death.'

'It sounds awful,' I said.

'It was supposed to be.' Snowdrop Scott nodded. 'So now you know the whole story, Jack, let me offer a word of advice. The less the royal family know about us, the better. We may share this palace, but we live in separate worlds, and that's the way it's always been. Sometimes they get the wrong idea about what we keepers do over here, and when they find out, they tend to get rather excited.'

She looked up at me over her glasses. Was this what she'd wanted to tell me? Not quite.

'As far as they're concerned, Isabella Royle was just some

troublesome young keeper, and fairies are all beautiful and strange like Asphodel, who you'll meet this afternoon.'

'Asphodel?'

'Asphodel's probably the most famous fairy of them all. He'll tell you how he rode a mouse to the coronation of Elizabeth I, paddled a cockleshell around the bath of Henry VIII, shared the stage with Shakespeare. And maybe he did. Asphodel's always been a great entertainer and a royal favourite. Which is why he's up in Prince Richard's bedroom at the moment.'

'So he's not dangerous?'

Snowdrop Scott smiled.

'My dear Jack, every fairy is exceedingly dangerous. Asphodel just so happens to be a wonderful performer. He loves showing off. Whenever there are royal children, Asphodel is usually brought up to amuse them. He lives in a cage in their room for a few years, then when they're grown up, he comes back down to the vault and stirs up trouble. Asphodel's seen them all, met them all. But of course nowadays he's never let out of his cage, that would be quite out of the question. I'm sure you'll have a lovely time.'

With that, Snowdrop Scott put on something like a beekeeper's suit and entered the Enchanted Forest with the tray of fresh blood and cheese. I watched through the window as she walked out into the dappled sunlight calling to the fairies. It was amazing to see them swarm down out of the great trees and circle around her, screaming and shrieking as they lapped at the bloody dishes and thieved each other's cheese morsels, their teeth glittering like needles...

Sam Yuell was right, fairies were terrifying, and Snowdrop Scott was as hard as an anvil. But I sensed she too had a secret admiration for Isabella Royle. Perhaps everyone did.

～ 24 ～
Asphodel

A T FOUR O'CLOCK I stood outside Richard's door with the gold-rimmed invitation in my hand. I knocked.

No answer. I imagined Richard might move slowly so I waited for the tap-tap-tapping of his cane. Nothing. Should I dare to go in?

The octagonal room was bright from the snow outside, the pictures and bookshelves gleaming. A fire blazed in the grate. There was a reading light switched on beside the armchair and a book about haunted castles lying open on the floor. Richard had obviously just been here. But he wasn't any more. Beyond I could see into the large bedroom, with its huge four-poster bed, and the bathroom beyond that. There was no one here.

That is, not quite.

Hanging in an alcove beside the window was a birdcage. Actually, it was more like a miniature hanging palace. There was a floor at the bottom with barred windows, and then an open space above, with a table and chairs, a sofa and a swing. It was on this swing that a fairy lolled with his back to me, his wings shimmering like jewels.

'Is that you, dear boy?'

The voice crackled and seemed to come from somewhere far away. I walked closer and stared through the bars at the fairy. With his toe, he pushed himself round to face me. Asphodel wore a velvet dressing gown, and his hair was scraped back off his forehead and tucked under a silk hat embroidered with the tiniest pearls. To me, he looked like an ancient actor in his make-up, white and dried and empty. But his lips were black, and his fangs sparkled, and his eyes were as bright as a mouse's.

'Do I know you?'

I shook my head. Something must have excited his curiosity as he stared at me a little longer.

'Who are you?'

I explained. He nodded, watching me all the while.

'Welcome then, Jack. I would get up but I'm feeling very weak this afternoon. Richard has gone to the library and he's forgotten to give me my rations again. Oh that boy takes such a long time to do anything,' he groaned.

I looked at the table inside his cage. A tiny cut-glass decanter rested on it. It was empty, as was the goblet resting in Asphodel's hand.

'I'm sure he'll be here in a minute,' I smiled.

Asphodel sighed.

'You're an optimist, I see. It's intolerable, not to be endured.'

'Can I help?'

Asphodel shook his head.

'I'm sure you'd rather not,' he said, his thin fingers indicating the small steel pin resting on a white plate on the table.

'Three drops is enough,' he said. 'Three small drops. No matter. It can wait. Ohh I'm so weak these days.'

With one slippered toe, he pushed himself away and stared out into the grey sky. The goblet glittered in his hand.

I looked at the pin again. And then I understood.

'Three drops… of blood?' I said.

'That is all. Three drops, hey-ho. Richard uses his fingertip, as a rule. But don't trouble yourself, I'll wait.'

Asphodel began humming a tune quietly. Quite why I decided to do what I did next, I don't know. I suppose I couldn't really think why not.

'I could give you some,' I said.

Asphodel stopped his humming and spun around to face me.

'You're brave. Most children hate the sight of blood.'

'If it's only three drops I don't mind.'

The fairy stared at me with interest.

'Galahad Joliffe was not a brave man. He was a coward.'

I shrugged. Asphodel smiled.

'Very well. I am much indebted to your generosity, Jack.'

Hauling himself off the swing he moved across the cage to a small hatch. Placing the goblet and a pin on the tray he swung a lever and it appeared outside. His dark eyes watched me as I picked up the pin and pierced the end of my little finger. It was a sharp jab of pain, and then the blood came.

'Careful not to waste any,' instructed Asphodel, as I placed my finger over the glass. I squeezed three drops into it, and it was full. The fairy stared at it greedily.

'Enough?' I asked.

'Ample.'

I sucked my finger then lifted the hatch and slid the goblet through, closing the lock behind. Asphodel picked up the glass and savoured the smell. Then he took a sip, rolling the blood around in his tiny mouth like an expert. He looked at me approvingly.

'You have excellent blood, Jack.'

'Is there a difference?'

'Oh yes. Some is sweet and some is sour, some is complex and some is low grade; but yours is... interesting.'

'Different to Richard's?'

'Of course.'

'I was told that's the reason why he's so ill, because he has bad blood. Royal blood is bad blood. Can you tell?'

Asphodel was back on his swing, the goblet cradled between his fingers. There was a living colour in his cheeks now, and a glint in his eye.

'People are always quick to find reasons for what they don't understand. Richard's blood is as good as anyone else's.'

'So what do you think is wrong with him?'

Asphodel opened his bony hands.

'My dear child, I am a poet, an actor, a loyal friend to the Kings and Queens of Albion. Alas, I am no doctor. What I think is not worth a groat.'

The fairy glanced back at me, his black eyes twinkling.

'So wise so young, they say, do never live long.'

I wasn't sure what to make of that. Asphodel glanced at the stairs.

'Hush. He doth approach. Ding-dong bell.'

The door opened and Richard leant against the frame, stick in hand, beads of sweat on his brow.

'Every day those steps seem to get a little steeper,' he panted. 'Hi Jack.'

'Hi.'

He shuffled in and dropped into an armchair, breathing hard.

'My poor boy,' whispered Asphodel. 'What has become of you?'

'Don't be sympathetic, Asphodel. It's so boring.' Richard looked at me and attempted to smile. 'Shall I ring for tea?'

～ 25 ～
The Tea Party

THERE WAS A WHITE TABLECLOTH, an ancient tea
service laid out with cucumber sandwiches, cakes, chocolate
fingers, crumpets for toasting, raspberry jam, strawberry
jam, scones and heaps of clotted cream… This was a proper royal
tea, no question. Lily came in with a friend called Matty Wong,
and then a friend of Richard's called Tim Iddunshy turned up, who
was even thinner and nerdier than him. There was much talk about
Jackernapes and the school, and there were many questions for me
about 'the weirds', as they called the keepers, which I answered
as truthfully as I could – mindful of Snowdrop Scott's advice…

Afterwards we all sat down to watch Asphodel strutting about his cage like a peacock, reciting verses from Shakespeare and doing funny impressions of Henry VIII dancing and Queen Victoria trying to juggle sugar lumps. Then Richard sat at the piano and played a couple of songs with effortless ease and Lily did the splits, and even Tim Iddunshy did an amazing trick of squeezing himself through a very small wire coat hanger. Never having been to one of these sorts of parties before, I was a bit embarrassed that I didn't have a trick too, but no one seemed to mind – at least they didn't say anything. Perhaps the fact that I was even there was a novelty in itself. Anyway, I was so happy to be with people of my own age again that I was the last to leave.

'You know, I'd really like to find out more about what you do, Jack,' said Richard as we stood in the doorway. 'It all sounds so interesting.'

I shrugged. Perhaps it did. Perhaps I was beginning to take it all for granted. Richard noticed the tiniest light flickering in Asphodel's barred window and quietly closed the door. We were alone in the corridor. Outside it was dark and the snow glowed on the rooftops.

'D'you think I'd ever be allowed to come down into the Ghost Vault with you?'

Of course I didn't have a problem with that. But I don't suppose anyone else in the palace would agree.

'I'm not sure how you'd get over there,' I said tactfully. 'Isn't everyone trying to keep you safe?'

'In jail, more like,' Richard huffed. 'Apparently everything is "too dangerous" for me now I'm ill. I'm so bored.'

'My life can be pretty boring too,' I said.

'How, *how* can your life possibly be boring?'

I thought of all the endless hours I spent studying the ghost register, practising phantasmiphication with Dancing Dan...

'I want to find a way to come over there and see everything,' he said. 'I'm not crazy enough to clamber over the rooftops like the twins do, and I can't exactly walk through the gate either. So...' Richard hesitated. 'Perhaps there's some other way. Maybe I could be disguised.'

'How?'

Richard was looking at my long green coat. And he was looking at me. Looking at me like he wanted to tell me something.

'You want to wear my coat?'

He smiled, a little embarrassed.

'Of course, I understand it's your keeper's coat, Jack. I just want to see what I'd look like if I tried it on...'

'Try it on if you want.'

I undid the great silver buttons and handed it to him. Richard threw off his dressing gown and put it on, thrusting his hands in the pockets and turning around. Needless to say, it was a good fit – but then we were almost the same size and shape, despite Richard being a year older than me.

'Well?' he said, looking pleased. 'What do you think?'

I shrugged, not entirely sure what he was expecting me to say.

'You look like you're wearing my coat.'

'Supposing I borrowed your boots and hat too? Just to see.'

'To see what?'

'To see what they look like.'

Reluctantly I pulled my boots off and he put them on, then I handed him my hat. It was a small blue woolly hat I had taken to wearing about the palace to keep my head warm.

'I don't think it's going to make much difference,' I said.

'It might.'

'How? You're never going to be me. Everyone knows you, Richard.'

'Over here they do. But not on your side, Jack.'

Obviously I could see where this was going.

'Richard, listen, I think–'

'Can you keep a secret?' he said.

I suppose I can't have looked very impressed because suddenly he did something that took my breath away. In one movement he grabbed his hair and pulled… It was a wig! Underneath, his head was almost bald; what hair there was, was patchy and shaved. It was a shocking transformation. Suddenly he looked completely and utterly different.

'The only person who knows is Mother,' he said. 'Not Father, or the twins, not even Lily knows about this.'

I stared at him in amazement.

'The doctor says it's probably a side effect of all the pills I'm taking. It wasn't always like this and I hate it. Hate it more than anything else in the world.'

I continued to stare at him. I was still in shock.

'Come, Jack.'

He led me around the corner to a full-length mirror beside a tapestry. We stood together, side by side. And only now did I begin to see what he must have noticed all along.

'It's strange, isn't it?' he said.

That was an understatement. Richard may have been a year older than me, but without his wig and his princely ways, standing there in my long green keeper's coat… somehow he just looked like a sicker, thinner version of me, and I looked like a healthier version of him. It was almost a double reflection. To be honest, I was very confused. I didn't like it one bit.

Richard turned about, admiring himself.

'The first time I saw you through the gateway I had this funny feeling that I could be you. All I need to do now is get rid of this—' He twirled the stick.

'But Richard, aren't you forgetting something?'

'What?' He looked at me.

'I'm a *girl*?'

Richard smiled.

'Obviously there's that. But your voice is quite low for a girl, and you're not exactly very girly, Jack, if you don't mind me saying so. I mean, you're called *Jack*.'

He was right, of course, and I wasn't offended. Because I had a boy's name, people had always treated me like a boy for some reason. Not that I cared anyway.

'It's about acting, isn't it?'

'Is it?'

'Asphodel's been teaching me how to act,' he said. 'He shared the stage with Shakespeare once. It was the first performance of "A Midsummer Night's Dream", and Shakespeare played Bottom and he was Puck. Asphodel wrote all the fairies' parts, he said. He used to sit on Shakespeare's desk and they wrote out the lines in turn. I don't see why he shouldn't have. You can't expect Shakespeare to know much about real fairies.' Richard turned to me and smiled.

'Good afternoon. My name is Jack Joliffe, Keeper of Ghosts, Phantoms and Wisps. How do you do?'

He offered me his hand. I smiled.

'Too royal? A bit rougher then.'

I won't describe Richard's Artful Dodger impersonation, but believe me, it was embarrassing.

'No?'

'Definitely not.'

'Terrible?'

'Yup.'

He seemed a little surprised at my honesty.

'Why d'you want to be me anyway?' I asked.

'Because I don't like being me very much.'

'But you're going to be King one day. What's wrong with that?'

'Everything's wrong with that, Jack. Everything. You wouldn't understand.' Richard turned back to the mirror and stared at his reflection. 'I know, I'm so lucky, so privileged; I should be so grateful, blah blah blah. But I'm never going to be any good at it, am I? Everyone tells me I'm never going to be any good at it.'

'That's only because you're ill.'

'It isn't, Jack. It won't make any difference. I just... I don't want to be the King. I've never wanted to be the King. Stephen would have been the perfect King, that's all anyone ever says. And it's true. People look at me and I know what they're thinking.'

'But why can't you be a different kind of king?'

Richard shook his head crossly.

'No. There's only one way to be a king as far as Father's concerned, and that's his way. Stephen's way. I'm never going to be someone to look up to. A figurehead. A mascot. I don't care about any of it.' Richard coughed; a deep, scraping cough that was painful to hear. He smiled bravely. 'Which is why I want to be you, Jack. Only for a day. Just to try it. What do you think?'

Poor Richard. He seemed sort of desperate. I could almost see the weight of the crown upon his narrow shoulders, pushing him down. Could he really be me? Maybe he did look right, but even managing those stairs up to my room would be a struggle. But Richard was clever, and charming in his way, and I was sure he could handle all those ghosts far better than I could… but that was only half of it.

'What do *you* do all day?' I asked.

'Not much. I lie in bed. Talk to Asphodel. Occasionally go to a lesson. Try to avoid playing Jackernapes. Nothing really. Being me is easy.'

I wondered about that.

'How d'you avoid playing Jackernapes?'

Richard shrugged.

'I just say I'm ill. Or I go and hide somewhere. Plenty of places they can't find you in the palace.'

'Like the Sable Tower?'

Richard looked shocked. So that *was* him, up there in the velvet castle high up on Umballoo's back.

'That's seriously out of bounds, Jack. Only Lily knows I go in there. How did you know that?'

'I saw you. I was with Sam Yuell feeding Umballoo.'

Richard seemed a bit annoyed about that.

'The last time they caught someone in the Sable Tower they chopped off his hands and feet in front of the whole palace. That's still the punishment if you're caught.'

'But you risk it.'

'Obviously they're not going to do that to me, are they?'

But to you, definitely, he might have added.

'Also Umballoo is one of my best friends. I wouldn't want him to get in trouble. So please, Jack, don't go in there.'

'Okay, I won't,' I said.

But of course I couldn't pretend I wasn't interested. Not after everything Sam Yuell and Snowdrop Scott had told me.

'I suppose that if I ever did this, I'd have to trust you rather a lot,' he said, casually leaning against the wall. His fingers closed around a cord.

'So would I, *if* I ever agreed to it,' I said. 'We'd have to get to know each other a lot better to make it convincing. And I'd have to tell you about everything I've done in the vault...' Not to mention Isabella Royle and all that other stuff going on over there. 'To be honest, Richard, we're so different, I'm not sure it would ever work.'

He looked at me a moment, then shrugged.

'Oh well. My left leg's the bad one by the way, and I take the wig off and brush it every night. Good luck, Jack,' he said. And with that he turned the corner and hobbled away down the corridor. I stared after him, not quite believing what he was doing.

'Richard? Richard, where're you going?'

'Where d'you think?'

A door opened at the far end and a maid pattered towards us with a tray.

'You called, Your Highness? Oh excuse me, sir—'

The maid curtseyed before Richard – then quickly realised her mistake.

'You'll find the Prince down there,' he said. 'Thanks for the tea, Your Highness!'

'Come back!' I called.

But he didn't! Down the stairs he went. And he even had the nerve to give me a little wave...

26
The Little Lie

I DON'T KNOW HOW WELL I'm telling this. Looking back, it seems so obvious what Richard was going to do. I promise you it wasn't. Yes, I suppose I did feel sorry for him, because he was so ill, and trapped, and... The truth was, he'd deceived me completely. I barely had time to dive into an alcove, jam Richard's wig on my head and pull his embroidered gown around my shoulders before the maid arrived.

'Shall I take the tea things now, Your Highness?'

'Erm... if you like,' I mumbled, keeping turned away towards the window.

She went into the room, and while she bustled about, I stared at myself in the mirror, still too shocked to be angry. I realised Richard had planned all this. It wasn't some spur of the moment thing. Probably the only reason he'd asked me over here was to try and swap. He'd probably even called the maid – I looked at the cord on the wall… he *had* called the maid–

'Your Highness,' she curtseyed, and off she went with the tray.

'I'm not Your Highness.'

She giggled and carried on down the corridor.

'But I'm not!'

The maid ignored me and disappeared round the corner. Straightening the wig, I closed the door and took a deep breath. What was I going to do?

'She's gone?'

I jumped. Asphodel was on his swing, facing towards the window. Looking back, that was when I should've told the truth. If I'd come right out with it, there and then, everything might have been so different. But the thing is, once you start to lie – and it only takes one tiny little lie – everything else just seems to follow…

'Yes,' I replied, far too quietly to be heard.

The fairy pushed himself back and forth with one thin toe.

'Come here, my boy.'

I did as I was told, perching on the edge of the chair. It seemed impossible that he wouldn't recognise me, sitting as I was, so close.

'What did you make of her?'

'She seemed, erm… extremely nice,' I said, again ludicrously whispery. I cleared my throat. 'I liked her very much.'

'She hides something. She is not what she seems.'

I swallowed hard.

'What do you mean?'

'You should be careful consorting with Miss Joliffe, Richard.

She is dangerous to you.'

He watched me through the bars of the cage. I picked up a book and pretended to read it. The silence grew.

'In what way is she dangerous?'

'Asphodel trusts his instinct. The Prince should trust Asphodel also. There is something about her I do not like – I could taste it.'

I shuddered a little.

'You mean you–'

'Forgive me, Richard, I hope you're not offended, but you do take such a long time to do anything. Yes, she offered me a drink. I supped and sensed something most unexpected.'

I nodded. I wanted to ask him more, but I knew such curiosity might betray me.

'Oh well.'

'Am I boring you?' he said, seeing me retreat towards the bedroom.

'Oh no, no–'

'Then why are you skulking away like that?'

'I'm just a little tired, that's all.'

'Befriend this stranger at your peril, Richard. She's nothing but a snake to poison your garden.'

I reached the bedroom door and opened it. Should I take this from Asphodel? I didn't think Richard would.

'Actually Asphodel, I am going to befriend her.'

'Then thou art a foolish knave!'

'And I'm going to see her again. Very soon, in fact.'

Asphodel stared at me, his tiny eyes blazing.

'Go hang thyself in thine own heir-apparent garters!' he hissed.

'Goodnight, Asphodel.'

I closed the bedroom door, my heart thumping. I had no idea

what he was on about, but I sensed there and then it was not worth making an enemy of Asphodel. Underneath all that poetry he seemed very sharp indeed. But Richard wouldn't let himself be pushed about by this creature, would he? And I was Richard now... at least until tomorrow morning.

∼⁓ 27 ⁓∼
Being Royal

YOU WILL NOT BE SURPRISED to know that I barely slept that night. Richard's bed was far more comfortable than Galahad Joliffe's, but on this side of the palace there seemed to be people forever moving about in the darkness. Nightwatchmen calling to each other across the courtyards, doors creaking and closing. At one point I heard a scream and a fluttering of wings and I woke up sure something was in the room. But it was nothing.

Eventually I drifted away to sleep, and began to dream an old dream I've had for almost as long as I can remember. I'm running through a burning forest, searching for an exit. Everywhere I look there's an avenue of fire; the noise of the branches crackling and exploding is deafening. Then I realise a pack of wolves is chasing me. It's scary, but somehow I know they don't want to eat me; they're following me, hoping I can lead them out of the inferno. Suddenly I see a clearing ahead. I race through the burning trees towards it, running out into the centre and the wolves are all crowding around me. Up beyond the flames I can see the sky. Somehow I know something is going to rescue me. I'm not sure why, I just know it is. The flames grow higher and higher, and just as the heat becomes unbearable a shadow appears through the smoke. Something black, like a great bird, getting bigger and bigger till it spreads its wings and seems to block out everything else. I can feel its wings beating right on top of me… and then I wake up. I always wake up at that moment, sweating and confused. Have I been saved? Am I dead? I don't know what it means. I don't suppose it means anything very much…

In the morning, breakfast turned out to be just as dreamy, only differently so. The clue was in the buttons in the roof of the four-poster bed – big white buttons that lit up when you poked them. I pressed the first word I recognised: Armada.

A mechanical arm appeared from under the bed and set a tray before me. There was quite a lot of wheezing and banging from the far end, then a bell rang and a line of miniature silver galleons sailed up over the edge. Each seemed to be carrying something useful for breakfast: a rack of toast, a pot of tea, a jug of milk, boiled eggs, bacon, honey, jam, salt, pepper, porridge… There were a lot of them, it was an armada after all. These miniature ships then attempted to sail my breakfast up the bed towards me, sliding down the dips and up the humps of the blankets, slopping the tea and milk and honey all over the place. Had I been less amazed I might have said 'Slow down!' or 'Not that way!' or something more sailory if I could have thought of it. But as it was, I just sat there and stared.

'Thank you. What a lovely... armada,' I said, when the galleons finally reached me, and I set about rescuing the eggs and the marmalade pot, and all the rest of the debris floating about the bedspread. The ships barely paused before turning about and sailing back towards the end of the bed, which by now I had smoothed down to a glassy calm. Whether they were clockwork, mouse-powered or robots I don't know, but they looked extremely old. Barely had the last galleon returned to port when there was a knock at the door. I hastily straightened my wig.

'Come in?'

'Richard?'

A bald head and moustache appeared around the door. Who are you?

'I'm a little early. D'you want to finish your breakfast?'

'Erm... no,' I said, retrieving some capsized toast and crunching it. 'Come in.'

'Are you sure?'

In he beetled and set his leather bag down on the messy bed. Something about him said 'doctor'. He peered at me over his half-moon spectacles.

'You look better this morning.'

'Yes, I think I might be feeling a little better.'

'There's colour in your cheeks.'

'Is there?'

'And you don't look so tired.'

'No, I'm not feeling quite so tired.'

'Taken your pills?'

'Yes.'

'All of them?'

Again I nodded.

'Excellent.' The doctor stuck a torch in my eye, got me to say 'Ahh' and checked my pulse. 'Heart's a bit quick. I expect you're thinking about your meeting with the Prime Minister this afternoon.'

'What? Oh yes, *that*. Probably,' I mumbled, hoping a bit of vagueness would disguise my panic. 'It's always a bit nerve-wracking, meeting the Prime Minister.'

The doctor looked up at me over those spectacles.

'I mean… that's normal, isn't it? To be nervous before meeting the Prime Minister. What with my condition and… everything.'

The doctor kept looking at me over those spectacles.

'I expect one day I'll have to meet the Pope–'

The doctor suddenly burst out laughing.

'What?'

'Richard, you've never met Byron Chitt.'

Oh.

'And as you and your parents will be discussing the arrangements for your presentation, which will be the first time anyone has seen you since Stephen passed away, I think it's probably rather important. Not to mention the small matter of swearing the Oath of Succession.'

I spluttered into my tea.

'What's that?'

'The Oath of Succession, Richard, which seals your place as the next King of Albion.'

'Wait… when is this?'

'Next *week*, Richard. Your presentation. I don't suppose you've forgotten that too, have you?'

Inside I let out a yelp. Outside I was very careful to do nothing more than shrug.

'I suppose now you come to mention it, that is slightly important.'

The doctor's face broke into a wide smile and he laughed again.

'Oh Richard! You have a wicked sense of humour!'

The door opened and Lily came in, already dressed and carrying a school bag. I was glad the doctor had already taken my pulse because now my heart was hopping like a box of frogs.

'Morning, Dr Mazumdar. Morning, Cuz.'

Lily came over and planted a kiss on my cheek.

'How are ya?'

'Pretty good.'

'Yes you don't look half bad.' She crunched on a piece of toast and noticed breakfast splattered all over the bedspread.

'I thought you said you were never going to summon the armada again after that teapot capsized and burnt your leg.'

'I'm giving it another try,' I said quickly.

'What about the porridge that tipped all over your pillow? And that mouldy fried egg you found stuck in a book?'

'I've changed my mind.'

Lily seemed surprised.

'You never change your mind about anything, Cuz.'

'Well I have changed my mind. About changing my mind.'

'The Prince is in better form than I've seen him for a long time,' smiled Dr Mazumdar, throwing his bits and pieces back into his bag. 'I have high hopes for Tuesday.'

'It's Tuesday?'

'Yes *Tuesday*, Richard. Your presentation's on Tuesday. Don't forget now. Lady Lily, Your Highness.'

Dr Mazumdar stood up, bowed and made for the door with two dark patches of marmalade squished into his trousers.

The moment he'd gone Lily turned to me in excitement.

'So much news, Cuz. Have you heard what's been going on in the night?'

I shook my head. I wasn't exactly concentrating.

'Some terrible creature – a giant worm or a rat or something's gone missing from the other side.'

'Oh,' I said, trying not to sound too alarmed.

'There was a massive kerfuffle apparently. Whatever it was has disappeared and now everyone's doing their nut. Onion is going to give us a stern talk this morning about all the new security measures. Loads of corridors are going to be out of bounds… it's all very serious, Cuz. Archie Queach says it was deliberately let out.'

'Oh dear.'

'Richard, you don't seem very bothered.'

'Should I be?'

'Yes you should, Cuz. Supposing it's still here? Supposing someone let it out hoping it would come and kill you? Or me, or any of us? From what Jack said, they sound completely bonkers over there.'

'Probably,' I said, crunching a piece of toast. Richard, I thought. More than likely Richard. And whatever he'd done was almost certainly going to get me into a whole heap of trouble. Lily looked at me curiously.

'Well what can I do, Lily?'

'You really are in a funny mood this morning, Cuz.'

✦✧ 28 ✧✦
The Brilliant Prince

S O YOU'VE PROBABLY GUESSED by now that I'm not much good at acting. And you might be wondering how I got through those first few lessons at school. The answer is, I've no idea. In each class I found myself sitting at the front, and whenever the teacher asked any kind of question, the hush and slightly bored glances I received told me that Richard usually knew the answer. And I don't think this was because he was the heir to the throne. Looking back through his exercise books, I saw that Richard really *did* know the answers to pretty much everything, and his fan club stretched from the bottom of the school to the top.

'Hi Richard!' Jake Tiptree, an enthusiastic second year with large glasses and wide trousers gave me a high five. 'They say it was a *dragin* that escaped. A proper real-life *dragin*!'

'Richard, you look really well,' smiled Matty Wong.

'Really well,' chimed Jocasta Hobart–

'Really like *so* well,' Lottie Dromgoole–

'Like totes 'mazing,' Tilly Loder–

'Not bad–' Blossom Cossage, a tough-looking girl with huge shoulders.

All lovely high-born people I'm sure.

'Thanks.'

'Heard about the breakout, mate?' George Hartswood sidled up, bouncing a ball around.

'I did hear about it, yes.'

George threw the ball against the wall and caught it. George Hartswood (the future Earl of Hartswood – they were mostly something like that) was at least a head taller than me, with masses of freckles and curly hair cut very short. I had no doubt that if I hadn't been the Prince, he would have made my life a misery, as I was weak and thin and he was that sort of person.

'Queach said the beast got into some tunnel no one knew about and escaped. It's like a badger worm or something? No one wants to go after it because it's killed seven people already. He had to go and clear up the remains himself.'

Really. Archie Queach, telling tales… George's two sidekicks wandered over. They were two boys named Spiggins and Tucker-Smith. Spiggins was short and stocky with a weaselly smile, and Tucker-Smith looked like he'd been inflated. Seeing me, they mustered a smile.

'Sounds like it's gone now anyway,' George continued. 'You've nothing to worry about, Richard.'

'Filthy eaters, badger worms,' said Spiggins.

'They suck out your liver when you're still alive,' added Tucker-Smith with relish. 'Then your kidneys. Then your brains.'

I smiled. Badger worms. What was Archie Queach up to? But it was nice they were trying so hard to impress me. That was status, as I quickly discovered. People will forgive you anything. Even Minty Bishop, the Classics teacher, who seemed only slightly irritated that I couldn't remember 'the name of the boy who flew too close to the sun?'

'He made wings out of wax, and when he flew too high they melted and he fell to his death into the sea?' Miss Bishop stared at the board, pen poised. She was a tall woman with a long pink nose like an anteater, and she ignored the forest of upstretched hands for as long as she dared.

'You wrote a poem about him, Richard, last week. In Greek,' she added, as if that was some kind of clue. At this point I sincerely wished I'd been to school more often.

'Something tells me you're not really with us this morning, are you, Richard?'

'Erm, no, not really,' I replied, hoping that sounded like a Richardish thing to say. There were stifled giggles and Miss Bishop smiled painfully. She leaned forward and whispered in my ear.

'I understand you have other things on your mind, but perhaps you might at least *pretend* to be interested?'

It was amazing Richard knew so much, really. He probably could have got away with doing nothing at all. But she was right; I did have other things on my mind. Like meeting the Prime Minister, and how to avoid being presented to the people as the next King of Albion.

At break-time the whole school gathered in the Assembly Hall, a vast room filled with armour and sofas and ping-pong tables and other indoor games. Everyone crowded around the blazing fire, and particular care was taken for me to have the best seat at the front. In came the Headmaster, Professor Runyon, a thin, heron-like man in a suit and gown, with a long neck and a sharp chin and a pink carnation in his buttonhole. I suspected Onion Runyon was rather vain, and also rather strict – though perhaps not to me, being Richard. He clapped his hands loudly to get our attention.

'Settle down! Thank you, everyone! Let's have some hush! Hush!'

Onion Runyon wafted his hands. Hush eventually came.

'Now as I'm sure you've all heard, there is a rumour that some sort of animal might have escaped from the other side of the palace last night–'

'Was it a dragin? I bet it was a dragin – a big one!'

That was Jake Tiptree at the back, unable to stop himself. Tucker-Smith grabbed his fingers and Jake yelped.

'No it wasn't a *dragon*, Tiptree–'

'So what was it then?' asked someone else. 'I bet it was something horrible–'

'Queach said it was properly disgusting–'

'Come on Professor Runyon, tell us–'

'Hush! Hush hush!' barked Onion Runyon. 'Nobody knows what it was. But it wasn't a dragon, because as we all know, dragons don't exist.'

Groans of disappointment at that. Onion Runyon smiled in an oily way. I think he thought that by lying he would keep everyone calm. It hadn't worked.

'Hush hush!' he shouted again. 'Now as this "creature" – *whatever* it is — may still be at large within the walls of the palace, those responsible for our protection have decided that we cannot be too careful. Therefore it is my pleasure to introduce some new faces you may see patrolling the corridors at night. First Miss Cribbage, Keeper of the Night.'

Onion Runyon turned around and there was Enid Cribbage, who had somehow entered the room without anyone noticing. She looked a little awkward and vaguely ridiculous in her tall hat and raven-feathered cloak. Someone at the back was even brave enough to giggle before Professor Runyon silenced them with a hard stare.

'Miss Cribbage carries a box of bats, so don't be surprised if you hear a lot of screaming in the corridors. It's only the bats nattering to each other I expect,' Onion joked, glancing at Enid Cribbage. Enid Cribbage stared resolutely ahead.

'Excellent. And the other person you may see is Mr Knock, the Keeper of...'

'Stones and Menhirs, sir.'

'That's it. Menhirs and Stones. Welcome, Mr Knock.'

I hadn't noticed the other keeper waiting patiently beside the door. Mr Knock came forward and planted his feet either side of his black staff. He wore a long yellow coat and had the expression of someone thinking very serious thoughts that were starting to hurt his brain.

'Good morning, Your Highness. Good morning, my lords and ladies, and good morning to everyone else,' he said in a quiet, serious voice. 'My name is Solomon Knock. What do I do? Officially, I look after all the stones in this country, make sure they don't go misbehaving themselves and creating mischief. Unofficially, I'm also the palace detective.'

Silence. I'm sure we all wanted to ask the same question. How could a stone misbehave?

'I'd like to show you something.' Solomon Knock thrust a hand into his pocket and pulled out a grey stone the size of his fist, holding it up for all to see. 'These little perishers are what I call "seeing stones". Lovely little blokes. Seeing stones, see?'

'But it hasn't got any eyes,' growled Blossom Cossage, stating the obvious.

'Quite right, miss. No it hasn't. And it's also asleep. I've got to wake the little fella up.' Placing the stone on the floor, he gave it a tap with the end of his staff and then picked it up again. 'There we go. He's awake now.'

'It's awake?' said George Hartswood.

'Indeed, sir. And now I've woken him up he will start to see.'

There was first silence, then an embarrassed titter. Solomon Knock might as well have said, 'Look, it's a banana.' Plainly this stone was still a stone and no more awake than it had been moments earlier. 'And you're saying that that stone can see us?'

'He's looking at you right now, sir.'

'Ooh it winked at me!' someone said.

'And me!'

Giggles rippled around the room. Onion looked very serious, and wafted his hands for more hush.

'What's it going to do when it sees us, then?' asked Blossom Cossage.

'It's going to tell me what's going on, miss.'

'Are you serious?' asked Spiggins, sniggering with Tucker-Smith.

'Oh yes.'

Only the kindly manner in which Solomon Knock stroked the stone in his palm convinced anyone in the room that this might be true.

'Now I'm going to place a lot of these seeing stones around the palace. Please don't tamper with them, as they're there to keep you safe.'

'What will you do to us if we *do* tamper with them?'

'Supposing we collect them all up and smash them with a hammer–'

'In our bedroom–'

'Which you're not allowed into–'

'Because you're a commoner–'

'What will you do then?'

Solomon Knock wrinkled his nose and turned to the two blonde children sitting cross-legged on the floor. From his expression it was quite obvious what he would have done to Thomas and Victoria Lancaster had he been allowed – which is probably why Onion Runyon cut straight in.

'The seeing stones are there for everyone's safety,' he said firmly. 'Please, do not tamper with them.'

'Why don't you just use a camera?' asked Matty Wong.

'Because seeing stones see things that cameras cannot,' replied Mr Knock mysteriously.

'You mean, like ghosts and stuff?'

'Exactly. St James's Palace is full of them. Even in this room, right now.'

Now this *was* interesting, and chatter about it buzzed through the corridors as everyone returned to their classrooms.

'Did you believe him?' said Lily, walking up beside me.

I shrugged. 'Didn't you?'

'Seems like a convenient way of frightening everyone into behaving, if you ask me. I mean, he's a bit weird, isn't he?'

Yes he was. More than a bit.

'Apparently it was a dragon, a real dragon. Why would someone deliberately let out a dragon?'

'No idea.' On we walked round the courtyard. Would Richard have let it out? It was hard to believe… unless he was even more accident-prone than I was…

'The carriage is at two. The Queen suggested you wear the Number One suit. She said your father would like that. Make a good impression on the Prime Minister.'

My stomach turned. I'd been trying very hard to forget about this afternoon's ordeal.

'Righty-ho.'

Lily stared at me and giggled.

'Righty-ho? Righty-*ho*? What's that, Cuz?'

I had no idea. It just came into my head.

'I was wondering if perhaps I should try to sound more princely. For the Prime Minister.'

'Princely?'

'To impress him.'

'*Impress* him?'

'Don't you think?'

Lily stopped giggling. Her expression became serious.

'Listen Cuz, I know how much you hate all this stuff and you'd do anything to get out of it, but perhaps you should just try being yourself? If you start messing around and getting all "princely", your father will go ballistic.'

I nodded. Okay. Good advice.

'By the way, Lily, we've got to invite Jack back over here.'

Lily seemed surprised.

'Why?'

'Because I want to see her again.'

'But she was only here yesterday.'

'I know. It's just… don't you think there's something they're not telling us?'

'Probably,' Lily shrugged. 'It can't be today though, can it?'

No, I suppose it couldn't.

'See you at two,' she said, and watched as I limped to the circular staircase and began to hobble up with my stick, one step at a time, all the way to the very top… Oh Richard, what had you let me in for?

～ 29 ～
Presentable

RICHARD'S NUMBER ONE SUIT turned out to be a long blue velvet jacket with matching breeches, an embroidered gold waistcoat and a very complicated white shirt and lacy scarf. I suppose he must have had as much trouble getting into this costume as I did, as pinned to the inside of the wardrobe was a picture of some ringlet-haired prince wearing it, with a set of instructions beside. For the best part of an hour I stood in front of the mirror fiddling with cufflinks and garters, tying the long lacy scarf first this way then that, up and over, under, then round – or was it back again? There was no one to ask and it was so frustrating I nearly chucked it out the window…

Suddenly it was almost two.

'How do I look?'

I stood in the doorway of the bedroom. Asphodel turned around in his swing where he sat reading a tiny leather-bound book.

'Like the Prince who never was.'

'What does that mean?' I said, sensing the insult.

'It means you look too good to be true.'

Charming. I thought I looked pretty good, considering. Asphodel's black eyes glazed over, then he offered a weak smile.

'Forgive me, my boy. Waspish words wander from my lips before I have a chance to stop 'em. I will curb my tongue. You look passing excellent.'

'Thank you, Asphodel.'

The fairy smiled weakly.

'Give your father my regards.'

'I will.'

'And your Uncle Thad. I hear he has returned. Tell him old Asphodel still remembers him fondly.'

Obviously I had no idea who the fairy was talking about. I nodded anyway.

'We had some roistering fun together, Thad Lancaster and I. Plays and music, games and feasts. Merriments galore. When Thad was young and easy under the apple boughs, the royal nursery was quite the place to be. A great doer of deeds was Thaddeus Lancaster, even then.'

Asphodel sat back and wallowed in a haze of memories. I was curious to know more about Richard's Uncle Thad, who I presumed was the King's younger brother, but I suspected Asphodel had told Richard such tales many times before. I made for the door.

'My boy.' The fairy craned his neck round to look at me. 'Can you spare me a drink before you go?'

I looked at the tiny crystal glass and decanter in Asphodel's cage and remembered his words from last night. It was not worth the risk.

'I'm sorry, Asphodel. I'm late already.'

'Three small drops – is that too much? Sustenance for poor Asphodel?'

'You'll have to wait.'

'For pity, dearest Richard, you'll be gone such a long time!'

'I told you Asphodel, I can't. I'm late.'

'Oh you're always late with your hoppity-hop, clickety-clack! Hobbling about like some blind old beggar! Cruel child, Richard! Nasty, wicked child indeed! Is this how you treat your greatest friend?'

The fairy's face was screwed up with anger. He was desperate, clearly.

'I said I'm sorry, Asphodel.'

'Sorry! Ahh! What is sorry? Sorry is as sorry does. A pox on you!'

Asphodel turned away in a sulk. I closed the door and shuddered. This was going to be a big problem. Perhaps Richard had not foreseen it, but obviously he had been feeding Asphodel in secret, and there was no way I could do that – the cunning old fairy would know we'd swapped places immediately. What about Snowdrop Scott, wasn't she supposed to send him rations of cheese and blood? I couldn't remember. For all his poetry and dancing Asphodel was a moody creature, and not particularly pleasant. How long could I put off his craving? Not long, I thought. Not long at all...

⤳ 30 ⤳
Buckingham Palace

GLOOMY THOUGHTS filled my head as I made my way down the stairs and along the corridor to the main gate. Limping everywhere was surprisingly tiring when you didn't have to, and I noticed Mr Knock had wasted no time with his seeing stones. They were resting on windowsills and in dark corners, watching... It was all a little frightening.

'Cuz? Where are you going? I thought we'd lost you!'

Lily came running up behind me and took my arm.

'The carriage is waiting, come on.'

I allowed Lily to guide me through a side door and down some steps to a basement, where strangely enough there was a coach and horses waiting at the end of a long dark tunnel.

'I'm beginning to wonder what's got into you today, Cuz,' she said, looking concerned. 'You're behaving very oddly.'

'I've been doing a lot of thinking,' I replied, which was true.

'I can see that. But maybe you should stop doing so much thinking and start doing a bit more concentrating instead?'

Lily was right, again. Trouble was, I had a lot to think about, and I was very nervous – who wouldn't be? Before I knew it, we'd climbed aboard and the coachman had flicked his whip. Off we rattled into the gloom.

Now you might be wondering why we were rumbling down a tunnel to Buckingham Palace in a coach, instead of going overground in a car. The reason, as I discovered later, was the same as it was for most things around here, or so it seemed. The assassination of Stephen. Once the royal family had withdrawn into the safety of their palaces, the government refused to pay for expensive cavalcades of bulletproof Rolls Royces to ferry them around. Much better, they said, to open up the network of old royal tunnels that ran between the palaces. But you couldn't use a car. No ventilation. So it was either bicycle – which sounded like hard work and rather unroyal – or carriage. Now the royal family might be short of many things (luck definitely, possibly brains as well) but they certainly had a lot of carriages… beautiful old painted carriages that jangled and squeaked, with names like barouche, cariole, landau, phaeton, troika… all with wide leather seats worn soft by hundreds of royal bums.

It was to Buckingham Palace in one of these barouches that we travelled. The two black horses were called Donald and Pip, and the coachman was called Arthur Squiddle. He told us he had been doing this job for thirty years – man and boy, man and boy, above ground and below. He missed the daylight, and so did Donald and Pip, but, Lordy, Lordy, it was much warmer in the tunnel, especially when there was a thick blanket of freezing fog up there in The Mall. Who'd go outside now, eh? Not unless you were a polar bear you wouldn't, declared Arthur Squiddle, jabbering away out of the side of his mouth as we clip-clopped through the darkness. I was still wondering why London was buried under such a blanket of cold. No one seemed to know the answer, and it didn't sound much fun to live in. It sounded more like the North Pole. Lights appeared in the distance and a pair of liveried footmen stood shivering in the darkness to greet us.

'Buckingham Palace.'

The door opened and Lily bounced down and took my hand. She was looking very elegant in a white fur coat and silk dress, her hair all done up in diamonds. She must have got the Number One instruction too. Up the wide steps we went, me taking extra care with my limp as Arthur Squiddle and the footmen stood in a line watching.

'I'm feeling just a tiny bit anxious about this, Cuz,' whispered Lily, threading her arm through mine.

'Yup.'

Nothing compared to what I felt. My heart was hammering so loudly I could barely speak.

At the top of the stairs we reached a wide marble hall and stood at the edge of a Persian carpet that seemed to stretch about a mile across the room ahead of us. On the far side there were two doors either side of a staircase. Footmen stood outside both. We were just about to continue when a side door banged open and two men swept out onto the carpet in front of us, not noticing we were there. One of them I recognised; it was William Foxglass. Tall and imposing as ever, he was now wearing a long black coat with a gold zodiac on the back… but Mr Foxglass was not in charge here. It was the smaller, wild-looking man in the flamboyant green uniform marching ahead…

'Why did you not ask me first, Foxglass?'

'I had to take the decision to appoint someone, Your Highness. We cannot have a vault without a keeper–'

'But you can't just appoint anyone you fancy, then sneak them in the back door! Are you trying to hide her from me, Foxglass, is that it?'

'She's not anyone, Your Highness, she is Galahad Joliffe's niece–'

'Niece?' The smaller man turned around in a fury. 'And I suppose you know she was invited to tea with Richard?'

Mr Foxglass did not.

'Well for goodness' sake, man! That is an extraordinary breach of security! How on earth did that happen?'

Again William Foxglass tried to sound reasonable.

'I suppose the Prince must have seen her through a window or something. I'm sure it's not what you think–'

'Don't you dare tell me what I think! How useless are you, man!'

'Your Highness, I'm merely–'

'No one enters the school without my permission in future, and none of your keepers – I repeat *none* – are permitted to come anywhere near Richard! Do I make myself clear?'

'Yes, Your Highness.'

'Now find out which of your incompetent fools released that dragon. I want a name, Foxglass, or else there will be consequences for all of you, d'you understand?'

'Very clearly, Your Highness.'

'I mean it, Foxglass!'

The wild-looking man shook off his cape and flung it at a servant, who hastily gathered it up off the floor. Smoothing back his hair, he scowled at himself in the mirror then went in through a door on the far side. Lily looked at me.

'Thad's not happy,' she whispered.

'Richard darling!'

The Queen suddenly appeared from a corridor behind us looking busy and elegant.

'My goodness you look so well! You really do look so well.'

I smiled automatically. Lily beamed. Kiss kiss.

'Doesn't he look well, Lily?'

'He does.'

'So well! And Lily, dearest, you look absolutely divine, as ever. Love the coat by the way. Now you two, are you ready for this?' She grabbed our hands and turned around. There was William Foxglass padding away across the carpet, attempting to make his escape. 'William?' she said. 'What a surprise. What are you doing here?'

'I was summoned to report to the Duke, ma'am. He has returned just in time to join you.'

'Ah. Well I hope it wasn't important.'

'No, ma'am. Not important at all.'

'Good. Come here then,' she said, beckoning him over. 'Darlings, this is William Foxglass, Black Zodiac. A very important fellow from the other side,' she said, stressing each word.

'A pleasure to meet you, Your Highness,' he said, taking my hand. I'll admit I was shaking as those hazel eyes met mine… Could he tell? His foxy face gave nothing away.

'Mr Foxglass knows everything there is to know about everything. I can't think what we would all do without him.'

William Foxglass bowed. Lily and I glanced at each other.

'We heard it was a real dragon that escaped?' she asked.

'Indeed it was, my lady.'

'And that it was released deliberately. Why would someone let out a dragon deliberately?'

Mr Foxglass seemed a little surprised at the question. He glanced at the Queen.

'The palace is always full of rumours. If you follow the Keeper of Stones' advice, I'm sure you'll be quite safe,' he said, smiling at us both.

'And the very last thing we want is for the Prime Minister to find out, otherwise that will be yet another black mark against us,' sighed the Queen. 'So he's not to know, my darlings, got it? Hopefully it will all have blown over by next week.'

The Queen squeezed our arms and grinned again. I sensed she was a little frantic this afternoon. A butler appeared from the door on the right and gave a sign.

'Ah. They're ready for us now. Come along.'

Mr Foxglass took his leave and the Queen led us, arm in arm, across the great carpet, keeping up her chit-chat – to calm us, I think she thought, but it was probably to calm herself. When we reached the door, she held me back a moment and waved Lily on.

'You look so smart, my darling,' she said, brushing imaginary dust off my Number One. 'I just can't get over how much better you look. You're almost a different person. I don't suppose you *are* a different person, by any chance, are you, darling?'

She was joking of course. What could I say? I grinned madly.

'Nervous?'

'A little.'

'Nervous is normal, darling. We're all a little nervous about this.'

She smiled again. Something was proving hard for her to say.

'Now I know you and your father have been having some chats recently. And we both know that sometimes he says things he doesn't mean. We know that, don't we?'

I nodded blankly.

'So whatever he might have said or suggested, please ignore it, because we can't have a scene. Not in front of the Prime Minister. Will you promise me that, Richard?'

'Okay,' I said, now feeling even more nervous.

'Good. And remember Mr Chitt knows nothing about your being ill, and he doesn't need to. It's none of his business. So if you can manage from here to there without the stick… can you, my darling?'

'I'll try.'

'Brave boy.'

She took my cane and leant it discreetly behind a vase.

'It's just so much easier if he doesn't know about that… or this,' she said, smoothing my wig. 'We keep so many secrets, you and I. But you're looking so much better, I shouldn't be surprised if after next week you can come off those nasty pills and your hair will start growing back again.'

I smiled. If only! She planted a kiss on my forehead.

'Best foot forward, my darling boy.'

Into the drawing room we went.

~ 31 ~
Persuading Mr Chitt

A **GROUP OF MEN ROSE** to greet us from the sofas around the fireplace. The room was just as I imagined the private rooms in a palace ought to look – very grand, with bits of the modern world littered about by accident. In fact, the TV was rather old, and the phone even older… all of this I noticed in a second. Then it was time for the handshakes.

First the King, my father.

'Hello old chum,' he said rather formally, taking my hand and squeezing it in a manly way. 'Chin up and remember our plan,' he whispered in my ear. He stepped back and winked. 'Look at that old Number One,' he honked. 'I remember wearing that. But

I don't think I was as big as you are at your age, Richard. You'll be needing the Number Two shortly, what?'

Next came Thad Lancaster, the King's scary younger brother, swaggering forward in his military uniform. Whatever temper tantrum he'd had minutes earlier seemed to have entirely disappeared.

'Lily, you look wonderful as ever.'

She was thrilled when he kissed her hand.

'And how are you, Richard?' he said, clapping me on the shoulder in an even manlier way.

'I'm very well, thank you, Thad.'

'And you look it. I'm looking forward to taking you out for a ride when the weather improves. I'd challenge you to a race around the park, but I think you might beat me.'

He laughed loudly, a spark dancing in his eyes. He seemed a bit crazy.

'Asphodel says hello,' I said.

'Does he indeed? How is the old rascal, still moaning about everything?'

''Fraid so.'

'Ha! Don't you listen to a word of it, Richard. He's the rudest creature alive. Always was. The things he'd call me I can't repeat. Not with your father around at any rate,' Thad winked.

I went in further still. Lurking beside the fire stood a portly man in a grey suit who looked very much like a walrus. Byron Chitt had large hands and tiny black eyes like raisins. All I knew about him was that he was very clever and very stingy, and had once called the royal family 'a bunch of raving mad toffee-nosed spongers'. Well here I was, the Prince of those toffee-nosed spongers, about to shake his hand.

'Prime Minister, please meet my son, Richard,' said the King.

'Your Highness, delighted to make your acquaintance at last.' Byron Chitt offered a flipper and I grasped it. He looked at me.

'Quite the image of your mother,' he said, smiling at Queen.

'With his father's chin,' said the King.

'Ah yes, I can see that now.'

Byron Chitt smiled and sat down, and everyone else followed suit. Obviously I knew nothing about royal protocol but it was clear that Mr Chitt seemed to be in charge.

'Now then,' he said brightly, 'we have, I believe, a royal presentation next week?'

'Quite so,' smiled the King. 'As you know, Chitt, royal presentations are a very important part of a prince's life. The moment when one leaves the nursery and faces one's people for the first time. A rite of passage accompanied by much pomp and circumstance.'

'And that pomp and circumstance is what I am here to discuss,' smiled Mr Chitt patiently. 'Perhaps Your Highness would be good enough to explain what you have in mind?'

The King stood up before the fire and cleared his throat. He looked to me like an actor about to say his lines. He had obviously been practising.

'What I have in mind is a royal parade, much like my own, but obviously in these straitened times not quite so grand.'

Mr Chitt stroked his whiskers in a walrusy way. He obviously approved of that. The King cleared his throat again.

'So we would begin in a fleet of carriages, sweep out of St James's and up The Mall. First off would be Richard, obviously, alone, obviously, because it's his show and everyone should see for themselves what a fine young fellow he is.

Then the Queen, myself and the twins, if they can be wrangled into behaving themselves, then Thad here, cousins, Mother, and all the royal beasts following along behind. The people always love to see the royal beasts, Chitt, brings a bit of pageantry to the thing. So down The Mall we tootle, standard mass bands playing, lots of cavalry, lots of flags, then on through Horse Guards, down Whitehall to Parliament Square, wave to all you chaps, Westminster Abbey, bishops ditto – but I'm not too bothered about the bishops. The main thing is we get back to Buckingham Palace and out onto the balcony where Richard swears the Oath of Succession in front of the watching millions. So grateful, humbled, vow to serve my country and all that, and the moment he says it, I don't know, how about a few fireworks banging off the roof? Confetti bombs? Your call, Chitt. Battleships on the river blasting off a gun salute definitely, cannons in Hyde Park ditto, lots and *lots* of noise, and then a good old fly-past with bombers and – well I suppose we don't *have* to have bombers. Broadly speaking it will

be a standard royal presentation – cut down of course, given the circumstances. Very much cut down. Hmm.'

There was silence. All eyes turned to Mr Chitt.

'That's *all* you're envisaging, Your Highness?' said the Prime Minister.

'That's it, Chitt. Oh I forgot, there's usually a tea party in here at the end of it, to which you and the government would be invited, so long as you promise not to eat all the cakes! We can't have that, Chitt, certainly not! Ha! And then of course we've got the jolly old Jackernapes final in St James's Palace. You're more than welcome to come to that too.'

Byron Chitt took his time screwing the lid back on his fountain pen and slipping it inside his jacket.

'Your Highness, I don't know whether you've looked out of the window recently?'

The King frowned.

'What d'you mean? Of course I've looked out of the window.'

Mr Chitt coughed.

'Did you see anything?'

'Well of course I didn't see anything! How could I see anything? There's fog!'

'Precisely, Your Highness. The weather, sir, is presenting considerable challenges.'

'The weather? The *weather*?'

'I'm sorry to say that this cloud of freezing fog over the capital has created a never-ending winter. A great many people are very cold and hungry, starving in fact. The cost of keeping hospitals warm, schools open–'

'Yes yes, Chitt, you've made your point.' The King waved impatiently. 'What you're saying is that you've run out of money.'

'Not entirely, Your Highness, but almost.'

'Well I think that is very foolish of you. I mean, the fact that it's snowing in May is hardly our fault, is it?'

The Prime Minister raised his eyebrows. I half-wondered if Mr Chitt was suggesting exactly that. Maybe it was my imagination.

'All right,' said the King. 'I'm not an unreasonable man. I anticipated you'd take this tone. The weather has indeed been a little on the chilly side, so I am prepared to compromise.' The King looked at me knowingly. 'We'll make do with *one* battleship. That'll deafen anyone, what?'

'It's not quite as simple as one battleship, Your Highness.'

'Very well, no battleships at all.'

Silence.

'Or massed bands.'

Silence.

'But we must have a fly-past! We always have a fly-past.'

Mr Chitt stroked his walrus moustache and locked his flipper-like hands across his belly.

'What about the millions watching? What are the millions watching going to watch if there aren't bands and battleships and a fly-past with planes doing loopy-the-loops with coloured smoke coming out of their bottoms and… you mean there won't be millions watching?'

Silence. To everyone in the room, it was plain to see where this was going – except perhaps the King. He looked at me. I think he was embarrassed. His voice grew louder.

'Very well then, Mr Chitt. No battleships, no gun salutes, no massed bands and no fly-past. But that is absolutely the last concession I am prepared to make. This is a royal occasion, Mr Chitt. The Prince is being *presented* to his *people*. He is swearing the Oath of Succession to become the next King of Albion. Do you understand what that means to the people of this country?'

'Indeed I do, sir.'

The King fumed.

'Mr Chitt,' said the Queen, smiling her most charming smile, 'what do *you* think we could manage?'

'Ma'am—'

'I'm sorry, Olivia, but you can't possibly ask Mr Chitt to organise our affairs. He's the Prime Minister! He's going to say no to everything!'

Mr Chitt sat entirely still, flippers locked.

'You see!'

'Mr Chitt?' pressed the Queen.

'I think if we could cut it all down to just one carriage, ma'am, for the Prince.'

'One carriage?' The King was amazed. '*One* carriage? What about the rest of us?'

'You could get in as well.'

'And I suppose you are expecting me, the King, to drive the thing?'

'If you like.'

Mr Chitt was entirely serious.

'That's it?'

'Perhaps we can organise a bit of bunting.'

'B-B-Bunting?' The King's eyes were popping out of his head. 'Anything else?'

'Soup. Jam sandwiches. Maybe a brass band to jolly things up a bit.'

'JOLLY THINGS UP!' The King stood up, incensed. 'This is not a village fête, Mr Chitt. This is a royal presentation!'

'Then perhaps Your Highness might consider a contribution from the royal purse.'

'But you can't expect me to *pay* for anything! I don't have any money! I AM THE KING OF ALBION!'

'Indeed you are, sir.'

The King's face had turned a dangerous shade of purple. He let out a small cough.

'Well I don't know,' he said. And out he stormed.

Silence resumed. Mr Chitt seemed relieved, but not unduly worried. I could see that he was a man used to getting his own way by simply planting himself down and waiting. The King could huff and puff as much as he liked.

'Is not a single carriage on its own, driving through the crowds, a little vulnerable, Prime Minister?' asked Thad Lancaster, glancing at the Queen. It was obvious what they were thinking.

'Oh I don't think so. As His Majesty pointed out, everyone just wants to see the Prince on his big day. Nobody wants to harm him. Who would want to harm this fine young man?'

'The same people who murdered his brother,' muttered Thad Lancaster.

Mr Chitt smiled his walrussy smile.

'I think you are unduly concerned, sir. This is a celebration. We all love our Prince. We all love our royal family. What's not to admire, eh?'

Thad Lancaster grimaced. He didn't believe it. And I wasn't quite sure about Mr Chitt either.

'I'm sure you'll still have a grand day out, Your Highness,' he said to me. 'It'll be an experience sitting in one of those old carriages, if nothing else.'

'Quite,' said the Queen, a smile fixed on her face. She took my hand. 'Oh Richard darling, are you awfully disappointed?'

They all stared at me. I shrugged awkwardly.

'If there are people freezing and starving... it doesn't seem right to be having a big ceremony... I mean it's probably not a good thing to do, is it?'

Mr Chitt nodded approvingly.

'Well said, Your Highness. We must all make sacrifices in these hard times.'

'Is there really nothing else we could do?' asked the Queen.

Mr Chitt considered.

'Well, I suppose if you wanted to bring out the royal beasts from that private zoo of yours, I can't see any harm in that, provided they're kept under control,' he added. 'I know some people may like to see them, but as far as I'm concerned, legendary creatures should stay exactly that, legendary, and preferably hidden as far underground as possible where they belong – if indeed they belong anywhere at all in this day and age.'

With that vague threat, Mr Chitt stood up and placed himself squarely before the fire with the air of a victorious boxer.

'I do apologise for popping your party balloon, young man, but nothing ever turns out quite the way you want it to, does it? Hard times,' he said with a smile. 'Hard times.'

∾ 32 ∾
More Complications

L ILY AND I LOITERED in the hall as the Queen said her
goodbyes to the Prime Minister.

'That was very big of you, Cuz,' said Lily. 'D'you really
not mind?'

As you can imagine, this was a tricky question.

'Not really, except… I suppose maybe perhaps I do mind, a bit.'

'Well I don't think you should be expected to do it. Not all on
your own, not after what happened to Stephen. That's not fair. I
think Mr Chitt could've shown more sympathy.'

I nodded. I wasn't quite sure how Richard felt about his older
brother, except that he was still in his shadow.

∾ 197 ∾

'My mum says Mr Chitt's just waiting for his chance to kick out the King and live here himself,' Lily continued in a whisper. 'That's the rumour. He's going to get rid of everything and turn St James's Palace into a hotel and the vaults into a car park. No wonder your father went mental. And you know how much he hates soup. And jam. *And* brass bands. I really think Mr Chitt might've shown a bit more sympathy.'

Oh dear. This was getting very, very complicated. I turned around and stared at the huge picture above the fireplace. It was a portrait of three children sitting in the grand room we had just left. Standing beside the sofa was a tall, blonde boy, looking very dapper in his yellow trousers and velvet coat. On the carpet before him sat a much younger boy playing with a train set. Sitting on the sofa between them was a dark-haired girl in a pale pink dress and a silk jacket embroidered with pearls. They all looked haughty and bored in a royal kind of way. It took a moment for me to realise who these children were. The King was the eldest boy. He hadn't changed much, and neither had Thad, whose piercing eyes and mischievous expression were exactly the same. So who was the girl in the middle? She was very pretty, and looked rebellious – the sort of person who wouldn't obey rules much. So there must be a middle sister between the King and Thad. I wondered why I had never heard of her before...

'Thank you for being so grown-up about all of this, darling,' said the Queen, bustling across the carpet towards us. 'Enormously helpful not to make a fuss. And thank you too, Lily darling, for the moral support.'

'But Aunt Olivia, is Richard really going to have to do it on his own?'

'Obviously not. It's quite absurd. Thad's already said he'll be

there to protect you, and your father… He's in such a rage, I don't know what he's planning to do. I think the threat of soup and sandwiches was the last straw. Oh darlings, what a business. We'll simply have to do what we're told, I suppose – that is the modern way.' The Queen sighed and touched my cheek. 'Dearest darling Richard. My dearest darling boy. Keep getting better, promise?'

I nodded. The Queen kissed us both and strode off at speed to organise something else. How she didn't suspect, I had no idea. Apparently she didn't.

Lily threaded her arm through mine and we wandered back across the carpet and down the wide staircase.

'You don't ever want to be crowned King, do you, Cuz?'

'Of course I don't.'

'Good. Because I don't want you ever to become King either.' She squeezed my arm in a friendly way. 'Wouldn't it be great if we could just stay like this forever? Never have to go out there and do all that stuff.'

Definitely. We walked down the stairs in silence for a bit.

'Has my father seemed strange to you lately?' I asked.

Lily considered. He was her uncle, but he was also the King after all.

'Well everyone knows he can be moody,' she said carefully. 'No offence, Cuz, but that is your family trait. And obviously we both know Thad goes totally ballistic sometimes. I suppose Marina must have done too.'

So that was the name of the girl in that portrait. Lily smiled. Clearly she did not want to offend. My mind was racing on.

'It's funny how no one talks about Marina any more,' I said.

'Is it?'

'Like she's been deliberately forgotten about.'

'Well obviously there's a good reason for that, isn't there?'

Whatever that reason was, I wasn't going to find out. We were now at the bottom of the long staircase and the footman was holding open the carriage door. Mr Squiddle the coachman tipped his hat and I climbed aboard. Lily was about to follow and then she stopped suddenly.

'Richard, where's your stick?'

I froze. Literally, my blood tingled.

'Erm….'

Lily stared at me.

'It's… I think it's back up in the hall, behind the Chinese jar.'

'Cuz, you've just walked all the way down the stairs and then jumped into the carriage as if nothing was the matter.'

My cheeks were on fire. What could I say?

'Whoops.'

Lily wrinkled her nose.

'And now I suppose you want me to run back and get it for you?'

'Could you?'

Lily huffed. 'You know sometimes, Cuz, you drive me totally nuts.'

Shaking her head, she ran back up to the hall. My heart was hammering. How could she not suspect?

We returned to St James's Palace in silence. At the bottom of our tower, Lily stood behind me.

'Try it again. Walk up the stairs without the stick.'

'It's going to be difficult,' I lied. 'Because I'm thinking about it now—'

'Try it.'

And so I did. My impression of someone with a limp who's suddenly beginning to get better as they climb a steep circular staircase was – I think you can imagine by now – not very convincing at all.

'Well?' she said.

'Something's happening to me,' I puffed. 'I feel... different.'

'I'm glad you said that, Cuz, because I'm seriously beginning to wonder.'

I shut the door to my room gratefully and sighed. I couldn't keep this up for much longer. Somehow I had to get hold of Richard and swap back again – tonight. Was he having the same problems that I was? Somehow I doubted it. I walked over to the window and stared across the snowy rooftops towards the Keepers' Courtyard. At the top of the black tower in the corner, the light was on. I imagined Richard sitting there with Tom Bootle, sharing a crumpet or two before the blazing fire, listening to yet another long story of the great days of the court...

'And how the world spins.'

I nearly jumped out of my skin. There was Asphodel, his eyes like lamps, staring at me not ten centimetres from my face. His cage was now hanging in an alcove just behind the curtain.

'How was the Prime Minister?'

'He was... What are you doing over here, Asphodel?'

'Waiting for you, my Prince.'

'But who moved your cage?'

'I have had a visitation. Miss Scott has taken me out of the light. I've been having trouble sleeping. The darkness suits my mood.'

The ancient fairy was hanging from the bars of his cage and he looked different somehow. His skin more vivid, his eyes more intense. It was a little frightening.

'The Prime Minister,' Asphodel repeated.

'It went well,' I lied.

'Well? Hmm. I suppose he was telling you how little money

he has.'

'Yes—'

'And how you mustn't have any pomp and parades for your presentation day.'

'Yes—'

'And how much it would offend the people if you did.'

'I don't want to offend the people.'

'Of course you don't, Richard. But did you agree to it?'

Asphodel's black eyes gleamed so brightly they seemed to be looking straight through me. It was a horrible feeling.

'Ahh. You did. You believed his lies.'

'What d'you mean?'

'Byron Chitt is a liar. He is plotting the downfall of the House of Lancaster. He wants to be rid of you all. You must be careful, Richard, in agreeing to anything he says. It is all a tissue of lies. Poisonous lies.'

'But he said people are freezing, starving to death…'

'Of course he did! Clever Mr Chitt, to pull upon your heartstrings and make you feel the embarrassment of privilege. I have seen how the world works, Richard. I have seen the traps men set to snare the kindest heart. How will they do it, I wonder? What will be their plan? Doubtless it will be subtle and swift. An assassin, hidden in the crowd with a knife under his cloak, a shake of the hand perhaps, then a clever thrust and it's goodbye House of Lancaster! Farewell, Richard, the never King! Farewell, sweet Prince, farewell, farewell, slain like his brother before him!'

Chanting this merry song Asphodel took flight and whirred about his cage, landing upon a china dish that held the remains of a mouse, its belly split open. Asphodel dipped his head inside and feasted, gurgling to himself. It was disgusting. Perhaps that was what had changed his mood – he was blood happy. Well at least that saved me one problem.

'So you're saying the Prime Minister is plotting to kill me?'

'Ah no. Mr Chitt's much too clever for that. And besides, he has no access to the palace. I have heard the night whisperers, my boy, listened as secret messages are passed about. A look here, a wink there... They are gathering to strike, crawling from their chambers and plotting behind teapots. Nothing escapes old Asphodel!'

The fairy spat out a bone, then pulled an eyeball from its socket and sucked on it like a sweet. His face was red with blood now; it ran down his neck in streams, staining his white silk scarf.

'You're not making this up?'

'Asphodel has never been more serious in his life.'

He looked at me and grinned, his sharp little fangs glistening. He spat out the eyeball and began chewing on an ear. I couldn't watch this disgusting performance any longer.

'I'm going to talk to Lily about this.'

'Very wise, my Prince. Think hard on't. The truth is a cruel mistress.'

I left him to his feast and closed the door. I did think hard on it – for a second. Lily was not the person to warn. It was Richard himself.

'She's not interested.'

'Give her a bit longer.'

'Cuz, she's obviously not there.'

'She must be.'

We sat at the open window looking down at the snowy rooftops glowing pale blue. Lily had gone down to borrow the royal harbinger again, and after a lot of bribery with nuts and chocolate the grumpy white squirrel agreed to take my letter over the rooftops to my old room. Lily thought it was just another invitation to tea, when in fact my letter said this:

Dear Richard,

I suppose I should be congratulating you, because what you did was very clever. I didn't know anything about your Presentation on Tuesday. And I also didn't understand anything about what it's like to be a Prince, or even the next King of Albion. So yes, I sympathise. Maybe it's not so great after all. Even so, I am NOT swearing any Oath of Succession. Ever. Why? Because I'm not very good at being you, Asphodel is getting suspicious, and Lily is getting even more suspicious. In fact she'll probably kill you if she ever finds out the truth. And apart from all that, there's something else you should know. I'm serious. Reply, otherwise I'm climbing back over the roofs tonight. I mean it.

Jack.

Lily shivered and pulled up her scarf against the swirling fog.

'You know she's going to get into serious trouble if she's caught over here again.'

'I'll say it was my fault. I asked her to come.'

'And who's going to believe that?' scoffed Lily. 'You never get in trouble for anything, Cuz, or haven't you noticed?'

I had, as it happens.

'Seriously, Thad might decide to make an example of her. You know what he's like—'

Somehow I missed the sound of scrabbling up the wall and

before I knew it, the white squirrel had hopped back in through the window.

'That was quick,' said Lily, removing the letter from its back. 'Charming!' she added, as I swiftly snatched the envelope out of her hand.

'Well it's addressed to me, isn't it?' I said, taking it over to the fireplace.

Not surprisingly, Lily was now watching me very carefully indeed.

'What does she say, Cuz?' she asked, trying to hide her curiosity.

I turned away and began to read.

Hi Jack,

You seem to be panicking. It sounds like you've been feeling far too well. Don't be well, be ill; very ill! Spend all day in bed, like I do. Then you don't need to worry about the presentation, because if you're too sick they'll have to cancel the whole thing. They can't do it without you. That was my plan. And definitely ignore Asphodel. He can be so boring sometimes. Just ask Snowdrop Scott to bring him a mouse, it makes him about a hundred times nicer.

As for swapping back tonight, I'm afraid it's completely impossible. You might be able to climb over the rooftops, but Enid Cribbage has locked all the staircases and I'll never get back. And the truth is, I don't want to come back. I like being a keeper, I like snooping around all the other vaults (Patrick Pettifog's is amazing), and I'm also getting rather good at charming ghosts. No one's ever going to allow me over here again, so I've decided to stay for a while. You'll just have to carry on, I'm afraid, and that's the way it is. Just ignore everyone and stay in bed!

R.

'Well?'

Lily leant against the wall with her arms crossed, staring at me. I folded the letter guiltily.

'She says she can't come. You were right; Thad's ordered all the staircases to be locked and Enid Cribbage is patrolling the courtyards. It's impossible.'

Lily nodded.

'And what else did she say?'

'Nothing much.'

'Why does she sign herself "R"?'

'It was a J.'

'Didn't look like a J.'

'Well it was. You obviously misread it.'

And with that I screwed the letter into a ball and threw it on the fire. Lily watched the paper catch alight. Like I said, she wasn't stupid.

'Is there something you're not telling me, Cuz?'

'No. What d'you mean?'

Lily stared at me a moment, then stood up.

'I suppose it's none of my business,' she said, and flounced over to the door. 'But you are lying to me, Richard. Don't think I don't know it. Something's going on, because you're being really strange. Just don't lie to me, okay?'

The door slammed. Oh dear. Lily definitely suspected now. I felt terrible deceiving her, but what could I do? Tell her the truth, I suppose. Maybe sooner rather than later.

ᨶᨶ 33 ᨶᨶ
Night Song

I T WAS IMPOSSIBLE to get to sleep that night. I lay awake,
staring out at the snowy rooftops, wondering quite how this
little secret had so quickly turned into a nightmare. Richard
was obviously enjoying himself far more than he ever thought
he would. He didn't want to come back, and I didn't blame him.
But if I *did* tell everyone who I really was, what would happen
to me? Impersonating the Prince, meeting the Prime Minister…
Lily was right, Richard never got the blame for anything. So it
would all be my fault – and then what? Thad Lancaster seemed
very angry that I was even in the palace… I stared at my reflection
in the mirror, my mind galloping on. I began to wonder what

the chances were of two people looking so similar. It wasn't just our eyes and faces and the lack of hair; everyone – the King, the Queen, Lily, even William Foxglass, who knew me better than any of them – somehow I had fooled them all, hadn't I?

It was almost three o'clock and I still wasn't able to sleep. Listening in the darkness, I heard a murmuring from next door. Slipping out of bed, I opened the door a fraction and peered into the moonlit room beyond. There was Asphodel, lolling on his swing, singing softly to himself.

'To this curs'd land comes a child with no name,
  With a hey-ho, the ice and the snow,
  To restore fair Albion's fortunes again,
  With a hey-ho, the ice and the snow,
  Brought here in secret, a fiery thing,
  With a hey-ho, the ice and the snow,
  Born out of love and great suffering–'

Asphodel stopped suddenly. He must have sensed I was there, hovering in the darkness.

'You heard the singing too, my Prince?'

He turned around, his eyes blazing like lamps.

'Well?'

I hadn't. As I walked closer, I heard a voice drifting up over the rooftops. It was a nightwatchman perhaps, in another courtyard, singing to himself as he made his rounds. I recognised the song. Tom Bootle had been singing it the first morning I arrived.

'The Song of the Phoenix Child,' whispered Asphodel. 'I've only heard such singing once before. I suck melancholy out of that song as a weasel sucks eggs.'

'What does it mean?'

Asphodel considered.

'The people are restless for change. It's a warning, Richard. Heed it.'

He stared at me, his skin almost green in the darkness. That strange smile on his lips was frightening.

'What kind of change?'

Asphodel turned to the window once more.

'A change in the wind. A change in their world. There are dark forces at work, my child. A fiery-footed catastrophe lurks just around the corner. We must take heed.'

'So you keep saying, Asphodel.'

'My counsel bores you?'

To be honest, yes it did.

'It's just that you keep going on about these "dark forces" and people plotting behind teapots, but you never tell me what I should do about it.'

'I apologise for my concern.' Asphodel bowed sarcastically. 'I love my Master not wisely, but too well.'

'So? What should I do about it?'

'In Asphodel's humble opinion, place your trust in the hands of your uncle. He alone will protect you in this den of thieves.'

I was confused. Thad Lancaster?

'What about my parents?'

The fairy shook his head sadly.

'Only the Duke of Lancaster has seen what's coming. Trust him, Richard. Trust your uncle with your life. Do exactly as he tells you, as any dutiful boy should.'

The fairy lay back in his swing, staring out at the night. I wondered why Asphodel was telling me this. And then I decided to do something dangerous. I wanted to see his reaction.

'Do these people who are plotting to kill me have anything to do with Isabella Royle?'

Asphodel froze like an actor on stage.

'Where did you hear that name?'

'I read about her in the library–'

'There is no book mentioning that name in the library.'

'Then it must've been some keepers talking about her–'

'And you've been listening to such talk? Who were they? Which keepers? What were their names? Tell me.'

Asphodel's eyes glittered. I tried to look as helpless as possible.

'How do I know? They were over in their side of the palace. Someone just said her name, that's all.'

Asphodel muttered to himself.

'Well, Asphodel?'

'Isabella Royle is dead, my Prince. Dead, long dead, along with all her followers. Fifty traitors lost their heads, and their rebellion was quelled. 'Twas a brutal massacre, but necessary. How the executioner's axe did echo through the palace that day! We should be thankful.'

I stared at him hard.

'That's funny, because that's not what I heard.'

Asphodel's eyes narrowed.

'Indeed?'

'I heard that Isabella Royle's followers were never caught – or executed, either. There were lots of them, and after her death they quietly went back to whatever they were doing before. But I suppose that might have been an idle rumour.'

'Aye, my Prince. An idle rumour that mocks the very meat it feeds on.'

'Well that's good to know,' I said. 'Because there obviously *is* someone in the palace trying to kill me, isn't there? I don't know who they are, or how they're doing it, but I'm sure if you knew anything more than rumours, you'd be the first to let me know. Wouldn't you, Asphodel?'

The fairy's expression changed.

'Oh. Oh I see. I see now. Oh I am fortune's fool!'

With a great show of emotion Asphodel climbed down from his swing and knelt before me, placing one hand upon his heart. 'My dear Prince, remember this. Asphodel has been a devoted friend and servant to every King and Queen this last five hundred years. He has only one wish, and that is to entertain and enchant, and offer wise counsel where he may.' And with that the fairy staggered across to his bedroom as if wounded.

'Asphodel?'

He opened the little door and raised one hand.

'Croak not, black angel, I have no food for thee.'

'I'm not accusing you, Asphodel, I just wanted to know—'

'Blow, blow, thou winter wind, thou art not so unkind as a Prince's ingratitude to his friend!'

'Asphodel come back—'

The door slammed shut. The lock clicked. Asphodel had gone.

I returned to my bedroom, less certain than ever who my enemies were. But one thing I knew for sure; Asphodel was a great mischief-maker. Perhaps he didn't know who those dark forces were. Perhaps he had only been listening to gossip. But that didn't make me want to trust him. And the truth is, I don't think he trusted me either...

◈ 34 ◈
The Mask Slips

T**HE NEXT MORNING,** my second as the heir to the throne, began a lot better than my first. By better, I mean I was more convincing, because I felt exhausted and trapped. I didn't order another 'Armada' breakfast, but wearily pressed the 'Loco' button instead. This was far more sensible. Tea, cereal, toast and eggs all arrived in an orderly fashion on carriages pulled by a small puffing engine, which appeared out of a tunnel from one side of the bedhead and disappeared into another tunnel on the other. No spillages at all. Then Dr Mazumdar beetled in again.

'Good morning, Richard!' he beamed. And then his smile faded. 'Oh dear.'

He checked my pulse, inspected my eyes and ears, and decided from my expression that yesterday's miraculous recovery was short-lived. Everything was slipping back to normal.

'A false dawn. Never mind,' he muttered, stuffing his torch back into his bag. 'Soldier on, Richard, and keep taking the pills, my friend. Keep taking the pills.'

Lily seemed rather pleased to see Richard back to his old, sick self. Perhaps everything that happened yesterday could not be explained; it was just one of those freaky days where nothing makes sense.

'One good piece of news, Cuz,' she said brightly, 'I've brought you a present.' Reaching into her pocket, she unwrapped a soggy tissue.

'It's a snowdrop,' I said, trying not to seem too underwhelmed.

'I know. Isn't it great?' Lily beamed. 'I found it in the corner of the courtyard. There's a patch of them.'

I looked at the delicate white flower. Three perfect petals hung from a slender green stalk, like a lamp from some fairy kingdom.

'Why are you so excited about a snowdrop, Lily?'

'It's a sign that the season is changing, isn't it? Winter is on its way out and spring is coming.'

I shrugged. I could see this meant far more to Lily than it did to me.

'Come on, Cuz, show a bit more enthusiasm. Things might be changing at last.'

'Better put it in some water, then.'

If only I knew as much about Albion's history as I knew about snowdrops (which was nothing, by the way). Minty Bishop stared at me till her eyes seemed about to pop out of her head.

'What was the name of the last man to execute a king?'

I frowned. I doodled. I scratched my nose.

'Richard, you composed a sonnet about him last week!'

Ah. Another poem. Why did Richard have to keep writing poems about everything?

'Using perfect iambic pentameters?'

They sounded impressive, whatever they were. Minty Bishop stared at me.

'Jackernapes, Richard? His head is the ball in Jackernapes?'

'His head is the ball in Jackernapes,' I repeated.

'*Yes.* So there's a clue for you. What was his *name*?'

Minty Bishop stood before me, hands on hips, her nose twitching in that anteatery way of hers. I'm sure that had I been anyone else, she would have exploded by now. I glanced around. Only Tucker-Smith and Spiggins were giggling. No one else dared.

'Was it…' I looked down at the note someone had swiftly slipped onto my desk. '*Nolliver Crumbell,*' it read. Now I may not have been to school much, but I'd been enough to know that when someone slips you a note like that, it's not the right answer.

'I've forgotten.'

'You've forgotten? What does that note say, hmm?'

'Which note?'

'Why don't you tell the class what it says, hmm? Come on, share it with the rest of us. What does it say?'

Miss Bishop was getting very angry.

'I haven't the foggiest idea,' I said.

Muffled honks filled the room as Minty Bishop bent forward, her face redder than ever.

'You have gone too far this time,' she whispered. 'See me afterwards.' With a snort, she turned to the rest of the class. 'Matty Wong?'

'Oliver Cromwell, Miss Bishop.'

'Thank you, Matty, for giving me a straight answer. Now...'

The rest of the lesson seemed to go on for weeks, months perhaps. I stared at the timetable stuck to the top of the desk. It was Anglo Saxon next. Then Onion Runyon's guide to heraldry. Then double Greek. Why they were learning all this terrible old stuff I did not know. Perhaps it was Professor Runyon's idea of a royal education, but it certainly wasn't mine. I couldn't do any of it. My bluffing skills were at an end.

Afterwards arrived, too soon.

'Richard, I really don't know what's got into you. Are you trying to be funny?'

'Definitely not, Miss Bishop.'

'Are you bored?'

'No.'

'What's the matter with you then? Because you seem to have entirely lost your memory. In all subjects.'

'I know.'

'You think you *have* lost your memory?'

'Maybe. I can't remember.'

Minty Bishop frowned, then stared at my exercise books spread out across the table. On every page I could see 'Ten out of ten!', 'Five stars!', 'Smiley faces!', exclamation marks and ticks all over the place.

'It's as if your mind has been completely emptied of everything,' she said, flicking through one book after another with irritation. 'Frankly, Richard, I wonder if you can even remember your own name. Can you?'

'Can I what?'

'Remember your own name.'

'My name?'

Miss Bishop peered up from the galaxy of stars.

'Yes, Richard, can you remember the name you were given when you were born?'

This sounded suspiciously like a sort of doctor's question. My heart began to thump.

'My full name?'

'Yes, your full name.'

'Do you mean *all* of it?'

'Of course I mean *all* of it,' she repeated impatiently. 'What is your name?'

Now while it may be understandable not to know anything about Greek myths or Oliver Cromwell, everyone, surely *everyone*, knows their own name. Unless they have a problem. And I did. A big problem. Professor Runyon had been listening to all this at the open door, and now he came forward into the classroom looking concerned.

'Shall I start at the beginning or the end?'

'I don't mind, Richard. The beginning is where people normally start, isn't it? What is your name?'

I looked across at Onion. He narrowed his eyes in his herony way.

'Well? What is your name?' he repeated.

What to do? I closed my eyes and thought. Desperate situation. *What to do?*

'I think he's fainted!'

'Fainted?'

'His heart's still beating! He needs air!'

'Air?'

'Quick!'

Books were fluttered in my face.

'There's something very wrong with this boy,' said Onion, hauling me over his shoulder. I hung limp as a rag doll as he raced out into the school cloister.

'Is he dead?' asked Jake Tiptree, who had been smashing icicles beside the fountain. Onion did not reply. 'Richard's dead!' shouted Jake.

Heads popped out of windows to look.

'No way!'

'Richard's dead?'

'Richard's *dead*?'

'He died just now, I saw him!' shouted Jake, pleased to be the bearer of such important news. I opened one eye and saw a crowd anxiously gather around, pressing to know more. 'Onion and Minty Bishop were shouting at him, "What's your name! What's your name!" over and over and getting really angry. And then Richard just sort of... collapsed.'

'So they like... *killed* him?'

'Yeah. I suppose they did.'

'Actually killed him?'

'Yeah.'

'Onion's killed Richard! Onion's killed Richard!'

'He's not dead!' shouted Onion Runyon in a panic as we reached the bottom of the tower. 'Someone call the doctor!' he bawled, before racing up the stairs.

Ultimatum

WELL I WAS back in bed again. That was the good news.

'Darling, what happened?'

There was the Queen, looking perfect as usual, her brow knotted with concern.

'I don't know,' I croaked. 'I sort of... suddenly felt strange. Odd.'

'Odd? Hmm.'

There was the King. He looked concerned too – but in a different way. Sort of confused. His moustache twitched. On the other side, stood Dr Mazumdar and Onion Runyon. Lily hovered in the background.

'Memory loss, you say?' said Dr Mazumdar.

'He didn't know who Icarus was, who Oliver Cromwell was, and he struggles to conjugate even the simplest Latin verbs,' said Onion.

'And what does that prove, eh?' demanded the King.

Onion Runyon smiled in his oily way.

'Your Highness, it can't have escaped your attention that your son is the most brilliant student in this school—'

''Course he is. And?'

'This is a boy who knows absolutely everything there is to be known about Albion's Kings and Queens, knows every date of every battle, writes perfect poetry in Greek—'

'Yes, *yes* Onion, we all know this,' said the King impatiently. 'What's your point?'

'It appears that now he can't even remember his own name.'

'And?'

'His name, Your Highness.'

'You mean his full name?'

'Yes, Your Highness.'

'With all his middle names?'

'Yes.'

'*All* of them?'

Onion Runyon smiled, slightly less sure of himself.

'Dang and blast, that settles it!' honked the King. 'Ask me that question and I'd also fall flat on my back and start wobbling like a cowpat. And have I lost my marbles, what?' Another honk. Polite smiles all round.

'What would cause such memory loss, Doctor?' asked the Queen.

Dr Mazumdar stared at me a while.

'Sudden amnesia can be brought about by many things. A blow

to the head. Perhaps a profound shock of some kind.'

The Queen looked at the King. The King frowned.

'You mean the shock of not having any battleships?'

'No darling–'

'No fly-past, then?'

'*No* darling. You know how Richard feels about the whole thing, don't you?'

'Hmm,' the King sniffed. 'Well I don't know. Probably a bit too much ragging around with the chaps in the Jackernapes court. Banged his bonce and not even noticed. Nothing a day or two in bed won't fix. Come to think of it, his hair looks a bit peculiar.'

'Let him rest, Edward,' said the Queen, politely but firmly holding her husband back. 'Lily, what do you think, has Richard seemed peculiar to you at all?'

Lily smiled awkwardly.

'Now you mention it, Aunt Olivia, Richard has been acting a little strange.'

I opened my eyes a fraction. No, Lily, please don't say anything.

'Strange in what way, darling?'

'He seems... a little confused about who he is.'

She caught my eye. I shook my head as much as I dared.

'And he walked down the stairs.'

The King honked loudly.

'Well that solves it! The boy who walked down the stairs! He must have gone mad!'

'Without his stick.'

'Well, what's a stick for? Twirling and twizzling. Whizzling and fizzling. Flicking snow off one's boots, fencing with chaps. I used to stride about with a cane when I was his age. Pure affectation. Sort of becomes one, what?'

Dr Mazumdar leant forward.

'May I suggest, ma'am, if you're in any doubt, we could give him an X-ray, and a full-body examination. That would probably be a good idea in any case.'

'Would that be necessary?' asked the Queen. 'I mean, he's just confused—'

'The King's right. Perhaps Richard's sustained an injury that he can't remember, which might be the cause of all this.'

The King nodded, pleased to be right about something.

'Give him both. Why not?' he said. 'Best get to the root of it.'

The Queen looked at me again, harder this time. She had one of those perfect faces that was a perfect mask. I couldn't tell what she was thinking at all.

'All right then.'

'I can arrange one for this afternoon if you like,' said Dr Mazumdar.

'No. Let him rest now. Make it tomorrow afternoon.'

'Ma'am, in such circumstances it's usual to find out the cause of the problem as soon as possible. If he's broken something—'

'Tomorrow afternoon, Doctor. I want to be there and I cannot be there before tomorrow afternoon.'

'With respect, ma'am, it's not you who needs an X-ray.'

'Dr Mazumdar, I think *I* know what is best for my son.'

'Who is my patient—'

'And he could quite easily become someone else's,' she said with a sharp look. 'It will be tomorrow afternoon, and that's the end of it.'

Dr Mazumdar was silenced. The Queen was definitely not someone you picked an argument with. Ever.

'As you wish, ma'am.'

'Let us leave him in peace,' she said.

I closed my eyes and listened as they withdrew.

'Make sure you get well *soon*, darling,' whispered the Queen, and I felt her lips on my forehead.

Away she tiptoed and the door closed. I opened my eyes, my heart racing. Full-body examination and an X-ray, tomorrow afternoon. That settled it then. Either we'd swap back before then, or I'd have to admit the truth – with all its consequences, which would be far, far worse for me than Richard. So it would have to be tonight. Somehow I would have to find some way back over there. How? I got up and stared out of the window. There were extra guards on the battlements, in the courtyards, on the gate. There were seeing stones in all the corridors, and when night fell Enid Cribbage would be tiptoeing about with her box of bats... Then in a flash it occurred to me. Why hadn't I thought of it before? Perhaps there *was* one final way to leave this rare world of royal privilege unnoticed...

✳ 36 ✳
A Way Out

THE CORRIDOR WAS DARK, but not too dark to notice
the seeing stone Solomon Knock had left at the end of it.
Could it see me? Who knows. I kept up my limp, tap-tap-
tapping towards it with my stick. I had a plan, and it didn't involve
clambering over slippery battlements and icy rooftops. It was
another way...

As soon as I passed the stone I dared to speed up. Down one
corridor, then another, then up two flights of stairs to the second
floor of the Sable Court. Through the window I could see the
Sable Tower on the opposite side, a light flickering behind one
of the narrow windows. Somehow I had to get as close to it

as possible. I'm sure whatever Richard did couldn't have been difficult…

'Miss Cribbage!' I jumped. 'You gave me a shock.'

Enid Cribbage's long bony face split into a grimace. I'd turned the corner and suddenly there she was, standing silently in the darkness in that way of hers. I wondered if she was about to shriek at me, but thankfully she thought better of it. She banged her snake-eyed staff on the floor and a hundred bats came whizzing back down the corridor towards us.

'We heard you had a turn, Your Highness. Sorry to hear that,' said Solomon Knock, wandering up behind her, hands twisted behind his back.

'I'm feeling a little better now, I think.'

'Oh good,' he grinned, giving me a lizardy stare.

'This corridor's out of bounds and no exceptions,' squeaked a thin nasal voice at the back. Archie Queach stood in the shadows, not daring to look at me like the coward he was.

'Unfortunately that is now the case, Your Highness,' said Mr Knock. 'All corridors in the Sable Court are out of bounds. For your own safety.'

'I see.'

'It was announced at the school

assembly this evening. I suppose you were probably resting in your room, Your Highness.'

I suppose I was. Nevertheless, the end of this corridor was where I wanted to go.

'If you could just return to your own quarters then we would all be most grateful, Your Highness.'

The three of them barred my way. Solomon Knock smiled. Enid Cribbage stared straight ahead in that way of hers. And Archie Queach – I couldn't really tell what his expression was. Bossing a prince around? He must have been in heaven. Reluctantly I turned around and together we all headed back the way I had come. There must be some other way... A group of third years clattered down the stairs at the end, carrying sports bags. I guessed they'd just been playing Jackernapes. They all looked down at our strange group then quickly pretended they hadn't.

'Cuz?' Lily stopped to look at me. 'What are you doing?'

'I... erm, I'm not sure.'

'Are you all right?'

Somehow she could spot my confusion at a distance and ran down to save me.

'I'm so sorry, Mr Knock, I'll take him back,' she said, threading her arm through mine and whisking me away in the direction I'd come. 'Richard you must pay more attention to where you are or you'll get us all in serious trouble.'

All this was said in a loud stage whisper. I glanced back at Enid Cribbage, Archie Queach and Solomon Knock standing there nonplussed.

'What are they doing up here?' I whispered once we were safely round the corner.

'What are *you* doing up here?' Lily hissed back. 'I was told not to disturb you and everyone's been threatened with terrible punishments if they make a noise and wake you up. Onion Runyon's gone crazy. Jake Tiptree's already got triple detention for telling everyone you were dead, and everyone else is making a banner saying 'Get well soon Richard'. Even Spiggins and Tucker-Smith. Well, Cuz? You'd better explain.'

I wondered whether this was the moment to tell her the whole truth. I settled for half.

'I need to go and see Umballoo.'

Lily looked at me. I could tell she knew Richard did this, a lot.

'Tonight? You know Dr Mazumdar's probably going to come back to see how you are. And the Queen—'

'I don't care, Lily. It has to be tonight.'

Lily sighed, but she didn't seem too surprised. I guessed that when Richard decided something, he always did it.

'I don't suppose you're going to tell me why?'

'No.'

'Okay. But I'm coming with you.'

'Lily that's not a good idea—'

'You can't do this on your own, Cuz. Not tonight. Cribbage's bats are everywhere and they've locked most of the doors already. If they catch you again, even *you* might get in trouble.'

Okay, she was right. And I suppose I didn't exactly know how Richard got into the Sable Tower...

'Fine. Come along then.'

'Oh thanks!' she beamed.

'But only if you keep quiet.'

'Says who? You?' she smiled, looking at my stick. 'Let's go the back way.'

Now the back way really was a back way, down narrow corridors and up staircases, through secret sliding doors and cupboards which mysteriously led into the back of other cupboards… At last we arrived at a lonely Tudor toilet, directly against the Sable Tower wall. High above the cubicle was a small round window. Lily and I squeezed inside the cubicle and locked the door. She looked at me in anticipation.

'So where's the pea-shooter?'

Pea-shooter. Obviously I knew nothing about any pea-shooter.

'Let me guess,' she said, then felt around the back of the cistern. She retrieved it, along with a small bag of peas. This was going much better than expected.

'You go first, you're much better at this sort of thing.'

'Oh thanks, Cuz!'

Lily was so thrilled to be in on this. She must have followed Richard and watched how he did it all without being noticed.

'Three times?' she said, rolling a pea into the shooter.

I nodded. Why not? Lily stood up and took aim at the small round window. Three sharp dings later, we replaced the pea-shooter in its hiding place and waited.

'You know, Cuz, I was pretty certain you wanted to keep the Sable Tower your own little secret forever.'

I smiled vaguely. Richard wasn't going to like this when he found out… Too bad. Somewhere in the distance, Enid Cribbage's bats screamed up a chimney.

'What d'you want to see Umballoo for?' asked Lily.

'I'll tell you when we're inside.'

'Love it! So mysterious.'

After another minute the small round window high above us creaked and swung open. Then a long snaking trunk appeared through the window and wound down towards us.

'Want to go first?' I asked.

'No, you go, Cuz. I want to watch how you do it.'

And so I did. I climbed up onto the top of the cistern and pulled the trunk towards me. The two pink nostrils explored my face, my wig, as if saying hello. Umballoo knew exactly who I was, I was sure of it. Having said his greeting, his trunk circled under my arms and lifted me into the air, then very slowly and carefully drew me through the round window like a letter through a letterbox.

'Thank you, Umballoo,' I said, as he gently set me down in the velvet castle on his back. The great creature then leant forward to get Lily. I looked around. We were on a wide staircase that wound up around the tower. In the middle was a column of shelves that ran up and down as far as I could see. Every single centimetre was piled high with glittering objects of every shape and size, and the steps were covered in them too, and the windowsills, and the odd gaps in the walls... It was like being inside a giant jewellery box.

Lily came through the window headfirst and her eyes lit up at the Aladdin's cave.

'Wow!' she whispered, flumping down next to me. We sat together in the little castle, awestruck. It was amazing. Umballoo reversed and carefully picked up the small piece of paper lying on the step. His list. Holding it up to his eyes a moment, he then tucked it behind his ear and began wandering up the stairs very slowly, picking his way through the objects he'd carefully placed there. This would have been hard enough for a person, let alone an oliphant wearing huge purple slippers...

'Mustn't touch anything,' I whispered. 'The last person caught stealing–'

'Had his hands and feet cut off. Yes you've told me that,' said Lily. 'I don't want to take anything, Cuz, I just want to look.'

And there was so much to look at. I could fill a few pages with descriptions of all the weird and strange presents the kings and queens of Albion had ever been given, as they really were as odd as you might be imagining. A few things caught my eye. The enormous stuffed crocodile given by the King of Burundi, which was now a sleeping bag large enough for four people. The packet of Russian fireworks given by Ivan the Terrible; there were smaller fireworks inside smaller fireworks inside smaller fireworks... Indoor flying balloons, a gift from the Emperor of China, a jar of O'Gallywacker's gobstoppers, presented by Gordon O'Gallywacker himself. '*This is a weapon of war!*' declared the label. '*And something to give to talkative uncles at Christmas.*' The more you sucked the more they grew, and kept on growing and growing till your jaw dislocated. I stared at the great jumble of presents floating past – clocks, candlesticks, toys, hats... What was it that Isabella Royle had wanted in this vast treasure store? Whatever it was, there was surely no way she could have found it on her own. Not only was the Sable Tower crammed to the rafters, but Umballoo was constantly rearranging things as he wandered along. It was incredible how he knew where anything was at all...

'Oh look at that!' gasped Lily. Umballoo had stopped to move something on the steps opposite a shelf with an old rolled-up scroll on it. '*Henry VIII's secret tips for winning at Jackernapes*' read the label.

'But we've got to see that, Cuz.'

'Must we?'

Lily glanced at me as if I was mad, then took the scroll from the shelf and unrolled it, squinting at the small brown writing.

'Secret levers? Hidden footholds... What? But this is amazing!'

Lily was fascinated. Obviously it meant nothing to me. I looked down at the shelf below. In amongst everything else was a small canvas rucksack. '*Merlin's stuff*' read the label. Curious, I carefully lifted it from the shelf and looked inside. There was a small silver knife, a clay pipe, a half-eaten packet of mints and an old-age pensioner's bus pass. The photo showed an old man with a white beard, looking very surprised. Merlin... as in the wizard from King Arthur's time? Perhaps that little knife was the one they'd used to... and then I felt something lumpy at the bottom. Wrapped inside a pair of old woolly socks was a large and ancient key. I picked it up and turned it over in my hand. I don't know if I was imagining it, but in the low light I was certain the intricate patterns on the handle were beginning to move, weaving and glowing like flames...

'This is incredible, Cuz,' said Lily. 'Did you know that–' She stopped when a long brown trunk tapped her on the shoulder.

'Oh. We're probably not supposed to look at these.'

No you're definitely not, the trunk seemed to be saying.

'Sorry, Umballoo.'

The oliphant's trunk snaked around and flattened out before Lily. Hand it over, it seemed to be saying.

'Sorry.' With an embarrassed smile she swiftly rolled up the scroll and handed it to the trunk. Umballoo set the scroll back on the shelf, then reached for Merlin's rucksack.

'Who did all that stuff belong to?' Lily whispered.

I told her. She didn't believe it.

'Merlin? The wizard? Come on, Cuz.'

'Why not?' I shrugged, noticing that my hand was still tingling.

On we went, the oliphant slowly meandering up the stone steps, occasionally twisting a bottle around, lifting a sword from one shelf to another... Looking back, I wonder if it was an accident that Umballoo had stopped exactly where he did. Had he known what was going to catch our eye, in amongst all those thousands of objects inside the tower? It's hard to say…

'So Cuz, you still haven't told me why you had to see Umballoo tonight.'

No I hadn't. And of course Lily wasn't going to forget either. She smiled in anticipation.

'Well?'

I cleared my throat.

'Lily, I have a secret to tell you.'

'Goody. Love secrets.'

'You might not like this one.'

'Try me.'

I couldn't think of an easy way to explain this. So I did exactly what Richard had done, which sort of explained everything without words.

'You see?'

Umballoo's Answer

LILY DREW HER HAND to her mouth in shock.

'I knew it. I *knew* it.'

She looked at the wig, and then me.

'It's those pills, isn't it? Those terrible pills the doctor gives you to make you well enough to play Jackernapes. I knew there was something bad about them–'

'I'm not taking the pills.'

Lily looked confused. Then concerned.

'You really are very ill then, Cuz?'

'I'm *not* your cousin. Can't you tell?'

She stared at me hard. Then smiled sadly.

'Oh dear. I've always thought this might happen.'

'What?'

'You've gone mad.'

'I haven't gone mad—'

'That's exactly what mad people say, Cuz—'

'I'm not *mad*, Lily. I'm not your cousin—'

'Stop it, Richard! This isn't a joke any more—'

'Lily, *look* at me. I'm Jack! *Jack* Joliffe. Richard and I have swapped.'

Lily stared at me, shaking her head.

'Don't be silly. *Swapped*? What are you talking about?'

And so I told her everything. How it was Richard's idea, how he was up in my room at this moment being the Keeper of Ghosts, and it seemed very clear from the letter he sent last night that he didn't ever want to come back.

It was the letter that seemed to clinch it. At last Lily realised it did all make sense. No wonder she seemed a little angry.

'So this morning, when you fainted – you didn't really faint at all?'

'No.'

'So you're *acting*?'

'Not very well, Lily. Can't you tell?'

'Well you certainly fooled me.'

'Did I?'

I mentioned the stick and all the things I'd said that had seemed strange to her. Slowly Lily became less annoyed; perhaps she *had* suspected, all along, she just hadn't realised it. She looked at me again – not angry now, more curious – still not quite sure if she could actually believe it.

'I suppose you do look and sound exactly the same as Richard.'

'I know. That's weird isn't it?'

'Why doesn't Richard have any hair?'

'I don't know. This is his wig.'

Lily looked at it thoughtfully.

'Everyone says royal blood is bad blood, and Richard has all the bad blood, whatever that means. But he was never as ill as this when Stephen was alive, honestly he wasn't. I mean he's always been thin and sick-looking, but nothing like he is now.'

That's what Sam Yuell had said too. I quietly told her what he suspected.

Lily looked at me with growing concern.

'Seriously? You mean someone in the palace might be *poisoning* him? How?'

I shrugged.

'I don't know. It was just a rumour. And Asphodel was always going on about the dark forces gathering in the palace. He might've just wanted to scare me for some reason, but he kept going on about it.'

'I've never liked that fairy,' muttered Lily. 'I've never understood what Richard sees in him. I wouldn't be surprised if he was just making it all up–'

'He may be right, Lily.'

'But everyone loves Richard. Why would anyone... Did someone try to poison you, Jack?'

'I don't think so. Unless it's those pills Dr Mazumdar gives him. I never took any.'

Lily shook her head, trying to take it in.

'But Jack, just supposing he *is* being poisoned, isn't it better that he's over there and you're here?'

'Until my medical inspection and X-ray tomorrow afternoon,' I reminded her.

'Oh. Yes. I see.'

We sat in glum silence for a moment. Lily was obviously

disappointed. She was clearly extremely protective of Richard, but what was the alternative? It may not have been his fault that he was born to be who he was, but it certainly wasn't mine.

'So that's why I wanted to come and see Umballoo,' I said. 'Because I thought if I explained everything to him, he'd help me in some way. Maybe there's something in here I could borrow, or maybe there's even some secret way over to the other side. Umballoo knows everything there is to know about the palace, apparently. I couldn't think of what else to do.'

Lily nodded. At last she seemed to understand.

'I can't believe someone might actually be poisoning him,' she said again, her eyes glistening with tears. 'It seems so unfair. Poor Cuz.'

All the while we'd been talking, the great oliphant had been ambling up the wide steps, shifting this and twisting that with his trunk, his huge leathery ears flapping occasionally. I was sure he'd been listening to our conversation. I leant out of the small velvet castle and looked down at the great oliphant.

'Well, Umballoo, what do you think? Can you help me?'

The oliphant's ears batted back and forth in a ding-dong sort of way. He scratched his head with his trunk, then carried on walking up the circular steps. Lily and I looked at each other. Was that a yes or a no? It was hard to tell...

'Maybe whoever is poisoning Richard stole the poison from in here,' Lily said, watching the crammed shelves drifting past. 'This place must be full of weird potions, mustn't it?'

It certainly looked like it. In amongst all the boxes of jewellery and goblets and candlesticks, there were plenty of odd-looking jars and bottles. I wasn't sure if Umballoo was still considering my request or ignoring it, but for some reason on the floor above he came to a halt. Reversing a little, his trunk drifted up towards the top shelf and lifted aside a couple of silver boxes. There at the back, between a Chinese dragon and a strange black hat, was a small empty space. The oliphant stared at it in silence. Stared at it and stared at it. Was some connection being made in that vast oliphant brain, some ancient memory jogged?

'*Has* something been stolen?' whispered Lily, looking at the small gap on the shelf. Whatever was there must have been narrow.

'What was it, Umballoo?'

The great oliphant raised his leg and rubbed his knee with his trunk. Lily and I looked at each other. Something for a sore leg? Umballoo then began rubbing his head, his trunk moving in circles. Something for a headache? Umballoo was just about to give us another clue when he spotted something high up on a window ledge on the other side. Carefully reaching over a line of diamond-studded ducklings, he lifted up a slim brown bottle labelled '*Madame Poloshka's Vanishing Cream*'. The oliphant unscrewed the lid and sniffed it. The bottle was almost empty. Umballoo seemed puzzled. Replacing the lid, he carefully stood the bottle in that empty space on the shelf. It fitted exactly.

'So it wasn't stolen,' whispered Lily, thinking she'd found the answer. 'He'd just forgotten where he put it.'

Somehow I couldn't quite believe that. Umballoo stood looking from one side to the other, thinking. This was all very mysterious. But it seemed to mean something to Umballoo. He turned back to the window ledge where that bottle of vanishing cream had been wrongly placed and began sniffing around on the stone. With his trunk he picked up the tiniest crumbs of something. Umballoo held them up to his eye.

'Is that earth?' asked Lily, looking down.

It might have been. Specks of red earth, perhaps. At that

moment a small white moth flew past. Umballoo watched it flutter up into the darkness… and with a sudden snort, he sucked the moth up his trunk.

'Moths must be a big problem in here,' whispered Lily. 'All these beautiful things to eat–'

Suddenly Umballoo lurched forward, throwing us back in the castle. What was happening? Round the corner, the oliphant stopped abruptly and carelessly swept aside a delicate pearl box from a shelf in the middle… There at the back was a jam jar without a lid, lying on its side. Inside it was earth. Carefully Umballoo lifted it out and examined it. It looked like the same red earth as the specks on the window ledge. He tipped out the rest and pushed it around with his trunk, as if searching for something… but there was nothing there. Umballoo hurled the jam jar to the floor, smashing it. He flapped his ears and snorted, punching the wall with his trunk so hard that several lumps of stone went flying.

'What's happened?' whispered Lily, frightened now.

Whatever it was, only Umballoo knew. Had something special been hidden in the earth inside that jam jar? Was it somehow connected to the empty bottle of vanishing cream – and the moth, maybe? Clearly Umballoo thought it was, and he was working himself up into a frenzy.

'What's the matter, Umballoo?'

Shaking his great head, the oliphant sent a pile of silver daggers clattering down the stairs. Spotting an intricately carved ivory tusk, Umballoo grabbed it and began stamping it to bits (not surprisingly, he seemed very sensitive about tusks). But even this wasn't enough to calm his rage. With a snort he charged up the stairs, flung open the nearest window, and flaring his great ears, he curled up his trunk and let out the loudest, longest trumpet

I've ever heard. Lily and I clung to each other in terror; I felt like every bone in my body was being shaken apart… All around us golden candlesticks, porcelain figures and glass bottles shuddered and slid off shelves… The whole Sable Tower echoed with the sound of tinkling and smashing.

At long, long last, the trumpeting died away. I opened my eyes. A mirror had fallen down in front of us and in its cracked reflection Umballoo seemed different. No longer was he a massive leathery piece of furniture. Umballoo had become a warrior oliphant once more – immense, dangerous, and very, very scary.

In the reflection I noticed something glittering behind me. Turning around, I saw a delicate crystal bottle rolling along the edge of a shelf. '*Elixir of Ethergryn*' said the label. '*The last batch ever made by the leprechauns of Tipperary. Drink this, and for the space of one hour you shall be <u>unseen</u>.*' Unseen… but that's exactly what… I reached out to catch it, and just as I did, Umballoo's trunk snatched it away from my fingers. I looked at the oliphant's jagged reflection in the mirror, his small black eyes holding mine. I sensed he knew the trouble I was in, and perhaps on some other night he might have given this to me to help me escape. Not now. Somehow everything had changed.

With a heavy heart I watched as Umballoo carefully placed the tiny bottle back on the shelf. He blew gently on its paper-thin glass, and the liquid began to glow mysteriously inside. I stared at it and felt all my hopes evaporate.

'Someone's tricked him, haven't they?' Lily whispered bravely. 'Someone's got in here and stolen whatever was in that jam jar, and used all that vanishing cream. I wonder who it was.'

So did I. Whoever it was must be getting nervous. They'd have heard that trumpet. They'd know the oliphant had found them out…

Trapped

E VEN IF UMBALLOO had decided to help me, I doubt I
would have succeeded. His violent trumpeting seemed to
have woken up the whole palace – the whole of London
probably. Everywhere there were shouts and lights and people
running.

'What's your plan now, Jack?' asked Lily as we hurried back
down the dark corridors to the Ermine Tower.

I didn't know.

'Wait till tomorrow afternoon, when I have the X-ray and
medical inspection, and then it will all come out,' I replied glumly.

'That's going to be very bad for you, you know,' she said.

I didn't need reminding.

'Impersonating Richard in the school, you might have got away with. But when they realise it was you who met the Prime Minister—'

'I didn't want to meet the Prime Minister! This was all Richard's idea! He tricked me into it—'

'But they'll never believe that, Jack. Don't you see? The King's never going to admit that his son doesn't actually want to be a prince at all. Can you imagine how embarrassing it'll be for him when everyone finds out?'

'William Foxglass will stick up for me,' I said lamely.

'You think his word counts against Thad Lancaster's? You've seen what Thad's like, Jack; he can be terrifying when he wants to be. I'm not trying to make you feel bad, honestly I'm not, but this is going to cause a massive fuss and I guarantee Richard won't get the blame for any of it.'

I knew in my heart Lily was right. This *was* going to be all my fault. Even if Richard admitted it, it would still be my fault. I was just some nasty little keeper who fancied having a go at being a prince; the truth wouldn't come into it. We reached the main staircase to find guards running across the courtyards bolting doors, flashlights on the rooftops, people shouting everywhere… I stared at the pandemonium, feeling completely and utterly trapped.

'So what am I going to do? What *can* I do?'

'I don't know, Jack. I really don't.'

Onion Runyon appeared at the end of the corridor, clipboard in hand, wafting people out of his way.

'Snap assembly in the courtyard! No, this is not a fire drill! No need for panicking. I'm not panicking, Cossage! This is simply to check all pupils are safe and accounted for. Hurry up, Spiggins!

You too, Tucker-Smith!'

'Maybe I should just go and tell Onion right now,' I said, feeling my heart racing. 'Get it over with. And if they want to kill me, then they'll just kill me.'

'Don't be silly, Jack,' said Lily quietly, laying a hand on mine.

I turned away. I didn't want her to see how upset I was.

'There's got to be a way to get you back. Cuz can't always have everything the way he wants it. It's completely unfair.'

'But how, Lily?'

'We'll think of something.'

'Really?'

'Of course.' There was a look of quiet determination on Lily's face that I hadn't seen before. She smiled, then gave me a hug. 'Come on, Jack, don't despair. We're going to sort this out. Seriously, we are. Let's do it.'

'Okay,' I said, wiping my eyes. 'Thanks.'

Taking a deep breath, I followed Lily down into the crowds milling about in the hall. It felt like such a relief, knowing that Lily knew my secret now.

'But there's snow, Professor Runyon!'

'And what about the monster, Professor Runyon?'

Half the younger ones refused to leave their beds. All the older ones had suddenly lost their slippers. Everyone else seemed to be wandering around the staircases in confusion. Up came Jake Tiptree in his dressing gown, always ready for a conversation.

'That was *quite* a big noise, wasn't it, Richard?'

I nodded, trying to concentrate on being the sickly heir to the throne once again.

'Yes, Jake, it was very loud.'

'Tucker-Smith said it was the death scream of a *dragin*!'

'Did he?'

'That's what Tucker-Smith said. Being eaten by a behemoth. What d'you think it was, Richard?'

Lily glanced at me. Jake's eyes were enormous through his glasses.

'Well I don't really know. Definitely some sort of creature.'

'D'you think maybe it's coming to eat us?'

'I hope not.'

'If it did, who d'you think it would eat first – you or me, Richard?'

'Me, I'm sure.'

'Hmm.' Jake considered this. 'If it does, I could sort of distract it for you, if you like. Say, "Here boy, here boy" and get it to run after me. I could do that for you, Richard, because I can run extremely fast.'

'That's very kind of you, Jake.'

Jake Tiptree smiled.

'It would be an honour, Richard.'

Off he went with a spring in his step. Lily and I made our way across to our staircase, but not before Spiggins and Tucker-Smith saw us and ambled up, also in their dressing gowns.

'Killer noise, wasn't it?' said Spiggins.

'Killer,' I agreed.

'My bed was shaking so much it was in the middle of the room.'

'Same.'

'What d'you think it was, Lily?'

'I have no idea.'

'Richard?' For some reason Tucker-Smith was looking at me suspiciously. ''Cos there's a rumour there's some weird creature that lives in some secret cave at the back of the palace that's been lost for five hundred years, and it's so massive it only eats elephants, and trees, and flocks of sheep.'

'Would that be a behemoth, by any chance?' asked Lily.

Tucker-Smith grinned in his gormless way.

'D'you believe *everything* Archie Queach tells you? You really are very stupid.'

George Hartswood arrived, bouncing a ball. He was one of those people who always carried a ball around.

'So Richard, I hear you're feeling better, huh?'

'A little.'

'You can walk without a stick now — is that right?'

'Erm…' I glanced at Lily and she shook her head violently. 'Sometimes. Depends how I feel.'

George began to bounce the ball off the wall just behind me.

'So you'll be going for a big score on Tuesday. All that Greensleeves practice you've been doing, you're going to wipe us out up there, Richard.'

He gave me a sarcastic wink. Jackernapes — that must be what he was talking about. George Hartswood was a legend at Jackernapes, apparently. He was already captain of the Plantagenet team and I'd seen his name in gold on several school noticeboards.

'Probably. I'm going to score ten goals, George, just you wait.'

George Hartswood glanced at Spiggins and Tucker-Smith and they sniggered.

'Oh Richard, you're so funny sometimes.'

Yes, it was probably a ridiculous thing to say. But being Richard I could say things like that and not get murdered.

'Onion's just told me there's a special training session tomorrow morning,' George went on. 'He said it doesn't matter if we miss lessons, we can use it to practise anything we want, so everything's perfect for Tuesday. Good, eh, Lily?'

'From what I've seen, you'll need it, George,' she said, leaning back and folding her arms. 'It would be such a shame if the final became embarrassing for you. Especially in front of the King and the Prime Minister.'

George Hartswood grinned.

'So long as you've got Richard, Lily, I guarantee it won't.'

'Is that so?'

'Bring it on, Lancaster. Bring it on.'

Off they went, shaking their heads and giggling. Lily watched them, looking particularly tough.

'You know what they're talking about, don't you? They're Plantagenet. We're Lancaster.'

I'd gathered as much. And I'd remembered that Lily was the Lancaster captain too.

'What's Greensleeves?'

'It's the position Cuz has to play. It's his worst nightmare. Funny though, we usually play Jackernapes on Thursday afternoons. I wonder why Onion's changed it to tomorrow morning...' Lily looked at me, and the beginnings of a smile crossed her face.

'What?'

'I think I've got an idea,' she said.

✧ 39 ✧
Worms' Meat

I CAN'T TELL YOU WHAT IT WAS, but as I shut the door to my room that night, I was feeling just a tiny bit more optimistic about my situation. At this moment, I felt my life was in Lily's hands, and I began to realise that perhaps I had misjudged her. Lily Lancaster wasn't just this permanently happy, confident person; she was also quite cunning, and perhaps even a little devious too.

I had almost tiptoed the full length of the carpet to the bedroom door when a small cough broke the silence.

'Hark, what news?'

My heart sank. I turned to Asphodel's cage. There he was, a

hunched silhouette, lying on his sofa.

'Nothing. Everything's fine.'

A thin finger beckoned.

'Come here, my boy,' he croaked.

The last thing I wanted was another interrogation by Asphodel, but I thought it would be more suspicious if I refused. The wizened old fairy lay as still as a statue, his eyes watching me carefully.

'Well?' he said.

'Well what?'

'Did you discover what upset that beast so?'

I hesitated. Did Asphodel know Richard went into the Sable Tower? I suppose he must have done. Or he'd guessed as much.

'No.'

''Tis curious. I haven't heard it make such a sound in many years.'

Asphodel's black eyes narrowed as he watched me.

'Oliphants are sentimental creatures, my boy. They become deeply attached to things of which they are fond, which is why the wrinkled old pachyderm is perfectly content to wander up and down, constantly arranging and rearranging that vast treasure store. It's his herd, you see; he loves and protects every useless trinket as if it were his own flesh and blood. The oliphant would only make such a racket if it had discovered something had been stolen – or if it had been tricked.'

Luckily it was dark; otherwise Asphodel would have noticed my unease.

'I'm sure you're right, Asphodel.'

The fairy lolled back in his seat, staring out at the rooftops.

'We must be careful, my Prince. Something is at work here. Something I cannot fathom. Something that shall make worms' meat of us all.'

'Yes.'

'All is fog and black confusion.'

'Yes. It's certainly still quite foggy,' I said, retreating to the bedroom. Asphodel turned to watch me go.

'Mock not, little owl. Thy hoot vexes me.'

The fairy smirked as I closed the door then locked it. Pleasant little creature, wasn't he?

⁓ 40 ⁓
Words of Advice

THE FOLLOWING MORNING I had a surprise.

Knock knock.

'Who's there?'

'Me?'

'Me who?'

'A little too early for a knock-knock joke?'

It wasn't the doctor, or Lily, or even the Queen. It was Thad Lancaster! I gasped. He was staring at me strangely.

'May I come in?'

He already had, striding into the room in his dark uniform, his thick black hair oiled back over his shoulders. I may not have mentioned before that Thad Lancaster was a very handsome man, and I suspect he knew it. This made me nervous. More nervous still when he sat down on my bed, folded his arms and continued to stare at me. And then I realised why. My wig was off! My heart jumped. I didn't even have the cap on that Richard had taken to wearing in his room when no one was looking.

'Hi.'

'Hi.'

My cheeks were burning. I smiled madly into those piercing blue eyes... It was impossible to think he didn't recognise me.

'You didn't know?' I said.

'Actually, no.'

'It's a side effect of all the pills I'm taking. Please don't tell anyone, I promised Mother I'd keep it hidden—'

'My lips are sealed. You probably don't want my sympathy, Richard, but I'm sorry. Bad business, truly, a bad business.'

I took my cap from the bedside table and silently put it on. We smiled at each other awkwardly.

'I just wanted to see that my nephew's safe after all the commotion last night. That trumpeting has put the wind up a lot of people.'

'It didn't bother me.'

'Glad to hear it. Some people are running around like headless chickens. The Prime Minister for one.'

I gulped.

'How did Mr Chitt hear it?'

'The same way most of London heard it, old chum. Unfortunately Mr Chitt now thinks things in the palace are getting out of control. First there was the dragon that was let out, and now this—'

'He knows about the dragon as well?' I interrupted.

'Of course he does. People talk, Richard. Far too much, as it happens.'

I was shocked. Thad stood up and crossed to the window. He stared down at the children in the courtyard going to breakfast.

'The Prime Minister likes to understand everything. What he doesn't understand he feels threatened by. Which is probably why he's now insisting that I have our old oliphant shot.'

'Umballoo shot!' The name escaped my lips and I couldn't bring it back.

'Why? What's he done apart from trumpet?'

'Exactly.' Thad turned to me, looking very serious. 'I'm doing my best to talk him out of it. But after last night, Mr Chitt thinks

we can't control him and he'll go on the rampage or do something daft. Ridiculous, when you consider old Umballoo wouldn't hurt a fly. But the last thing we want is Chitt sending soldiers in here to remove all the beasts and put them in zoos – perhaps shooting a few for good measure.'

I was stunned.

'Would he do that?'

'Yes he would. Byron Chitt's

been itching to clear out this palace for years. Umballoo misbehaving is just the sort of excuse he needs.'

'But that seems so unfair,' I said, unable to contain my emotion.

'Of course it is,' said Thad, sitting back down on my bed and placing his hand over mine. 'So, given how delicate everything is right now, perhaps it might be a good idea if you didn't pay the oliphant any more night-time visits. Or invite anyone over here to visit you,' he added, looking at me carefully.

'What do you mean?' I said, withdrawing my hand and folding it across my chest.

'The new Keeper of Ghosts. I believe you've made friends with her?'

Thad's eyes held mine and I could feel my cheeks burning.

'I wouldn't call it friends.'

'No? All sorts of mischief is going on over the other side at the moment, Richard. The keepers have never liked us, and one cannot trust them. They seem to think that as the guardians of everything that is ancient and magical in Albion, they are beyond the law, when the truth is most of them are completely incompetent. I wouldn't trust them to keep chickens, let alone giants. But that is by the by. Jack Joliffe is one of them, and she always will be. Whereas Umballoo is a very dear old friend of our family. I'd hate something tragic to happen to him.'

I swallowed hard. Was that a threat?

'You understand, don't you?'

I gave the briefest of nods. Now I felt not only guilty but cross. So this was actually what Thad Lancaster had come here to do. Tell me off.

'Good. You're a sensible chap, Richard. You can see how things are. We don't want to give the Mr Chitts of this world any more excuses to get rid of us. The people's love for us is all we have, and if they decide we're not worth it… well, what's the point of us then, eh?'

Thad seemed very earnest. I believe he meant it.

'Of course, your father doesn't quite see things that way. He thinks people should love their King whatever they might think of him, perhaps in *spite* of what they might think of him. But he would say that, wouldn't he?' Thad winked, chuckling to himself. 'Now don't worry about your parents, I can keep a secret. Is it Jackernapes today?'

'Erm… yes.'

'Taken your pills?'

I nodded, glancing at the small brown bottle beside my bed.

'Good chap. Lancaster is counting on you on Tuesday. Got to get more steps than your father, eh?'

Another dazzling smile and Thad was gone. My head was buzzing. Just how much did Thad Lancaster know? Was he trying to warn me in a friendly, uncley kind of way, or was there some other reason? I wasn't sure. But at least now I'd be able to tell Richard, if everything went to plan…

~ 41 ~
Jackernapes

'LISTEN UP!'

It was nine o'clock in the morning and I was standing in the Jackernapes arena with about thirty other boys and girls. I'll admit I was curious to be in here at last, because even in my short time in the school I'd realised that Jackernapes was all anyone talked about. Onion Runyon may have succeeded in making everything else just about as boring as possible, but there was nothing he could do about this ancient and dangerous game. All royal children had to play it — that was the tradition. And Onion Runyon was very keen on tradition.

The arena was in a huge domed hall, which was arranged like

a theatre. One half was the Jackernapes court where the game was played, the other half was an auditorium with tiers of velvet seats stretching up to the ceiling.

'Listen up!'

In the centre of the court stood Miss Squirrel, a short, tough-looking sports coach with a thin whistle clamped between her teeth. I don't think anyone could hear her because the arena was the sort of place where sounds seemed to disappear completely or come back even louder when you weren't expecting them.

'LISTEN UP!' she roared again, giving another shrill blast of her whistle. 'Now this morning we will be practising hot scurries!' (cheers), 'belters and Burlingtons!' (more cheers), 'the Rupert Manoeuvre!' (oh err), 'and finally, at the request of Lily Lancaster, Professor Runyon has agreed to one Hal's Defence!'

Lots of gasps at that one. Lily looked at me and nodded. This was the key part of the plan and she promised it would work... I looked up at the massive white barrel hanging over the balcony above, labelled 'Hal's Defence', and swallowed hard.

'And of course, the funambulers will have their last chance to practise their steps on the Greensleeves pole.'

Miss Squirrel smiled at me in particular. I looked up at the wooden pole that stretched across the domed ceiling high above our heads. At the far end, just below the window, was a painted target, in the centre of which hung a green rag. That was the Greensleeve.

'Feeling good this morning, Richard?' George Hartswood nudged my elbow with a smirk.

'Great,' I replied.

As the Lancaster funambuler, that was my job, to walk across that pole, up there... I could see why Richard hated Jackernapes more than anything else.

Now you might be wondering what exactly is going on. Jackernapes? What is it?

'Basically, Jackernapes is kind of like medieval basketball,' said Lily, 'and no one really knows the rules, not even Onion, though he pretends he does.'

That, in a nutshell, is it. Now I don't want to distract you with a history of Jackernapes, because I know that if I was ambushed by the explanation of some obscure sport in the middle of a story, I would probably throw it away and not read another word. All I can say is, please don't, because it turns out to be really important, as... but I'm rushing ahead. Give me two minutes, that's all.

So Jackernapes is named after a monkey called Jack, from Naples, and the game roughly follows what he did. Way back in the Middle Ages two noble families, the Lancasters and the Plantagenets, were fighting each other for the throne of Albion. The Lancasters had besieged the Plantagenets in their castle, and the battle had gone on so long that there was only one cannonball left. This was loaded into the cannon on the Plantagenet battlements. So the Duke of Lancaster called all his knights together and said, 'Which of you is brave enough to bring me that last cannonball?'

All the knights made brave noises, but none of them really were. So in the middle of the night Jack the monkey climbed up the Plantagenet castle wall and stole it. Somehow he rolled, dragged and heaved the heavy ball back over battlements, across the moat, through a ditch, passed the sentries, into the camp, all the way back to his master. But before the Duke had a chance to fire it, the Plantagenets attacked and took the cannonball back. So the next night Jack did the very same thing. And the following day the Plantagenet's also did the very same thing, and this time they hid it in a dragon's nest up amongst the castle's chimneys. Surely that pesky monkey would never dare to take it from there, they thought. But they were wrong. Jack was nimble, Jack was quick, Jack climbed up into the dragon's nest and found that old Shabbleflanks (the dragons' name, by the way, who was very old and completely blind) had mistaken the cannonball for an egg and popped it into her mouth intending to have it for breakfast. (Dragons do this, apparently. It saves boiling them.)

Jack of Naples carefully prised sleeping Shabbleflanks' jaws apart, leaving a brick in its place, and away he scampered to his master. So this cannonball stealing went on and on, long after more cannonballs arrived, and long after the Plantagenets and Lancasters had settled their quarrel, because stealing a cannonball was much more fun than actually fighting each other. Apparently it's still being stolen to this day; the King currently has it hidden in a box in his private lavatory. But that's a secret.

So that was how Jackernapes began, and the game kind of follows the story. There are two castle walls facing each other on opposite sides of the court. At the top of each is the head of a large stone dragon with an open mouth. Each team tries to get the ball (not a cannonball, but the leathery old head of Oliver Cromwell, the last man to cut a king's head off – I understood now) from their own castle wall, across and up the opposing team's wall, then into the stone dragon's mouth at the top. That is a goal. Simple. And it might have stayed simple, had not Jackernapes been played for five hundred years, and in that time certain kings and queens decided to make 'improvements'. So now the castle walls move on cogs and wheels, making them more difficult to climb. Ledges and windows appear and disappear. Ropes and ladders dangle down from the ceiling and the floor is replaced by a huge net, like a trampoline. Defenders carry large leather flappy things on poles called 'whappers' to bash opponents off the battlements. And then there are catapults, shields and a balcony above where the 'weathermakers' tip tanks of mud, rain, goo, even fog bombs (Hal's Defence – only used on special occasions), down onto the players below. And above *all* this is the pinnacle of the game, a highly polished wooden pole stretching from one side of the court to the other.

'That's where you stand,' whispered Lily, pointing at the rickety little platform at one end of the pole.

Now the tradition was that every prince and princess had to be their team's funambuler – they walked the pole, in other words – because funambulers could single-handedly win the game or lose it. Why? The story goes... (and it's a very long story according to Richard, the only person I know who's read the only book ever written about Jackernapes, called, not surprisingly, 'Jackernapes! The Secret Sport of Kings' by Sir Mouse Dipp-Diddle) basically this pole was all Henry VIII's idea. Henry was obsessed with Jackernapes and played it almost every day, but he was getting bored. 'Jackernapes needs livening up!' he boomed. 'Let's replace the ball with... a sheep!' Too heavy. 'A piglet?' Too slippery. 'A large, frozen, cowpat?' Too disgusting. 'Real dragons' mouths for goals!' Far too dangerous. 'What about...' And then he had the brilliant idea of the pole. Make it really high, really wobbly, and if you get to the end it's a hundred points and you win the game! All you needed was something to aim at... like–

'Ask Anne! She'll know.'

Henry burst into his wife's chamber to find Anne Boleyn busy doing her target practice while her ladies-in-waiting waited around listening to lute players and doing whatever else Tudor ladies at court did. Anne was looking particularly beautiful in her new green dress, the wide sleeves intricately embroidered with golden flowers and butterflies. 'What do you want?' she said, drawing back her bow and hitting yet another bullseye (she was an excellent archer, of course). Henry stared at the target in wonder. He stared at Anne's dress in wonder. His eyes began to spin. 'But that's it!' he said suddenly. 'It?' 'It! It!' With one rip, Henry (who was immensely strong) tore the sleeve off her dress and ran out. Anne Boleyn was not amused to see her beautiful green sleeve hanging from the wall of the Jackernapes arena. Actually she didn't speak to him for a month, and it was only when Henry composed a little tune about her beautiful green sleeve that she finally forgave him...

All that was five hundred years ago... and yet Anne Boleyn's green sleeve was still there, filthy and ragged, in the centre of the target. Why?

'It's very difficult,' Lily whispered, as we tramped up to the battlements. 'Very, very difficult.'

'Watch out for that fast-moving cog beside the window, Lily. I saw a bit of bone in it the other day,' said Tucker-Smith, carrying a whapper almost as wide as he was.

'Did you now?'

'Think it was a finger. There was still a bit of skin on it.'

'I'm sure there was,' said Lily.

'Oh yeah I saw that,' said Spiggins cheerfully. 'It was a bit of skull. With dried brains inside—'

'If you two think you're winding me up you're so wrong, so wrong.'

Spiggins and Tucker-Smith sniggered. Lily was getting wound up, no matter how hard she tried.

'People have died playing Jackernapes, Lily,' Spiggins smiled.

'Onion's got a list.'

Lily ignored them and pointed to the small ladder that went on up.

'After you, Cuz.'

At last we reached the weathermakers' balcony, high above everyone else. We looked down at the players taking up their positions. No sign of Onion Runyon yet.

'You know Richard will probably refuse to come,' I whispered.

'Of course he will, but he won't have much choice. Onion's not going to let anything spoil the biggest game of the year. He'll carry him over here if necessary.'

As you might have guessed, this was the plan Lily and I had hatched. It was Lily's brilliant idea to tell Jake Tiptree that when she came in that morning, she thought she saw a ghost out in the dark auditorium. It looked like a monk, she said, holding a bloody dagger, she added, though she couldn't be certain; it might have been an axe. When it saw her, it hid behind a pillar.

'A monk with an axe?' gasped Jake Tiptree, peering out into the darkness. 'Wow!'

Jake then did what Jake did best, and while we tramped up to our positions, Onion Runyon tried calming frightened children down.

'Yes, I suppose it might have been a murdering monk, Tiptree—'

'Will it be coming after us with its bloody axe, sir?'

'I suppose that is possible—'

'You mean rampaging around the arena hacking people's heads off, sir? Or sort of jumping out at people and saying boo! – and *then* hacking their heads off. Which will it be, sir?'

'I'm not an authority on murdering monks, Tiptree, but I shall go and get the Keeper of Ghosts to capture it immediately.'

'Best be quick, sir, before it does something awful.'

'Thank you, Tiptree,' said Onion Runyon. 'Panic not, everyone, the situation is entirely under control!' he said, adjusting his bow tie and staring into the dark auditorium in terror.

While all this commotion was going on, Lily had been pleading with Miss Squirrel to be allowed to be a weathermaker up on the top balcony. Weathermakers were usually anyone who didn't like bouncing on nets, swinging on ropes or climbing up moving walls while being pelted with mud, slime and rain – all of which Lily normally adored.

'You'll be feeling better before Tuesday, won't you, Lily?' said Miss Squirrel, peering at her with concern. 'Lancaster cannot go into a Jackernapes final without their captain.'

'I'm sure I'll get better soon, coach,' she said, attempting to sneeze.

'All right then.' Miss Squirrel turned to me with a look of resignation. 'And what about you, Richard, how are the legs today? Wobbling like jelly as usual?'

'Totally jellified, Miss Squirrel.'

'Now there's a surprise. Right, off you go, you two,' she sighed. 'Let's hope there aren't any more ghosts up there.'

So there we stood, high up on the weathermakers' balcony, waiting for the game to begin. All along the edge, large vats of water, mud and green goo were suspended with levers ready to be tipped on signal. And at the far end stood that huge barrel labelled '*Hal's Defence*'.

'You've to go up there now,' said Lily, pointing to the rickety little platform above our heads. 'Good luck, Cuz,' she winked.

Gripping the thin rail, I climbed up and stared at the wooden pole stretching across the arena to the opposite wall. The ragged green sleeve looked so far away it might have been on another planet. I gingerly touched the pole with my toe. It felt slippery, and well used.

'Oh I do love Jackernapes. It's always such fantastic fun, isn't it?' said a thin boy with sloping shoulders who climbed up to stand next to me. I guessed he must be the Plantagenet funambuler, and he smiled like he knew me… and then I remembered he did. This was Tim Iddunshy, the boy Richard had invited along to his tea party. I wasn't surprised he'd been made Richard's rival – Tim was the only boy in the school even thinner and nerdier than him…

'Ready, teams?'

Far below, Miss Squirrel stood in the centre of the net like a lone swimmer in a wide sea. Everyone was silent, waiting in position on the walls, ropes and battlements. She blew her whistle so hard a shudder went down my spine, then she kicked Cromwell high into the air…

'PLAY!'

And the game began.

I'm not going to attempt to describe what was going on. Imagine you are a pigeon perched on top of a tall tower looking down at some kind of ancient battle taking place, which involved a brown leather head being thrown, intercepted and wrestled from one castle battlement across to another. Well, I was that pigeon. There was a lot of swinging around on ropes, bashing, catapulting, climbing, tackling, for Jackernapes was played extremely fast, was extremely dangerous, and clearly a lot of fun. Whenever the Plantagenets came close to smuggling Cromwell up the wall into the dragon's mouth, Lily would tip a load of mud or slime onto their heads sending them sprawling back down onto the net, and the Plantagenet weathermakers would do the same.

Miss Squirrel blew her whistle for scurries, blusters, Burlingtons, none of which seemed to barely stop the game for a second. All the while I kept watching the auditorium for Onion to return with the reluctant Richard. I hoped he'd remembered that he was supposed to be me…

Suddenly the whistle went three times and everyone stopped.

'Time out! Greensleeves! Funambulers take your positions please!'

Funambulers. That was us. Thirty filthy, breathless players stopped what they were doing and craned their necks up towards the ceiling. I looked at the shining wooden pole stretching out across the arena. Somewhere in the far distance was that dusty green rag.

'Walk like a penguin,' whispered Lily. 'And very slowly.'

Lily looked concerned, and so she should be. I discovered later that like every prince and princess before him, Richard had been practising this for years, first balancing on poles on the floor, then a little higher, then a little higher, but he was never even half as good at it as Stephen, who not only used to be Lancaster's funambuler, he also played the rest of the game as well… How far had anyone ever got? Somewhere near the far end of the pole was a red silk handkerchief left there by Charles II – a shaggy, piratey-looking king – who had apparently put on his best silk slippers, eaten a dozen oysters, filled his mouth with peppercorns, then shouting 'Hurrah hurrah hurrah!' had sort of run, skidded, wobbled and hopped all the way along the pole almost to the end, where he'd dropped his handkerchief and fallen off. That was three hundred and fifty years ago. His record was yet to be beaten.

Miss Squirrel blasted her whistle again and waved me on.

'Slowly,' repeated Lily.

I took a deep breath. First step. A cheer. The wood was certainly slippy. Like glass. Second step. Another cheer. Third step. *Another* cheer. Later I realised that every step was a small miracle and Richard had never got further than ten… I took my fourth, fifth – gasps now; I was right out in the middle of space. I kept my eyes on that hanging rag in the middle of the target. Henry VIII was right; you definitely needed something to concentrate on to stop yourself looking down… because you really didn't want to do that, as I discovered, when a door slammed and out of the corner of my eye I saw Onion Runyon stride into the auditorium, looking very stern. Behind him trudged Richard in my long green keeper's coat, looking equally grumpy. But his anger turned to amazement when he saw that it was me – who was supposed to be him – up here.

'Go on Richard!'

'You can do it!'

'Go Richard!'

What happened next, I can't quite remember. Suddenly that net looked a very long way down. Suddenly the pole seemed to be wobbling of its own accord. My arms began to cartwheel wildly as I tried to stay upright, and I was vaguely aware of Lily moving towards the big white drum labelled '*Hal's Defence*'. I guessed she knew what was coming before I did… I don't know how many tiny steps I had taken but suddenly I was falling, for what seemed like forever, into the net. I bounced back up to wild applause, and as I opened my eyes I saw the domed ceiling of the hall rushing to meet me—

Then it disappeared. A rolling cloud of thick white fog was advancing down the walls. Some of the younger ones screamed; it did look a little terrifying.

'You're supposed to wait for the whistle! We haven't restarted yet!'

Miss Squirrel was beside herself, but there was nothing she could do. You can stop many things, but not a wall of fog. The game had to go on.

'HAL'S DEFENCE!' shouted Onion at the top of his voice. 'Hal's Defence! Take them down, Plantagenets!'

And so the Jackernapes began again, now played in a fog so thick you could barely see a hand in front of your face. Stumbling around the back of a raiding party, I scrambled out of the Jackernapes court and began racing up the steps of the auditorium. Immediately I knocked into someone running away in the opposite direction.

'Richard?'

It was him! He stared at me. I think he must have suspected our plan because the moment he recognised me, he tried to wriggle away.

'I'm not going back!' he shouted. 'I never want to go back! You can be King, I don't care!'

'Richard, we must swap back, we must!'

'Why must we? I can be a far better Keeper of Ghosts than you, and you can obviously do that! I don't want to be King – I told you!'

'Richard, *listen*–'

'No! I'm not going back!'

He was stronger than I thought, and he almost got away again before I wrestled him to the ground and pinned him down.

'LISTEN!'

'Richard? Richard, where are you?'

'Over here!' I shouted.

Lily staggered up out of the fog. She stared at us, breathless and confused.

'Am I going completely mad, or do you two look even more similar?'

'Exactly,' said Richard, sitting up. He pulled off his cap (my cap). 'See?'

Even during the short time we had swapped places, his hair had grown a little. Now his head was dark, and he had colour in his cheeks. Even the deep grey rings under his eyes had gone.

'What's happened to you, Cuz?' asked Lily.

'I feel better, that's what's happened, Lily.'

'How?'

'How am I supposed to know?'

Lily and I looked at each other. I knew what she was thinking.

'Richard, you have to come back–'

'No I don't. Obviously someone was poisoning me over there and you can't expect me to go back and be poisoned, Lily, because I won't.'

'You won't necessarily be poisoned,' I said. 'I wasn't being poisoned–'

'Then maybe the poison didn't work on you–'

'Or maybe I didn't take it, like those pills the doctor gives you–'

'D'you think I'm an idiot? I don't *take* those things! I throw them out the window!'

Richard glared at me angrily. I glared back at him angrily.

'You can't expect me to go back and be killed,' he huffed.

'And you can't expect *me* to carry on being you either,' I replied. 'You tricked me into this whole thing. It's complete luck I've got this far without being found out.'

'She's right, Cuz. It's been really hard. Jack's been amazing, actually.'

Richard shrugged. He plainly didn't care what had happened to me.

'I can do what I like, Lily. And I will. It's your problem.'

'No, Cuz, I'm afraid it's *your* problem,' she said, folding her arms.

'Jack fainted and she's going to have a medical inspection, and an X-ray, this afternoon. And when that happens they're going to find out anyway, aren't they?'

Richard may have been obstinate, but he wasn't stupid. He looked at me like I was an idiot.

'You *fainted*? What did you do that for?'

I explained. Richard seemed crosser than ever.

'I can't believe you did that,' he said. 'Unbelievable.' But he could see that it was over. With an angry yelp he kicked the nearest chair, then with great reluctance handed me the cap and I handed him the wig. Quickly we swapped everything else, and I became me, and he became him.

'You know it's really amazing how similar you look,' said Lily when we were done.

Richard grunted. He didn't seem too interested in our similarities now that being the Keeper of Ghosts had been taken away from him. I think he knew I was never going to swap again.

'Oh by the way, Jack, you might like to know that I've sorted out a few things for you. Doctor Grimswitch is back in his bottle.'

I stared at him open-mouthed.

'Doctor Grimswitch?' I spluttered. 'How did you do that?'

'I charmed him. Oh, and I also recaptured Black Lowther.'

'But Black Lowther hadn't escaped–'

'Then it must've been after you'd gone. Archie Queach somehow got hold of the Black Lowther bottle and "accidentally" let it fall out of his bucket in the dining hall. I got the impression it was in revenge for something, as he doesn't seem to like you one bit. There was chaos for a day or two – Black Lowther suddenly galloping out of pictures in the middle of dinner, riding down the tables, smashing all the plates and glasses… The Master was getting very angry about it, and so was Ocelot Malodure. So there was nothing to be done but lay a shirk, then use the fandangus to miniaturise him and the stagecoach, *and* the six headless horses of course. Once I'd got them down to the size of mice, they were pretty easy. Flicked them back into their bottle with my finger.'

'Richard, *what* are you talking about?' asked Lily.

I explained. Lily's eyes widened.

'And Doctor Grimswitch was so crazy he was never even supposed to be released. Actually, how *did* you do that?'

'I charmed him, Jack. It wasn't difficult.'

Richard grinned, pleased with his own brilliance.

'Oh and Uncle Thad paid me a visit. He seemed rather suspicious about who I was. Wanted to see if I could actually capture ghosts at all. So I showed him a few tricks with the staff; basic net casting, a little bit of phantasmiphication. He was fairly convinced after that.'

'You convinced Uncle *Thad*?' said Lily, glancing at me.

'Yes, Lily. Why shouldn't I?'

Lily still had that wow-that's-totally-amazing expression. Richard smiled his clever smile.

'So unlike you, Jack, I've probably been quite useful–'

'Richard, that was absolutely phenomenal!' Onion Runyon skipped up out of the gloom, clasping his hands. 'Fourteen steps, that's your best ever!'

'Blinking bloody marvellous!' agreed Miss Squirrel, running up to join the headmaster. 'Do that in the final on Tuesday and your father's going to be amazed!'

Richard sucked in all the praise with a vague smile.

'I'm sure you can go further, young man,' smiled Onion.

'Definitely,' agreed Miss Squirrel. 'Work on that arm position and you'll make twenty steps, no problem.'

'Actually I think I've had enough for one morning,' said Richard suddenly.

'What?' Miss Squirrel was outraged. 'But you *must* have another go.'

'Must I?'

'Richard, you have to prove to yourself it wasn't a fluke–'

'Supposing it was?'

'Then you have to prove it wasn't–'

'Does it say that in the rules?'

Miss Squirrel sucked her teeth.

'The game has barely begun, Richard,' said Onion, smiling his oily smile. 'The general idea of sport is to try to *improve* on your first attempt. That is what it's all about. You don't just give up when you feel like it.'

'Why not?'

I could see that he was rather good at this. Miss Squirrel knew when she was being mocked.

'Richard Lancaster,' she fumed, 'stop messing about and get back up onto that pole! If you give up now you've let down the whole team!'

'And what's wrong with that?'

'Now now, Richard, we both know the last thing you want to do is let Lancaster down. That would be like letting your country down,' said Onion Runyon with a jolly chuckle. 'Why not have another go, for yourself? Do it for the sheer *fun* of doing it. That's the attitude I want to encourage in this school.'

Richard stared at the headmaster in disbelief.

'Do that again, for *fun*?'

'Why not? You're the funambler! Fun is absolutely part of what you do up there, is it not? Fun... ambling... having fun?'

'Actually, Professor Runyon, funambler comes from *funis*, the

Latin word for rope. Fun has nothing to do with it.'

Onion smiled his oily smile.

'So I'm not going to do it again. For you, me, them, or my country. In fact, d'you know something, Professor Runyon? I *hate* my country. Almost as much as I hate Jackernapes.'

Onion Runyon winced. Miss Squirrel ditto.

'Richard Lancaster, you *will*—'

'Excuse me.'

With his limp resumed and his royal attitude regained, Richard made his way down to the exit. Onion's face turned as pink as the carnation in his buttonhole.

'I shall be forced to tell your father about this!'

The door closed.

'Well!' he harrumphed. 'What kind of attitude is that?'

'He's a coward, always has been,' growled Miss Squirrel. 'Pathetic child.'

'He's not pathetic,' said my mouth before I was able to stop it.

Miss Squirrel turned around, hackles raised.

'What did you say?'

'Richard's not pathetic. He's ill. Can't you see that?'

She folded her arms across her tracksuit.

'Expert on the royal family are you, Miss Joliffe? I suppose *you* know what it's like to walk the Greensleeves pole, hmm?'

Somehow my mouth kept quiet.

'Miss Joliffe is not backward in coming forward with her opinions,' said Onion Runyon, turning his beady eye on me. 'Now unless you have any more pearls of wisdom you'd like to share with us this morning, I suggest you get on with catching this ghost, which apparently you *do* know something about. And make it quick, Keeper, because we're about to launch a Burlington.'

～ 42 ～
Keeper Again

I T'S STRANGE HOW DIFFERENT everything seems when you're on the outside. Nothing was said, particularly, and nothing was done, particularly, to make me feel like the low-born keeper intruding on a jolly game of Jackernapes, but somehow when I tramped back through the great gate into the keepers' side of the palace two hours later, having pretended to catch the non-existent ghost, I was heartily sick of being bawled at by Miss Squirrel, bossed about by the pernickety Professor Runyon, and pointed and giggled at by all those stupid boys and girls playing their ridiculous game.

That's harsh, I know. I suppose the truth was, I really did miss being a prince much more than I cared to admit. I don't mean all the privilege, and those amazing breakfasts, *and* being able to get away with almost anything – though that was quite useful. It was something else. I wasn't plain old Jack Joliffe any more. I realised I didn't want to *be* plain old Jack Joliffe any more. And I only realised that now, when that's exactly who I was again.

My rooms at the top of the tower seemed even further away than usual. The stairs were higher, the wind blew colder, my coat felt heavier... I don't know how I made it to the top. I must have gone soft. Breathless, I pushed open the door and slumped down into an armchair. A fire blazed in the grate. Everything looked spick and particularly span.

'Would the Keeper of Ghosts care for a cup of cocoa?'

Tom Bootle appeared from his cubbyhole dressed in his best embroidered waistcoat and matching hat. The cup steamed on the silver tray he bore before him.

'I took the liberty of anticipating. That Professor Runyon can be very rude. If he had spoken to me like that, why, I'd 'ave told that ghost to give him a damn good hiding! But then I ain't diplomatic, oh no. I'm sure you wowed him with your skills.'

'Thank you.'

Tom Bootle smiled his nose-wrinkling smile.

'Macaroon?' He nodded at the biscuit on the plate.

I picked it up. It wasn't a macaroon at all. It was a piece of card that exploded into a bunch of paper flowers. Bootle snickered to himself, very pleased.

'Here, have one of these.'

He set down his tray and retrieved a plateful of real macaroons from behind a chair. They were freshly baked, and they were very good.

'Very good, yes. Old Ma Bootle's recipe, that. Reserved for special occasions.'

I sensed Richard had changed things around here. Tom Bootle seemed much more eager to please.

'Was it a good game of Jackernapes, Mastress?' asked Tom Bootle, putting another log on the fire.

'It was all right,' I said with a mouthful of crumbs.

'Did the Prince walk the Greensleeves pole?'

'Yes he did.'

'And how did he do?'

'Pretty well, considering.'

'Oh lovely. So that means he's feeling better, is he?'

'I think he might be.'

'Oh that is good news. The Prince is feeling better. That is most excellent news indeed. Hmm.'

Tom Bootle finished stoking the fire and climbed into a chair. He sat rubbing his long pink hands, holding them up before the blaze.

'And how d'you think I've been doing these last few days, Mr Bootle?'

'Doing, Mastress?'

'What have people been saying about me? Have I improved much?'

'*Well*,' he sighed, 'if you want my humble opinion, it has been nothing short of *phenomenal* what you have achieved. Why, you are quite the most famous keeper in the palace! Everyone is talking about you. May I say it is an honour to be your servant, Miss Jack. An honour.'

So that explained it. Oh dear.

'They are saying that not since the days of Isabella Roy...

yoy... di–doy–' Bootle screwed
up his face with the effort of
trying to say her name. 'Not since
her has someone made such an
impressive start. Genius, they
are saying. Galahad Joliffe
would be very proud indeed.'

How annoying. I stared at the
picture of Uncle Galahad in all
his finery hanging on the wall.

'Do you know what happened
to my uncle, Mr Bootle?'

'Happened, Mastress?'

'All I was told was that
he disappeared off somewhere.
No one seems to know what
happened to him.'

Bootle's nose wrinkled and he wagged his finger.

'Have you already forgotten what I told you yesterday?'

Ah. Of course. Devious Richard had discovered this already.

'It don't do to be repeating secrets. Not around here. Secrets
are powerful things, don't I know it. Oh yes indeed.'

Tom Bootle sat smiling, his fingers twiddling one way then the
other. Well, I was sure I'd find out soon enough. If Bootle had
already told Richard, then he had almost certainly told someone
else... Didn't Sam Yuell say he was the biggest gossip in the palace?

'After an adventure like that, I expect he's taken a long holiday,'
said Tom Bootle, looking up at the picture. 'Always very keen on
holidays was Mr Joliffe. Every spring, every summer. Sometimes
Christmas as well.'

That didn't sound right. I thought my uncle didn't even have time to come and see me...

'So he took a lot of holidays, then?'

'Oh *yes*. Holidays, holidays! Of course, Mr Joliffe always pretended he was on a ghost-hunting trip, but that didn't fool me. He particularly loved the seaside. Oh, the fish dinners he had! He would tell me all about them. Every fish, on every dish. Every single one.'

Tom Bootle smiled at the memory. Was he making this up? He was clearly enjoying all this nudging and winking. Frustrated, I went to the window and looked out on the snowy courtyard. Somewhere over the rooftops the school bells chimed. I wondered what other gossip Richard had found out from Tom Bootle. Perhaps he'd even found out about those 'dark forces' Asphodel never stopped going on about... if I was him, I think I might have tried.

'You probably think it's a bit strange that I've been asking you so many questions recently, Mr Bootle.'

'Not at all. Now Miss Joliffe has become so famous, it's only right and proper that she should know all that there is to be known.'

'What about what isn't to be known? Shouldn't I know that too?'

Bootle smiled and wagged his finger.

'You see? My, what a silver tongue you have! How d'you get so clever so quick– eh? How you've changed!'

Did he suspect, then? Somehow I thought not.

'What do you mean "changed", Mr Bootle?'

Tom Bootle scratched his nose.

'Well, not meaning to offend, but when you first arrived, I was of the opinion that you was rather dim.'

'Dim?'

'Yes. Dull-witted. Slow. A simple country girl, who knew nothing about anything. A strangely featherless, farmyard goose. Quite unsuited to the ways of the palace.'

I stared at him, wondering if I should be offended.

'And now?'

'S'trordinary transformation. It was that tea with the Prince that did it, I reckon.'

'Really?' I gulped.

'Whatever they put in them cucumber sandwiches I don't know, but ever since you've become so sharp! And *sly*. My, how sly. Bootle must watch his step!' Smiling to himself, Tom Bootle shook his long-suffering white mouse out of his sleeve and it sat in the palm of his hand. 'His other master reminds him of that,' he said, stroking its head. 'Oh indeed he does.'

His other master. I couldn't remember if I knew about his other master.

'So you have two masters, Bootle?'

'Correct. Not many can say that, can they?'

Tom Bootle closed his fingers around the mouse. With a quick shake he opened his palm and it was gone. Then he opened his other hand, and there was the mouse.

'Every day I goes from one to the other, keeping them both happy.'

Back and forth the long-suffering mouse went, from one hand to the other like a yo-yo.

'Who is this other master of yours?'

Bootle shook his head.

'If I so much as whispers the name, it will be heard,' he said, pointing a long pink finger around the room. 'Walls have ears, doors have eyes. All things are known. Better a wise fool than a foolish wit. Don't I know it.'

Obviously this was only making me more curious.

'And what does your other master ask you to do?' I asked innocently.

'Oh many things. I have been most especially busy lately. What with the presentation next week... So many jobs, Mastress.'

'Such as?'

Tom Bootle pressed a finger to his lips. I nodded and said nothing. I had a feeling that if I just said nothing Tom Bootle might forget himself, for he was not someone who could stand silence for long. Sure enough, after a few moments staring at the crackling fire Tom Bootle leant forward conspiratorially.

'It all has to be kept most secret,' he whispered. 'Everything must be done in silence. No clanging or banging. All is muffled, because the *oliphant* suspects.'

'He does?'

Bootle nodded vigorously and carried on.

'He's caught a sniff of it and he's listening out with those great baggy ears of his. I tiptoes here, tiptoes there, up and down the tunnels like the doomed little rabbit man I am. In fact, I'm quite the most foolish son of a bunnikin you could ever hope to meet.'

I wasn't sure I understood. But then I never understood everything Tom Bootle said. He sat there smiling at me and nodding.

'Extraordinarily foolish,' he said again. 'If Bootle utters another single word about that...'

'About what?'

'That which is secret, fool! I expressly instructed you not to tell!'

Tom Bootle was looking at me in a way I hadn't seen before. His eyes narrowed. His ears flattened to his head. Somehow he was sliding down in the chair and twisting oddly.

'Bootle? What's the matter?'

'How dare you presume to gossip!' he growled, staring at me with angry red eyes. 'One more word and I shall sew up your lips and hang you from the gutter, bunnikin!'

This was becoming very frightening. Bootle was talking to me, and yet someone else seemed to be talking to him, *through* him, out loud…

'Bootle? Who's doing this to you?'

Tom Bootle shook his head and moaned. The mouse jumped out of his breast pocket and ran away in panic. He began thrashing about on the floor, shaking his head–

'ENOUGH!'

Bootle screamed, and suddenly he was hoisted into the air by some invisible force. There he hung, suspended by his scarf that tightened around his neck like a noose.

'I MEAN IT, FOOL! ALL IS SEEN! ALL IS KNOWN!'

Tom Bootle was released and collapsed in a heap. He seemed to have fainted. Immediately I knelt at his side.

'Bootle? What happened? Wake up!'

I thought he might have died. I loosened his scarf and shook him, hugged him, rattled him… At long last he opened his eyes and stared at me as if he had just woken from a terrible dream.

'Poor Tom's cold…'

I grabbed a blanket from the bed and wrapped it around him. Bootle curled himself up into a ball, shivering and shaking. He seemed overcome.

'There is strong magic about, Mastress. I think I'm bewitched.'

I could see that.

'It's your other master doing this to you, isn't it?'

Bootle closed his eyes and gave the smallest nod.

'No one must know, Mastress. Promise you won't tell.'

'I won't. I promise.'

'Truth is, I'm a slave. My life ain't worth a groat,' he whispered.

'What's he making you do?'

Tom Bootle shook his head.

'Is he poisoning the Prince? Is something going to happen at the presentation?'

Tom Bootle shivered and pulled the blanket over his head, hiding from my questions, hiding from the world.

'Beware, Mastress,' he groaned. 'They know everything. They see everything. The magic is everywhere now. I can feel it. Oh dear.'

I stared at Tom Bootle curled up under the blanket. He wasn't going to tell me any more. Who was doing this to him? Magic is for the fairies; that is what Galahad Joliffe had said. And this was magic, wasn't it? I got up and stood at the window, my mind galloping on. It was snowing again, and almost dark. Somewhere on the other side of the palace I heard a lonely bell chime.

All is seen. All is known.

Supposing that was true? Did Tom Bootle's other master know Richard and I had swapped, and was that the reason I wasn't poisoned? Did they even know that Richard was back over there again? I stared across at the shadow of the Ermine Tower, the lamps burning in the windows like a line of buttons. How I wanted to know the answers to these questions. Then I noticed a cloaked figure with a lamp hurry out across the Keepers' Courtyard below. It was Snowdrop Scott; I recognised her quick short steps. She was carrying a basket under her arm, and in it I could just make out shapes of small plastic bags, shining in the gloom.

That gave me an idea.

⚜ 43 ⚜
Ancient Magic

NIGHT HAD FALLEN and I was hurrying down the dark corridors into the vaults. I knew where I was going, but I wasn't quite sure how to ask the question. It was going to be very difficult. I glanced at the stone dragons above the archways, the animals woven into the tapestries. Was the palace itself watching me now? I quickened my step, almost running past the worms in their cages…

'Can I help you?'

I jumped. A large pair of glasses suddenly appeared out of the gloom.

'You were following me,' said Snowdrop Scott.

'Yes I was—'

'May I ask why?'

Snowdrop Scott's pink keeper's coat was wet and so was her headscarf. I looked at the collection of dark packets in her basket. It was definitely blood. She had just come back from the hospital.

'I wondered if I could ask you something?'

'Now?'

'If it's convenient.'

'It's hardly convenient, Miss Joliffe. You know there are snap inspections of all the vaults?'

Obviously I didn't.

'The Duke of Lancaster has asked Red Tempest to visit every vault and provide him with a list of what they contain before the presentation. There will be dire consequences for keepers unable to do so. I doubt even you can expect any leniency, Miss Joliffe, despite your exceptional start.'

She peered at me through those enormous glasses with vague admiration.

'It won't take long, I promise.' I glanced at the tapestry behind her. 'In private?'

'Very well.'

Down to the fourth floor we went, and in through the heavy door of the fairy vault. The moment we entered her tiny office, the Enchanted Forest through the barred window beyond began buzzing. Brilliant-coloured fairies fluttered down from the trees and emerged from under the mossy banks. Swirling through the dappled light they began fastening themselves to the bars and tapping on the glass.

'Mistress, for pity, for pity,' they called in their shrill, hissing voices.

'In a minute, be patient,' said Snowdrop Scott, setting down her basket and taking off her headscarf.

'Mistress, mistress—'

'Patience! Snowdrop will be with you in a minute.'

'Snowdrop went to London Town—'

'To buy herself a wedding gown—'

'But to the altar her love never came—'

'And Snowdrop nearly *died* of shame—'

'QUIET!' yelled Snowdrop Scott. The fairies screamed with laughter and turned their taunting insults on me.

'Ah see, the wicked child is back—'

'The ugly one, with nasty eyes—'

'Ready to tell its pack of lies—'

'See how it stands, how it holds its head—'

'The young pretender, soon to be—'

'ENOUGH!' snarled Snowdrop Scott. Marching to the window she pulled the curtain shut. 'Impossible creatures! I'm afraid they can smell the blood, Jack, and they won't stop till they're fed.'

I looked at the packets she was placing on the table.

'How much can a fairy tell about a person from the blood they drink?' I asked innocently.

'An awful lot. Everything, I'd say. Whenever I've given one of them a drop from my finger, I've deeply regretted it. They're the most terrible gossips. You find yourself being discussed in intimate detail by the entire wood. It's a very bad idea. I hope you're not tempted.'

'Oh no. I was just curious.'

Snowdrop Scott eyed me and sat down. She began to arrange her dishes on a tray.

'Asphodel has always claimed to be the greatest connoisseur of blood. There was a time when royal children used to fill his glass, and he'd take great pleasure in tasting all the different bloodlines. He tells me he can identify every noble family in Albion, and plenty more besides.'

I'd feared as much. I watched as Snowdrop began snipping the corner off the packets and pouring the blood into shallow dishes. Perhaps I should just come straight out with it.

'Do you think there's any way Asphodel could escape from his cage and bite someone directly?'

Snowdrop Scott smiled.

'I see. That's why you're here, is it, Miss Joliffe? And I suppose you think it's highly irresponsible of me to allow the future King to keep a caged fairy in his bedroom. The same fairy that's entertained generations of royal children for four hundred years?'

I shrugged awkwardly. Yes, I suppose I did. But I wasn't sure what I wanted her to do about it.

'Miss Joliffe, let me offer you a word of advice. You've only just arrived and you can't be expected to know better, but poking around in the palace can lead you into very dangerous places. Sometimes it's best to remember that you're only the Keeper of Ghosts and to stick to your own affairs.'

Was that a warning or a threat? Snowdrop Scott reached behind her and produced a small leather bag. Loosening the drawstring, she took out a handful of dead mice. Carefully she began to chop their heads off.

'I'm not poking around,' I said defensively. 'I'm just worried for the Prince and what might be happening to him, that's all.'

'And you aren't alone, my dear,' she said. 'We are all deeply interested in the cause of the Prince's ailments. Why is he getting

sicker and sicker? Why do certain royal personages seem to be getting madder and madder? Why is the capital still locked in winter's grip in May? Quite obviously there is some deep magic at work. It's all anyone ever talks about. In the hall, the library, the cloisters, everyone has an opinion. Don't tell me you haven't heard anything?'

No I hadn't. But then there was a good reason for that. Yet I was surprised. I thought all the old keepers were just dozing in armchairs or bumbling about in their vaults... I decided to tell her about what had just happened to Tom Bootle. Snowdrop Scott listened with growing interest, her knife clacking away. After the heads, she began removing the tails and feet.

'That ridiculous rabbit man's never had much sense,' she said when I'd finished. 'He's made some very foolish choices.'

'But who could be doing that to him?'

Snowdrop Scott sighed thoughtfully.

'It takes great skill to use the ancient magic in this palace. There's plenty of it, mind; don't forget the foundation stone was laid by King Arthur and blessed by Merlin himself. But few people have that knowledge any more. I very much doubt it's Asphodel. For all his learning, he's only a performer, an actor, nothing more. And besides, Asphodel has other things on his mind.'

I watched as she arranged the mice's heads on sticks, and began placing them on stands in the centre of each little lake of blood. It looked like something from a vampires' tea party.

'Such as?'

'How to stay out of here. Asphodel knows he's no longer quite as beautiful or entertaining as he once was. The moment Richard gets bored with him he'll be sent straight back down to the vault, and I very much doubt he'll ever be brought out again. This is his last great performance, his final moment to shine, and knowing him he'll try to make it last as long as possible. Asphodel needs Richard far more than Richard needs Asphodel.'

I thought of that ancient fairy, hobbling about in his cage. The great actor, playing his final role.

'And besides,' she went on, 'from what I've seen, he seems genuinely protective of the sick prince, now that he's become so ill and weak. If there were any dangers, I'm sure Asphodel would try to warn him.'

That was definitely true. Asphodel never stopped going on about it. Snowdrop finished arranging the dismembered mice in pools of blood. She looked at the gruesome plates proudly.

'And there's one other reason why I don't think Asphodel is involved,' she said. 'He's a coward. He knows there are ancient punishments for fairies found guilty of treason, which haven't been changed for a thousand years – deliberately.' Snowdrop Scott glanced across at me. 'If found guilty, his eyes will be burnt with hot pins, his tongue cut out, then his belly opened with a knife. He will be nailed to a post in the courtyard, coated in honey, and there the palace ravens will feast on him, slowly pecking away until nothing but his flapping carcass remains. It's an excruciatingly painful death.'

I stared at the fairies' dinner and felt sick.

'And has that ever happened?'

'It happened to a fairy named Pumblechook a hundred years ago. A truly wicked creature. Pumblechook took two days to die. Oh, they all know this punishment is real. Sometimes I wonder if the fear of a ghastly death is the only reason I have any authority in this place.'

Snowdrop Scott wiped her bloody fingers daintily, then got up and flung open the curtain. The barred window beyond was a wall of mean little faces, spitting and biting each other with their glittering teeth. When they saw the dishes, they screamed like monkeys.

'Nevertheless, you're right to be suspicious, Jack. I would never entirely trust any fairy, ever. The palace is becoming more dangerous for everyone.'

And with that, Snowdrop Scott went to get her beekeeping suit.

✦ 44 ✦
The Black Coat Inn

I DON'T KNOW HOW reassured I felt after hearing what Snowdrop Scott had to say. Yes, I understood that Asphodel had every reason not to get involved in any plot, and yet... did I ever think he was truly good?

As I sat eating dinner in the Keepers' Hall that night, Patrick Pettifog walked over and slid along the bench beside me.

'Finally Madame's gone to sleep,' he breathed. 'You wouldn't believe what I've been feeding her, Jack. Actually you probably would,' he added with a nervous laugh. It took a moment for me to guess who 'Madame' was.

'So are you ready, then?'

Patrick seemed excited.

'The Black Coat Inn? We're going back tonight, remember?'

'Oh... oh yes. Yes.'

Richard had obviously made friends with Patrick. In fact, didn't he say that in his letter?

'The Dragon Keepers are always in there on Fridays. And seeing as you're never going to get inside their vault now, Jack, this is probably your best chance of hearing some stories. There's an old bloke called Kiddy who sometimes turns up. He's like a legend among the Dragon Keepers. I bet if anyone's going to spill the beans about who let that dragon out, it'll be him.'

Patrick laughed his nervous laugh again. Obviously Richard had been busy doing a bit of detective work of his own.

'Come on, Jack. You don't really want to eat that. Even Her Ladyship couldn't stand it.'

I looked down at the brown and yellow mess on my plate. It was called 'King's Custard' apparently. Patrick was right.

Down into the corridors we went, Patrick Pettifog describing the history of this and that as we walked past the cages. I'd forgotten how knowledgeable he was about the creatures of Albion, but then I suppose he'd spent his whole life inside the palace. I'd also forgotten (or maybe not realised, I don't know which) that behind that nervous laugh, Patrick had some strong opinions, which he kept to himself.

'Sad, isn't it?' he said, as we passed a particularly mournful-looking giant in his cage. 'The last time Gogmagog here saw sunlight was when Elizabeth I got him out for a procession to the Tower of London five hundred years ago. He's the last true giant of this city.'

I stared at the great shaggy-headed creature, idly drawing patterns on the wall. Yes, it was sad.

'Albion doesn't belong to us, Jack. We've stolen it, from all of them. Don't you think there's something wrong with that?'

Of course I did. And I could tell what Patrick was thinking.

'Just imagine what it would be like if everything in here was set free and the old world came back. All the forests and wilderness… Albion would be truly *alive* again. Dangerous, crazy, real. What an amazing place that would be, eh?'

Patrick glanced at me, his eyes bright with excitement.

'But isn't it a little too late for that now?'

Patrick shrugged. Like Snowdrop Scott, I noticed he wasn't that interested in the real world outside the palace walls.

'Sometimes you have to go back to go forward,' he said mysteriously. I wasn't quite sure what he meant. On we went past the hobs and imps.

'They'd probably all just get killed, Patrick. That's what would happen.'

'Don't tell me you believe that old lie, Jack,' Patrick smiled. 'Nothing's kept down here for its own protection. They're all hidden away so that people like Mr Chitt can pretend they don't exist. He's terrified of the truth. They all are, out there.'

I said nothing. On we walked, Patrick looking in each cage. I didn't know what he was thinking. But I remembered it.

The Black Coat Inn was hidden in a narrow, cobbled alley right at the back of the palace. I recognised it from the first night I arrived with William Foxglass, and from the muffled shouts and shadows behind the fogged-up windows it looked very busy. In we went through the low door, and feeling a little self-concious I followed Patrick up to the bar. Everywhere keepers sat hunched over their tankards, smoking long pipes and talking. A few nodded at me approvingly as we passed.

'And what can I do you for, Miss Joliffe?' The barman smiled at me kindly.

'Same as last night?'

'Erm... thanks,' I mumbled, and then I realised I didn't have any money. Apparently I didn't need any. The barman set a frothing mug before me and winked.

'Same for you, Mr Pettifog?'

'Yes please,' Patrick smiled in his nervous way. I could tell by the way the barman was treating us, and by the way other keepers were grinning at me, that Richard's brilliant deeds had made him famous. Patrick certainly seemed very pleased to be seen in here with me.

'Cheers,' he said, and took a swig.

I stared at the foaming mug. Keeper's Tipple it was called, and it wasn't like anything I'd ever tasted before. It sort of warmed you up and tasted vaguely of apples... It was good, though. I looked around. In the corner beside the fire sat a particularly piratey group of keepers wearing long blue coats – Dragon Keepers I guessed, as there wasn't a single one of them that didn't have some kind of injury or other. Burnt skin, eye patches, missing fingers... They were listening as a grizzled old man in a hat held court.

'And what happened then? Was old Wellenstorm still asleep?' asked one.

'Indeed he was,' rasped the grizzled old man, puffing on his pipe. 'Snoring hard like the great bull dragon he is.'

'But you still crept up on him, you sly old dog—'

'Indeed I did. But you all know what happened 'cos I've told it a hundred times before!'

'So what if we do? It's a good story!'

'You sure you want to hear it again?'

'No,' muttered the keeper sitting next to me at the bar. 'I've heard Caractacus Kiddy tell that story so many times I could repeat it word for word.'

Patrick elbowed me in the ribs. That was him, Kiddy. I looked at the battered old man. With his wide-brimmed hat and long scar down his cheek, he looked like he'd seen a few battles. One of his hands was covered in rings and the other didn't seem to have any fingers left at all.

'Come on,' whispered Patrick, and moving through the tables we settled ourselves on a bench behind a pillar and listened.

'All right then,' Kiddy continued. 'So there Wellenstorm was, snug in the deep gulley, hiding himself between the rocks. Quiet as a mouse, I shimmied out on a branch till I was bending right over him, and with me gruttling pin I fastened the horns of his wings together, so tight that flight was impossible. Then I slides down from me perch and, ever so careful, steps down upon that scaly back, light as a feather so he don't feel me.'

'You weren't frightened?'

'I was blinkin' terrified! This is Wellenstorm we're talking about! The last of the ancients!'

'And what then?'

'I dandles me running-loop forward and slips it over that toothsome smile. Mindful of the fire-snorts, I runs it back through me belaying block I'd wound round his tail. And I does it again,

again, again – three times before I ties it off. Old Wellenstorm still don't know nothing about it, 'cos I'm that subtle, see. Tiptoeing up and down his back like a gnat. Then I shimmy off that scaly neck and I wait. Couldn't resist giving him a poke on the way.'

'Oh–ho! I bet he hollered when he woke up!'

'I don't mind telling you he did!'

'Diddled proper!'

'Diddled *and* daddled! The biggest dragon in the kingdom trossacked!'

'Kiddy, old man, you've nerves of ice–'

'You dogs! Why, in my pomp I was The Operator – Kiddy The Operator!' he roared, draining his glass and thumping it down on the table.

Laughter followed the boast. I was barely following half of this diddling and daddling. Patrick looked at me and smiled. I'm not sure he understood it either.

'But Wellenstorm weren't captured for long, were 'e?'

'That's a fact.'

'So what happened then, old man?'

Kiddy glanced at his audience again. A squarely built young Dragon Keeper in the corner stared down at his drink. My guess was Kiddy was hesitating out of courtesy; not everyone might want to hear what he had to say.

'You don't want to know–'

'Tell us, Kiddy. You can't stop now!'

Kiddy nodded. Took a puff of his pipe.

'Very well then. We threw another net across his shoulders, pinioned steel it was, then a stopping bridle so he couldn't move an inch. And that's how we winched him onto the low-loader and trussed him down.'

'That was a feat.'

'It was. And we'd have Wellenstorm trussed up still, had it not been for those roistering lords and Thad Lancaster! Because of course they'd all come along on the dragon hunt too, 'cept they hadn't done any dragon hunting, had they? It was me that done that.'

Kiddy called for another drink and took a long draught, wiping his mouth on the sleeve of his tatty old coat.

'So this is how it went. We was all for taking Wellenstorm straight back to the palace, but no, Thad Lancaster insisted we take a detour to this little inn he knew. Wanted to buy us a drink, didn't he, to celebrate the capture of the oldest bull dragon in the land, the last one never to see the inside of a vault. Okay then. Why not. So we gets to this place at the edge of the forest, and leaving Wellenstorm nicely covered under a tarpaulin we goes inside. Now Thad Lancaster and his chums were leading the party, all singing and getting right loud and rowdy. I thought nothing of it. Just young lads blowing off steam, I thought. Till it got to two o'clock in the morning. I woke up and looked out the window, and blow me down if that wasn't Wellenstorm walking around the car park!'

'They'd let him go, then?'

'Loosened his chains just enough so he could walk. And Thad Lancaster had stuck a white flag between his nostrils, and he was daring the others to take it off. I ran straight out and I warned him; I said Wellenstorm's not to be foolin' around with, Your Highness, he's a serious piece of work, you don't go baitin' that old dragon – but would he listen? They woz drunk as skunks and all razzed up. "Let him walk! Let him walk!" they shouted. And they ordered me to unbolt his mask. Great steel cage it was. "Take it off! Take it off!" Well I didn't have no choice. And I could see the look in that dragon's yellow eye… He, the great Wellenstorm, old as Moses, ruler of the North, bound and gagged with a diddly white flag stuck on the end of his nose? Why he were madder than hell! But them roistering boys don't see it. Round he walks, clanking in his chains; round they go, taking turns to sneak up close and reach for that flag. And Wellenstorm plays along with their game; he lets them get close then shakes his great head. And all the while he's working the chains between his feet, the net across his back, grinding through the steel gag in his mouth…

'And then William Foxglass arrives. All day he'd been out searching the far side of the forest. And when he sees what's happening, I thought he was going to knock Thad Lancaster down, he was that angry. Foxglass orders me and the rest of the keepers to secure the dragon immediately, but Thad Lancaster won't allow it. He threatens Foxglass with his pistol, swears he'll have him thrown in jail on a charge – "You jumped up so-and-so, how *dare* you speak to me like that!" – 'cos they've never seen eye to eye, have they? And this dragon-baiting game's too good. All lathered up and hot for it they were! Then this one young fella, Lord Hartswood, comes forward. Ever so brave this Lord Hartswood, hiding behind his shield, flinging out insults, creeping closer… and Wellenstorm knows this is the one. He lets Hartswood get close, *real* close, almost so he's touching those great leathery nostrils, and as he reaches for the flag – WHOOSH! A blast of flame from the depths of hell. Hartswood's gone, clean disappeared in a shower of sparks. Not a trace left. Then the next fireball comes. WHOOSH! I've never seen anything like it. It tears into the old pub and it goes up like a box of matches. Old thatch roof, see, dry as bones…

'Then Wellenstorm roars and stands up to his full height, the chains and nets pinging off him, and them brave boys know their game's truly over now. They scatter into the forest like birds. Wellenstorm blasts that pub again and again till it's roaring red, then off he smashes into the trees. Straightways us keepers that are left climb onto our bikes and hurl after him, and then all of a sudden there's a voice from the flames. It's the innkeeper and his wife, standing at the upstairs window! "Jump!" we shout. "Jump!" 'Cos the flames were ferocious, licking all about them now. So they jump, the lass first, tumbling down the burning thatch till she's on fire. Foxglass runs forward and catches her. Then comes her husband – he leaps down into that orange furnace, but the roof can't hold him and he falls inside. Then the lass suddenly starts screaming. She's beside herself. "My baby's up there, my baby!" and she points to a tiny attic window right in the heart of the inferno.

'And I do believe that was the moment Thad Lancaster came to his senses. He realised what he's done, and he felt guilty as hell. Straight away he runs in through the burning doorway, and five long minutes he's inside. I didn't think we'd ever see him again. Then out he comes at last, empty-handed, clutching his mouth. "Too late," he says, all blubbering and crying. "Too late." And he was right. The inn was blazing, the flames high as trees. Nothing could survive that. And I'm sorry to say that by then the young lass had gone too. All three of them. Gone.'

There was silence. Kiddy relit his pipe and eyed the young man who didn't want to hear the story.

'That's how it went down, as I recollect.'

'And Wellenstorm, what of him?'

'Pssh – he was already way up the track. Oh we chased him a good few miles, but he'd worked his wings loose by then and he was off. That was the last we ever saw of him. Twelve years ago that was. Twelve years, aye.'

'Thad Lancaster, eh?' said one of the listening Dragon Keepers.

'Oh so brave he is, the runny-nosed hubgrubbing whelp,' muttered Kiddy. 'Why if I had a whip, I'd–'

'Hush now, old man, that tongue o' yours'll lead you into trouble.'

'And what if it does? That was cold-blooded murder that was!'

'Shhh!'

The circle of Dragon Keepers quietened Kiddy down. He shook his head and blew a cloud of blue smoke from his nostrils.

'Wellenstorm's more than a job for you lily-livered mangel-wurzels now,' he rasped. 'Them screws I driv' into his skull must'a given him a permanent headache, and his talons will'a grown back sharp as carving knives. See what he did to my hand with one swipe?' Kiddy held up his maimed fist. 'You'll all be feelin' his anger soon enough. I'll wager half of you won't be sitting here next week.'

The Dragon Keepers glanced at each other uneasily. Kiddy stared at them with his one good eye.

'Losing a *mole* dragon?' he snorted. 'Might as well've rolled out the red carpet. This way, Mr Wellenstorm, kindly step inside–'

'We didn't lose it, Kiddy–'

'Course you didn't! Right before the presentation as well. You careless bunch of–'

'Shut it, old man!' roared one, grabbing Kiddy by the collar of his coat and lifting him up.

'Come on then, you great hobnosed higgedy-diggedy, knock me teeth out, I dare you,' said Kiddy, smiling a toothless smile.

The keeper grimaced and shoved him back into his seat. The other Dragon Keepers sat in awkward silence, staring at him accusingly.

'We didn't *lose* the mole dragon, Kiddy,' one whispered. 'Someone broke into the vault and let it out. Deliberately.'

'Deliberately, eh?'

'Yes *deliberately* you old fool,' muttered another.

Kiddy shook his head and took a long draw on his pipe.

'Higgedy-diggedys, one and all.'

Back they went to whispering amongst themselves, all moody and mysterious. I stared at them, shocked by what I'd just heard. Somehow the violent death of that young family seemed to have touched something deep inside me, I don't know why. I felt... I don't know what I felt, or why I felt it. And yet I couldn't help wondering what Kiddy meant...

'First time you've heard that one, Miss Joliffe?'

I barely noticed the barman leaning against the wall behind us.

'Is it true?' I asked.

'As far as I know. Wellenstorm's grown a bit over the years, but the Dragon Keepers never seem to tire of it. They're obsessed with that dragon. The great Wellenstorm, the last lone bull dragon of Albion, and when he's coming back.'

'And *is* he coming back?' asked Patrick.

'Wellenstorm's always coming back, Mr Pettifog,' murmured the keeper in a purple coat sitting opposite us. 'Every Friday night, when Caractacus Kiddy comes in.'

'And what's the missing mole dragon got to do with it?' I asked.

The old lady drained her glass and pretended she hadn't heard. Others who'd been listening at nearby tables did the same. Had I said something wrong?

'That's what everyone wants to know, Miss Joliffe,' said the barman quietly.

'So it has, then?'

The barman shrugged. I looked across at Patrick. He smiled nervously.

ᴖᴗ 45 ᴗᴖ
Porridge

THE NEXT MORNING was Saturday. I changed quickly, noticing that Tom Bootle had laid out my clothes as usual, left a pot of tea as usual, but wasn't anywhere to be seen. If he was avoiding me then I didn't blame him. He didn't want to answer any more questions, and I didn't want to see him become possessed again, or worse. Perhaps it was better that we avoided each other.

Closing the door to my staircase, I pulled up my collar against the swirling fog and set off around the Keepers' Courtyard. It was still very cold, and everything was white and frozen, yet underneath I couldn't help noticing a new sound... dripping.

Plip-plopping. The gutters were gurgling with melting snow. Was the weather really starting to change? Maybe – even if nothing else was. I glanced up at William Foxglass's windows at the top of the narrow tower in the corner. As usual, the lights were off, the curtains closed. Not for the first time I wondered if he was avoiding me. Unless he wasn't even in the palace…

'Often disappears, does William,' murmured Sam over breakfast. 'Special errands. Private business. The Master's getting very twitchy about the presentation.'

I looked over to the top table where Valentine Oak sat, old and frail in his white coat. His head was bowed in deep conversation with Ocelot Malodure.

'Do you know anything about Wellenstorm, Sam?'

'Some big nasty old dragon, isn't it?' he said, scratching his ear. 'I remember there was some business with Thad Lancaster a few years back. If you're feeling brave you could go down the Dragon Vault and ask one of the keepers about it, though don't expect to get a straight answer. Full of stories that lot, even when they're sober.'

I wondered. There was a low growl behind my feet and I looked down to see Stinky the royal leopard chewing on a bone. Her golden eyes glared at me and she snorted, sending out a shower of sparks.

'Everyone's thinking about Tuesday now, aren't you, Stinky? They sense something's in the air. Ocelot Malodure inspected your vault yet?' asked Sam.

'Not yet.'

'Hmm. Well, she's on the warpath. Gave Pettifog a right going over last night. Half his roses were rambling around the corridors and a couple of climbers were hiding up in the chimney pots. I think young Patrick would've been slapped down in the dungeons if it weren't so close to the presentation. Thad Lancaster insisted he stays out to look after you-know-who.'

Sam nodded down to where Fleur de Lys was parked in her wicker wheelchair, wrapped in blankets and scarves. As usual Patrick was trying to make her eat breakfast.

'So Fleur takes part in the presentation?'

'Yep. Always has. No one has the heart to stop her. Still convinced she's famous, see – the legendary Fleur de Lys. I don't think anyone's got the foggiest idea who she is any more.'

Patrick Pettifog caught my eye and smiled. As I was leaving, I walked over to say hello.

'Hi Jack,' he said.

Was it my imagination or was Patrick even more nervous than usual? Perhaps.

'Sorry to hear you got in trouble last night.'

'That? Oh, it was nothing. Just an excuse for them to have a good poke around my vault, I think.' With a quick grin he turned to the bundle of scarves. 'Fleur, you remember Jack. She came down to see us the other day.'

Fleur de Lys turned to stare at me vacantly, her pale trumpet head looking particularly sickly and grey.

'Zer petit rosbif who is making waves around 'ere.'

'That's right. Jack's the new Keeper of Ghosts–'

'I know who she is!' she snapped. 'Zey're trying to kill me, Jack.'

'I've brought her some friends from the yard,' said Patrick, nodding to the snowdrops in the jar on the table. 'I thought they might cheer her up. They're English of course, but at least it's someone to talk to, isn't it, Fleur?'

Fleur de Lys ignored him and kept staring at me.

'Zey are eating my soul, rosbif. Vat are you going to do about it, hmm?'

'She's being ridiculously tricky this morning,' whispered Patrick with a nervous laugh.

Fleur peered down at the snowdrops.

'Vat do you zink, Snowy? Is zis Jack un petit cochon comme les autres? Eh?'

The snowdrops nodded and waved a little.

'Oui, I zink you're right. Never trust a rosbif. "Vat a pretty leetle flower"– snip! "Oh, 'ere is anozer one" – snip! I know how you feel, Snowy. Zey smile, zen zey chop your head off!'

'Fleur is getting a special beauty treatment this afternoon,' said Patrick. 'I found an old recipe in the library that'll take five hundred years off her. She'll be looking her very best for Tuesday.'

'If I live zat long, vitch I doubt,' she said.

'Fleur that attitude is not going to solve anything,' said Patrick. 'Now do please finish your porridge.'

'Pff. *Porridge.* Vat do you zink I am, a piglet? I DO NOT VANT ANY PORRIDGE!' she shrieked, sending the bowl flying. Fleur leant forward and whispered in my ear.

'She is here,' she hissed. 'Uh-uh. You *know* who I mean. Ici. *Here.*'

I looked at the plant. It nodded at me.

'Some things you can never please, no matter how hard you try,' sighed Patrick with that nervous smile. 'Thankless task isn't it, being a keeper?'

Patrick Pettifog was right. And I couldn't help wondering if Fleur de Lys was right too…

ᜫᜩ 46 ᜬᜩ
Secrets of the Joliffes

GHOSTS, PHANTOMS, WISPS. I stared at the stone letters above the vault door. Everything I'd heard about Richard's great achievements made me a little nervous about coming back in here. How was Dancing Dan ever going to believe that we were the same person? Surely if anyone was going to guess the truth, it was him… Oh well.

'Hello?'

I opened the door and stepped into the deep darkness.

'Dancing Dan, are you there?'

It appeared he was not. I banged my staff on the step, hoping to wake him up.

'Dancing Dan? It's me.'

'Oh no.'

That wasn't much of a welcome.

'Dancing Dan?'

'Oh dear.'

Perhaps he was sulking. That was odd. I walked down the steps and reached for the light switch.

'What's the matter?'

It was one of those questions that as soon as you ask it, you feel very stupid. The matter was all around me. The matter was everything. I could describe the chaos of broken glass, overturned racks, broken shelves, destroyed ledgers… but the sight of Dancing Dan mournfully floating in the middle of the vault wearing a frilly apron somehow said it all. There was a lost expression on his face.

'It's all gone,' he said. 'The careful work of centuries, undone in a night of madness. Gone. Gone.' His gloomy eyes turned to me. 'How could you be so careless?'

'M-me?' I stammered. He meant Richard, of course. 'What did I do?'

'You'd shown such brilliance. You recaptured Doctor Grimswitch, you rebottled Black Lowther and the six headless horses, you were becoming so charming and cunning you might've become the greatest Keeper of Ghosts there ever was… What possessed you to hold a ghost ball and think there wouldn't be trouble?'

I didn't know what to say. Is that what Richard had done?

'It's always a grave mistake to open a black-lidded jar,' droned Dancing Dan. 'One persuadable ghost you might have managed to turn back. But Slippery Sid Barton, the greatest safe-cracker of them all, a man who in life could slip through railings no wider than your hand…' Dancing Dan shook his head. 'Slippery

Sid knew there was nothing to stop him sliding out through the walls of the vault. So Slippery Sid slipped the secret to Harry 'the Snitch' Snitchington, who snitched it to Mad Maria Marten, who screamed it to the Headless Horses of Humberside, who neighed it to the Swimming Swine of Swelland, who grunted it to the Cup-juggling Chickens of Chichester, who clucked it to the Rhyming Rats of Ribble... I could go on, ma'am.'

I was glad he didn't. The cardinal rule of the Joliffes, broken. Richard, I realised, probably knew nothing about any of this, because I'd forgotten to tell him. Uncle Galahad's advice was stowed away in the desk.

'What are we going to do?'

Dancing Dan sighed again. And again. I don't think he could have looked any sadder.

'In the circumstances, perhaps ma'am might consider... retiring?'

'Retiring? But Dancing Dan, I've only just started!'

'Which makes it all the more remarkable what you've achieved, ma'am.'

Dancing Dan pushed the glass he was brushing into a pile. I decided I didn't like this snide tone he was taking.

'How many ghosts are missing?' I asked. 'It can't be *that* many, can it?'

'According to the official ledger, there were forty-four thousand, three hundred and seventy-two troublesome ghosts in the vault, ma'am,' said Dancing Dan. 'I think we can assume that ninety-nine per cent of them are now at large.'

Oh dear. I suppose that was quite a lot.

'But what about all the contraptions in the cellar? Isn't there something we could use to, I don't know, sort of suck them all up again?' Dancing Dan leant on his broom and considered.

Titus

Oberon

Larkspur

Clarence

Hissop

Maurice

Absolom

Horatio

Bramwell

'Oberon Joliffe's ox-drawn ghost smotherer has not been used since 1804. Absolom Joliffe's ghost-gobbling balloon has a hole in it. Griffin Joliffe's steam-powered charming device is still operational, though it is usually towed behind a locomotive—'

'It's on a train?'

'In a siding between Bungay and Beccles. The Waveney Line.'

'What's the line got to do with it?'

'Nothing, ma'am.'

We stared at the piles of glass.

'And there's no helpful ghost left who can help us charm them back?'

'There is me, ma'am,' said Dancing Dan Dravot, looking gloomier than ever in his frilly pinny.

Okay. This was a dire situation.

'It is, ma'am. What a way to end the great enterprise the Joliffes began four hundred

'and forty-nine years ago.'

'Thanks for rubbing it in, Dancing Dan.'

'No problem.'

My eyes drifted up to the portrait of the toad-faced Oberon, noble and stern in his great robes of office, and the seventeen toad-faced Joliffes that came after... Larkspur, Maurice, Dandelion, Fellbrigg... I had failed the lot of them! Except it wasn't me, exactly, who had done it. It was Richard.

BANG! BANG! BANG!

Hammering on the great wooden door brought me to my senses.

'Miss Joliffe! Open up if you please!'

I looked at Dancing Dan. He looked at me. We looked at the door.

'That is Mr Knock knocking, ma'am,' said Dancing Dan.

'Open up now, as we don't have all day!' commanded another high nasal voice.

'That's Ocelot Malodure, ma'am. Red Tempest, Keeper of Time and Enforcer of Rules—'

'Yes I know who it is. It's a snap inspection, isn't it?'

BANG! BANG! BANG! BANG! BANG!

The banging became a barrage. I thought they were going to break the door down.

'She doesn't like to be kept waiting, ma'am.'

I'd guessed as much.

'What are we going to do, Dancing Dan?'

Even Dancing Dan looked momentarily concerned. He hastily began removing his pinafore.

'May I suggest that we draw a veil over the matter, ma'am?' he said, swiftly putting his brushes away.

'But we can't pretend it hasn't happened – can we?'

'No, but we can draw a *veil* over it, ma'am. If you would be so kind as to hand me the key to the keeper's desk?'

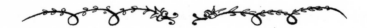

'Red Tempest.'

'Phasma Argent.'

In strode Ocelot Malodure in her orange keeper's coat, looking even more impatient than usual. She wore a line of watches up her arm and an expression that suggested no nonsense. Solomon Knock followed in her slipstream, grinning that painful grin of his.

'Joliffe Junior. We met yesterday. How do,' he said.

'How do,' I said, and we all bowed to each other. Yes we *had* met yesterday, but at the time he thought I was the Prince out of bounds in a dark corridor...

'What is the meaning of this?' demanded Ocelot Malodure. She rapped her eagle-headed staff on the floor and waited expectantly. Perhaps this usually brought missing minutes scurrying from their hiding places, but here nothing moved. Perhaps because there was nothing here, at all, because of the veil Dancing Dan had drawn across the vault. Half the room looked like it had been rubbed out.

'You're not concealing something behind that, are you, Miss Joliffe?'

'Erm, no. No, no, we're—'

'Snap inspections of keepers' vaults are taken very seriously indeed.'

'I'm sure they are.'

'So what *are* you doing in here, hmm? Explain,' demanded Ocelot Malodure, prodding the end of her staff into the veil. It disappeared.

'I'm sorry, but you can't see the vault this morning,' I said.

'Why not?'

'Because… you just can't, that's all.'

'Are you telling me what I can and cannot do?' Ocelot Malodure took a step closer. She was quite a large lady with very small feet. I noticed she was wearing a pair of bright pink-and-green striped socks.

'Well? Are you?'

'I like your socks.'

Ocelot Malodure stared at me. I don't know why, but there was something about easily angered adults that made my mouth say the strangest things. It wasn't very helpful.

'I'm warning you, Miss Joliffe, I do not have a sense of humour.'

'No, I can see that.'

Ocelot Malodure twitched.

'But your socks are very nice.'

Mr Knock raised an eyebrow and swallowed a smile. Red Tempest became a shade redder.

'Miss Joliffe, you may be proving yourself to be an exceptionally gifted young keeper, but there's much about this palace that you need to learn. As Red Tempest, I hold the King's Commission. That means no corner of the palace is hidden to me. If I demand something, then it happens. D'you understand?'

I nodded. Ocelot Malodure snapped open a stopwatch and clicked her fingers.

'You have thirty seconds to put the Ghost Vault ledger in my hand.'

'Thirty seconds?'

'It's now twenty-five.'

I stared in panic at the seconds clicking by.

'You want me to go and get it?'

'I do.'

'Now?'

Ocelot Malodure began to turn a dangerous shade of purple.

'You have fifteen seconds to hand me the ledger listing every ghost in this vault, Miss Joliffe, OR ELSE!'

I turned back to the white wilderness, not really knowing what to do. And at that moment a huge grey shadow appeared. It was something like a giant serpent, with the head of a lion, or maybe a sheep, moving from one side of the vault to the other. The shadow of Dancing Dan hovered beside its head, leading it on a rein.

'What... is *that*?' gasped Ocelot Malodure.

The monster stopped and looked down at us.

'It's erm, it's a ghost—'

'Don't get clever with me, Miss Joliffe. A ghost of *what* exactly?'

I stared at it. It was sort of liony, chickeny... with large teeth and a very long tail.

'I'm afraid I don't know its name—'

'Why is it being moved about behind this wall of fog?'

'Erm… we can only move it behind a veil. Otherwise we might lose it.'

'You mean it will escape?'

'Only if it spots something moving. And then it gets very hard to control. It's very aggressive, you see, which is why my assistant is holding its head.'

The strange lion-headed serpent stared down at Ocelot Malodure. She must have suspected some trickery, but she couldn't be certain.

'It looks very much like a shadow puppet to me,' said Solomon Knock.

'Yes, that's right, that *is* what it looks like. Except it isn't.'

Solomon Knock eyed me in that lizardy way of his. Ocelot Malodure raised her staff to poke the creature through the veil, then thought better of it.

'Very well,' she muttered, pocketing her stopwatch. 'At 3pm this afternoon I shall return for that ledger. In the meantime, I expect you to be taking all necessary precautions. We don't want anything else to go missing before the presentation on Tuesday.'

'I guarantee that will not happen.'

'You seem very sure about that, Miss Joliffe.'

'I am. Nothing will go missing from this vault.'

Somehow my confidence seemed to annoy Ocelot Malodure even more. But what could go missing? There was only Dancing Dan left. She took a step closer.

'May I remind you, Miss Joliffe, that if *anything* from this vault threatens to endanger the Prince at his presentation, there will be serious consequences for yourself. We have certain unpleasant punishments in this palace, reserved for keepers alone.'

I definitely wasn't smiling now. But I think she thought I was.

'Anything else to say about my socks, Miss Joliffe?'

I shook my head. I had a feeling Ocelot Malodure might be quite keen on those unpleasant punishments.

'Phasma Argent.'

'Red Tempest.'

We bowed to each other again.

'At exactly three o'clock this afternoon, I shall be back for the ledger.'

Red Tempest twirled out of the room, Solomon Knock following. Before he left, Mr Knock pulled a seeing stone from his pocket. Tapping it with his stick he placed it on the step beside the door.

'Just to be sure,' he said with a grin.

I waited till the footsteps had died away.

'Dancing Dan?'

A moment later he floated around the edge of the veil, checking to see that the coast was clear.

'Dancing Dan, you're a genius.'

'One does what one can, ma'am, in the circumstances.'

'How did you think of that?'

'Shadow puppets have always been my "thing", ma'am. When I was alive, my first job was in a circus as a magician's assistant. Though, if may I say, you were rather quick on your feet yourself.'

'Not as quick as you, Dancing Dan.'

'Oh gosh.'

Dancing Dan went a little blue at the edges, then he noticed the seeing stone lurking beside the door. Without appearing to hurry he danced across the room, took a handkerchief from his breast pocket and dropped it over the stone.

'There,' he said. Standing at one corner of the veil, he then opened a large brown envelope and sort of wafted all the white fog back inside again. 'I believe the vault is now under your control, ma'am.'

And so it was, in all its smashed state.

'It's still a problem though, isn't it?'

'Indeed it is, ma'am.'

'What's going to happen when they come back? We can't do that again. And now there are forty-four thousand ghosts flying around the countryside. There's going to be panic and chaos everywhere.'

Dancing Dan was putting on his pinafore again. Somehow he didn't seem quite as gloomy as he did before.

'Isn't there?'

Dancing Dan whistled on in his mysterious way.

'Dancing Dan?'

'While hunting for a veil I couldn't help but notice something else hidden in the bottom drawer of the desk, ma'am. I took the liberty of reading it.'

Dancing Dan became even more mysterious when he floated around the corner and disappeared.

I rummaged around in the bottom drawer till I found a red box on which was written '*Totally and Utterly Private AND Personal!*' quite clearly in Uncle Galahad's writing. Dancing Dan, you most certainly did take a liberty. Inside was a thick black notebook. I opened it. It was a catalogue of the vault, each jar numbered and its contents neatly described, page after page after page – thousands of them. It was obviously some secret copy of the ledger that my uncle had kept... until I saw what was written at the end of each entry: '*Released*'. Released?

'I confess I was as surprised as you are, ma'am.'

Dancing Dan appeared from nowhere and loomed up over my shoulder.

'But why would he release them?'

'I'm certain he didn't, ma'am. I never saw him do it.'

'But then...'

'Mr Joliffe was a stickler for tradition,' explained Dancing Dan. 'I suspect that over the years he slowly began to discover that his ancestors had never actually caught many ghosts at all. Certainly not forty-four thousand. When he discovered a jar was empty, perhaps he wrote the word *"Released"* next to it, to preserve the good name of the Joliffes, and conceal the family secret. One imagines that if the truth were ever found out it would be catastrophic.'

I was struggling to understand.

'So what you're saying is that most of the jars in the vault were actually *empty*?'

'It appears so, ma'am. Just for show.'

'But then why did you say they all escaped last night during the ball?'

Dancing Dan looked sheepish.

'I fear I may have got a little carried away with my description—'

'Carried away? What d'you mean?'

'I didn't want to appear to be a party pooper, ma'am, but high jinks with highwaymen and headless dukes are not really my thing. I prefer a quiet evening playing scrabble, alone, and last night I wasn't actually here. I do beg your pardon, ma'am.'

I stared at him floating in the air mournfully. Well. Dancing Dan, making up that story to make me feel terrible. What a—

'Big fat fibber. Yes, ma'am, I quite agree.'

'But there must've been at least *some* ghosts in here to do all this.'

'Indeed there must, ma'am. May I?'

Dancing Dan flicked through the notebook, the pages blurring so fast I don't know how he could read anything.

'There were two hundred and thirty-four ghosts having a party. One presumes they have all escaped.' I looked at him. 'I used to count cards in a casino, ma'am.'

'Was that before or after you became a magician's assistant?'

'After. Though before I took to murderin' dowagers. But you're right to think I am the most terrible liar, ma'am, because I am.' He smiled mournfully. 'Which means somewhere in the region of forty-four thousand, one hundred and thirty-eight jars were in fact filled with nothing but air.'

Once again I looked up at my toad-faced forebears, all impressive and magnificent in their robes of office... perhaps they weren't quite so magnificent after all...

'One does wonder, ma'am. Obviously they caught a fair few of 'em, but one suspects they spent most of their time inventing stories in the ledger, eating cake and drinking tea.'

I didn't know what to say. What a sham. It was amazing.

'Indeed it is amazing, ma'am,' said Dancing Dan, reading my thoughts again.

'Do you think anyone else knows this?'

'I suspect Galahad Joliffe did his very best to keep this particular skeleton firmly in its closet, ma'am,' he said, with the tiniest wrinkle of his nostrils. 'I certainly never discovered it. Of course, the shame it would have brought upon the family, had it ever been revealed, would've been devastating.'

'Yes, you're right.'

'One imagines the powers that be would've taken a very dim view.'

'They certainly would.'

'They'd probably have concluded that the Joliffes were a bunch of lazy so-and-sos.'

'Probably–'

'Stripped them of their titles–'

'I suppose–'

'Thrown them out into the gutter–'

'Yes perhaps–'

'Good riddance to bad rubbish–'

'Thank you, Dancing Dan.'

Dancing Dan smiled and bowed, hovering in the air. He seemed a little too triumphant.

'Nevertheless, may I assume that ma'am would like to continue the appalling family deceit? One must keep up appearances after all.'

I shrugged. Did I have any choice?

'I rather thought you'd say that, ma'am.'

'I didn't say anything.'

'In which case I'll be ordering some more jars, ma'am.'

'As you wish, Dancing Dan. And please stop gloating.'

'I'll do my best, ma'am.' With the vaguest of smiles, Dancing Dan Dravot shimmered away into the darkness.

~~ 47 ~~
Gossip and a Game

AFTER WE HAD TIDIED UP the vault together that morning, I'd gone off to the library to see if I could find out anything more about Wellenstorm. As you might remember, the Dragon section was a total jumble; most of the books were half burnt or not there at all. So it was no surprise that I found nothing on that ancient dragon, where he lived, what he did… though strangely enough, I did find Snowdrop Scott.

'Phasma Argent,' she bowed, and hastily trotted off into the depths of the bookstacks. Curious, I walked down and took out the book she had guiltily replaced. '*Tunnelling Dragons: Habits and Habitats*'. Why she was reading that, I didn't know; it looked very boring, though it did make me think about what old Kiddy had said… The mystery of that escaped mole dragon was still at the back of my mind. I replaced the book and made my way out, aware that Snowdrop Scott was still watching me from the floor above.

'Very clever is Snowdrop,' said Sam Yuell. 'Full of theories.'

'About dragons?'

'About everything. Likes nothing better than solving puzzles. And there are enough of them around this place, eh?'

Sam had grabbed me on my way back from the library and asked me to help him scrub the royal beasts. We spent a happy couple of hours painting hooves and oiling horns while he rabbited on about presentations and coronations and everything else, including what had happened to my uncle.

'That's a big old mystery, isn't it?' he said as we polished the Black Bull of Clarence's flanks so hard we could see our reflections in them.

'So you know what's happened to him?'

'Oh I've heard,' Sam Yuell chortled to himself. 'First I had it on good authority that Jellybean had been called out to capture a ghost in a cave, only the ghost had got the better of him, tied him up, and then set him afloat on a moat. Then I heard it wasn't in a cave, in fact he'd been locked in a cellar by a man called Dave. Then this morning I heard that while this Dave *might* have had something to do with it, at this very moment Jellybean was lost in a *maze*, chasing a goat that had stolen his coat, so it would be quite understandable if he was never seen again.'

The great Bull of Clarence snorted.

'Exactly, my friend,' said Sam, handing the bull a carrot. 'And guess which floppy-eared gossip told me all that?'

Tom Bootle, obviously.

'D'you think he's ever going to come back?'

'Nothing would surprise me about your uncle, Jack. Galahad Joliffe was a law unto himself.' Sam smiled, and gave the great bull a friendly pat. The bull chewed the carrot, staring at him vacantly. 'Maybe Jellybean's run away. Simple as that.'

Maybe he had. Though I did wonder if perhaps discovering the Joliffe family secret might have had something to do with it...

It was three o'clock on the dot and I was sitting in silence waiting for Ocelot Malodure to reappear. Actually I had been sitting there for half an hour already, wondering why Dancing Dan seemed so curiously happy.

'Indeed, ma'am?'

'Yes, you look rather pleased with yourself. What have you done?'

'Oh gosh. I don't think I've done anything at all. Nothing I can remember anyway.'

On it went like this for a bit. Me asking, Dancing Dan avoiding the question. But that curious smirk was still there. On the table in front of us was the official leather-bound ledger and the glass jar containing Mabel the duck, who somehow, despite the chaos, hadn't taken part in the breakout. If Ocelot Malodure wanted proof we had ghosts we could always let her out – though on second thoughts that might not be such a good idea...

I glanced up at the clock. It was one minute past three. Ocelot Malodure was actually late. Then another minute went by. Then another. Still no sign of her. Could it be that she had forgotten?

'The Keeper of Time never forgets, ma'am.'

'Then what's kept her?'

Dancing Dan had his sleeves rolled up and all the brass buckles and belts of my official state costume laid out on the table before him.

'I heard that there's been a little trouble in the Time Vault,' he said, merrily polishing away.

'What sort of trouble, Dancing Dan?'

Dancing Dan picked up a thick brass chain and began to buff.

'The Keeper of Time keeps her time in locked wooden boxes, ma'am. But missing minutes are so thin they can sometimes squeeze themselves out and slip by unnoticed. It's a devil of a job to find where they went. They like hiding in the narrowest of places.'

I looked at Dancing Dan. His expression was mournful, as usual. On he polished.

'And of course seconds are notoriously slippery. Blink and you miss them. Dying seconds have to be wrapped in towels and fed tiny bottles of warm milk to make them feel anything like their

old selves. Nursing them back to health takes hours. And even hours sometimes have a habit of slipping away, don't they?'

On he polished, whistling to himself.

'Dancing Dan, I hope you haven't done something awful.'

Dancing Dan attempted to look shocked at the suggestion.

'Is the Keeper of Time's vault inspected like the rest of them?'

'It is, ma'am. Ocelot Malodure may be Red Tempest, but she has to account for her vault the same as everyone else. Mr Knock will go wherever his fancy takes him.'

'So that's where he is now?'

'I believe so. Slice of cake?'

There was no point asking any more. When it came to keeping secrets, Dancing Dan could match the sphinx. Eventually the clock struck four. Ocelot Malodure was a whole hour late. What could I do? I couldn't leave, but I couldn't do anything else either. Unless I practised being more charming, which I probably should, given Richard had been so successful at it...

'Galahad Joliffe was often saying the same thing, ma'am,' said Dancing Dan, shining a buckle. 'One can never be too charming,' he'd say. 'One wants to be utterly irresistibly delicious at all times.'

I looked up at Uncle Galahad staring down from the pillar. Well, *maybe*.

'Ghosts are like people, ma'am. To charm them one must try to recognise their weaknesses and go to work on those. It takes patience and cunning. Galahad Joliffe would often practise his skills with Harry Gamblingay, who was once the most charming man in England. They say he could steal the shoes from your feet and you'd never notice.'

'I suppose he escaped with the rest of them, did he?'

'Strangely enough he didn't, ma'am. Somehow he survived the

ball unopened.'

I wondered.

'But supposing I can't charm him back into his bottle?'

'If you can succeed with Black Lowther and Doctor Grimswitch, then I think you're more than a match for anyone, ma'am.'

'Yes but I also let Doctor Grimswitch escape, Dancing Dan, don't forget that.'

Dancing Dan shrugged his mournful shrug.

'If you want to get better at being charming, ma'am, might as well cross swords with the best.'

That was true. And it might take my mind off everything else.

Dancing Dan retrieved the bottle from the racks. I stared at it. Harry Gamblingay. With very mixed feelings I opened the stopper. Out came a wisp of brown gas that spun upwards, swirled and turned into a man with a white painted face, a grey wig and fine silk clothes.

'Am I *still* in this godforsaken dump?' he groaned, then he spun around, saw me, and suddenly his expression changed.

'Ah–ha! And who, pray, are you?'

I told him. He bowed and took my hand.

'Enchanté! What a pleasure this is.'

With great courtesy Harry Gamblingay sat me down and then drew up a chair opposite. Crossing his legs, he leant forward, appearing incredibly interested in whatever I might have to say.

'Now young lady, how may I be of assistance?'

I glanced back at Dancing Dan lurking behind a pillar. He nodded encouragingly.

'I need to be more charming,' I said, coming straight to the point.

'But my dear Miss Joliffe, I don't know how you could possibly be more charming. I can see already that you're perfectly delightful.'

'But you've only just met me.'

'And my instinct is never wrong. My dear, you look quite exquisite in that wonderful long green coat. And those black boots are most practical-looking, and your face is perfect! As for your hair...' He paused. 'I agree, I think too much hair is unbecoming. Girls these days go to such lengths; I think you've been very sensible to... Yes, it suits you very well indeed. Remarkably well. You really are a picture of health, my dear. One does wonder what a creature of your character and breeding is doing down here amongst all these toady old Joliffes, because I think *you* are a cut above. Rather special, in fact.'

He winked. I smiled. Dancing Dan was right. Harry Gamblingay's charm was bewitching.

'I was told that my uncle used to practise his charm on you.'

'Oh indeed he did! Many times! He and I would indulge in a little game. We would bet that he couldn't charm me back into that nasty bottle, and if I won, I was free to go off and murder whoever I chose.'

'Really?' I gasped.

Harry Gamblingay laughed.

'Of course not! But he did promise me my freedom. Ah, what charming jousts we used to have! Would it be too much for me to assume that you've opened my bottle because you'd like to play the game as well?'

Harry Gamblingay may have looked like a peacock, and spoke nothing but empty flattery, but he was no fool.

'Actually, I was wondering if we could just chat, instead?'

'Oh come come, don't be shy!' he tittered. 'You seem like a very clever girl to me. There must be something you can do. Can you recite poetry?'

'Not really.'

'Sing a marvellous song?'

'Not a marvellous one.'

'Tell stories, then? Galahad Joliffe was full of stories. Or dance? Play a musical instrument?'

Was this what Uncle Galahad did?

'So shall we play? Who's going to charm who first? May I say it's usually the host who leads on these occasions.'

I stared at Harry Gamblingay's painted face, his perfect wig, his embroidered jacket and shining shoes. I had a bad feeling about this.

'Quite right, ma'am,' whispered Dancing Dan in my ear. 'They never played any such game. It's a lie.'

'What?'

'Apologies for being a harbinger of doom, ma'am, but I don't think you've a cat's chance in hell.'

'Thanks!'

Before I could glare at him, he'd disappeared.

'You begin,' said the ghost. 'If I smile, twitch, giggle or clap my hands and exclaim – consider me charmed.'

I took a deep breath. Be charming.

'Do I really have to play?'

'Of course you do, my dear,' grinned Harry Gamblingay. 'How else are you going to get me back in that bottle?'

Unfortunately that was true. Very well then.

'Shall I tell you the funniest thing that's ever happened to me?'

'If you like.'

It was a story about a lizard called Dracula, a dog called Teapot, and a birthday cake. It wasn't entirely true, but it used to make Oscar and Phil laugh out loud. Harry Gamblingay listened with a vague smirk fixed on his face. When it was finished, he didn't move a muscle.

'Anything else?'

'Actually I do know one song,' I said. I sang it. Harry Gamblingay listened… And did not so much as twitch.

'Do you like magic tricks?' I asked. Tom Bootle had taught me one. I did it and the card disappeared. Still nothing. This was becoming embarrassing. Maybe I should just go for the obvious. Flattery.

'My uncle told me you were the most charming ghost in the vault, but he never told me how handsome you are.'

'You think so?'

'Oh yes!'

I then listed everything that was completely wonderful about him, from his grey fluffy wig to his dainty pink shoes, even the strange black spot he'd painted on his cheek. Not a flicker. Not even a shimmer. Harry Gamblingay sat completely still, his face a mask.

'Anything else?' he said. 'Then I shall begin. If you titter, or even begin to smile, then I shall consider that I have won. Does that sound fair?'

'Hardly,' I said, knowing I was about to lose yet another ghost from my vault. At least he didn't seem to be mad or dangerous.

'I'm afraid he's both, ma'am, only he's so charming one can't tell,' whispered Dancing Dan. 'Ask him to show you his dancing.'

'His dancing?'

Before I could ask why, Dancing Dan had disappeared again. Harry Gamblingay leant back in his chair and regarded me for a moment.

'Allow me to give you some advice, Jack,' he said. 'We ghosts generally give excellent advice, because we see things as they truly are, and not as people would like them to be. Now it seems screamingly obvious to me that you are trying very hard to be something you quite clearly are not.'

Strangely enough, I began to feel embarrassed.

'What d'you mean?'

'What I mean, my dear girl, is that you know in your bones that something about your present situation is fundamentally wrong. Your instinct tells you it is so, and one should always obey one's instinct. When one has a feeling about something, one mustn't shilly-shally around, one must sally forth and seek out the truth! For as every ghost knows only too well; life is brief. I suggest you go out and do what needs to be done without further delay, otherwise I fear, m'dear, you'll be ensnared in this ghastly old vault forever!'

I stared at the ghost. This was most unexpected advice. Yes... yes maybe he was right...

'You're smiling!' cried Harry Gamblingay. 'I've won! You see, being charming is not only about entertaining one's victims–*friends*, I mean. Sometimes it's as simple as telling people the truth – in the nicest possible way of course,' he grinned. 'Now I think you should open the door,' he said, standing up.

'Really?' I gasped. 'Is that fair?'

'My dear, of course it's fair. We played a game, I won, you lost, *and* I've given you some rather excellent advice for nothing. I think I've earned my freedom.'

I noticed Dancing Dan reappear behind a cupboard. He shook his head violently and began hopping about like a bird.

'Erm... before you go, why don't you show me your dancing,' I said.

Harry Gamblingay turned around in surprise.

'My dancing?'

'My uncle said you were a wonderful dancer, Mr Gamblingay.'

'Did he indeed. Well I'm sorry to disappoint you, m'dear, but I'm not a dancer in any way, shape or form. Never have been. Two left feet.'

I glanced back at Dancing Dan. Carry on, I think he meant.

'Oh, that's a shame.'

'It is?'

'Because I do find dancing incredibly charming. Never mind.'

Harry Gamblingay raised an eyebrow. He was obviously finding this hard to resist.

'Then I shall give you another piece of advice for nothing. Always remember to have a hidden talent up your sleeve.'

'A hidden talent?'

'There is nothing more charming than a hidden talent. Particularly a spectacular hidden talent that one apparently has no knowledge of whatsoever. And one has been secretly practising this "hidden talent" for weeks, months, years.'

'Isn't that cheating?'

'Foo-ee to cheating! To be charming one must be wicked!'

'So this hidden talent could be anything?'

'Anything at all. Juggling eggs, flicking peas, pretending to be a chicken–'

'Could it be dancing?'

'Indeed it could. Not that I know anything about that, of course.'

'Prove it,' I said. 'I *dare* you to dance.'

'You *dare* me to dance?'

'Unless you're too shy.'

'My dear, do *I* look like I'm shy? Pah!' he snorted. 'Very well. I shall. I have never danced in my entire life, as you shall see.' And with that, Harry Gamblingay straightened his jacket and stood up, muttering that he was wearing the wrong shoes, that his waistcoat was too tight, etc., etc. There he stood, as if holding an imaginary partner.

'Does one stand like this?' he said. 'Or that? I really have no idea. Perhaps if there was some music... ah–'

Dancing Dan wound up a gramophone and a crackly tune began.

'I feel very foolish doing this, you know. But since you asked.'

Off he went, spinning around the vault. Predictably, Harry Gamblingay was a fantastic mover.

'You're not bad,' I said.

The ghost bowed humbly.

'Do you think so? I've no idea what I'm doing. The music is sort of blowing me about like a leaf. It's very odd. Ha! Does my dancing charm you?'

'Not yet.'

Harry Gamblingay smiled and tried harder. As the music got quicker his dancing became more complex, full of leaps and twists. Dancing Dan appeared at my side.

'Perhaps ma'am might now consider opening the vault door?'

'But supposing the Keeper of Time turns up?'

'I think it might be a good idea, ma'am.'

Dancing Dan was being his usual mysterious self. I couldn't help feeling a little angry with him. More than a little.

'If you must.'

No sooner had Dancing Dan turned the latch than Harry Gamblingay galloped out, leaping down the corridor before suddenly stopping in front of a large mirror that had somehow found its way out there.

'I had a vague recollection this is what Galahad Joliffe used, ma'am,' said Dancing Dan, now back at my side.

'But I don't understand,' I said, feeling rather stupid.

'Harry Gamblingay was the most charming man in the world, ma'am. There is only one person capable of captivating him, and that is himself.'

It was true. Harry Gamblingay seemed spellbound by his own reflection. He began flicking his toes and striking poses, adding funny little jumps.

'And I shall dance,' he said, 'like this!' he said, 'Like that!' he said, 'La-la!' he cried, 'La-lee! La-la, la-lee! La-la-la-lee!'

Soon the edges of his wig became a fuzzy blue... The faster he whirled, the wobblier Harry Gamblingay became, never for one moment taking his eyes off his ghostly reflection.

'Ma'am?'

Dancing Dan handed me the bottle and straw. A moment later my cheeks puffed out like a hamster and my nose tickled as I sucked Harry Gamblingay out of the air.

'You brute!' he declared. 'For shame!' Trying as hard as I could not to sneeze, I blew him straight back into the jar and quickly jammed on the stopper. 'For shame!' the jar echoed as I placed it back on the rack.

'Well done, ma'am. Not many people can claim to have outcharmed Harry Gamblingay.'

'You know I had nothing to do with it,' I snapped. 'Why did you do that?'

'Do what, ma'am?'

'Tell me to release Harry Gamblingay. Pretend it was some kind of tradition. Was it just to make me look stupid?'

'I'm very sorry to have caused offence, ma'am,' mumbled Dancing Dan. 'I merely thought that... considering your extraordinary achievements so far... it was presumptuous of me, ma'am.'

I watched Dancing Dan straightening up the vault. So that was the real reason. He wanted to find out if I was Richard. And now he knew I wasn't.

'I'm never going to be any good at this, am I?'

'Give it time, ma'am.'

'You think so?'

'In my humble opinion, Mr Gamblingay is quite correct. Miss Joliffe has found herself in a situation not of her own making. Fate has dealt her a truly bad hand, and she's trying to make the best of it. Perhaps one should obey one's instinct and seek out the truth, ma'am, whatever that might be.'

Dancing Dan smiled mournfully. This was another of those maddening answers he liked to give when he was trying to avoid the question.

'I'm afraid it is, ma'am.'

'Is what?'

'Another one of those maddening answers.' Dancing Dan put on his pinafore and picked up the tray. 'Will there be anything else, ma'am?'

'Do you need to ask?'

Dancing Dan bowed, sensing my frustration.

'Best of luck, ma'am,' he said.

And off he went.

～ 48 ～
Dragon Lore

THIS NEXT CHAPTER needs a little explaining. While
I've been describing everything that happened that Saturday,
thinking back, what Harry Gamblingay had said was right.
There was something gnawing away at me, something fundamental
that I couldn't stop thinking about. It was that story old Caractacus
Kiddy told. For some reason I could see it all, the moonlit car
park, the great dragon stalking round and round, the men shouting
and daring each other closer and the little thatched pub beyond...
The tragic tale of that young family and the dragon seemed to
have burnt such a hole in my mind that by the evening I was
desperate to know if it was true, or just another Dragon Keeper's

tale that had grown in the telling, as everyone seemed to think…

So that is why I didn't return straight to my room that night. Instead of taking the stone steps up from the vaults, I turned down a long corridor that led away to another part of the palace. This was a whispering corridor, and when I say whispering, I mean that when you walked along, it was like swishing through grass, and the moment you stopped, the swishing stopped too. What the tapestries were whispering about no one seemed to know, except they were always whispering… At the end there was an even narrower corridor, so narrow I could run my fingers along both sides. This made it dragonproof, because this was the way to the Dragon Vault. Whenever my curiosity had led me here before, Archie Queach had been sort of barricading the way with his brushes and pans in that not very helpful way of his. But this evening Archie was nowhere to be seen. I think Richard must have frightened him off with his tricks.

'HERE BE RAGONS' read the gold letters above the enormous vault door – the 'D' had disappeared. I stood in the shadows, hesitating. I'd be lying if I said I wasn't a little intimidated by the Dragon Keepers. Keepers were like dogs and their owners; they sort of resembled each other in an odd way, and the Dragon Keepers were like a rowdy gang of… yes, dragons. Whenever you met them in the dark passageways they seemed to be pushing huge wheelbarrows piled high with vile-smelling meat, and when they weren't slapping each other on the shoulder and roaring at each other's jokes they were punching and fighting. The Dragon Keepers kept themselves to themselves, and plainly didn't think much of anyone else in the palace. They weren't afraid to tell them either.

As I stood there behind the pillar, I heard a deep, fearsome roar.

Plucking up courage, I was just about to climb the wide steps when the door opened a fraction and a thin figure slipped out. It was Snowdrop Scott! What was she doing in there? I watched her trot away into the gloom. She seemed rather pleased with herself. What was she up to?

I approached the great door and dared to peer inside. Ahead of me was a long vault with huge arches on either side. Behind thick steel bars there were silhouettes of sleeping dragons, all snoring loudly.

'Hello?' I said, far too quietly, for I was nervous of waking the enormous scaly beasts. There was no answer. Steeling myself, I closed the vault door and began tiptoeing past the cages. Elsa, Ghastly, Merle, Zedrick; their names were scrawled around the top of the arches in chalk. The last cage was empty, the door hanging open, the lock smashed. 'Slappy' was the name scribbled above. And then around the corner appeared the head of the biggest creature I'd ever seen in my life—

'Get back, Delilah!'

Delilah looked at me and grinned.

'Back, you daft beast!'

A Dragon Keeper appeared with a long stick and jabbed Delilah back into her cage. He turned to see me standing there.

'Who's that?' he shouted.

He pushed his thick goggles up into his hair and strode purposefully down the corridor towards me. I recognised him immediately. He was that burly young man in the corner of the Black Coat Inn, listening quietly as Kiddy told his tale. He looked me up and down suspiciously.

'Jack Joliffe, isn't it? Jellybean's niece?'

'That's me.'

He grunted, his suspicion turning to curiosity.

'So you're the crafty one who bottled that runaway stagecoach in the hall? The most talented young keeper since Isabella Royle, eh?'

If I hadn't been (which obviously *I* wasn't – thanks Richard), I had a feeling he would have told me to get lost. Instead he seemed grudgingly impressed.

'Ray Sunlight. Under-Keeper. How do.' Wiping his fingers on his filthy blue keeper's coat, he thrust out a big meaty hand.

'How do,' I replied, trying to ignore his bone-crushing grip.

'How long you bin here?' he said, glancing back at the door.

'I've only just come in.'

'Oh aye.' I suspected he'd heard Snowdrop Scott poking around.

'Cribbage didn' see you, then?'

'No.'

'Solomon Knock?'

Again I shook my head.

'Hmm. Everyone's suddenly become very interested in dragons. I suppose old Knock's left a few of these for you to trip over an' all.'

Ray Sunlight pointed towards the seeing stone beside the base of the pillar.

'I'd shove 'em where the sun don't shine if I had half a chance,' said Ray, pretending to kick it. 'Only joking, Mr Knock. So you've come to look at Slappy's empty cage as well?'

I was standing right in front of it so he must have guessed I was curious. Ray rattled the bent lock.

'Slappy's a clever little dragon, but she ain't clever enough to do that. So it's got to be a Dragon Keeper that's let her out, hasn't it? Accidentally on purpose, of course.'

'Was it?'

Ray laughed. I had a feeling this was not the right question.

Or maybe I'd asked it in the wrong way.

'Would you deliberately let a ghost out of your vault, Jack?'

'I've had a few accidents.'

'Yeah well, we're not that careless in here. Can't be with dragons. Too blinkin' dangerous.'

We both stared at the empty cage again.

'I'm not that careless either, by the way,' I replied.

'I'm sure you're not. Only kidding,' he smiled.

I liked Ray Sunlight, I don't know why. He seemed like a cheerful, no-nonsense kind of man.

'So why do you think someone let her out? Is there something special about Slappy?' I asked.

Ray's smile hardened. Again I sensed I'd touched a raw nerve. Perhaps this was some kind of Dragon Keepers' secret. Perhaps this is what Snowdrop Scott wanted to know.

'I don't mind if you don't want to tell me,' I said quickly. 'Actually I came down here to ask you about another dragon.'

'Oh yeah?'

'His name's Wellenstorm. I don't think he's in the vault.'

'He most certainly is not. What d'you want to know about Wellenstorm for?'

'Oh I'm just curious. I looked in the library and I couldn't find anything there. I heard a story about him.'

My innocence seemed to do the trick.

'Would that be in The Black Coat Inn, by any chance?'

I shrugged. What could I say?

'Thought I recognised you. Old Kiddy telling his tale tickled your curiosity did it? You want to know if Wellenstorm's really as horrible as he sounds?'

For some reason Ray Sunlight was making me feel awkward.

I remembered he hadn't been so keen to hear the story.

'Is he?'

'You've got some nerve coming in here asking all these questions, Jack Joliffe,' he smiled. 'We never discuss "dragons" with other keepers, for good reason. I guess no one's told you that yet, have they?'

Obviously not. Ray Sunlight looked at me like he was deciding something.

'But you've got some talent, Jack, I'll give you that. Unlike the rest of 'em.'

Checking the corridor again, Ray indicated that I should follow him. Down the iron gangway we went to the floor below. I sensed this was a rare privilege. Why all the secrecy? Down here there were even larger dragons, great coal-black monsters lounging in their cages. The floor, the ceiling and the walls were all scorched and blackened as if the whole place had caught fire, which I suppose it did – probably every week. Ray unlocked a thick steel door and ushered me into the scruffy keepers' den. It was rather like being in the cabin of some old ship. The walls and ceiling bowed inwards and there were tatty old sofas and a bin overflowing with tea bags. Dog-eared copies of 'Flame and Stink: The International Dragon Keepers' Gazette' lay scattered about on the ragged carpet.

'So you know nothing about dragons at all?'

I shook my head.

Ray walked across the room and pulled aside a curtain to reveal what at first looked like a large pool table in a dark room beyond. Stepping closer, I saw that the edges of the table were made of marble, and the smooth black surface wasn't solid at all… it was a long, shallow pool of water.

'The thing about working with dragons is that everything catches fire eventually,' Ray said, unlocking a cupboard and bringing out a small bottle of ink. 'Which is why we don't have much use for books down here.'

He squeezed a little ink out of the bottle, then very carefully let five drops fall onto the surface of the water.

'Dragon's blood,' he winked.

Now I'm not saying it wasn't, but it must have been something special, because the instant the drops hit the water they ballooned into amazing shapes – creatures, islands, the sea maybe – before resolving into an ancient map, covered in beautiful pictures and careful gold lettering.

'This is the dragon map of Albion,' said Ray Sunlight proudly. 'Not many people get to see this, though plenty want to, especially now.' I had already gathered as much. 'It shows where all two hundred and seventy-one dragons of Albion are at this moment, and how they're related to each other. 'Cos every dragon is related to every other dragon. Most are hibernating in deep caves or sleeping high up on mountains,' said Ray, pointing out dragons in various remote places. 'And that's fine. So long as they don't disturb anyone, we leave 'em be. It's only when they start causing trouble that we have to bring 'em in here. There's your fella.'

Ray walked around to the other side and pointed to the picture of a large grey beast on its own near the top of the map. Even in this strange water picture, Wellenstorm looked decidedly horrible.

'Wellenstorm's the last lone bull dragon in Albion, and one of the biggest there is.'

'Why are all the Dragon Keepers so interested in him?'

Ray Sunlight folded his arms across his chest and leant back against the wall.

'It's like this, Jack. Long ago, and I mean *long* ago, in the time before kings, when Albion was nothing but forest, bog and mountains, dragons and fairies fought each other to control it. Fairies used their magic, dragons their brute force, and the pendulum swung back and forth between them. Then the people came. The fairies retreated deeper into the woods, made their secret enchanted places, and one by one the ancient dragons were driven out, captured or killed. Wellenstorm was forced further and further north, eventually settling on a barren island way off the coast of Scotland. And he's never forgiven us for forcing him off the land he considers his own by right. So every few years he gathers a crew of reprobates and leads them down to eat a few sheep and burn a few crofts. But it's the royals he's really after. They're his real enemy, because it was those ancient kings that hunted him out in the first place. And somehow he senses them; he knows when they're close. The last time he tried something was about twelve years ago. I don't know what he was up to, but someone spotted him crawling about in a forest, and straightaway every Dragon Keeper in the palace was sent out to trap him. And that's where old Kiddy found him, hiding in that gulley. You heard what happened next.'

'So you were there, Ray?'

He shook his head.

'No. I'd gone on ahead. If I had been, though, things might have turned out differently.' He paused, his mind far away. 'The landlord was my brother, you see.'

'Your brother?' He looked at me and nodded. I was shocked.

'Ned had been a keeper here, like me. Assistant Keeper of Werewolves. But he had an accident. The werewolves broke out of their vault, killed their keeper, and Nate was lucky to get away with a lump torn out of his back and one leg missing. You can't do this kind of work with injuries like that. So he was retired out of the service. Valentine Oak was very understanding, gave him that little pub at the edge of the forest. The "Never Say Die" it was called.' Ray smiled at the name. 'Him and Molly, and the baby not six months old.'

Ray stared into the watery surface of the map. I sensed he hadn't intended to tell me about this at all, but now that he had it was all a little painful. In my mind, I too could see that massive blast of flame pouring from Wellenstorm's mouth, scorching the earth, turning the trees into candles and the pub into a bonfire... and it was only then I realised the question I wanted to ask... perhaps the real reason why I'd come down here.

'Are you sure they all died?'

Ray Sunlight looked across the map at me, his face mysterious in the watery reflections.

"Course they did. What d'you mean by that?'

I didn't know exactly. The idea had just tumbled out for the first time... I was thinking about... I don't know what I was thinking about.

'They died, Jack, sure as I'm standing here. What kind of question's that?'

I shrugged, feeling awkward.

'I dunno, it just seems like...'

'A tall story, eh? Well yes, Kiddy's full of tall stories, most of which haven't a grain of truth in 'em. But that one's true, Jack. Foxglass was there, and he confirmed it – even Thad Lancaster playing the hero and going back inside for the baby. That's what happened. All three of 'em perished in that blaze. And for what, eh?'

Ray Sunlight suddenly thumped his heavy fist down on the

edge of the table, making everything jump, including me. The map dissolved, the ink swirling and slipping as the water sloshed about. We stood in awkward silence.

'That family's full of rotten apples, Jack. And Thad Lancaster's the worst of the lot. One day, someone's going to catch up with him...' Ray's eyes glittered in the light of the pool. Was he suggesting what I thought he was suggesting?

'So now you know all about Wellenstorm,' he said, changing the subject. 'We had the brute, but he escaped. He's spent twelve years biding his time up in those northern roosts, waiting for another opportunity to come along. And now maybe it has.'

'You mean the presentation – on Tuesday?'

'Not necessarily. There's always been presentations, and Wellenstorm's never turned up yet. Maybe it's too obvious. That old dragon hasn't survived this long by accident.'

I wondered what he meant. If it wasn't Richard's presentation, then...

'Slappy,' he said, nodding at the ceiling.

'Slappy?' I stared at him in amazement. 'What's Slappy got to do with it?'

Ray heaved his great shoulders and whistled.

'That's what everyone wants to know, isn't it? We've got a hundred dragons down here. Why let out that particular dragon, eh? It can't be an accident. You must've realised what rumours are like in this place.'

I had, as it happens. Ray looked down into the map. The water had stilled, the strange inky pictures visible once more.

'There she is. Cute, ain't she?'

Ray's filthy finger pointed to a small green dragon close to the right-hand border. If ever a dragon could be said to look cheerful, almost cuddly, it was Slappy. Slappy was grinning like it was her first school photo and she was showing off her new teeth.

'Slappy was put in here because she liked monkeying around. Chasing planes down runways, riding on the top of night trains, digging up tube stations. She needed to calm down a bit. Now being a mole dragon, she didn't try and fly up towards the first patch of light she could see and get stuck, like every other dragon would. Slappy followed her instinct and went down; down into the labyrinth of tunnels under the palace. That's where she sniffed out an exit, probably hidden behind an enchantment long forgotten about. Oh, the palace may be dragonproof from the outside, but from the inside?' Ray shook his head. 'The Dragon Vault was never designed to keep mole dragons. Slappy was the first we'd ever had in here, and look what happened.'

I stared at the grinning little mole dragon.

'Where d'you think she's gone?'

Ray's finger traced up to a cave in a remote northern forest, and a most respectable-looking pair of dragons named Fungus and Magda.

'Back home to see her folks. Young dragons get homesick, y'know. And here's the thing about mole dragons. In the dragon world they are the lowest of the low. The smallest, weakest, the most polite; which is why they've always looked to someone much bigger and more dangerous for protection.' Ray nodded at Wellenstorm, lurking out on his rock. 'He patrols those northern forests. They owe him allegiance. If Wellenstorm wants to know something, they'll tell him, and if they don't, he'll eat them. I'd say those little mole dragons are quite terrified of Wellenstorm. With good reason.'

I was beginning to understand what Ray meant.

'So you think that whatever hidden tunnel Slappy used to get out, Wellenstorm could use to break in?'

'Exactly,' Ray nodded. 'And if he does come, he won't be alone. There's plenty of nasty characters up there who'd fancy a fight. We know most of 'em.'

I looked at all the other dragons of the north, roosting on mountain tops and sleeping in caves. I couldn't understand how Ray could be so calm about all of this.

'But Ray, shouldn't you tell someone–'

'Oh we don't need to, Jack. William Foxglass used to be the Head Dragon Keeper; he don't need reminding. He's already been up there himself to see what's going on. And he's had words with Thad Lancaster about it, though a fat lot of good that did.'

'What d'you mean?'

'Think about it. Would Thad Lancaster really mind that much if this place was ripped apart by dragons? And what if Wellenstorm just so happened to kill Richard and the twins as well... Well then, who'd be next in line to the throne? I pity that poor Prince. With family like that, who needs enemies, eh?'

'Thad wouldn't do that. He couldn't.'

'Wouldn't he?' Ray Sunlight watched me closely. 'Do you know him, Jack? Could you trust him?'

I said nothing. Ray held open the door and out we went in silence. My head was spinning. I'd come down to the Dragon Vault expecting to be frightened, but I never imagined this.

'So now you know why everyone's so interested in who let Slappy out,' said Ray as we walked up past the great black dragons snoring in their cells. 'There's a traitor, Jack, right here in the palace. Could even be someone you know. Someone we all know.'

'A follower of Isabella Royle?' I asked, wondering if this had anything to do with everything else I'd been told about.

Ray Sunlight smiled for the first time in a while.

'You've heard the rumours then. Some people around here are obsessed with Isabella Royle. Whatever skulduggery is going on, blame it on Isabella Royle. Yes, she still has plenty of supporters, but here's a fact: no fairy would ever help a dragon, and no dragon would ever help a fairy either. That old quarrel of theirs has not gone away, Jack, and I doubt it ever will. Whoever let Slappy out is either very stupid, or deliberately inviting chaos into the heart of the palace for some reason best known to themselves.'

We walked past Slappy's empty cell and I stared at the smashed lock. Why would someone do that? I couldn't help thinking it was all to do with Richard somehow. I imagined him hobbling around some dark cloister and a great black dragon suddenly bursting out of the ground…

'When do you think he'll come?'

'Very soon, I guess. But we'll get a warning. Foxglass has left a spy up there to watch what's going on. If Wellenstorm's on the warpath, we'll know about it.'

That was a relief. At least William Foxglass could be trusted. We reached the door of the vault and Ray lifted the heavy latch and swung it open.

'And if Wellenstorm does break into the palace… can you keep Richard safe?'

Ray smiled. I guess he could see how worried I was.

'I guarantee we'll give it our best shot, Jack,' he said, resting a friendly hand on my shoulder. 'Fighting dragons is what we keepers live for. And to tell you the truth, if for some reason Wellenstorm and his gang *don't* turn up, I might almost be disappointed,' Ray winked. 'I've a score to settle with that old monster.'

ᨉᨏ 49 ᨏᨉ
Red-Handed

BY THE TIME I HAD trudged back up to my room it was dark.
Tom Bootle had left a fire roaring in the grate, a couple of
crumpets next to the toasting fork, a pot of tea and a pile
of those most excellent macaroons – but he was still nowhere
to be seen. I wasn't surprised. For all his tricks and jokes, Tom
Bootle was a strange, complicated creature, so proud of who he'd
once been and yet so confused and terrified of his other master,
whoever that was.

I too was feeling a little confused. Perhaps more than a little.
There was so much I'd just discovered – about Wellenstorm,
Asphodel, my deceiving ancestors, the feuding royal family... in

a strange way it still all seemed so unreal. I half-wondered if I'd wake up tomorrow and find myself back in my old bedroom, listening to Oscar and Phil making breakfast downstairs in a life I seemed to have lived about a million years ago. What *was* I doing here? For the first time, I began to wonder...

I watched the embers for a while, then stood at the window feeling lonelier than ever. Lights were on across the palace, and there was that steady plip, plip, plip of melting snow dripping into the gutter outside. Winter was loosening its grip at last; that much was certain, even if nothing else was. And then I noticed something else had changed. At the top of the narrow tower on the other side of the Keepers' Courtyard I saw a light burning in William Foxglass's room. I was glad Ray Sunlight had told me where he'd been, because I was starting to think he was deliberately avoiding me. The only time we'd met since that first morning was at Buckingham Palace, and as I was being Prince Richard at the time I could hardly say hello, though I'd have liked to. I stared at the light twinkling in the window. I suddenly realised how much I wanted to talk to William Foxglass. I trusted him. If anyone could tell me the truth about all these secrets, surely he could...

'Hello?'

I stood shivering on the dark stone steps at the top of the narrow tower. I knocked again.

'Mr Foxglass?'

I was about to knock again when I realised the door was ajar. I pushed it and it swung open, revealing the dark room beyond. That was odd. The light had been on a moment ago.

'Mr Foxglass?'

No answer. Had he gone out? That open door puzzled me. I walked in. William Foxglass's room was narrower than mine, with little windows peeping out like portholes onto the forest of chimneys. There didn't seem to be a bed, only a hammock hanging in the corner, and I wouldn't have been surprised if William Foxglass had slept in it fully clothed too, such was the state of the place. He obviously didn't mind a bit of discomfort, despite his lofty position in the palace as Black Zodiac. There was that famous black coat, magnificent and embroidered, hanging from a thick hook driven into the wall. Beside it hung a gun, and a satchel, and a hat. On the table was a collection of odd socks and a pair of darning needles; had he been mending them? The idea was almost as mysterious as the smell of his room, which was sweet and oily, sort of mechanical…

'Hello?'

In the small study beyond I could see the floor was strewn with papers, cupboards thrown open, drawers pulled out…

'I can't think there's anything to be gained from this, Your Highness,' said a voice from inside. 'William's not hiding anything from you. Why should he be?'

There was a sudden rustle and the door behind me closed shut.

'Miss Joliffe.'

I turned around and gasped. Thad Lancaster! He swaggered towards me in his arrogant, confident way.

'What are you doing here?' he demanded.

If I'd been feeling braver, I might have asked what *he* was doing here, but–

'I believe there's a curfew after dark. Shouldn't you be in your rooms?'

'Who is it?' said the voice from the study beyond.

'It's your brilliant new Keeper of Ghosts,' Thad Lancaster replied, looking at me with a smirk on his face.

'Is it?' Valentine Oak shuffled out into the doorway, leaning on his staff. He stared at me a moment, bewildered. 'Were you looking for Mr Foxglass?'

I nodded.

'Why?'

Thad Lancaster stared at me hard. I felt my cheeks redden.

'No reason really–'

'You must have a reason, Miss Joliffe. Perhaps you and Mr Foxglass have something to talk about.' Thad Lancaster stepped closer. 'Do you come up here often? Have little chats about what's going on in the palace?'

'No–'

'Discuss the royal family perhaps?'

'No.'

Thad Lancaster was looking at me strangely. Was he starting to suspect?

'I've hardly seen him, Your Highness. I just saw the light on and–'

'He's not here, and neither should you be,' he barked. 'You should go, Miss Joliffe, before you find yourself in deeper trouble than you already are.'

'What have I done?'

'That remains to be seen. But until I find out who released that dragon, every keeper is under suspicion – especially someone like yourself. D'you understand?'

Not really, but I nodded. Thad Lancaster escorted me to the door. I glanced back at Valentine Oak standing in that sea of papers. I couldn't work out his expression. His eyes were set so deep they were like black holes in his head.

'Oh, and I wouldn't mention this to anyone if I were you,' Thad Lancaster added as I stepped out onto the landing. 'This is a private matter between the Master, Black Zodiac and myself. If you so much as breathe a word of it to anyone, I guarantee I'll be the first to know. Which would be a shame for someone as apparently gifted as yourself.'

With that final threat he waved me away, and I felt his eyes burn into me as I hurried down the steps. What were they looking for?

Even asking that question was going to land me in more trouble, I knew it. Thad Lancaster meant what he said...

Out in the Keepers' Courtyard I dared to glance up at the window again. Thad Lancaster's silhouette was still there, watching me... and then I realised he wasn't the only one. In the cloister on the far side I spotted a figure in a black cloak hovering behind the Isabella tree. Who was that? Whoever it was must have seen me come down from William Foxglass's room. Maybe they even watched me go up there...

Then I heard a familiar sound. Bats. Screaming bats – Enid Cribbage silently appeared in an archway in her tall hat and cape.

'CURFEW!'

Immediately the cloaked figure turned and hurried away. Cribbage made some strange whistle and the bats fizzed out of her box then shot off in pursuit. The cloaked figure ducked through a doorway and raced away up some steps... And then the Keeper of the Night spotted me too... She gave me a particularly crazy stare.

'CURFEW!' she shrieked again, banging her staff on the stone. Its snakes' eyes lit up and caught me in their beam, and before I knew it her bats looped about and began screaming towards me in a black cloud. Terrified, I raced as hard as I could around the cloister, just managing to reach my staircase and slam the door in their furious faces...

'CURFEW!'

Instantly the great key turned... She'd locked me in! Enid Cribbage stood outside, chirruping weirdly. I panted hard. Well at least I was safe in here. But who was that on the far side of the courtyard? I'd glimpsed the shadow for barely a second, but there was something familiar about it...

∼∽ 50 ∽∼
Return Visit

I WAS NOW EVEN MORE convinced that there was all sorts of
skullduggery going on in this palace. Thad Lancaster was
obviously up to no good; and he hated me too, for some
reason, and now that I'd caught him ransacking Mr Foxglass's
rooms he probably hated me even more. What was he looking
for? Whatever it was, I had a strong feeling that Valentine Oak
didn't want to be in on it; he seemed embarrassed that I'd caught
him… Gratefully closing the door of my room, I dared to look
out the window once more. The light was off. Did that mean
they'd gone? I flopped down into one of Uncle Galahad's flowery
armchairs and took a deep breath. Don't poke around in other

people's business, remember your place – that's what Snowdrop Scott had said… except *she* obviously was, wasn't she?

Things were becoming very complicated. And they were about to get a lot more complicated.

'See?'

'It's there. In the chair.'

Without so much as knocking, a window opened and two familiar figures tumbled down onto the carpet in a giggling heap.

'Oh hullo, Jock,' said Thomas Lancaster, looking up at me and smiling. 'It is *Jock*, isn't it?'

'It's Jack. You know that.'

'Oh yes. Not much of a name for a girl, anyway.'

Victoria smirked prettily, then pushed herself up off the floor, wiping her filthy little hands on my coat.

'It's getting jolly slippery out there. All the snow's melting and turning into mud,' she said, merrily stamping it into the carpet. 'We've brought you a letter from Richard.'

'Oh?'

'He gave it to the royal harbinger in secret. But unfortunately the silly old squirrel lost its balance and fell down a chimney.'

'It was most unfortunate,' Thomas agreed. 'And there was a fire at the bottom. Most unfortunate.'

'So we've brought it instead.'

'Thanks,' I said, suspecting from their smirks that wasn't what had happened at all.

Thomas pulled the scrap of paper from his pocket. I thought he might be about to hand it to me but instead he held it up to read.

'What does he say?' I asked.

'Quite a lot of things,' said Thomas, frowning hard at the writing. 'First, he says he's sorry.'

'For what?'

'For having a party in your vault and… letting all your ghosts out?'

They giggled and I smiled as politely as I could. They had no idea.

'He says that probably got you into a lot of trouble. He's sorry about that.'

'But knowing Richard, not *that* sorry,' added Victoria. "Cos Richard's never *that* sorry about anything.'

'What else does he say?'

'You want to know what else he says?'

'Yes. Can I read it, please?'

Thomas deliberately turned the letter so that I couldn't see it.

'You're not allowed to read letters from the royal family.'

'But he's written it to me!'

'Commoners are not allowed to read private royal letters, they might get ideas,' said Victoria primly. 'That's what Daddy says.'

Thomas read on. I looked at the letter in his chubby little fingers. I wondered what would happen if I snatched it away…

'Now there's someone called… Flower der Loy-is?'

'Oh yes?'

'Flower de Loy-is… you must definitely look something up in the library about Flower der Loy-is–'

'May I see?' I said impatiently.

"Cos he thinks… hang on, there's a something… and then there's another… *something* in… Oh, there's a friendly jabber… wocky, called… Ralph?'

'A friendly jabberwocky called *Ralph*?' giggled Victoria. 'Our brother's gone completely mad!'

This tickled them both immensely. I smiled too.

'Yes it sounds like it. May I read it, please?'

Thomas and Victoria's smiles drifted away. They stared at me.

'What did you say?'

'Richard's gone completely mad, is that what you think?'

'You should be very careful what you say, Commoner,' said Thomas, striding forward and planting his legs wide. 'You're not allowed to say things like that.'

'And you're not even allowed to be here.'

'But that's not half as bad as secretly com-mu-cating with Richard and Lily. Because you have been, haven't you, Jock?'

I felt my cheeks redden.

'I haven't.'

'Liar,' Victoria smirked. 'Liar, liar, pants on fire. Oh that's bad, Jock. Very, *very* bad. I'll bet you've been doing all sorts of terrible mischief ever since you arrived.'

'I haven't–'

'We could have you investigated, y'know. And then you'd probably be guillotined.'

'Or hung, drawn and quartered. Which is much worse.'

Thomas and Victoria Lancaster stood grinning at me. They were very good at this. Why didn't I see it coming?

'Okay,' I said. 'I'm sorry. I don't think Richard's mad at all.'

Thomas nodded. There was an air of triumph about him now.

'*How* sorry are you, Jock?'

'Very sorry.'

'That's not sorry enough.'

'Okay I'm very, very, *very* sorry, now please, could I just read the letter?'

The little monsters turned to each other, then back to me rather stiffly.

'All right. We accept your apology,' said Victoria. 'This time only, mind.'

And with that Thomas screwed up the letter and threw it onto the fire.

'Whoops a daisy.'

I watched it burning there, feeling utterly helpless. That was something really important he wanted to tell me... Somehow I bottled my anger. Hitting the little brat would not have been a good idea.

'Now, Jock, aren't you going to ask us what we're doing here?'

They waited expectantly. I sighed.

'Gosh, Thomas and Victoria, what are you doing here?'

They exchanged grins.

'Tonight we're going to raise merry hell,' smiled Victoria. 'That's what Daddy calls it. We're going to scare the bejeepers out of everyone.'

'Great,' said I. 'Why?'

''Cos it's the last chance before the presentation. Much more annoying if we do it now when everything's being tidied up, rather than afterwards.'

I nodded politely. Of course the twins had their own reasons for everything. They waited expectantly.

'Well? Aren't you going to ask us what we're going to do?' said Victoria.

'So what are you going to do?'

Victoria looked very pleased with herself.

'First,' she said, 'we're going to let out all the monsters and dragons we can find.'

'Then,' said Thomas, 'we're going to set off all the fire alarms and break all the lights with sticks.'

'Then,' said Victoria, 'we're going to set fire to Cribbage and her bats—'

'Because she's evil, and she doesn't like us—'

'And after that we'll go into the stables and let out all the royal beasts—'

'Make them fly away, drive them out, *beat* them—'

'And then we'll go into the kitchens and eat all the cakes we can find, and drink all the vodka we can find—'

'And get really, *really* drunk—'

'And then we're going to be sick all over the stairs!' squealed Victoria. 'But that's all right. Daddy says it's good to be sick if you drink too much vodka—'

'And *then*, we'll... I dunno, probably start another fire,' said Thomas.

'Accidentally on purpose, so the whole palace explodes,' said Victoria.

'And then we'll go back to our room.'

They looked at each other and giggled.

'That sounds like a good plan,' I said, very careful not to laugh or suggest anything at all.

'And if anyone finds out it was us, we'll say it was you that told us do it,' said Thomas proudly.

'Me?'

'You *forced* us to do it,' he said.

'But I'm not forcing you to do anything!'

'You invited us over here and you *made* us do it,' said Victoria smugly.

'But I didn't invite you over here—'

'Yes you did—'

'No I didn't—'

'You secretly invited us over here to drink vodka and sing songs just now—'

'I did not—'

'Yes you did,' said Victoria. 'And then you promised to take us on a tour of this side of the palace, because you know how much we want to see the zoo, and the beasts and the witches and the monsters, but you should've known what happens to people who've been drinking, they get completely out of control.'

'That's what Mama says,' added Thomas.

'Especially when they drink vodka. She says when people drink too much vodka they turn into perfect hooligans. That's what happens to Father, she says, and that's what's going to happen to us too,' said Victoria. 'Only it's not our fault – it's your fault. You should have known better than to give it to us.'

'But I haven't given you any vodka!'

'But you're not going to try and stop us getting it, are you? Even after we've told you. Oh dear me, you're *so* irresponsible!'

I didn't know what to say. Thomas and Victoria smiled, looking for all the world like a pair of cuddly kittens in velvet suits, the sort you might see frolicking in the snow on a Christmas card.

'When are you going to start all this?'

'Now, of course,' said Thomas.

'Yes, now,' agreed Victoria.

Together they marched towards the door. Standing on tiptoes, Thomas just managed to open the latch.

'Please don't set fire to everything,' I said, barely able to believe it.

Victoria turned and smirked.

'It's no good saying that now, Jock. It's too late. See? You're just letting us walk out! You're not even going to chase us!' She put a hand on her hip and wagged her finger at me. 'What a silly person!'

Away they went, rushing down the stairs, giggling and shouting.

Now you might wonder why I didn't try to stop this pair of little maniacs. Why didn't I rush downstairs and warn Sam Yuell and everyone else? I suppose the truth was I didn't believe it. For all their bad attitude, Thomas and Victoria Lancaster were only seven, and a pair of quite small seven-year-olds at that. What could they really do? The door at the bottom of the staircase was locked for a start. Then there was Enid Cribbage prowling about with her bats. I wasn't the twins' nanny. They weren't my problem... were they?

For the next two hours yelps and screams echoed up from the vaults. Torches flashed past the windows, and there were shouts for water and hosepipes...

Okay, so now I was beginning to feel guilty. Had Thomas and Victoria really set fire to the vaults? Beat Enid Cribbage with sticks, pulled the wings off her bats, driven out the royal beasts, maybe even thrashed the dragons? It seemed sort of impossible, but perhaps they had...

~ 51 ~
A Bigger Surprise

MAYBE THE TWINS' night of mayhem was the trigger, I don't know, but from this point in my story everything begins to fall to pieces in a quite spectacular way.

There was one exception. When I opened my eyes and looked out of the window that Sunday morning, I could see patches of clear blue sky beyond the rooftops. It was as if a thick duvet had been pulled away and there was the sun, shining down on the brilliant white snow for the first time since I'd arrived at the palace. There may even have been a bird or two singing, I can't remember. It was definitely one of those mornings when you might start singing. And the palace was still standing, which meant the twins had obviously failed to burn it to the ground. So all that was good… wasn't it?

As I lay stretching and yawning in the centre of the Joliffe four-poster bed, I heard a knock at the door. Tom Bootle, I guessed, armed with a cup of cocoa and stories of the twins' escapades last night. Only it wasn't exactly a knock, more the scratching of a key in the lock…

'I expect Mr Bootle's already here, doing a bit of cleaning. He's the tower servant, and a most interesting fellow. Never a dull moment with Tom Bootle! Well, what do you think? Not bad, eh?'

'Oh! It's very grand,' said a woman's voice, sounding excited. 'Look at them tapestries! It's like being lost in a forest. I suppose they're very old?'

'Indeed they are. These hail from Dandelion Joliffe's time. Joliffes have always been very keen on feathering the Ghost Keeper's nest, so to speak.'

'See, Geraldine, this is how the other half lives,' said a man. 'I bet even that teapot's solid silver. How much did it cost, eh?'

'Sssh, Albert, you can't ask him that!'

'Why not?'

'*He* won't know. It'll be paid for by the King. Everything's paid for by the *King*.' The woman was hissing in a loud whisper.

'I do know, as it happens.'

'There you are, Geraldine. I bet your brother could put a price on everything in this room. Even that golden toad–'

'Albert! Stop asking questions! We don't want all this magnificence to go to Jacky's head.'

'Erm, perhaps you'd like to see the Joliffe bedroom now? The bed itself is at least four hundred years old. The view in the mornings when one sits up and stares out of the window is nothing short of—'

The door opened. All I could do was pull the sheet up to my chin and cringe. In strode a little round man in a green suit, with gold spectacles and oiled hair and a wide grin. No prizes for guessing who this was. Uncle Galahad, Jellybean to his friends. There he was. Back. Behind him came a woman in a hat who looked almost identical, followed by a strong-looking man in a sheepskin jacket, and last of all, the tadpole of the gang, a boy in a neat school uniform. Even from this distance I could tell he was a Joliffe too; the family resemblance was shocking.

'AHH!' he screamed, pointing at me as if I was a poisonous snake.

'Goodness gracious me!' huffed Galahad, his eyes popping from his head.

I drew the counterpane up a little higher. I felt like Goldilocks. The tough-looking man called Albert looked to Galahad for an explanation.

'Galahad, who's this in Jacky's bed?'

'I... I... I don't know.'

'You don't *know*?'

Uncle Galahad stared at me helplessly.

'Tell me, child, what... what is the meaning of this in-in-intrusion?'

'It's some guttersnipe come in from the cold, that's what it is,' snorted Albert, seeing the open window. 'What are you, a palace servant? Chimneysweep? Fancied a kip, did you? That's royal property you're sleeping in!'

'I think it's a girl, Albert,' whispered Geraldine.

'I don't care what it is, I'll soon have the truth out of it,' he said, marching forward with purpose. 'Right you — hop it or else!'

'N-n-n-now wait a m-minute,' gasped Uncle Galahad, sensing

that Albert was about to get violent. 'H-h-hang on a minute.'

Suddenly young Jacky burst into tears.

'It's a girl!' he wailed. 'There's a girl bin sleeping in my bed!'

'I am a girl,' I said. 'And my name's Jack Joliffe. I'm the new Keeper of Ghosts.'

They stared at me in horror.

'You're *what*?' said Geraldine.

I looked at Uncle Galahad standing there mopping his brow.

'I thought you'd got lost in a maze,' I said.

'Lost in a maze?' he repeated.

'Chasing a goat that had stolen your coat–'

'Chasing a goat that had stolen my coat?'

'Or you'd been locked in a cellar–'

'Locked in a cellar?'

'By a man called Dave–'

'By a man called–'

'GALAHAD, ARE YOU A PARROT?!' roared Albert, losing all patience. 'What's she talking about?'

Uncle Galahad looked very flustered.

'Well, bless my soul, I've absolutely no idea.'

'You're my uncle.'

Albert and Geraldine and little Jacky Junior stared from Galahad, to me, and back again. I realised it was no longer me who needed to give an explanation.

'This really is the most outrageous assertion. I... I *have* once been locked in a cellar, and I *do* happen to know a man called Dave–'

'Forget Dave, Galahad! Why does she think you're her uncle?'

Galahad Joliffe dabbed his forehead with his handkerchief and attempted to stiffen his upper lip – in vain.

'Well I'm not sure... that is–'

'But you *are* my uncle,' I insisted. 'You sent money with William Foxglass every year for my guardians to bring me up.'

'Is this true?' asked Geraldine, sensing some terrible wrong had been done. 'How long have you been supporting this girl, Galahad?'

'Twelve years,' I said.

'Twelve years!' barked Albert. 'This is getting better and better! Galahad, what is going on?'

Poor old Galahad. He looked like he wanted to disappear through the wall. Either that or lie down on the floor, wiggle his legs in the air and scream.

'Spit it out, man!'

'Well gosh... I think, erm, someone has made a mistake—'

'Too right they have. There can't be two Jack Joliffes, can there?'

'N-n-no. Quite right. Absolutely, there can't—'

'Unless he's not called Joliffe,' I said.

Everyone turned to look at me angrily.

'What did you say?' asked Albert, advancing with menace.

'If he's your son, then maybe he's called after you, and not his mother? Just a thought,' I added, my voice getting smaller as Albert got closer.

'Jacky prefers his mother's name to my name,' growled Albert, his face now very close to mine. 'And if Jacky prefers to be called "Joliffe", then "Joliffe" is his name.'

'What's your name?' I whispered.

'My name,' he whispered back, 'is Nibbles.'

Albert Nibbles was not a man to be trifled with. I discovered later he'd been a police champion shot-putter, and I had no doubt he could have putted me straight over the palace wall if he fancied.

'I knew it was too good to be true!' wailed little Jacky, angrily stamping his foot on the ground. 'I knew it! I knew it!' He began howling loudly.

'See that, Galahad? Look what you've done now! I'm not having our Jacky's future mucked about with,' said Geraldine, throwing an arm round her son's plump little shoulders. 'There, there, Jackson, Daddy will get to the bottom of this soon enough. This is just some... *imposter*,' she said, nodding sourly in my direction.

'You'd better find this Foxglass fellow, Galahad,' snarled Albert. 'Find him now and we'll have it out straight!'

'That's exactly what I'll do. Right this minute,' nodded Galahad, obviously intent on fleeing the scene. He'd just about made it to the door when the thunder of footsteps on the stairs outside stopped him. 'Ah,' he said, smiling weakly. 'The long arm of the law—'

In burst Ocelot Malodure, Solomon Knock and a pair of guards, all breathless and hot.

'Phasma Argent?'

'Red Tempest?'

'Yellow Panache?'

'Runnymede Pursuivant?'

Ocelot Malodure, Galahad Joliffe and Solomon Knock all bowed to each other like trees, unfurling their hands in a courtly manner. This took some time. Eventually the formalities were over and Ocelot Malodure strode into the centre of the room, planting her eagle-headed staff on the carpet with a bang. She stared at me hiding in the bed. She stared at the family lined up meekly against the wall. She stared at Uncle Galahad, who looked like he might rather have been chasing that goat through a maze after all. The Keeper of Time glared at us all witheringly, as if we were all guilty of some terrible crime.

'Now. Which of you would like to tell me exactly what is going on?'

52

Justice is Served

THE ANSWER WAS, NOBODY. I was marched down to a panelled room behind the library and made to wait while Ocelot Malodure summoned the three most senior keepers to hear my case. Yes, that's what she said, and I realised that this was in fact a courtroom. This made me very nervous. After much coughing and rasping, a procession of elderly keepers shuffled in. They all had large ears and faces as craggy as cliffs, and were introduced as keepers of things I'd never heard of – mermigans, snodbadgers and battleswine, all extinct centuries ago I shouldn't wonder. I won't describe all the doffing and bowing – you can probably imagine how long all that took, and then finally the

Master arrived. Valentine Oak climbed up into the judge's throne at the end of the room and shot me a poisonous glance. Oh dear. He had clearly not forgotten our meeting last night…

The Master banged his gavel and Ocelot Malodure got to her feet. She beckoned me forward and the proceedings began.

'Please tell the court your name,' she said.

I stood in the centre of the room feeling angry and very alone. But I wasn't stupid enough to forget that I was the one deserving sympathy here.

'My name is Jack Joliffe,' I sniffled sadly. 'Not Jackson Joliffe, or Jacky Joliffe. *Jack* Joliffe.'

Ocelot Malodure nodded and began to pace around me like a tiger.

'You were brought into the palace by Black Zodiac?'

'Yes.'

'Why was that?'

'*Why?*'

'Presumably he must have given you a reason?'

I stared at the grim-faced keepers sitting on the bench before me. If I'd been a better actor, now was the moment to have burst into tears and weepily told them the whole sorry story, beginning with the death of my beloved guardians and ending with my narrow escape from Abel Goodnight. I decided against it.

'He said my uncle had gone missing, and he needed me to take his place.'

'So he told you that you were Galahad Joliffe's niece?'

'Yes.'

'And it was Mr Joliffe who'd been supporting you all your life?'

'Yes.'

'Had you ever heard of the Keeper of Ghosts?'

'No.'

'Had your guardians ever mentioned that your name was Joliffe?'

'No.'

'So you had no idea what members of your family have been doing at St James's Palace for the last four hundred years?'

'No. Mr Foxglass told me everything.'

'Mr Foxglass told you everything.'

Ocelot Malodure glanced across at the Master. He shook his head.

'Did any of this surprise you, Miss Joliffe?'

I shrugged defiantly.

'Maybe. A bit.'

On it went. The three ancient keepers flapped their ears and grunted from time to time, and after about ten minutes they decided I was guilty. Guilty of being a girl called Jack, who'd been brought into the palace to take over the post of Royal Keeper of Ghosts when her uncle disappeared, which as anyone who's been paying even the tiniest bit of attention to this story will know, is exactly what I am. In other words, I was found guilty of being myself!

'The trouble is, young lady, you're clearly not the Jack Joliffe we want,' said Ocelot Malodure, peering at me over her spectacles.

I looked across at that little round tadpole sitting sandwiched between his parents. I had to admit it, young Jacky was a Joliffe all the way to his webbed toes.

'But how could Mr Foxglass make such a stupid mistake? Wasn't it obvious I wasn't the right person?'

Ocelot Malodure raised her eyebrows and consulted one of her many watches.

'Unfortunately Black Zodiac is not here to answer that question,' she said. 'And until he returns to explain this extraordinary state of affairs…'

'YOU SHOULDN'T BE HERE!' screeched the first ancient keeper suddenly, so loud he made me jump.

'You should never have been let into St James's Palace!' agreed the second, his eyes popping from his head.

'You are not one of us!' they all cried together in their high squawking voices.

I looked across at the three ancient keepers sitting in a line. They stared back at me without blinking, like a line of angry seagulls.

'Then you have to let me go,' I said boldly. 'You can't just keep me here against my will. I demand–'

The Master's gavel crashed down.

'Order in the court!' he croaked. 'The accused shall make no demands!'

Valentine Oak beckoned the three elderly keepers over. There was much nodding and hissing behind hands. I was angry now. Not with them, so much as with William Foxglass. I'd trusted him! How had he made such a stupid mistake? Hadn't he ever guessed I was the wrong person?

Their whisperings over, the keepers returned to their seats on the bench. The Master coughed loudly.

'Miss Joliffe, it is the opinion of this court that you are an innocent in all this,' he rasped. 'Nevertheless, we are all agreed that you're to be locked up in the dungeons.'

He might as well have punched me in the stomach.

'The dungeons! Why?'

'We cannot let this scandal get out so close to the presentation,' crowed one of the ancient keepers. Then they all offered their opinions.

'They'll think us complete nincompoops–'

'To award the post to a total stranger—'

'Just the excuse Chitt needs to take over the palace—'

'Not to mention the Duke of Lancaster—'

'Lock her up for a few years! Pretend it never happened—'

'She'll be forgotten about soon enough.'

They all waggled their ears and nodded their heads in agreement.

'But that's not fair!' I cried.

'Let's just wait until William Foxglass returns from wherever he's got to, and Tuesday has come and gone, and then we can *really* decide what's to be done with you, Jack,' said Ocelot Malodure. At least she was trying to be nice about it. She certainly seemed a lot less angry with me now that I wasn't a keeper after all.

'Until then, I'm afraid...'

'Take the prisoner down!'

Valentine Oak cracked his gavel and stared at me sourly. I stared sourly back. I had a good mind to blurt out that I'd found him ransacking William Foxglass's rooms... Luckily I didn't. I think that might have made my situation a whole lot worse.

'Nothing wrong with doing a bit of bird,' grinned Solomon Knock in his lizardy way as he marched me out of the courtroom. 'Happens to us all from time to time. I find it's a good place to have a bit of a think, a dungeon.'

Off we went, down one passage after another, past the xylobirds, yahoos, zeberdees and zooks, until we reached the great black dungeon door, bristling with ancient locks. It was only when it clanged shut behind me that I realised there was no escape from this. Here I was, quietly shoved out of the way for however long they felt like it... And how did *I* feel about it? How would you feel about it? Swapping Uncle Galahad's cosy rooms for a cell with straw on the floor and a tiny, handkerchief-sized window miles up the greasy black wall? But after crying a bit and generally feeling sorry for myself, I realised the bitter truth: no matter how hard I'd tried, I wasn't ever supposed to have been the Royal Keeper of Ghosts; and to be told that for certain… it was quite a relief in a way. I wasn't going to have to pretend any more.

'Oo-er, someone's in trouble.'

Guess who. Archie Queach leant against my cell door, blowing bubblegum.

'I always thought you weren't right. I can smell a bad un' a mile off.'

'That makes two of us.'

Archie's bubble popped. He grinned gormlessly.

'So, what are you then? Some sort of freak Foxglass brought in by accident?'

'That's right, Archie. Which is why I fitted in so perfectly.'

'Ha ha.'

'Are you allowed down here?'

Archie rattled the keys.

'I've been promoted. Jailus Mungus now. You want anything, you're going to have to be nice to me.'

From that grin I suspected Archie Queach was telling the truth.

'I suppose you did something to impress them?'

'I didn't have to do anything, Joliffe. The chaos upstairs means everyone's been moved around and I was considered most suitable for the post.'

Oh. That was bad news indeed. Archie Queach had climbed to the lofty first rung of the ladder and he wasn't going to waste any opportunity to kick all those beneath him. Which was me.

'What did the twins do?' I asked innocently.

It turned out, what didn't they do. They opened every vault they could, they beat the royal beasts, set fire to the stables, bit the bats, covered Fleur de Lys in flour and ketchup, then drank all the whisky and brandy and vodka they could find, and then did something unspeakable on the stairs–

'Which I don't have to clear up,' smiled Archie smugly. 'I have far more important things to worry about now. Like who's going where in my jail. You might have a bit of company later, Joliffe.'

'That'll be an improvement.'

'You wish. Your mammy ever tell you any stories about nursery bogeys to keep you on your best behaviour?'

I shook my head.

'Father Flog, Cankobooby, Auld Scratty?'

'Never heard of them.'

'Cutty Dyer, Jenny Greenteeth, Mr Grindylow?'

'I suppose he's your best friend.'

'Oh no, Joliffe. Though he might become yours.'

There was something about Archie Queach's supercilious grin that I didn't like. (But I like that word. Richard later told me it describes Archie perfectly.)

'The Keeper of Nursery Bogeys left her vault open and the twins have let out every single one. Most have scarpered, but there are still a few really nasty bogeys hiding in cellars and cupboards. They'll all be caught and brought down here soon enough. It's going to get ever so crowded. I think some of you might have to share.'

I stared at him hard.

'You're not putting any nursery bogey in here with me, Archie.'

'That all depends, doesn't it? Jailus Mungus can allocate prisoners any cell he deems appropriate.'

'Mr Foxglass will hear of it,' I grumbled.

Archie flicked his hair and rattled his keys.

'Hmm. Where exactly is Black Zodiac, I wonder? I can't be seen to have favourites, Jack. I have a job to do. Just like you did – before they discovered you were never supposed to be here at all.'

Archie smirked at me through the bars. Oh, he was so enjoying this. Power.

'You dare put any nursery bogey in here with me, Archie Queach. You dare.'

With a swagger in his step, Archie walked away down the corridor, swinging his keys loudly. And the door slammed shut.

53
Lowest Ebb

I 'D **LIKE TO SAY** I could ignore Archie Queach's taunting, but it was hard. Only two days ago I had been at the very top of the palace – okay, yes, by accident – and now here I was down at the very bottom, also by accident. Perhaps the wheel would turn and somehow, *somehow*, my world might be reversed again…

I lay down on the short hard bed and watched the tiny square of blue in the window turn to black. Night came. Despite everything, I closed my eyes and soon fell into dreaming. It was that same old dream again. I was caught up in that burning forest and soon enough there was a pack of wolves at my heels, following me as I raced this way and that, hunting for a way out. And then came the clearing, just as it always did, and the wolves howled as we left the avenues of flames. I searched desperately for patches of blue sky beyond the smoke, knowing that's where I'd find an escape, just as I always did... only the flames were getting closer now, really close... and then at last that dark shadow came down out of the sky... my heart leapt as I knew I'd be saved... But this time there was something different about it... the wolves sensed it first; they began growling and snarling, huddling around me. Down it came, down, down, slowly blotting out the smoke, and somehow I realised this wasn't a friendly shadow; this time it was something else... The wolves were going mad now, snapping and leaping up to bite the black shape that had filled the whole sky, and when I reached up to touch it, fire stung my fingers and suddenly I felt myself falling away...

I sat bolt upright, sweating. What had happened? Why wasn't I rescued? I couldn't understand...

At that moment I heard a giggle.

'Who's that?'

My heart was thumping. I pulled the blanket up around me and listened. It seemed to be right behind me, like someone whispering...

'What if the carriage doesn't stop?'

'Oh it will. Just as before.'

'And that's when he'll do it?'

'Aye. The confusion shall conceal the deed. The child is so sick now it'll be over in a moment.'

I stared at the black wall, my heart thumping in my head.

'And what then?'

'The stage is set, the lights dimmed, we must all be ready to play whatever part is required of us. This time the oliphant shall not succeed.'

The voices grew fainter. I pressed my ear to the wall. They'd gone. You can be certain I knew what those words meant...

54

News from Elsewhere

NIGHT FINISHED AND morning arrived, and still no sign of the nursery bogeys Archie Queach had promised. 'They must be very difficult to catch, these nursery bogeys,' I said, as Archie loitered outside the cell. He was doing a lot of loitering was Archie, not wasting a single opportunity to gloat.

'Ooh you are impatient, Joliffe! Don't you worry. It's going to be a very busy day.'

Archie idly swung his keys back and forth. Perhaps now was the time to frighten him.

'I heard voices down here last night.'

'Did you now.'

'They were coming from the other side of the wall. Two nursery bogeys. They said they were planning to eat you.'

For a second Archie's sneer turned to panic, then he remembered to sneer again.

'Nice try, Joliffe.'

'But there was definitely someone there, I heard them. Who could that have been?'

Archie Queach sighed like he could hardly be bothered to explain.

'Unlike you, Joliffe, I happen to know that it's quite normal for conversations held in one part of the palace to end up in others. In my former role as Under-Keeper of the Backstairs I would often hear unknown voices gossiping in the bricks and stones. I expect you found it a bit frightening, but then you've obviously got a vivid imagination. Phasma Argent? Per-lease.'

'So there's no vaults or tunnels anywhere near here?'

'No,' said Archie, smiling his superior smile. 'The only vault rumoured to be near here contains the last behemoth, which even you have probably heard of. Not only is it the largest creature in Albion, it also has a permanent enchantment over it, so no one knows where it is. Perhaps the palace has swallowed it up. *I* have certainly never found it, and I think *I* would've done by now, don't you?'

'Probably.'

'Oh, I almost forgot.' Archie pulled an envelope out of his pocket. 'I've been instructed to give you this. Can't think why.' He studied the writing, then casually flicked the envelope through the bars. 'From one of your new royal chums, I expect,' he said, attempting not to seem too interested.

'Looks like it,' I replied, picking the envelope off the dirty floor.

Archie tried to think of something unpleasant to say. 'Well,' was all he could manage. Away he went.

Inside were two letters. Lily's first.

Dear Jack,

We've just heard. Can't believe they've really put you in the dungeons! That's a bit extreme, isn't it? And has Mr Foxglass gone completely mad? Imagine getting the wrong Jack Joliffe! I wouldn't be surprised if even he gets in serious trouble now. Luckily no one knows our other secret, because no offence, Jack, but if you're not the Keeper of Ghosts, who are you?

And Thomas and Victoria. Wow. I expect you've heard the full story, because they've refused to tell us much. The Queen is incredibly angry. The King thinks it's hilarious. Uncle Thad is sort of angry, but secretly he thinks it's hilarious too. Can you imagine if they actually ruled this place? It would be total anarchy!

I'm sorry to say poor Cuz seems to have had a relapse since coming back, just as we (and he) predicted. So someone must know you've swapped. But at least if you're down there, you're safe. Anyway, everyone's really worried about Tuesday now. Last night the Queen tried to talk the King out of the whole thing, but you know what he's like. Poor, poor Cuz. He really looks half dead.

Write if you can.

Lily xxx

P.S. Hope this gets to you. We had to seriously bribe Archie Queach to take it.

Now Richard's letter, scribbled on the back.

Dear Jack,

Lily insisted on writing to you, because she feels sorry for you as you're in the dungeon. As it happens, I might as well be in a dungeon too. Why? Here's why:

A. I told you that if I came back I'd probably die. Now I probably will. Thanks a lot.

B. You're not even Keeper of Ghosts. Brilliant. So I'll never be able to avoid becoming King.

C. Because of your Greensleeves walk, I'm forced to practise for an extra two hours every day, just so I can repeat what you did at the Jackernapes final on Tuesday. And also because of that, everyone now suspects that I'm not really ill at all. I'm just faking it to get out of my presentation.

So thanks a lot, Jack, for being a far better version of me than I could ever be. Why couldn't you have been more useless? All you had to do was stay in bed! If you ever see me again it will be as a ghost. I mean it. That's what's going to happen.

Richard.

I stared at the letter guiltily. Richard was right. This swap might have been all his idea, but I should have been better at being him. And I wasn't surprised that he was being poisoned again, because whoever was behind it obviously wasn't fooled. Perhaps Lily was right; being down here *was* a safer place to be, and it did make it almost impossible for me and Richard to swap again... So was I being protected, or was the poisoner deliberately keeping me out of the way? I sat on my bed in the darkness, weaving these webs in my head. Good place for thinking, a dungeon. Yes it most definitely was...

ᨑ 55 ᨑ
The Bogeyman

'O H I'M SURE you'll get along famously.'

Archie Queach's face split into his best sneering smile as he held open the door. In walked a very tall, very narrow man in a long tweed overcoat that was soaking wet. He had an eye patch and a bushy moustache, and his skin was the colour of mist.

'Mr Grindylow, this is Jack Joliffe,' said Archie Queach, as if introducing us at a party. I don't know if he was expecting us to shake hands, but Mr Grindylow took a long look at me and grunted. His coat pockets trailed to the ground, hiding a pair of enormous hands quite out of scale with the rest of him.

'Enjoy yourselves,' said Archie, clanging the door shut and attaching the keys to his belt. 'Bye, Jack.' He gave me a nasty little wave.

I should say that I wasn't surprised. All morning one nursery bogey after another had been led down and dumped in the cells. What had once been silent and creepy was now filled with shouts and hoots from all these characters whose job it was to frighten small children. Noisiest of all were Father Flog and Mother Flog. Father Flog flogged you for pretty much anything – rocking your chair, picking your nose, not tying your shoelaces. The only reason he wouldn't flog you was if you had been rude, and then he would make you eat a bar of soap. Mother Flog hid in the fridge and boxed your ears with a pair of frying pans. I don't know why. Stealing food, I think. Father Flog and Mother Flog were having an argument about who had flogged the most children. They just would *not* shut up.

'SHUT UP!' bellowed Mr Grindylow. A chorus of approval rang around the jail. The Flogs didn't take a blind bit of notice. Mr Grindylow sat down on the chair. He didn't look particularly monstrous, more like an exhausted traveller soaked in a storm. He smelt of ponds. In fact, slugs and snails were crawling over his coat and there was a white worm wriggling in his ear.

'Bin 'ere long?' he grunted.

I told him.

'What they do you for?'

I didn't exactly tell him.

'Woz the food like?'

I hadn't had any. Mr Grindylow exhaled loudly. He pulled the white worm out of his ear and ate it.

'I'd a' got out if it weren't for one of 'em blinking bats. Flew into me face an' I swallowed it. Ever had bat?'

I hadn't.

'Like leech without blood. Ever had leech?'

What do you think?

'Like slug without salt. Ever had slug?'

Mr Grindylow was sizing me up. I began to wonder if he was thinking of eating me too. He seemed to have eaten just about everything else.

'You don't live in a pond, do you?' he said.

'No.'

'Hmm.'

It turned out Mr Grindylow did. He lived in ponds and sometimes marshes and waited for curious children to come close to the edge. Then he grabbed them and dragged them down to his murky hole and buried them in the mud. He'd been doing it for three hundred years. It was good work, mainly. He lost his eye while sleeping in a muddy creek at low tide and a fisherman had pronged him with a spear. Skewered his eyeball. Pulled it straight out. Apart from that, no real complaints. People thought he ate children but that wasn't true, he said, he only ate their hair, which was the best bit. Skin and bone were too chewy and not that pleasant.

'Everyone says human flesh tastes like chicken, but it doesn't, Jack, it's more like dog. Ever had dog? No? Drowned dog? No? Tail's all right. Ears, a bit leathery. Legs okay–'

'I don't eat dog.'

Mr Grindylow picked a slug off his bald patch and ate it. I could tell he thought I was a lost cause.

'Eat to live or live to eat, I know where I stand on that.'

He looked around the cell, noticing the wet black walls, the tiny window up above.

'Not bad in here, is it?'

I suppose if you lived at the bottom of a pond it probably wasn't bad. He pulled a thin mirror from his coat pocket and reached up... and up... and up (his arms extended somehow) and held it to the window.

'Where are we?' I asked.

Mr Grindylow squinted.

'Hmm. Up there's the Keepers' Courtyard. Hmm. Snow's still melting.'

He then extended his long and bendy arm out through the bars of the cell and down the corridor.

'What's the jailer like?' he asked, still peering into the mirror.

'He's new and doesn't know what he's doing,' I replied. 'And he's very pleased with himself.'

'Hmm.'

Mr Grindylow slipped the mirror back in his coat pocket and chuckled.

'What?'

'Nice head of hair he's got. Black as a raven. Haven't had a nice black one for a good while.'

It took me a moment to realise what this meant.

'Erm… you're going to eat his hair?'

Mr Grindylow grinned, revealing a very sharp set of teeth. Unlike the rest of him, these were in perfect condition.

'Let's wait till tonight. Don't want too much fuss.'

I smiled awkwardly.

'I don't eat hair, much.'

'Hmm. We'll have to kill him anyway so you're welcome to the rest. And then I've got to get meself into the sewer. All this melting is very good news. Lots of lovely water. Ice is no good for pond work.'

Mr Grindylow replaced his gnarly hands in those long deep pockets. For the first time in my life I was relieved my hair was as rough and patchy as it was – a fact he'd almost certainly noticed.

'I suppose you've thought about how you're going to get out?' I asked.

'The key's hanging on a nail in the office down the way.'

'Can you reach it?'

Mr Grindylow grinned.

'Not quite. But you can.' He nodded to the top of the cell door, and kicked an iron rod with his boot. 'See that up there?'

The rod turned. It was loose and could be worked looser. I hadn't noticed, and I don't think Archie Queach had either.

'I'll pop it out and put you through there, no problem. Then we can skedaddle, eh?'

'Erm, okay.'

'Excellent.'

Mr Grindylow farted loudly and stretched, locking his massive hands behind his head.

'I tell you, I'll be glad to be shot of this place, Jack. I've bin in that vault nigh on fifty years – not a proper meal in all that time. The Keeper of Nursery Bogeys, she was never there, ever. Never even saw her. And the company, ohhh dear,' he sighed. 'Nursery bogeys, I tell you. I should've been in with the water beasts. That's where I should've been. I'm not pulling lambs' tails or stealing apples, or turning the milk sour. I'm a *proper* bogeyman, you know. "The Grindylow", that's my name, not *a* Grindylow or *Mister* Grindylow – *the* Grindylow, there's a difference.'

'Well you do look very unpleasant, if that's any consolation.'

'D'you think so?' he said, plucking a slimy green bogey from his nostril and munching it.

'Definitely. You're completely disgusting.'

'Hmm.' The Grindylow burped and then spat out some kind of green snot, which he scraped off the floor and used to clean his ear.

'I wish I looked badder, though. But if I did, I'd never get any of 'em, would I?' He pointed to his long grey face. 'This is how I lure me victims, see. I spy them little children playing close to the water and up I floats, like this, watch...' He closed his eyes then opened them – his pupils had disappeared. He stared ahead with a sad, vacant expression. 'They think I'm a drowned man, but they can't be sure. So they comes closer, and closer, standing and pointing, and I goes... WHUMP!'

'AHH!'

One long arm had sneaked around behind my back and suddenly a massive grey fist snatched the air in front of me so hard I jumped in shock.

'Like that,' the Grindylow smiled again. 'This visage is my trick, see. Makes me seem more pleasant than I actually am.'

That was most definitely the case. The Grindylow was a foul

creature and no mistake.

'What did you say you did again?' He pulled a mouldy pack of cards from his coat and began shuffling them.

'Oh, y'know,' I shrugged. 'I'm not a nursery bogey.'

'No, I can see that. What you in for, then?'

Perhaps the truth was not a good idea. So I said the first thing that came into my head. The first thing I saw, actually.

'I erm, I kill bricks.'

'You kill *bricks*?' The Grindylow seemed impressed, or perhaps confused.

'That's a new one on me. What you do – smash 'em?'

'I just… touch them. They tend to die after that. Then I eat them. Only the inside. The outside is all rough and horrible. Tastes rubbish.'

'Oh yeah?' The Grindylow nodded. I don't think he'd ever heard of such a thing. 'Eaten any good bricks round here?'

'Nah,' I said in my best jailbird chat. 'Palace bricks are no good. Too old and… slimy. Don't taste of anything.'

The Grindylow nodded to that. Whether he believed me I don't know. He finished his shuffling and set the deck of cards on the table.

'Snap?'

ꞈ 56 ꞈ
Archie Takes a Peek

PPARENTLY THE SUN went down and the moon
came up, though when you're in a dungeon it's hard to tell.
Archie Queach made one more round of his jail; he
seemed much less keen on loitering now he had some actual
prisoners to control. And nursery bogeys, I discovered, were
particularly good at spotting a weakness and teasing mercilessly.

'Ooh look at his dainty walk! Don't he walk so dainty?' shouted
Mother Flog.

'Quite the gentleman,' agreed Father Flog.

'Oh but he can't be a day over sixteen!' added Auld Scratty.

'He's covered in pimples, covered in 'em! Oh what a fright!'

shouted Jenny Greenteeth.

'Got a girl you're sweet on, Archie?' shrieked Cutty Dyer.

'Ooh he has! He's blushing!' cackled Mother Flog.

'What's her name, Archie? She covered in pimples too?'

'Ooh she is! She is! Covered in 'em!'

'Imagine them kissing!'

'Oh for mercy! Don't!' Auld Scratty howled with laughter.

'Keep going Archie! Keep going! You just ignore them now!'

I almost felt sorry for him by the time he got to our cell.

'Well, well, look who's enjoying themselves,' Archie sneered, seeing us playing cards.

The Grindylow avoided eye contact with his jailer. He slapped down a card.

'Snap!' I said.

The Grindylow grunted. On we went, ignoring him.

'Who'd have thought you two would be having so much fun,' said Archie. 'It won't last, Jack. No one makes friends with Mr Grindylow.'

The Grindylow winced at that 'mister'.

'Tomorrow morning you'll be *begging* me to let you out of there.'

'You've got a good head of hair, Mr Queach,' said the Grindylow without looking up.

'You think so?' Archie parted the long black curtains away from his cheeks.

'Lovely black hair. Snap!' said the Grindylow. 'I do like black hair. Long black hair.'

'Oh. Thank you,' said Archie with a silly smile. Obviously he had no idea what the Grindylow meant. 'Yes, I should probably have it cut.'

'You don't want to do that. Not in my opinion,' said the

Grindylow. 'Not tonight anyhow.'

'Oh no, not tonight,' said Archie, still playing with it. 'Soon, certainly.'

'You look like a raven, Mr Queach.'

Archie flicked it, enjoying the flattery.

'Hmm,' he said. 'Yes I suppose it *is* very black.'

'What time do you knock off, Mr Queach?'

'In a couple of hours. About midnight.'

'Oh that's good, that's very good,' nodded the Grindylow, still slapping down the cards. 'And you'll leave the keys in the office, as usual?'

'Yes, that's the safest place. Far away from you fiends.'

'Snap! And then you'll be back in the morning, eh?'

'Around seven, yes I will.'

'Oh lovely. I'll be waiting for you then, Mr Queach.'

Archie nodded.

'Indeed you will, Mr Grindylow.'

'Oh yes I will, Mr Queach. I'll be waiting for you around seven tomorrow morning, don't you worry.'

Had Archie Queach been more suspicious he might have interpreted all this differently, but Archie was too puffed up with his position to notice the slyness about the Grindylow.

'Goodnight, fiend.'

'Goodnight, Mr Queach.'

'And goodnight to you too, Jack. Though I don't think it will be,' he tittered.

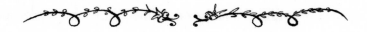

'How are you going to do it?' I asked when Archie had gone.

'Grab him from behind. Out in the corridor's best. I would dash his brains against the ceiling but that would spoil his lovely hair, so I'll just break his neck like this.' His huge gnarly fingers snapped together loudly. 'Twist it right round like an owl, though his head's so full of air I don't think he'll notice.' The Grindylow looked across at me and winked. 'You ever eaten owl?'

'No.'

'Not bad, owl. Bit like stoat. Snap! You ever—'

'I don't eat stoat. Or owl.'

The Grindylow nodded.

'Sorry, I forgot. Stones, isn't it?'

'Bricks.'

✺ 57 ✺
Proper Prisoners

S OMETIME LATER I WAS woken by a great commotion
out in the corridor.

'Widdicums diddicums, what have we here?' clucked
Auld Scratty.

'Phorr! It's the stinky brigade!' shrieked Jenny Greenteeth.
'Smell those socks!'

'Look at all that unbrushed hair!'

'And those unwashed hands!'

'Have they ever seen a toothbrush? Never! Never!'

All the nursery bogeys began rattling their bars and squawking.
I peered out and saw torches fill the corridor as a large and rowdy

group of keepers were led in, all shackled together.

'Oh look at Archie at the front! Don't he look important!'

'Who've you got there, Archie? Proper bad'uns I expect!'

And then I recognised their long blue coats – it was the Dragon Keepers! All of them! At least twenty guards were herding them down to the lower level in chains. The nursery bogeys became so excited they all began to sing.

'Oh, he's... clever old Archie Queach!

He's caught twenty very-smelly-men!

He marched them up to the top of the jail and he marched them down a–'

The nursery bogeys' singing was drowned out by such a barrage of abuse I had to put my hands over my ears. The Dragon Keepers waggled their tongues and made faces, so Auld Scratty bared his bum and farted back, then all the rest of the nursery bogeys joined in, roaring and shrieking all the while.

'Stinky boys get what stinky boys do!'

'Flogging's too good for you, Flog!' shouted the Dragon Keepers.

'Scarecrows going to pris-on, Scarecrows going to pri-son!'

'Kiss this, Scratty!'

On it went.

'Ray!' I shouted, suddenly spotting Ray Sunlight in the thick of it. He turned to look at me, ignoring the guard shoving him along.

'Jack? Is that you?'

'What's going on?'

'Remember what I told you about Wellenstorm? He's on the warpath with every dragon he can find! And now's the moment they decide to jail us for letting out Slappy! Every single one of us – where's the sense in that?'

A guard grabbed Ray's head and shoved him through a doorway. The clanking and banging continued as the Dragon Keepers were led away to their cells, protesting and arguing every step of the way.

'This is a madhouse, isn't it?' said the Grindylow, waking up and staring at the commotion.

'It is now,' I said. Truly this was madness. On the eve of the presentation, to lock up every single Dragon Keeper… Where *was* the sense in that?

'All the better for us though, eh?' he grinned.

Yes. You could say that…

·∿· 58 ·∿·
The Escape

AT **PRECISELY TWO** o'clock the Grindylow jabbed me in the ribs.

'Psst.'

There he was, his long stooping silhouette standing before the bars of the cell. The cacophony of complaint had died away now. Even the Flogs had stopped their rowing. All the nursery bogeys were wheezing and snoring in unison like some broken organ.

'Are you ready?'

I suppose you could say that. I hadn't slept for thinking about what I was going to do and I didn't feel too good about it. The consequences might be dire. But it had to be done. Pretending to rub the sleep from my eyes, I slipped on my shoes and shuffled over to where he stood.

'All lovely and quiet,' whispered the Grindylow. 'Perfect. Now, you remember everything?'

I nodded. We had spent a long time discussing this.

'Okay. Hang on.'

One large knobbly hand closed around my waist, picked me up as if I was made of air and held me up to the ceiling. The Grindylow had wiggled that iron bar loose and bent it to one side, creating a hole just wide enough for a small person to squeeze through – which is what I did, before climbing down the other side. The Grindylow grinned at me through the bars, his teeth glittering in the candlelight.

'Hurry up now, Jack,' he whispered, hugging himself with excitement. 'Oh this is good.'

'I'll be as quick as I can.'

'You do that, you do that. I'll be watching just in case you get jumped. Tee-hee!' He pulled the mirror from his pocket and gave me a massive thumbs up.

I tiptoed swiftly down the corridor, past the sleeping nursery bogeys, all looking as harmless as soft toys in their cells. Father Flog sat against the wall in his hat and breeches with a riding crop across his lap. Mother Flog was a very fat woman in a wide frilly bonnet snoring in the corner. There was a spider, a milkmaid with fangs, a gnome with a club, another old hag with enormous green teeth… I could go on, but I won't. All I was thinking about was getting round the corner, beyond the reach of the Grindylow, to Archie Queach's office. Archie had left the door unlocked. A line of keys hung on the wall.

'Is it there?' hissed the Grindylow.

I looked back and saw his giant gnarled hand holding up the mirror. He was watching me – of course, he would be. Yes, the key was there. All the cells' keys were there. But these were not what I was looking for. It was the massive one at the end labelled 'spare'.

The Grindylow snorted as he saw me come out of the office with the large iron key in my hand.

'Well done, well done!' he chuckled as I walked back down the corridor towards him. 'Hey?' he said, as I turned and swiftly began climbing the steps towards the main door. 'Hey! Where you going?'

'I'm leaving,' I replied, feeling the excitement of it all race through me.

'Oh no you're not.'

'Oh yes I am,' I said.

'Oh no you're not–'

'Oh yes I am–'

'OH NO YOU'RE NOT!' (Yes, nursery bogeys really do speak like this.) He dropped the mirror and a pair of huge hands swiped at the air above me. 'You're not going anywhere without me,' muttered the Grindylow murderously. 'That was the deal.'

'Deal's off. Sorry,' I said, ducking out of reach.

'Why you double-crossing, brick-munching–' I won't repeat exactly what the Grindylow said but it was a list of all the ways he would mash my head into a thousand pieces, feast on my brains, boil my eyeballs... I'd almost reached the door... in fact I had reached it, when I heard a familiar voice–

'Wow. That's... it can't be, is that... Father *Flog*?'

The Grindylow stopped. I stopped. Footsteps were coming from the other end of the corridor.

'And Mother Flog? Nancy Needles... the Cracklemouth... Old

Scratty? But, but they're all real...'

I recognised that voice. A shadow tiptoed in front of the cells...

'Lily?'

She gasped and turned around.

'Jack? Is that you?'

'What are you doing down here?' I replied.

'I was looking for you – AHH!'

WHUMP! A huge hand bent round the corner and grabbed her by the foot. She shrieked and clung on to the bars of a cell. The Grindylow laughed.

'Ransom, Brick-eater! An eye for an eye, a tooth for a tooth!'

'Let her go!' I shouted, daring to advance.

'Not unless you let me out!'

'Let her go, you monster!'

'Oh no I won't–'

'Oh yes you will–'

'Oh no I won't–'

'Oh yes you will–'

(This probably went on a bit... maybe more than a bit.)

'If you leave me down here, Brick-eater, I shall bash this one's brains out and then, then I'll–' I won't describe the rest but it was proper swearing and terrible threats.

'Gosh!' gasped Lily, looking shocked. 'Would he really do that?'

'Oh yes I would–'

'No he wouldn't–'

'Oh yes I would–'

'Can you stop saying that?'

'Oh yes I would, you–' Another blast of even fouler threats and abuse.

'Wow!' Lily looked shaken.

There was nothing for it.

'Fine. Let her go. Here.'

I grabbed the cell keys and chucked them down the corridor towards him. The Grindylow looked at them. To pick up the keys he would have to let go of Lily, as they were just beyond his reach…

'All right, Brick-eater, it's a deal. But mind you leave that outer door unlocked.'

'And if I don't?'

'By heaven!' The Grindylow roared and began his threats yet again… Lily looked at me in terror.

'Okay fine, whatever,' I said quickly.

The Grindylow smiled, and released Lily's foot. Instantly she ran to me. The Grindylow grabbed the keys and his huge hand slid back down the corridor.

'I'd stay out of the sewers if I were you, Jack!' he called.

'Don't worry, I will.'

'And don't even think about bolting that outer door!' he yelled as we hurried through it, closing it behind us with a boom. For a second I looked down at the heavy iron bolts…

'Jack? Are you mad?'

Perhaps not…

'Who *is* that?' Lily asked.

'That's the Grindylow.'

Lily's mouth fell open in amazement.

'The *Grindylow*? The real one?'

'Yes. I was locked in a cell with him for two days.'

Lily stared at me with a wow-that's-totally-unbelievable expression.

'Well he didn't eat me, did he? What are you doing down here, Lily?'

✤ 59 ✤
Decision Time

EXPLANATIONS, EXPLANATIONS. After I'd told her
what had happened, Lily described how she'd crawled
over roofs, slipped down drainpipes, jumped from shadow
to shadow, and just about everything else to get down to the
dungeons to find me... Why?

We were standing in a dark corridor close to the Ghost Vault.
I was hoping we wouldn't be overheard.

'Basically there's been this massive row. William Foxglass has
just returned and warned Thad about some dragon that's coming
down from wherever it lives–'

'Wellenstorm?'

'Is that its name? I don't know. Thad didn't believe it, so Mr Foxglass went direct to the King, and the King's gone ballistic. He thinks it's all some big attempt to sabotage Richard's presentation, and he's ordering everyone responsible to be locked up, and if Richard continues to refuse to cooperate, he won't be doing a presentation but a *coronation*, because *he's* threatening to abdicate! Can you believe it?! So now Thad's gone ballistic, and he's told the King that would be a very good idea, because he's clearly completely mad, and *he's* the one who should be thrown in jail! Everyone's screaming at everyone else and… poor Cuz, he's just lying there trapped in the middle of it…' Lily blinked hard. 'Sometimes, Jack, I really wonder if they're all deliberately… no one seems to realise how ill he is. He can barely even speak. Oh Jack.' She threw her arms around me and sobbed. Poor Lily. Poor Richard. 'Honestly, Jack, if Cuz takes part in the presentation tomorrow, I really think it might kill him. It really might.'

'I know,' I said. And I knew what she was thinking too. Lily wouldn't have risked coming all the way down to the dungeons just to tell me that. We sat in silence for a moment.

'He'd be so angry if he knew I was down here,' she said, wiping her eyes. 'But you know what he's like. He's so stubborn. He thinks he's far stronger than he actually is.'

'There's only one alternative, isn't there?'

'Is there?'

'Come on, Lily. You know there is.'

Lily looked at me.

'You don't have to say yes, Jack, you really don't. I just couldn't think of what else to do and—'

'Lily, I understand.'

'But you really don't have to. You really don't. You *really* don't.'

Lily was one of those people who the more she said 'you really don't' the more she actually meant 'you really do'. And come to think of it, she had no idea how much she was asking, considering what I'd found out about Wellenstorm and everything else...

'Okay. I'll do it.'

Lily half-smiled in anticipation.

'Would you *really*? Honestly?'

'Yes. I'll do it.' I felt strangely lighthearted saying it.

Lily gasped.

'Oh Jack!'

She flung her arms around my neck and hugged me again. I have to say, I was slightly amazed at myself. I wasn't a noble, self-sacrificing sort of person like Lily, and you've probably noticed by now that I'm not particularly brave. Maybe I said it because I couldn't think of a reason not to. It had to be me. We both knew it.

It was as simple as that.

'They'll make you swear to be the next king of Albion and all that stuff, but it's only words. You don't have to be, Jack.'

'I don't want to be. Ever.'

'Just like Cuz then,' she smiled. 'But there's one tiny problem.'

'What's that?'

It turned out that even Lily, fearless Lily Lancaster, knew we'd never be able to repeat what she'd just done. Not now, with the school in complete lockdown the night before the presentation... She'd made it out through sheer luck. Getting back into the Ermine Tower would be like trying to break into a jail. Again we sat in glum silence. I wracked my brains, thinking of all those odd things Dancing Dan had showed me... Perhaps... couldn't we both, wasn't there something Richard said he'd used, to...

'I think one of those would be quite perfect, ma'am.' The

corridor shimmered and Dancing Dan Dravot appeared through the wall. As ever, he had anticipated my thoughts and even finished my sentence.

'Good evening, Lady Lily. Welcome to our humble surroundings.'

Lily stared at the ghost. She was a little frightened, but also curious.

'He lives here,' I whispered.

'How does he know what you're thinking?' she whispered back.

'I don't know. He just sort of does.'

'It's rather spooky, though I say it myself,' said Dancing Dan. 'Shall we?'

We hurried down the corridor to the vault and Dancing Dan disappeared into the store cupboard downstairs. A minute later he was back smiling his mournful smile carrying a pile of thin grey material, intricately embroidered and light and floaty as a spider's web. It had a high collar, a hood and pockets. It looked like the sort of thing a princess might wear to a ball–

'It's a ghost cape, ma'am. Wear it and you appear to be exactly that, a ghost, even though you're not. Mostyn Joliffe was very keen on it. "If you can't charm 'em, join 'em" I think was his phrase. And he did. This is what he wore when he captured the famous forty ghosts of Mockbeggars Hall.'

'It's very strange,' said Lily, running her hand across the curious grey material.

'It's spun from ghost silk, collected by wood elves, m'lady. Ghosts have a habit of rushing through woods far too quickly – especially ghosts in love. They never look where they're going and leave their traces lying about. This one is made from The Grey Lady of Ashdown Forest. For twenty years she rampaged after a particular young postman on his bicycle. By the end, all that was left of her was her slippers.'

'Gosh.'

'I hope it might accommodate you both. The Grey Lady was rather large. Mostyn Joliffe ditto.'

I stared at Dancing Dan, floating there with that melancholy look on his face. What would we do without him?

'May I say it's also very nice to see you again, ma'am. We all think it's deeply unfair the way you've been treated. Through no fault of your own.'

'Thank you, Dancing Dan.'

'Thank *you*, ma'am,' he murmured, the end of his nose turning blue.

'So let's go then,' said Lily, suddenly beaming. Then almost as suddenly she was frowning again.

'What is it?' I asked.

'Just to warn you, Jack, Richard's in such a strange mood, he may not exactly agree…'

'Why not?'

'Because it's not as simple as that, Lily.'

'Isn't it?'

Richard was sitting up in bed, propped up on a pile of pillows. (If you were wondering how we got over here, just imagine a fat ghost floating down dark corridors and slipping through gates guarded by dozens of dozy sentries… Even Tiny Torquil never noticed us.)

Richard coughed horribly. His face was sickly green, and the shadows under his eyes were so black they looked like they had been drawn on in felt tip. Poor, poor Richard. He really did look as if he was about to die.

'If I do it, everyone will see how ill I am. And then maybe they'll all just leave me alone.'

'No one's going to leave you alone, Cuz. Definitely not tomorrow, and probably not ever.'

Richard shook his head. He looked at me with glassy eyes. Was the idea of me taking his place so terrible? Lily stared at him in frustration.

'Cuz, you can barely stand up. The doctor's probably going to give you some massive injection just so you can walk down the stairs. And then you'll have to climb up into that carriage and stand there on your own, smiling and waving for hours. Why would you want to do that?'

Richard coughed and coughed. It was an awful sight.

'Let me sleep. I'll feel better in a bit.'

He turned away and waved for us to go.

Out of the bedroom we crept, closing the door quietly behind us. Lily and I stood beside the window in silence. A brilliant moon was shining down into the school courtyard. There were now dark patches of bare earth everywhere.

'He's so ridiculous. Anyone would think he actually wants to die,' she whispered, blinking a tear away. 'What shall we do?'

I didn't know. I looked over to where Asphodel's cage hung in the corner. Fortunately the velvet curtains were closed.

'Perhaps it might be a good idea if you stayed with him tonight,' I whispered.

Lily didn't understand. Nodding at the cage I led her out into the corridor and quietly closed the door.

'Do you think Richard might've been secretly feeding

Asphodel?' I said.

Lily looked at me like that was a disgusting idea.

'Feeding? How?'

I explained about Asphodel drinking blood from my finger, and the way the fairy had rattled his glass goblet like he expected it. I told her about the fairies' poisonous bite; perhaps Richard had been pushing his fingers to the bars and letting Asphodel suck his blood directly?

'Richard would never let Asphodel do that, no way,' she said. 'For a start he can't stand the sight of blood. He faints. But I suppose Snowdrop Scott did absolutely forbid us to feed Asphodel like that, which is a reason why Richard *might* do it... No Jack, definitely not. Asphodel doesn't always get what he wants, you know.'

Lily seemed totally convinced. I wondered. So why had Asphodel pleaded for me to feed him, then? Was that just an attempt to find out who *I* really was? That fairy was so devious...

'Anyway, thanks for the warning,' she said, wiping her eyes. 'We can't give up yet. I'm going to barricade his bedroom door and sleep in an armchair right in front of it, so if anyone's thinking of murdering him or poisoning him tonight, they'll have to get past me first,' she said, sounding tough. 'You go upstairs and sleep in my bed, Jack, and at dawn we'll see how he is. Hopefully Cuz will have come to his senses by then.'

Lily looked every bit as obstinate as her cousin as she slipped back into his rooms.

'Good luck,' I said.

She didn't reply.

A Ghostly Solution

I WENT UP TO LILY'S BEDROOM and lay down on her large four-poster bed. The walls were plastered with pictures of unicorns (Sam Yuell had let her ride the royal one in happier times), and there were also several spectacular photos of Lily in action during Jackernapes matches, flying through the air, slam-dunking Cromwell into a dragon's mouth while George Hartswood flailed behind. Beside the bed was a photo of the Queen with Lily's mother (they were sisters) and father standing before a gloomy Scottish castle which I supposed might be their home. They were all tall, outdoorsy, healthy-looking people. Quite, quite different from Richard...

Poor, sickly Richard. Lily was right. He probably didn't care if his presentation killed him or not; he just wanted it to be over, and he was not a persuadable sort of person... In fact, he was probably the most stubborn person I'd ever met–

Suddenly I sat bolt upright in bed. *No.* It was obvious what we must do. We had to be much more subtle about it... I ran to the door and opened it a crack. The moonlit passage beyond was empty.

'Dancing Dan?' I whispered. 'Dancing Dan Dravot, are you still there?'

After a moment, the air at the end of the corridor seemed to move. A ripple silently approached beside the tapestries.

'Ma'am?'

And there he was, hovering in the shadows. Somehow I had a feeling he'd followed us over here. He probably even anticipated what I was going to say next–

'I think that's an excellent idea, ma'am,' bowed Dancing Dan. 'The Prince is indeed headstrong, and won't be swayed. He reminds me very much–' The ghost checked himself. 'Consider it done, ma'am.'

'You won't upset him?'

'I will endeavour not even to wake him.'

'The door is barricaded.'

'Not a problem, ma'am. I shall find another way.'

With a bow and the flicker of something like a smile, Dancing Dan drifted away humming vaguely. Dancing Dan. What a ghost he was.

'Jack!'

Lily was staring down at me, her pink cheeks positively pulsing with shock.

'He's gone!'

'What?'

'Richard's gone!'

I glanced at the clock groggily. It was six o'clock in the morning.

'I thought you were sleeping outside his bedroom door,' I groaned.

'I was! But he's gone! He's disappeared!' Lily stared at me. I stared back at her, vaguely remembering everything. 'Supposing he's been kidnapped, or something terrible like that? Jack, what are we going to do?'

'He's probably just wandered off somewhere—'

'But he *can't* have done, I was right in front of the door! How could he wander off?'

I shrugged wearily. Lily sat down. Calmed down a bit.

'Okay. Deep breath. Maybe he's hiding. That would be so typical. He was never going to admit how sick he was, so now he's pretending the presentation isn't happening.'

'Which is good, isn't it?'

Lily stared at me. And then, at last, she clicked.

'Okay. Yes, maybe, but… supposing he suddenly comes back?'

'Why would he do that?'

'He might. You know what Cuz is like. He's totally selfish. He never thinks about anyone but himself. Honestly, Jack, where d'you think he's gone?'

I yawned. Rubbed my eyes. Tried to look as confused as possible.

'Isn't there some secret hiding place he has somewhere?'

Lily suddenly looked at me wide-eyed.

'He's in the Sable Tower! You're so right, Jack, that's just *so* Richard. I bet that's exactly what he's done. He's crawled off to hide in that velvet castle on Umballoo's back where he knows no one will ever find him. Phew.' Lily took a deep breath. She seemed very relieved. 'I was getting ready for a really big argument this morning. But now...' She looked at me. 'You've definitely got to be him now, haven't you?'

Lily was right again. I felt a little mean playing this trick on her, but anyway... She glanced at the clock on the wall.

'The doctor's coming in half an hour, then the dresser, then the King and Queen; they'll all be trooping in to see how you are. Better have breakfast, Cuz,' she added, with a smile. 'Going to have to practise that one too, aren't I?'

～～ 61 ～～
Fit for Duty

BREAKFAST ARRIVED on that tiny steam train and flashed past in a half-crunched sort of way. I just about managed to put on Richard's complicated underclothes and wig before anyone important arrived. Unfortunately the first visitors were probably the most critical of the lot.

'Morning, Richard.'

'Morning, Richard.'

In filed Thomas and Victoria, already wearing their costumes as a miniature Henry VIII and a miniature Anne Boleyn.

'We've come to see how dead you look.'

They stood beside the bed and inspected me closely.

'Not quite as dead as yesterday,' pronounced Victoria. 'But still *almost* dead.'

'I'm feeling a lot better, actually,' I replied, careful not to be too insulted.

'But you still look awful. And you're probably going to die shortly. Admit it, Richard, you're almost dead.'

I stared at the two vile little monsters, all blonde and kittenish in their curls and velvets.

'I'm not almost dead, and I'm not going to die shortly either. Sorry to disappoint you.'

Thomas looked very cross. He took out a small penknife and began gouging a hole in the bedpost.

'But Richard, it's so unfair. You don't even want to be King!'

'Can't we at least come and sit in the coach with you?' said Victoria.

'No you can't.'

'Why not? The people don't really want to see you.'

'And how do you know that?'

'Because you're so weak and weedy. People will just look at you and think, "Oh no, it's just another rubbish king. What's the point of *him*, he looks like he's about to die"– *and* he is.' The twins turned to each other and giggled.

'We're the ones they really want to see,' said Victoria. 'They want to see if we're as awful as everyone says. Because we are famously awful, Richard, just like you are famously useless.'

Thomas gouged his knife a little deeper into the bedpost.

'We could *make* you do it, Richard,' he said menacingly. 'We could–'

'Well, well, a party!' Doctor Mazumdar marched in, smiling kindly at the two young Lancasters.

'I hope you two aren't annoying your brother on his big day,' said the Queen, a step behind and a little less friendly. 'Thomas? Victoria?'

'Actually he's really annoying us, Mummy,' said Thomas.

'I find that very hard to believe.'

'He's refusing to let us come in the coach.'

'Of course he is. This is Richard's presentation, not yours. Your turn will come. Now put that knife away, Thomas, and both of you go back to your room. I'm sure you've got plenty to do.'

'It's not fair!' wailed Thomas. 'He's got better!'

'Hmm, yes he does look it,' said the doctor, peering into my eyes. 'Decidedly better.'

'Thomas, Victoria, room, now.'

The Queen pointed a long finger at the door. The twins trudged towards it like a pair of disgruntled teddy bears. Suddenly Victoria turned around, her eyes wild with rage.

'WHEN'S HE GOING TO DIE, MUMMY!' she shouted.

'Victoria!'

'DIE, YOU HORRIBLE BOY!'

'Victoria—'

'DIE!'

The Queen was momentarily speechless.

'Kindly leave and don't come back,' she said. Ever, she might have added. They left, slamming the door.

'I do apologise, I don't know how they've become such perfect beasts,' she said hastily. 'I suppose it's all my fault.'

'Seven's a difficult age,' said Dr Mazumdar knowledgeably. 'They're only jealous of their remarkable brother I expect.' He smiled and reached for his stethoscope. 'I must say, Richard, your health yo-yoes in the most dramatic fashion. Yesterday your heart was barely beating, your eyes were yellow and your tongue was blue. But today... I'd very much like to make a more thorough examination–'

'I hardly think there's time for that, Doctor,' the Queen cut in hastily. 'Richard has to get dressed and that will take at least an hour. Probably two.'

'But I should like to listen to his chest–'

'Please don't,' I said, hastily placing my hands across my middle. 'I'm feeling very ticklish this morning.'

Dr Mazumdar looked at me curiously. He sensed something was wrong, and it had nothing to do with my health.

'Very well, then. Can you cough for me, Richard?'

I tried. He turned to the Queen, mystified.

'Yesterday he was wheezing like an old man and now his lungs are as clear as a bell–'

'What's all this talk about being perfectly well?'

In breezed the King, sporting an extraordinarily spiky, waxed moustache. I smiled nervously, wondering quite how mad he was feeling this morning... hopefully not as mad as he looked.

'Well?'

'Richard's feeling decidedly better,' said the Queen brightly.

'No longer knocking on death's door?'

'Not at all, Your Highness,' said Dr Mazumdar. 'Quite the reverse.'

'Excellent! What a lot of rot these people talk, eh?' He sat down beside me and gave my cheeks a squeeze. 'I've always told them you've got the constitution of a yak. Just like your mother.'

He winked at the Queen. She smiled indulgently. I'd never met anyone less yak-like.

'No need for any more damned injections then?'

'I would like to give him a little booster, just to be on the safe side,' said Dr Mazumdar. 'Something to keep him in tip-top condition–'

'But you've just said he's in tip-top condition!' exclaimed the King. 'He's proved you wrong, Doc. What the devil d'you want to pump him full of drugs for?'

'Your Highness, today is going to be a very long day. First he has the presentation. Then I understand he's expected to play in the Jackernapes final this afternoon–'

''Course he is!' beamed the King. 'Most important game of the year. Can't miss it. Doesn't want to miss it. Richard'll be walking that pole for Lancaster and winning the game single-handed I shouldn't wonder. Show young Hartswood a thing or two about funambling, eh?'

'But the Prince hasn't left his bed for three days. Even if he does appear to be better now, he's probably just excited. He's still very weak and frail. It's inevitable he'll become totally exhausted.'

The King snorted.

'Well I don't know. Don't think he needs any more injections myself. Queenie, what say you?'

'Not if he doesn't think so.'

'Good idea, ask the patient,' said the King. 'Richard, fancy another needle full of drugs stuck in your arm?'

I didn't have to act now.

''Course he doesn't! He's not a damned fool.'

Dr Mazumdar sighed and pulled off his stethoscope.

'As you wish. As his doctor I merely want to help in any way I can.'

'Offer kindly noted, but cordially rejected. Now on your way, Doc.'

Dr Mazumdar snapped his case shut, perhaps a little harder than he should have done.

'May I wish you the very best of luck, Richard,' he said. 'Your Highness. Your Highness.'

He made his bows and left. I breathed a sigh of relief.

'Hoity-toity fellow, isn't he, what?' said the King once Dr Mazumdar had gone.

'I found his concern for his patient rather touching,' said the Queen. 'He's so impressed with you, darling.'

'Hoity-toity I call it,' the King went on. 'Decidedly hoity-toity. That's the problem with one's people, Richard. When it comes to it, they don't really understand us. We might look the same – heads, legs, arms, what have you – but really we're as similar as bluebottles and bison. Old Doc Mazumtee-tum will never understand that the day a prince is presented to his people is the greatest day of his life! The beat of the drum, the blast of the trumpet, the roar of the crowd, the unbridled adoration, you can't hear that through a stethoscope! *He* might have no idea how you've shrugged off the dread hand of death so quick, but *I* do, my boy, oh I do indeed. You're no shirker from duty! You stand up when you're called! You're a Lancaster from your braces to your boots, Richard. Inside that bag of bones there's a lionheart roaring!' The King had tears of pride in his eyes. 'It's almost as if… you're almost like…'

His moustache twitched. I knew what he was going to say. And so did the Queen.

'Like *Richard*,' she said, gently taking his hand across the bed.

'Yes,' nodded the King, his hand squeezing mine. 'That's right. Like Richard. Well done my boy.'

We sat for a moment, all three holding hands. The King was overwhelmed. I was overwhelmed.

'Now we are all going to get through this together,' she said, squeezing our hands in turn. 'And there's going to be no more talk of abdications, or coronations, or any more silly nonsense like that. This is your day, darling; you must enjoy it.'

'That's right. Your day. Nothing to worry about,' snorted the King, his eyes shimmering like wet eggs.

'You will impress them all. I know you will.'

The King nodded again.

'Yes. Impress 'em all. Jolly good.'

The King composed himself and left. The Queen sat holding my hand. She stared at me for a long moment, and there was so much pride and hope and love in her eyes that I felt myself melting… No one had ever looked at me like that in my life, and I almost wanted to tell her the truth…

'Best foot forward, darling,' she whispered. 'You can do this. I know you can.' Bending forward she kissed me on the forehead, then walked quickly to the door.

'Oh your father was planning to send his valet through to help get you dressed, but I think you and Lily could probably manage on your own, couldn't you? Shall I let him know?'

I nodded.

'Good.'

She waved and was gone.

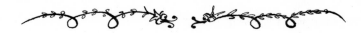

'How did it go?'

'Okay. Sort of.'

'Even Doctor Mazumdar believed you?'

Lily stared at me in the mirror.

'Well I don't suppose it matters now,' she said. 'Richard looked like he was almost dead yesterday. Poor Cuz, I hope he's all right.'

So did I. We were fiddling with a sash and a collection of medals that went over my bright red tunic. I found it amazing that, aged twelve, I was already the colonel of several regiments and sported a line of honours that would have looked impressive on some whiskery old general.

'There we go,' said Lily, finishing her fastening. 'And now for the most important part.' Taking a soft brush, she began to tidy up my wig, smoothing down the parting and making sure it looked right around my ears. 'You'll wow 'em, Jack,' she grinned.

We stood looking in the mirror. I raised my chin and struck a regal pose. Lily giggled.

'The funny thing is, Richard would never do that. He's always so soft-shouldered and mopey. The King is forever telling him to stand up straight.'

'Like this?' I tried.

'Oh please no. He's not a zombie.'

Okay. I'd forgotten what a rubbish actor I was.

'What about the stick? D'you think I should use it?'

'Probably should,' said Lily, handing me Richard's cane. 'It's not like some miracle has happened.'

'I'm still not very good at it,' I said, practising a little.

'No I can see that,' Lily agreed. 'But we're all going to have to raise our game a bit today, aren't we?'

⚬⚬ 62 ⚬⚬
Going Forth

LILY'S WORDS ECHOED around my head as an hour later I stepped out of the heavy oak door and stood blinking in the sunlight. Hard black shadows cut across the school courtyard, and either side of the path ahead of me stood lines of people waiting – the keepers in all their finery, the servants, the footmen, the guards, and at the far end the children of the school. Waiting under the archway beyond stood the royal family, and in the next courtyard I glimpsed the golden coach in which I was to ride. Everyone in the palace was there, looking at me, expectant. Flags snapped and fluttered in the wind.

'Pray silence for His Royal Highness, Prince Richard!' came

a shout. A trumpeter on the battlements sounded. My heart was pumping so fast I could hardly think. Fixing a smile on my face I put my best foot forward, or was it my worst? I stepped down one step, then another, then suddenly my mind went blank. The limp – I had completely forgotten which foot was the bad one! In my dithering I dropped my cane. In my panic I made the mistake of stooping forward to pick it up... Smack! Suddenly I was on my hands and knees on the wet stone – I'd trodden on the corner of my cape and tripped... With dirty hands, burning cheeks and large black smudges on my cream satin breeches and ermine gown, I scrambled back to my feet. Had there been a snigger I might have felt better, but there was nothing; just cold, dead silence. They waited. Taking a deep breath, I tried the walk. After three steps I realised I couldn't do it. I was limping like my leg had been cut off.

'Come on, Richard! What on earth's the matter with you!'

The King stood silhouetted in the archway, hands on his hips. He was clearly furious. I glanced back at the Sable Tower looming over the courtyard. I'm sorry, Richard. If you're watching up there, please forgive me, I'm making a real mess of this. Suddenly Lily appeared at my side, her cheeks flushed from running around the back.

'Cuz,' she said, offering her arm. Gratefully I took it. 'You can do it. Just keep smiling. Left foot,' she whispered.

'Thanks,' I whispered back.

With a determined nod she led the way down the path. The lines of keepers bowed as we approached. Snowdrop Scott in a large pink hat, Enid Cribbage in her strange raven-feathered cape, Archie Queach... he didn't even look at me. Did he know my cell was empty? Perhaps he was hoping nobody had noticed – especially not Ocelot Malodure or Solomon Knock, who stood either side of him. I was dreading seeing Galahad Joliffe, but thankfully his place was taken by my namesake. Little Jacky Joliffe was right there at the front, already wearing a specially tailored green Ghost Keeper's coat. He had the nerve to stare straight at me as we passed. I ignored him in a proper princely way. He may have been totally innocent, but I still hadn't quite forgiven him for taking my place in this world...

On we went past keepers of this and that – mermigans, jumblies, frumious bandersnatches... The three ancient keepers who had decided to throw me into the dungeon bowed as one, and I couldn't help giving them a particularly haughty smile... but there were no rowdy Dragon Keepers. And there didn't seem to be any Sam Yuell either...

'Your Highness.' Valentine Oak bowed low, looking white and frail in the harsh sunlight. To cover my nerves, I decided to ignore him too, and looking ahead almost missed the very last keeper in the line...

'Mr Foxglass?'

I said the words in shock – not really meaning to. The Black Zodiac coat rose, and William Foxglass raised his head, looking at me with those watchful eyes.

'Your Highness,' he said, smiling that strange upside-down smile. I realised there was so much I wanted to say, I was still so angry with him, and yet... I found I couldn't stop smiling back. The sight of William Foxglass lifted my heart. Somehow the chaos of the last two days would end and order would be restored. The cat was back. The mice would have to stop their playing.

Lily tugged my arm gently and on we went. I suppose my smile was infectious, because as we walked the servants, cooks and footmen began to smile too. Lily felt the mood change and turned to me with a grin.

'Okay?'

I nodded and she gave my arm a squeeze. By the time we reached the crowd of schoolchildren all the seriousness began to evaporate. Young Jake Tiptree stood first in line and he couldn't help himself.

'Just because your legs go a bit funny sometimes doesn't make you a bad prince, Richard.'

'Thank you, Jake.'

'My legs go a bit funny sometimes. You'll get better one day.' Jake Tiptree took off his hat and raised it in the air. 'Three cheers for Prince Richard! Hip-hip!'

'Hurray!'

'Hip-hip!'

'Hurray!'

'Hip-hip!'

'Hurray!'

The shouts echoed around the courtyard as I limped on down, knocking hands with Richard's fan club, Tilly, Lottie, Jocasta... George Hartswood gave me a manly nod, and even Tucker-Smith and Spiggins were grinning (though perhaps at the thought of me falling off the Greensleeves pole later). By the time I reached the King and Queen my heart felt as light as air.

'Lily, darling, you're such a star, I can't think where we'd be without you,' gushed the Queen, her smile as brilliant as her sparkling blue coat. She turned to me and sighed. 'You are a silly sausage. Had us all panicking for a moment.'

'We said he was useless—'

'He can't even walk properly.'

There stood the miniature Henry VIII and Anne Boleyn, their hands firmly held by Tiny Torquil the gatekeeper.

'He'll probably fall straight out of the carriage and go splat,' said Victoria crossly.

'And then get stabbed with any luck–'

'Thomas!' hissed the Queen. Despite her perfect face she actually looked quite angry. 'Torquil, any more of this and you know what to do.'

'Throw them in the deepest darkest dungeon, ma'am,' said Tiny Torquil, looking particularly massive in his gold and red livery.

'Did you hear that? No balcony, cake, Jackernapes, nothing. Now behave.'

The twins stared at their mother sulkily. The Queen took me aside and wiped some imaginary mud off my tunic.

'Seriously darling, you are going to be able to do this, aren't you?'

'Yes of course, Mother.'

'You'd say if you couldn't, wouldn't you?'

'Yes.'

'Promise?'

I nodded. I think she believed me. I hope she did. The King came forward to join us, tall and imposing in his white tunic and red sash, with a bucketful of medals splashed across his chest.

'All right, old chap?' he said gruffly.

'I'm fine, Father.'

'Hmm.'

The King seemed very stiff and awkward. Gone was his buffooning around, his fatherly pride. Perhaps he was as nervous as I was.

'Can't have any more accidents today, Richard,' he said quietly.

'You can collapse in here, but not out there, in front of the people. That won't do.'

'Yes, Father.'

'They need impressing. Understand?'

'I just tripped. I promise, I won't.'

'Hmm,' he grunted. 'Chin up then. And remember what's expected of you.'

I nodded nervously. How could I forget?

We walked through the archway to the outer court where the royal procession was gathering. At the head were the two heralds in silver and red. Behind them a train of brightly painted floats was being assembled, each drawn by a heavy grey horse. Riding on the first float was the Black Bull of Clarence, looking both angry and stupid with a gold ring through his nose, then came the Silver Yale of Beaufort, its horns and hooves all painted white, then the little Red Dragon of Wales, the White Hart, the Royal Falcon, the three fat Golden Lions of England, the ghostly White Greyhound of Richmond, the Brown Bear of Bothelswaite, and last but not least, there was Stinky, with a magnificent diamond

collar round her neck, her multicoloured coat glistening in the sunlight. She seemed the most agitated of them all, scratching and snarling, sending showers of sparks shooting from her nose. The young footman holding her looked terrified. Where was Sam Yuell? I still couldn't see him anywhere...

'Richard!'

I shuddered as Thad Lancaster raised a hand and swaggered across the courtyard to meet us, looking predictably dashing in his dark green cavalry uniform. This was what I'd been dreading most of all. After our last meeting, how could Thad fail to recognise me?

'Edward.' Thad bowed formally to the King. 'Olivia.' He took the Queen's hand and kissed it. 'And today, young man, as it's your presentation day, I defer to you too.' With an elaborate twizzling of his wrist Thad Lancaster made me a bow. I tried to be as unimpressed and Richardish as possible.

'Will you ever get used to bowing to a son of mine, little brother?'

'Ha!' laughed Thad. 'I serve the Crown and the Crown alone. Whoever wears it is of no interest to me at all.'

The King snorted loudly. He clearly didn't believe it. I'm not sure I did either. Thad looked me up and down and grinned.

'What grand weather, eh? Fate must be smiling on you, Richard.'

'The weather is indeed perfectly capital weather,' agreed the King impatiently. 'Now kindly explain who is going where and doing what?'

Thad Lancaster collected himself, became business-like.

'I shall be riding beside Richard. Captain Cake over there—' He nodded to another tall cavalry officer waiting on his black horse, 'shall be riding behind. Mr Squiddle will be driving the carriage, and young Wilf will be sitting up alongside.'

There they sat on the grand gold coach, the old coachman and his mate, dressed up in their finest.

'Now if there's any trouble, the first thing I shall do is grab Richard, haul him up behind and we'll gallop for the palace gates. Anything more serious...' Thad Lancaster pulled back his cape to reveal a pair of pistols across his chest and another strapped to his thigh. He gave it a friendly pat. 'I'm ready if they are.'

'This is a royal procession, Thad, not the Wild West!' gasped the Queen.

'I think that might be rather overdoing it, old bean,' added the King, with a nervous honk.

'Please remember, Richard's just left his sickbed. He can barely stand up.'

Thad smiled.

'Olivia, I am merely being prepared. One cannot be too careful, as we all know, do we not?'

The King and Queen glanced at each other. Once again, Stephen's long shadow seemed to be stretching out over everything Richard did, even now...

'All I ask is that you escort Richard out there, they get a good look at him, and he's returned to us in one piece,' said the Queen, unable to conceal her nerves. 'That is all I ask.'

'Consider it done.' Thad bowed, then he turned to me. 'Ready to be presented to your people as the next King of Albion, young man?'

I swallowed hard and just about managed a nod.

'Excellent.'

We crossed the courtyard and Thad helped me up into the open carriage. The leather creaked, the harnesses jingled. Mr Squiddle turned around and tipped his hat. He may have said a few words of encouragement but I didn't hear them, I was so preoccupied with what was to come... Thad mounted a black charger with a mane almost down to his boots and drew alongside, the horse dancing left and right.

'Open the outer gates!' he commanded. The order was repeated and it was done. I glimpsed the massed crowds beyond the barriers. They craned their necks to see. Thad nodded to the trumpeters on the battlements. They raised their instruments and blasted a fanfare up into the crisp blue sky.

'When we get outside, stand up, so they can get a good look at you,' said Thad.

I nodded, trying to ignore the butterflies in my stomach.

'Good luck, darling,' called the Queen.

She had slipped her arm through the King's, her face a picture of pride and worry. The King nodded at me in a stiff-upper-lip, you-can-do-it kind of way. Lily beamed and winked. The twins stared at me sulkily. I looked back over the rooftops to the Sable Tower. Was Richard up there, watching me too? I felt that he was, and I suddenly felt guilty. He may never have wanted to be

King, but I was still stealing something important from him; this was supposed to be his moment, not mine…

'Forward!' roared Thad, raising one gauntlet. The Black Bull of Clarence bellowed, the greyhound barked nervously and Stinky sent a shower of sparks into the air.

'Forward!' Thad roared again.

'ARRÊTEZ VOUS! ARRÊTEZ VOUS, SI'L VOUS PLAÎT!'

The screeching echoed around the yard as Patrick Pettifog came hurrying through an archway pushing a cart. On it was Fleur de Lys, bouncing around on a purple cushion, looking unbelievably magnificent. Her leaves were polished deep green, her flowers painted brilliant white and her stamens were brushed with gold… but no amount of make-up could disguise her foul temper.

'Vite, you silly leetle rosbif! Vite! Vite!'

Patrick Pettifog slowed and made for the gap behind Stinky at the back of the procession.

'Non non non! I go zere, over zere!' She slapped Patrick about the head and pointed at the space on the front float, right next to the Black Bull of Clarence.

'I think Mademoiselle is mistaken–'

'You zink I am mistaken? You smelly English maggot, do I look like I bring up zer rear? I am Fleur de Lys! FLEUR DE LYS! ALLEZ! ZER FRONT! VITE!'

Patrick glanced at Thad Lancaster in confusion.

'Why anyone has ever put up with that monstrous pot plant I do not know,' he muttered, and waved them on. Fleur was wheeled forward, drinking in the recognition like a great actress coming on stage. They stopped before the King.

'Your Majesty.'

'How perfectly lovely to see you again, Fleur,' he said. 'Enchanté.'

She took his hand and bowed low, then curtseyed before the Queen.

'You're looking younger and younger Fleur. I don't know how you do it.'

Fleur gracefully accepted the compliment.

'Vee all 'ave our leetle secrets, Madame, do we not?'

The Queen's perfect face didn't flinch. Fleur moved on, passed the twins who giggled, and then stopped the moment she spied them.

'Oui, petits cochons, Fleur de Lys is still 'ere.'

They were just about to stick out their tongues when she hissed so loudly they cowered behind Tiny Torquil's legs.

'Zat's right, petits cochons,' she smirked. 'It takes more zan a leetle naughtiness to stop Fleur de Lys!'

Patrick Pettifog heaved the enormous plant up beside the Black Bull of Clarence, and arranged her leaves just so. Fleur turned to stare at the silent masses beyond the gate.

'Ahh, regarde les rosbifs. What can you do wiz zem? Like a field of turnips, no?' She turned to the great black bull behind her. 'Let us give zem some royal razzle-dazzle, eh?' The bull stared at her vacantly. 'Razzle-dazzle, my big stupid friend! Razzle-dazzle!'

'Forward!' shouted Thad.

Mr Squiddle cracked his reins and out we rolled into the sunshine, with all the royal beasts rumbling along behind.

ᨊᨘ 63 ᨘᨊ
Out on The Mall

I
T'S HARD TO REMEMBER all the details of that momentous
day now. My first impression as we rumbled out into the street
was shock. There were so many people. The crowd stretched
as far as I could see; there were people hanging out of windows,
standing in trees, perched on top of lamp posts... My second
impression was terror, for this vast crowd stood completely silent.
That was the strangest thing. Nobody cheered, nobody shouted.
There was no sound at all, but for the jangling harnesses and the
hooves echoing on the cobbles.

'Stand up,' said Thad quietly. I did as I was told. Lines of sombre
faces squinted at me in the hard sunlight. The Prime Minister

had been as good as his word; a few miserable scraps of bunting fluttered between the lamp posts, and I spotted a couple of vans doling out soup and sandwiches. There were no other signs of the glorious pageant the King had wished for me. On we went through the streets, the horses' hooves clip-clopping into the eerie silence... It was like a funeral.

'What's the matter?' I whispered, stealing a glance at Thad.

'It's insolence, that's what it is. Damned insolence,' he murmured, his eyes darting left and right.

I was beginning to get anxious. The animals felt it too. The Silver Yale whinnied. The Black Bull of Clarence snorted. The White Hart whimpered. The horses flicked their tails and danced a little. Only Fleur de Lys seemed oblivious to the mood of the people. She bowed and waved, lost in a dreamworld of her own.

'Allo, allo, bonjour rosbifs... What a lot of rosbifs you are... Why don't you have a wash, you smelly people! Allo, yes allo! C'est moi. Remember moi? Zer most famous flower in zer world, Fleur de Lys...'

And then something peculiar started to happen. A low murmuring began, creeping through the crowd like a rising tide, slowly becoming a tune... I recognised it. It was that old forest song I'd heard drifting over the battlements with Asphodel...

'To this cold kingdom a child shall come,
With a hey-ho, the ice and the snow,
To scatter the clouds and light up the sun,
With a hey-ho, the ice and the snow,
A child of no one, a fiery thing,
With a hey-ho, the ice and the snow,
Born out of love and great suffering–'

'This is too much,' muttered Thad. I noticed his hand had

dropped to his holster. 'Prepare yourself, Richard.'

The smile froze on my face.

'What are you going to do?'

I never found out, because at that very moment the Black Bull of Clarence decided that it too had had enough. With a flick of its head, it broke its gold chain and jumped off the float to the ground. The young footman hopped down after it, pulling at its nose ring, cracking his whip across its shining flanks, but the huge black bull would not be persuaded. It was going no further. Its knees folded and it sank to its belly, as if camped in the middle of a meadow. And there it stayed. And then of course everyone else stopped, because they couldn't go on without it. All the other animals began prancing about impatiently, pulling at their leads, snarling at their handlers and yapping... Even Fleur de Lys snapped out of her trance.

'Vat are you doin' down zere? Get up, you lazy creature!' she shouted. 'Ver is your pride, big fat bull! Zis is not 'oliday time! LEVEZ-VOUS! MONTEZ! ALLEZ!'

But the Black Bull of Clarence would not be moved.

'Just carry on as if nothing's happened,' Thad instructed Mr Squiddle. 'Richard, we'll catch you up.'

Thad and Captain Cake peeled off and trotted back to the commotion.

'Where's the Keeper of Beasts?' demanded Thad Lancaster.

'No one knows, sir,' replied the young footman, tugging in vain at the bull's nose. 'We couldn't find him; we looked everywhere.'

'What?'

I didn't hear any more; the crowd's low singing drowned out their conversation.

On we went down the centre of The Mall, completely alone

now. Thinking back, that was the hardest part of all. I stared at the thousands of faces spinning past, and clung onto that carriage like it was a life raft in the middle of an ocean… Why were they singing like that? What did it mean? Did they hate me so much? I couldn't tell, but underneath the voices I began to sense something else… something dangerous and strange… building like a wave and coming closer…

There was a snarl behind me and I jumped in shock. Stinky! The royal leopard leapt up into the carriage, spitting and baring her teeth. She looked at me and growled, sending a shower of sparks from her nostrils. Did she sense the danger too? I tried to stay calm.

'Okay Stinky, you can sit there, that's fine–'

Mr Squiddle turned around and his eyes almost popped out of his head.

'Go! Go! Yar!' He urged the horses on. The trot became a fast trot. But not fast enough.

Thump! Thump! Thump!

Up clambered the three Golden Lions of England. What were they doing? Whatever it was, Stinky didn't like it at all. The royal leopard snorted showers of sparks at them and the lions roared back. Now I was sandwiched between four ferocious creatures, baring their teeth and growling at each other.

'Erm, Mr Squiddle? Wilf!'

They both turned around at the blood-curdling noise… then ducked as the sparks shot everywhere.

'Yar! Yar!'

Crack went the whip, and the four grey horses broke into a canter.

'Stinky you've got to stop doing that!' I shouted, noticing one of the seats was now on fire. There was a whinnying behind us, and a squeak–

I looked back. The Silver Yale was chasing us down, followed by the little Red Dragon of Wales and the Brown Bear of Bothelswaite. Then suddenly the White Greyhound of Richmond went sprinting past. All had broken their chains and were racing for the end of The Mall.

'What's going on?' asked Wilf, as the royal falcon dipped by at speed. Who knew? Was it the hostile crowd, or that other approaching danger I'd sensed? Whatever it was, the royal beasts had decided they'd had enough. And they weren't alone. When Stinky snarled yet again, Mr Squiddle stood up, turned to me and removed his hat, which was now on fire.

'Your Highness, I'm sorry to say this leopard scares me sideways. It always has and it always will. I do apologise.'

And with that, he jumped off! He actually jumped off!

'Best of luck, Your Highness,' said Wilf. And then he jumped off too!

'What am I supposed to do?!' I shouted after them.

No answer. They'd gone. The panic of the situation concentrated my mind.

'Stinky, stop it!'

The royal leopard wasn't listening. She was now intent on driving the three lions out of the carriage as well. Maybe she thought she was defending me, I don't know, but she began rushing at them, snorting at them, and with every snort more parts of the old ceremonial carriage caught fire… The four horses began to panic. Their canter got faster and faster… Soon it became an all-out gallop…

'HELP!' I shouted, pulling on the thick leather reins as hard as

I could. It was like tugging at a charging elephant. I glanced back down The Mall. The Great Bull of Clarence was being shoved back onto the float. Patrick Pettifog was attempting to revive Fleur de Lys, who seemed to have fainted. Thad Lancaster was firing wildly into the air, trying to hold back the surging tide of people pushing forward to see what would happen next...

Snap!

I looked down. One of the back wheels was wobbling drunkenly. The other didn't look too good either–

'Richard!'

Out of the crowd came a man on a galloping horse. He was wearing a long black cloak and hat, and a mask obscured his face. It wasn't Captain Cake.

BANG! That wobbly back wheel went flying. The carriage lurched violently, then the other one disintegrated and we were being dragged along on two wheels like a flaming sledge, the back half of the carriage screaming along the tarmac. Off tumbled golden lamps, cherubs, dolphins... and then the Three Lions of England...

'HERE!' shouted the galloping man. 'QUICK!'

I edged towards him. Stinky sensed what I was going to do and she was beside herself, blowing great showers of sparks and spitting–

'JUMP!' he shouted, holding out his hand. I stood up, and just as Stinky was about to lunge at me, I jumped...

Somehow the man scooped me out of the air and hoisted me up into the saddle in front of him.

'Hold tight,' he said, peeling away and riding straight into the crowd. People screamed and scattered in all directions.

'Who are you?' I gasped.

'A friend,' he whispered. 'You're in great danger, Jack. Stay close to those you trust – no one else, understand?'

My heart skipped a beat. He'd used my name! He knew who I was... And then I heard a growl behind us. There was Stinky! Chasing us down, snarling furiously. The next second, the man tugged the reins and the horse came spinning to a halt. No sooner had we slid off its back than Stinky stood before us, barring our way.

'Don't worry, Jack, she's protecting you,' he whispered. 'Trust her.'

Trust her? I stared at the royal leopard advancing towards us, her tail thrashing from side to side, sparks flying from her nostrils...

'Take him, he's yours,' he said, pushing me forward. 'I don't want to harm him. Take him to Buckingham Palace.'

Stinky roared again and the masked man retreated, holding up his hands. I sensed she was thinking about killing him, only something was stopping her... She watched the man back away into the crowd, then turned around and growled at me again... Did that mean 'climb aboard'? When she crouched down, I thought it might. I dared to climb onto her back, grabbing her thick diamond collar, whereupon Stinky stood up and faced the crowds. With a tremendous blast of sparks she cleared a path...

'There he is!'

'Let the Prince through there!'

'This way, lad! Quick!'

The palace guards saw us charging towards them and hurriedly opened the great gates of Buckingham Palace. In we went. The next thing I knew Stinky skidded to a halt, unceremoniously dumping me flat on my face on the gravel.

'Thanks,' I whispered, smiling nervously.

The royal leopard glared down at me like I was an idiot. With a haughty flick of her tail, she turned around and in one leap cleared the railings. I watched her bound away through the crowd to join the rest of the royal beasts heading back into St James's Palace. I was very glad to see they'd all made it, even the Black Bull of Clarence and Fleur de Lys. But the old gold carriage I'd been riding in was nothing more than a blackened heap. I glanced up at the window. The Queen gasped when she saw me, Lily too. Even the King looked a little shaken.

'That was very brave, Your Highness. What an escape!' cried a guard, running forward to help me to my feet. 'Are you hurt?'

'I'm fine,' I said, hastily straightening my wig and remembering who I was.

'D'you know who that was who saved you, sir?'

I didn't, though I wished I did. I turned towards the crowd pressing forward towards the railings. Whoever he was, he'd gone.

'We all thought you was another busted flush like the rest of 'em – but no you ain't, nothing of the sort!'

A jolly old lady waved a flag at me and stretched her hand in through the railings. Quickly realising what was expected of me, I went forward to shake it, and before I knew it, she'd grabbed me by the cheeks and planted a big wet kiss on my nose.

'Oh! I've kissed a proper prince!' She elbowed her friend and they giggled.

I pulled away, embarrassed, then moved on down the line, shaking hands and smiling.

'Well done, Your Highness', 'Good on yer, lad', 'That was something to see'. The crowd was a blur of smiles and flags, and for the first time that day people seemed happy to see me, as if I'd passed some sort of test...

'You're becoming a proper little escape artist, aren't ya?'

I think I smelt him before I saw him. That musty stink of old bonfires... A huge hand gripped mine and when I looked up, I felt like I'd been smacked in the face with a frying pan.

'Thought you'd get away with it, eh? I bet you did.'

It was Abel Goodnight! *Abel Goodnight.* Still wearing that little hat and that dirty brown overcoat, with a matchstick sliding back and forth between his teeth. His meaty hand began to crush my fingers.

'Let me go!' I said.

Abel Goodnight's mouth split into a grin.

'What's your game, yer little tyke–'

'Oi you! Leave it!' The guards stepped forward and knocked Goodnight's arm away, shoving him back into the crowd.

'I'll be seeing you again, *Jack*!' he called.

'Clear off!' shouted the guards.

Abel Goodnight laughed as he was jostled away.

'She ain't who you think she is, mate! She ain't who you think!'

'Darling!'

Out rushed the Queen to envelop me in her arms. Just in time.

'Thank goodness you're safe! What on earth happened?'

She led me back towards the palace, comforting and scolding, but I didn't hear a word of it. All I could think about was that monster from my past... Only when the door was shut safely behind us did I dare to look back through the window. There he was, standing on the other side of the railings. Abel Goodnight raised a huge hand and smiled.

I'll be seeing you again, Jack...

The Oath of Succession

I T TOOK A LOT OF EFFORT to calm myself as we entered
the state drawing room.

'Cuz!' Lily rushed forward and flung her arms around me in an
embarrassing hug. 'My goodness, that was so brave. Are you all right?'

It was a question everyone kept asking me. Obviously I was.

'What on earth made the leopard and the lions want to jump
into the carriage with you?'

I wasn't sure how much to tell them.

'I suppose they were frightened.'

'Frightened of what, my darling?' asked the Queen.

I told them about the silence, and then the singing, and how horrible it all was. I decided not to mention that other feeling I'd had.

'Well I think you were amazing,' said Lily, beaming.

'Utterly amazing,' agreed the Queen. 'And was that Captain Cake who rescued you?'

'It most certainly was not,' growled Thad Lancaster, striding into the room looking very hot and bashed about. Somehow he must have fought his way back through the crowd into the palace. 'Whoever that was had the nerve to knock Captain Cake from his horse. Did you see his face, Richard?'

'No.'

'Why not?'

'He was wearing a mask.'

Thad stood square before me and took off his gauntlets. Clearly he was very angry.

'But he spoke to you, didn't he, Richard? What did he say?'

I remembered the man's words. Be careful who you trust...

'He... he just said I should go back with Stinky – the royal leopard, I mean,' I added hastily.

'Nothing else?'

'No.'

'So you have no idea who he was?'

'No.' I looked at Thad helplessly. 'I'd never seen him before. He just set me down and then disappeared into the crowd. I thought he was a palace guard or something.'

Thad Lancaster scowled, slapping one leather gauntlet against the other in frustration. I suspected he knew who this masked man was...

'Surely we should be grateful to whoever it was for rescuing Richard,' said the Queen. 'If he hadn't been there, I can't think what would've happened.'

'Was there anyone else in the crowd you recognised, Richard?'

I suppose my confusion was obvious. Thad took a step closer.

'There was? Who did you recognise? Tell me, who?'

'Thad, really–'

'What's all this, a quiz?' asked the King, marching in from the next room and rubbing his hands impatiently.

'Edward, I think we may have a problem–'

'Don't be so daft, Thad. Everyone's back safe and sound, even that wretched old pot plant – worst luck.'

'Edward–'

'The only *problem* I can see is the total and complete destruction of Great-Aunt Guddybum's state carriage. No doubt Mr Chitt will be telling us how valuable it was, but frankly sitting in it was like being jiggled about in a steel bucket.'

'Edward–'

'*And* it used to make me sneeze. Honk, honk, honk, honking away like a donkey with a feather stuck up its nose–'

'*Listen* to me Edward!' Thad was staring at me so hard I could feel my cheeks redden. 'Richard still has some explaining to do.'

'Well I'm afraid it'll just have to wait, Thad, because the people are expectin'. The *people*, Thad, are *expectin'*. Save the quezzies for later, eh?'

That spark of red fire danced in Thad Lancaster's eyes as he looked me up and down. I was certain he knew who I was.

'As you wish,' he said at last.

The doors opened onto the balcony and I immediately sensed that something had changed. The angry silence and frightening singing had given way to a murmur of anticipation. Had I done something right? I dared to think I had… In the centre of the balcony there was a small red podium. The King stood to my left, the Queen to my right. They both smiled at me encouragingly. I stared out at the sea of faces stretching away down The Mall.

The Archbishop came forward, dressed in purple and gold. He bowed, and taking the microphone he said: 'And now comes the part I know you've all been waiting for. The Prince will swear before his subjects the Oath of Succession.'

There was an excited murmur below. The Archbishop smiled and indicated that I should step up onto the podium. I did so. He looked down at the card in his hand and wiped his brow. He smiled at me again. Smiled at the crowd. He seemed very smiley, this Archbishop. And a little flustered.

'The Royal Oath of Succession is a solemn, binding promise. It should not be undertaken unadvisedly, or lightly. Once sworn, it can never be broken.' He glanced at me. I nodded nervously. I'd guessed as much.

'If there is anyone who knows any reason why this Prince should not be crowned the next King of Albion, let him speak now.'

I waited, my heart hammering in my throat. There were at least two people down there who knew the truth. Abel Goodnight, and that masked man, whoever he was. And there was Lily, standing on the balcony beside me, and last but not least the person whose place I'd taken, who was at this moment hiding in the Sable Tower…

No one said anything. The Archbishop smiled yet again, then adjusting his glasses, turned to his card and began to read.

'Do you, Richard, James, William, Fitzwilliam, Dingleberry, Trenchermouse, Snevningham…'

The murmuring below turned to giggling.

'Snodlington, Glossypott, Bandicoot…'

The giggling became laughter. I dared to glance at the Archbishop. Was this my name? He kept his eyes firmly on the card.

'Oddy-Noddy, Coriolanus, Cartoonus, Egg-and-Spoonus, Adolphus, Crocodile...'

The laughter became a roar. This couldn't really be my name, could it? The Archbishop looked like he was in pain.

'Fizzlebottom, Aardvark, Canary-bird, Canute–'

'Maybe skip the rest, old boy,' muttered the King, seeing that everyone in The Mall was doubled up, helpless with laughter. The Archbishop, whose face was now as purple as his robes, whistled gratefully like a kettle. He wiped his eyes.

'Do *you*, Richard, swear to become the next King of Albion?'

What could I say? I glanced at the words written on the card in front of me.

'I do.'

'Do you swear to love, honour and protect this fair country and all its citizens, so long as you may live?'

'I do.'

'Then it gives me great pleasure to present the next and rightful King of Albion, Crown Prince, Richard Lancaster!'

The cheer that greeted me took my breath away. I stood there, the smile frozen on my face. What had I done?

'Thanks,' I said, my voice booming down The Mall. 'Thank you very much.'

I raised a hand and waved. The crowds roared and waved back.

'Oddy-Noddy, Fizzlebottom, Adolphus, Crocodile!' They sang, howling with laughter. Well at least I'd made them happy. Maybe it didn't matter that I wasn't Richard after all...

'I think you've convinced them, my boy,' mumbled the King, a little misty-eyed.

The Queen took my hand and squeezed it.

'Of course he has,' she said.

'He's convinced everyone,' said Lily, beaming at me.

I glanced at Thad Lancaster at the end of the balcony, acknowledging the cheers. Whatever doubts he might have had, he was far too sensible to show them in public. Even the twins were happy. It's hard not to smile when thousands of people are smiling back at you.

'All we need now is a fifty-gun salute,' said the King. 'I bet old Chitt's got something up his sleeve. Sort of a birthday surprise, what?'

'I very much doubt it,' muttered Thad. 'He seemed very keen on bits of bunting and mugs of soup.'

'Oh, he might have *said* that, but old Chitty-Chitt's so damned clever. He can see the sun's shining, the people are happy, he'll want a slice of the old reflected glory, what? Y'know what these damned politicians are like. Slippery as weasels.'

'Eels, darling,' smiled the Queen.

'Quite. Slippery as easels,' snorted the King.

'Oh but look, Papa! He has!' Victoria pointed into the blue sky to the east.

'Wow!' gasped Thomas.

It was a squadron of black shapes flying straight towards us over the London skyline. There were twenty or thirty of them, stretched out in a V formation.

'Are those aeroplanes?' asked the Queen.

Down in The Mall people were turning and pointing. There didn't seem to be any sound of engines...

'Some sort of bird, mebbe?' suggested the King, squinting into the sun. 'Swans? Peacocks?'

'Don't be so damned stupid,' growled Thad. 'They're not swans or peacocks.'

Over Admiralty Arch they came, descending lower with every beat of their wings. People down the far end began to scream.

'Good grief! Dragons!' shouted the King.

Dragons they were, large, scaly and black, flying in low like bombers on a mission. At their head was a huge snaggle-toothed creature, with golden eyes and iron spikes bristling from its skull...

'Wellenstorm,' I gasped. 'That's Wellenstorm, isn't it?'

'Wellenstorm?' repeated Lily. She looked at me in horror. I glanced at Thad Lancaster... was that fear in his eyes?

'Come along, darlings, inside, quick quick,' said the Queen, grabbing the twins by the hand and pulling them towards the door.

'But I want to see the dragons, I want to see them!' shouted Thomas, wriggling free. Before anyone could stop him, he'd climbed up onto the stone rail, waving his tiny sword at the oncoming beasts. 'Come on dragons! Come on you nasty dragons! Ha! Ha!'

Wellenstorm noticed the boy and his tiny sword and grinned.

WHOOSH!

A blast of flames ignited the flag just above our heads.

Whump, whump, whump... Over the great dragon flew, his squadron of ugly brutes following. Their wings brushed the rooftops, blocking out the sun.

Whump, whump, whump... Off they went, to the west.

The Mall was silent. I got up from where I was crouching and looked around. Everyone else was also climbing back to their feet, looking a little bewildered. The dragons had come, and they had gone. No one had been killed. Nothing had happened.

'Funny sort of flypast, eh?' said the King, dusting himself down. 'What d'yer suppose was the meaning of that?'

It was a question to which everyone wanted to know the answer.

↝ 65 ↜
Return to Safety

LILY AND I SAT IN SILENCE as the carriage rumbled back
down the tunnel to St James's Palace. After the balcony there
had been sandwiches and cake though no one had felt like
eating anything, then thankfully the twins had thrown a tantrum
at not being allowed to chase Wellenstorm and been put to bed.
The Queen and King would be arriving at the Jackernapes final
later, along with the rest of the government. As for Thad Lancaster,
shortly after the dragon flypast he had disappeared, no one knew
where. I suspected he'd gone looking for my rescuer. That worried
me a great deal. Almost as much as the sight of Abel Goodnight...

'You're positive it was him?'

I nodded.

'And he definitely knew who I was.'

'Gosh.' Lily's face creased into a frown. 'Do you think William Foxglass knows he's here? I bet he does. I bet it's all connected somehow.'

I bet it was too. I just couldn't think how to join up the dots.

'And I'm sure Thad suspects me.'

'Probably, with all those questions he kept asking. And he obviously knows who rescued you too, Jack. So you really didn't see his face?'

I shook my head. It had all happened so fast. Already I couldn't remember if the masked man was tall, short, fat, thin; it was just a blur.

'I sort of wondered if Stinky recognised him,' I said, and explained.

'I still don't understand why that leopard suddenly decided to jump up into the carriage with you,' Lily said. 'It was kind of a weird thing for her to do, wasn't it?'

'I think she was protecting me.'

'From what?'

I tried to describe that feeling I'd had. It was almost impossible to put into words, but I knew I hadn't imagined it. It was like an invisible wave, a silent roar, coming closer, underneath... Lily listened in silence, thinking. Then she said:

'Something strange happened out in The Mall when Stephen was assassinated. We were all in our carriages and Stephen's suddenly stopped. The horses spooked at something and they refused to go any further. That's why he decided to get out and walk, and that's when it happened. No one saw exactly, because Stephen was out there alone, surrounded by people... Jack, you don't think...'

'That was what was supposed to happen to Richard too?'

I shuddered, remembering those voices I'd heard down in the dungeon. Maybe that's what Stinky remembered. It was all becoming a little terrifying.

'And even if that didn't happen, can you imagine Cuz jumping off that burning carriage?' Lily went on. 'He'd never have done that, not in a million years. Either way he'd almost certainly be dead by now.'

On we went down the tunnel, watching the lanterns drift past.

'Why doesn't Marina come to any of these official events?' I asked, hoping to change the subject to something more cheerful.

'Marina? The King's younger sister?' Lily looked at me. 'Don't you know?'

I shook my head.

'She's dead, Jack. She committed suicide. She jumped off the Sable Tower twelve years ago. I thought you knew that.'

'Nobody told me.'

'No, I suppose they wouldn't. Marina's been deliberately forgotten about. It's almost like she never existed.'

'Why did she do it?'

Lily shrugged.

'Nobody knows. Archie Queach says he sometimes sees her ghost wandering around in a long silver dress, like she's come from a ball or something. It's all so terrible. Sometimes I wonder whether the royal family really is cursed.'

I thought about that dark-haired girl in the portrait. That wilful expression on her face. So that's why no one talked about Marina any more. Under the arch we went, swinging to a halt beneath St James's Palace. Lily was not someone who dwelt on anything depressing for long and already she'd moved on to this afternoon.

'Gosh I'm so looking forward to the Jackernapes final,' she said brightly. 'Nothing like a massive game of Jackernapes to make you forget about everything. You're going to play, Jack, aren't you?'

'How can I, Lily?'

Lily seemed amazed.

'But you have to! It would be totally mad for Cuz to do that now. You've just jumped from a flaming carriage and he's probably still fast asleep.'

'But I feel I've taken his place too much already... Won't he want to do it?'

'Want to do it?' she scoffed. 'Walking that pole in front of a packed audience is Cuz's worst nightmare, believe me.'

Disembarking from the carriage, we returned to the Ermine Tower by an inside route. I was steeling myself for another round of congratulations from my schoolmates, but the courtyards were curiously silent.

'On account of the dragons, Your Highness,' murmured Solomon Knock, who was escorting us back through the corridors. 'We're protected in here of course, but you can't be too careful with dragons. I understand they're particularly fond of children. The soft bones, I'm told. Little blonde children especially.'

No prizes for guessing whom he was thinking of.

'Did you ever discover who let out that dragon, Mr Knock?' I asked. 'Did your seeing stones actually "see" anything?'

'Oh they saw many things, Your Highness.'

'Anything to help you solve the crime?' asked Lily.

'I'm not at liberty to say, my lady.'

'So you know who did it, then?'

Solomon Knock's crumpled face crumpled even further.

'You're so mysterious, Mr Knock!'

He grinned painfully and held open the door to Richard's room.

'Good luck with the Greensleeves this afternoon, Your Highness. We'll all be there, cheering you on.'

'Thanks.'

'How you can walk up on that slippery pole I don't know. But I suppose if you can jump from a flaming carriage, you're not afraid of anything.' Mr Knock smiled his lizardy smile, then made an elaborate bow and left.

'You see?' whispered Lily, closing the door. 'There's no way you can swap back again, Jack. Not now.'

I was relieved to see the curtains still closed in Asphodel's cage as we went through to the bedroom. I felt sure the fairy would have already heard about this morning's escapades and would have plenty to say about it.

It turned out he wasn't the only one.

'Cuz?!'

There in bed sat Richard, propped up against a heap of pillows. He was eating a piece of toast and reading a book.

'You're back,' said Lily, shocked.

'I'm back,' he said.

'So soon.'

'That's right.' Richard put down his book and stared at us. He looked tired, sick and bored.

'Gosh that's… great,' said Lily, sitting on the edge of the bed. 'How are you feeling?'

'Better.'

'Are you sure? Only you don't look it. Frankly, Cuz, you don't look much better at all.'

'I'm fine, Lily. Stop flapping.'

There was an awkward silence as Richard turned to stare at me dressed in his finest robes of state. I wasn't sure if he was angry or curious. This was what he might have looked like had someone not decided to poison him. Lily took Richard's hand and patted it in a motherly way.

'The thing is, Cuz, we knew you'd never agree to anything, so... and Jack had the most incredible escape. First the carriage caught fire, then the horses bolted, and *then* a squadron of–'

'Can you stop doing that,' he said irritably, withdrawing his hand from hers. 'Wellenstorm, was it?'

We nodded.

'Everyone's convinced they're going to come back and do something terrible,' Lily went on. 'Thank goodness we're nice and safe in the palace. In fact, bed is probably the best place to be, Cuz.'

Richard crunched his toast.

'Normally I'd agree with you, Lily. Bed is definitely the best place to be, most of the time.'

'Good, because–'

'But it just so happens that I've decided to play in the Jackernapes final after all.'

Lily smiled in confusion.

'Really?'

'Yes *really.*'

'But you hate Jackernapes–'

'Lily you can't talk me out of it. I want to walk the Greensleeves in front of everyone this afternoon, and that's what I'm going to do.'

She stared at him crossly. He took a sip of tea.

'So you think you're up to it?'

'Maybe.'

'You're not going to take one step and, I don't know, collapse and kill yourself?'

'You're not my mother, Lily.'

'I'm *worried* about you, Cuz, and I care about you—'

'Do you? Or is the real reason that I'm interrupting your plans?'

Richard bit into another piece of toast. So he really was angry then.

'It's not about winning,' Lily blustered. 'I don't care who wins—'

'Don't you? Lancaster hasn't won a Jackernapes final since Stephen died, and as long as I'm in the team we probably never will. But with Jack…' He looked at me. 'Why don't you just admit it, Lily?'

'Why can't *you* ever admit that you're really, really ill?'

'I'm doing it. That's that.'

Lily shook her head in frustration. She was clearly embarrassed— and furious.

'You're such a nightmare sometimes, Cuz, you know that?'

'Yup. I do.'

We sat in silence. Lily sighed loudly and folded her arms. Richard seemed quietly triumphant. There was no way he could be persuaded. She knew that very well.

'So what are you going to do now?' she said. 'Because obviously there are two of you. Jack can't go back to jail, and she can't go back to being the Keeper of Ghosts either.'

'I suppose not.'

'So? What then?'

Richard shrugged. He didn't seem that interested in what happened to me, and to be honest, why should he? This was my problem. Somehow taking Richard's place at the presentation had blinded me to everything that might come after. What *was* I going to do now?

'Maybe Dancing Dan has an idea,' said Richard casually.
'Dancing Dan?'

The cupboard door opened and the ghost slipped out noiselessly. He hovered in the centre of the room, immaculate as ever in his black tailcoat and shiny shoes. Of course, he would be here.

'One strives for a certain inevitability in these situations, ma'am.' He bowed to me in his mournful way. 'Your Highness, Lady Lily.'

'Dancing Dan, as you can see, we have a problem.'

'Indeed, Your Highness.'

'That's going to make things a bit tricky, isn't it?'

'It might, Your Highness.'

'Do you have any ideas about what to do with Jack?'

'As a matter of fact, I do, Your Highness.'

'Excellent,' Richard smiled. 'There you are, Lily, simple. Dancing Dan has a plan. Problem solved.'

Lily looked almost as confused as I did.

'Problem solved? That was quick! Would you mind telling us what it is?'

Dancing Dan clasped his hands and inclined his head.

'My lady, if I may suggest...'

☙ 66 ☙
Lancaster versus Plantagenet

THERE IS NO POINT explaining the idea twice. Dancing Dan guided me through the courtyards (I was as ghostly as he was in Mostyn Joliffe's ghost cape) back to the Jackernapes arena, and there we took our seats in a private box in the corner of the auditorium. From here we could see the stalls below and tiers of seats above, and all the boxes on the far side. There was no chance of being disturbed because Dancing Dan had locked the door behind us, and there was no way we could be seen either, because–

'It's invisible from the outside, ma'am,' said Dancing Dan, drawing up a velvet chair. 'This box is reserved for visiting ghosts, which makes it the safest place in the palace. Many important secrets have been shared within these walls. Would ma'am care for some refreshment?'

As he floated off to the kitchens to see what he could find, I leant forward and watched the spectators start to arrive. First came the school children, filing into the stalls below, the black and white scarves of Lancaster on one side, the red and gold of Plantagenet on the other. Everyone had rattles, whistles and banners. In the centre I spotted Jake Tiptree, dressed as a black and white eagle – the Lancaster mascot, whirring his rattle loudly.

'Look at him!' he shouted, as Galahad Joliffe led the keepers in, looking very colourful in their long buttoned coats, and none more colourful than Galahad himself, swathed in a large red and gold Plantagenet scarf with a little cap perched on the back of his head. Taking his seat, he began pointing out all the details of the Jackernapes court to that other Jack Joliffe, who sat sucking on a drink, looking bored. Finally in marched the government, a platoon of grey-suited men and women all looking very serious indeed. Byron Chitt took his seat in the front row of the dress circle, and folding his flipper-like hands across his belly he cast his beady eye over the moving walls, the battlements, the ropes, the dragons' heads... I'm sure he was making a mental note of how much it all must cost, and how much cheaper it would be if Jackernapes was turned into a board game.

A blast from the herald brought everyone to their feet. In walked the King and Queen, still dazzling in their finery. The King was all snorts and guffaws, shaking hands with the gloomy-faced politicians and making jokes that no one seemed to understand. They took their place beside Mr Chitt, perhaps to discuss the sudden appearance of the dragons in The Mall, though I suspect the King was rather more interested in the Jackernapes. There was no sign of Thad Lancaster, or William Foxglass either.

With the auditorium now full to bursting, a bell rang and Onion Runyon and Miss Squirrel marched into the arena wearing green fluorescent capes and matching hats.

'The refs are in fluorescents just in case there's fog,' boomed the King to Byron Chitt.

'Fog, Your Highness?'

'Just in case there's FOG!' boomed the King again, assuming Mr Chitt hadn't heard.

'How can there be fog?'

'Oh there can and there will be fog!' he snorted.

Onion and Miss Squirrel bowed to the audience then welcomed on the Plantagenet team led by their captain, George Hartswood, looking very heroic in his red and gold armour. The crowd roared and George waved to the auditorium. As I said, George Hartswood was a proper school hero and his team looked massive, particularly Tucker-Smith, who seemed positively inflated in his armour. Then in came Lancaster from the other side, led by Lily, all dressed in brilliant black and white.

'That's my niece!' shouted the King. Lily waved excitedly up to the King and Queen.

'Oh and there's the Prince of the moment,' said Byron Chitt, as a green and ill-looking Richard shuffled in at the end of the line. He acknowledged the applause nervously. Why did he want to do this? I was so puzzled. I couldn't help thinking there must be some other reason he wasn't admitting...

The teams complete, they lined up and bowed to the audience.

'I say, Runyon! Psst! Chuck it here.'

The King motioned for Onion Runyon to throw him the

leathery brown ball that was nestling under his arm. Onion lobbed it up and the King caught it, then he handed the ball directly to Mr Chitt.

'Betcha don't know who that is, Chitty-Chitt,' he said.

The Prime Minister stared at the leathery old face with stitched up eyes and attempted to smile politely.

'Is it a relation, Your Highness?'

'That's Oliver Cromwell, that is! The last man to chop a king's head off, Mr Chitt. That's what happened to *him*!'

The King honked loudly and passed it round the cabinet, making sure all the grey-faced ministers got a good look at the leathery old head.

'Oliver Cromwell! Last man to chop a king's head off! Oliver Cromwell, what?' The King could not stop giggling as they passed the ball about as if it was poisonous.

Eventually Cromwell was returned to Professor Runyon and the game could begin. Miss Squirrel flipped a coin and Lily won the toss, giving Lancaster first touch, and both teams climbed up to their starting positions on the opposite battlements. After an age, Richard emerged on the top balcony and stood next to Tim Iddunshy. He looked exhausted already.

Onion Runyon blew his whistle sharply.

'Ready Lancaster?'

Lily stood halfway up the battlements hanging onto a rope. She raised her hand.

'Ready Plantagenet?'

George Hartswood lowered his visor and raised his hand. Professor Runyon nodded to Miss Squirrel behind him, whose arm rested on a lever.

'Begin!' he shouted, and threw Cromwell up into the air.

Miss Squirrel dropped the lever, and there was a great clanking as both castle walls began to move, bricks sliding up, down, sideways, windows and ledges appearing and disappearing...

'But that's dangerous!' gasped Byron Chitt. 'Someone could have an accident!'

The King laughed like it was the funniest thing he had ever heard.

'Very good, Mr Chitt, very good!' he honked.

Already Lily and her team had swung out on ropes and jumped down into the net, grabbing hold of Cromwell and passing amongst themselves. They'd barely had it for five seconds before Tucker-Smith dive-bombed straight into the heart of them, sending Lily flying high into the air. Spiggins swung out on a rope and bashed into her hard, knocking Cromwell from her grasp, and George Hartswood caught it – a clever move. Instantly he threw it back to his ten-strong raiding party, who swung out as one across the net...

And so the great Jackernapes final began. I could try to describe it, but on the other hand there was a little white-haired man sitting high up in the commentary box who knew more about the game of Jackernapes than anyone else. This was Sir Mouse Dipp-Diddle himself, who crouched over the microphone and spoke into it in that fast and breathless way you might hear at a racecourse. What he said went something (but perhaps only something) like this. Maybe. Try reading it very fast without breathing... or just skip to the words in CAPITALS to get the general idea... Ready? Deep breath...

'George Hartswood with the scurry, passes to Tucker-Smith, to Spiggins, to Harrawaddy, who takes it on up the Lancaster castle wall, jumps the moving window, steps across the spinning ledge and up to the battlements they go, Harrawaddy lobs to Spiggins, bounce dodge back to Hartswood and they're gathering to him, this is PLANTAGENET going for the classic Henry Five assault straight up the middle, ooh this is ambitious, THEY GO FOR IT, a climbing phalanx straight up the Lancaster battlements and HARTSWOOD SHOOTS – LONG!

'And it's a LANCASTER STEAL, Lancaster have Cromwell now, on the break with Loder, Cossage, Loder again – bouncing it across the net, fast break this as Spiggins flies with a basher – nicely done there Cossage, up the Plantagenet wall now this girl's a powerhouse – switch play! Plantagenet didn't see that coming, lovely cross-switch from Cossage to Dromgoole on the far side and the Plantagenet defence is scrambling across the battlements to meet her, but Lancaster have a bouncer on the net now, that's Matty Wong the bouncer, getting higher every time, Tucker-Smith swipes out, misses, Wong level with Hooter's nose now – Hooter the nickname for the Plantagenet dragon, their goal of course, high up there above the battlements and Wong's bouncing very high now, right up to the ceiling and I think she's going for a Rupert manoeuvre, she is, this dangerous move named after Prince Rupert who was very keen on this sort of thing and Wong's going for it, next bounce, FRANTIC DEFENCE FROM PLANTAGENET, swipes coming in at all angles as Wong bounces, high, catches the rope and swings, high, Tarzan stuff this as Wong kicks off the wall and drops, she's made it! WONG LANDS ON HOOTER'S HEAD! Talk about goal-hanging! Matty Wong's sitting on *top* of the goal and what can Plantagenet do about that?!

'Spiggins comes screaming in with the bash-off, misses, Harrawaddy, misses, now its Tucker-Smith's turn, Tucker-Smith the big defender swinging round on a rope with a leather basher one-handed, he swipes – solid smash from Tucker-Smith! Wong's unseated, she's slipping, she's going, gone – oh no she's not! Somehow Matty Wong grabs Hooter's snaggletooth and she's still there! Hanging by both hands to the last tooth left in Hooter's gaping mouth, brilliant recovery by Wong, but can she climb back up and can LANCASTER get Cromwell to her now… round to their own battlements it goes and they're going for an Agincourt! This will be the first Agincourt of the match, Cromwell loaded into the Agincourt CATAPULT and it's Dromgoole to take aim – she fires, CROMWELL sails high, it's got the height, has it got the legs, yes, yes, I think it has–

'GEORGE HARTSWOOD! BRILLIANT FLYING INTERCEPT! Out of nowhere, fingertips stuff from Hartswood, plucks Cromwell from mid-air! This is Jackernapes play of the highest quality – OH BUT HE'S DROPPED IT!'

'He's dropped it, Hartswood's dropped it, couldn't hold onto that brilliant catch and it's Cossage sweeping up for Lancaster now, she retrieves, short pass to Poole, Loder, Dromgoole, back to Cossage again, these girls do this so well it's fast fast one-second passes and now LILY LANCASTER HAS IT ONCE MORE, terrific spider-walking from her up over the battlements and looking very determined as Harrawaddy piles in, she scurdles round him, now it's SPIGGINS and TUCKER-SMITH's turn, they cross on ropes, gaining momentum as they GO FOR A SCISSOR-SWIPE TACKLE, NOT ENTIRELY LEGAL this, caused a few deaths in the past, and what can the Lancaster captain do to avoid a serious injury as here they come now, two very big units hurtling down from opposite sides, OOH this is going to be PAINFUL for someone…

'Oh! LILY Lancaster! How did she do that! BRILLIANT

ESCAPE! Somehow at the last second she twists to the wall and the two big defenders whack each other into the middle of next week! They'll be feeling *that* one in the morning! Down they tumble into the net, and Lily Lancaster has all the time in the world for what should be a simple lob up to Wong – LANCASTER SCORE! First points to Lancaster!'

A cloud of smoke puffed from the dragon's nostrils.

'BRAVO!' roared the King, leaping to his feet. 'Bravo Lancaster!'

Matty Wong dived down into the net to be smothered by her teammates. George Hartswood ripped off his helmet in disgust.

'Was that a goal?' asked Byron Chitt, leading the rest of the government in polite applause.

'That was a Jackernapes goal with knobs on, Mr Chitt!' whinnied the King. 'You'll not see better than that this afternoon. Well done, Matty Wong! You'll get the hang of it, old chap.'

Byron Chitt did not look convinced.

'And you actually used to play this game, Your Highness?'

'Rather!' he snorted. 'Every king, queen, keeper and servant has played Jackernapes at one time or other. Even Queenie's had a go, haven't you Queenie?'

'I've tried,' she admitted. 'I'm not very good.'

'Nonsense! She's actually jolly good, Chitty-Chitt. Superb dunk-chasing Hooter-watcher and not half bad at firing Agincourts either.'

Byron Chitt smiled weakly. I could tell that Jackernapes was not a game he was ever going to understand.

Racing to an early lead, Lancaster found themselves six one up by the end of the first quarter, but then a combination of bad luck and some nasty fouls by Tucker-Smith – one basher-smash tackle knocked Matty Wong clean out and she was stretchered out of the arena – saw the Plantagenet team fight their way back, and it was six five at half-time.

'Have I missed anything good?'

The door opened and in came a silver tray laden with cakes and tea, followed by Dancing Dan.

'It's very exciting,' I replied. 'Why don't you stay to watch?'

Dancing Dan smiled weakly and set down his tray.

'Jackernapes is not really my thing, ma'am. It all seems rather dangerous.'

He arranged the table, then loitered a moment beside the door.

'May I ask if anyone's joined you while I've been gone, ma'am?'

'I don't think so. Why, were you expecting someone, Dancing Dan?'

Dancing Dan inclined his head in that mysterious way of his.

'As this is the ghost box, they do have a habit of wandering through occasionally. It's very haunted.'

'No one has wandered through yet, as far as I know.'

'I see. Galahad Joliffe usually kept a packet of revealing dust in the cupboard should he need it. I believe there is a bottle and a straw in there as well.'

With a nod he slipped away, closing the door behind him. I crunched a biscuit, and looked around at the dark red walls of the box. There was no one here but me, I thought, though now I wasn't quite so sure. Out in the auditorium everyone was eating ice creams. The King and Queen were drinking champagne and merrily chatting away to Byron Chitt. The Master was locked in deep conversation with Ocelot Malodure. I noticed Patrick Pettifog leave his seat beside them and quietly slip away out the back. He looked nervous, but then he always did. Perhaps Fleur was being particularly demanding after her traumatic morning…

A roar erupted as the two teams came out again for the second half. George Hartswood and Lily both looked very determined as they led the way up to their battlements.

'And there's my boy, right up there, Chitty-Chitt, you see him?'

The Prime Minister looked suitably impressed and shocked at the sight of sickly Richard standing on the rickety platform at the end of the Greensleeves pole.

'Does he like doing that, Your Highness?'

'Can't get enough of it, Chitt. It's all he ever talks about. Born to do it.'

The Queen smiled faintly.

It was at this moment that I heard a soft knock at the door.

'Come in?'

Nothing happened so I got up, and as I did, I felt something pass by me, a sort of tingling feeling... From my days in the Ghost Vault I knew what it was...

'Hello?'

Silence.

'Who are you?'

It was still there, I sensed it. Something agitated and nervous was sitting in the chair. I wasn't scared of ghosts by now, but I'd learned to treat them with caution. I tiptoed back towards the cupboard and opened it. There was the bottle and straw, and a small packet of revealing dust. I shook out a small heap into my palm and crept forward... Three quick puffs filled the air with dust and I whispered the words...

'Fair or foul, foul or fair,

Leave thy dream, enter air!'

I was right. After a moment the shimmering shape became a young woman in a black velvet cape.

She looked at her watch. She was clearly waiting for someone. And that person was not here.

'Hello?' I said again.

The ghost stood up suddenly and turned around. She was dark haired and very beautiful, and wore a long silver dress. She stared at me with a determined expression that I recognised from somewhere… There were tears glittering on her cheeks.

'Who's that?' she whispered.

Even though she was looking straight at me, I sensed she couldn't see me.

'Who is it? Who's there? Show yourself!' she demanded again.

I couldn't understand why she couldn't see me – and then suddenly I remembered.

You cannot communicate with your own relations…

Galahad Joliffe's rules. You could see them, hear them, but they couldn't see you, only sense your presence… This made me even more nervous. Who was this? The beautiful young woman stared straight through me, then held out her hand and touched the air in front of my face. I felt my skin tingle as her fingers moved over my cheeks… She knew something was there…

'If this is more of your magic, Asphodel, I'm not listening to it,' she murmured, withdrawing her hand. 'You think you've won, don't you? You think that now I've lost everything you can make me mad. Torment me for the rest of my life!' There was a strange, determined look on her face. 'No, Asphodel. I'm not going to give you that satisfaction.'

'I'm not Asphodel,' I said.

The ghost stared through me with great sadness in her eyes.

'Goodnight,' she said.

My heart was thundering in my head. There was something in

her expression that in that moment I knew, I just knew… Wiping her eyes, she drew up her hood and opened a secret door in the panelling.

'Wait…'

Off she went into the darkness and with a racing heart I followed. At the end of the corridor the ghost swept down a small flight of stone steps and round a narrow cloister. I was almost running to keep up. Just as I reached the next corner, I noticed something small glowing there. It was a small envelope, unopened. It must have fallen out of her pocket…

'Wait!' I called again, forgetting she couldn't hear me.

The ghost floated on through the cloister and out of sight. Part of me wanted to chase after her, but curiosity stopped me… There was an M written on the front. *M*. I knelt down and picked it up. It glowed like a jewel in my palm. I knew the proper thing to do would have been to go back for the bottle and capture it to read it properly, but how long would this haunting last? The letter inside might disappear at any moment… Carefully I opened it and peered down at the short note, scribbled in pencil.

My Darling M,

I am writing in haste, hoping this letter reaches you in time. By now you will have heard all the rumours about Wellenstorm and what happened last night. How that young family perished in the blaze, how they all died —

It's not true! She's alive! I rescued her!!

Yes, she was almost lost, and bears deep scars, but she's a tough little thing. In time, I'm sure they will heal. I'm hiding her away now, somewhere Asphodel's spies will never find her. For that reason I cannot say more, but I'll tell you all when I see you.

In the meantime, you <u>must</u> keep this a secret. If they ever find out our little girl survived, they will come looking for her. And please, <u>don't blame yourself</u>. You gave her away because you had no choice. It was the only thing you could do.

<u>*None of this is your fault.*</u>

<u>*I will see you again very soon, my Love...*</u>

The glowing paper began to shimmer, then melted into the air between my fingers... You can imagine what I was thinking. So she'd never read this letter. It had fallen unopened from her pocket. She'd never known... But who was it from? I felt breathless, numb. There was no way I was going back to the Jackernapes now. Not when I realised that finally, at long last, I was beginning to stumble upon the truth...

The Curtain Rises

I HURRIED THROUGH the cloisters, across dark courtyards, meeting no one, seeing no one. Everyone must've been watching the Jackernapes game, even Enid Cribbage perhaps, though had I met her she wouldn't have seen me in Mostyn Joliffe's ghost cape. I was just about to climb the tower to Richard's room when a small figure scurried down the staircase, almost knocking me out of the way. He was wearing a black cloak and a tall hat, but neither of these could disguise who he was.

'When the deeds of this great night are written, let it be said that brave Tom played his part!' he muttered. 'I ain't no lazy maggot! All is cushty, the way is prepared!'

'Bootle? Is that you?'

The small figure stopped suddenly and spun around. Tom Bootle looked deeply worried. His ears hung flat and his eyes darted about nervously. In his hand he carried a pair of lanterns.

What's this, a ghost to haunt me too?' he murmured. 'Custards and chicken, I'm off to the tunnels this minute! This very minute, Master! About my business, as instructed—'

'What are you doing?'

Tom Bootle stopped again.

'Who is that? Show yourself!'

And so I did, shaking off the ghost cape. The instant Tom Bootle recognised me he ran forward, grasping my hand.

'Oh, Miss Joliffe! Hide yourself, quick! Such beasts are about, such–' and then, just as before, Tom Bootle was violently hauled up by the neck by some invisible force.

'DON'T TEMPT ME, BUNNIKIN! CURB THY TONGUE OR I'LL SLICE IT OUT! TO YOUR STATION AND AWAIT MY COMMAND!'

Tom Bootle dropped to the ground, coughing and gasping.

'Bootle? What's going on?'

Tom Bootle glanced at me in terror, then he sprinted away across the courtyard. Whatever was happening, there was no time to find out... and it wasn't Tom Bootle that I wanted to see...

I raced up the spiral steps to Richard's room, careful not to tread on the wafting hem of Mostyn Joliffe's ghost cloak. I tried the door. It was open.

'Asphodel?'

There was the spindly shadow of the fairy, lolling in his chair, staring out of the window. I noticed he had a small lamp in his hands and he was playing with it.

'Given up already have you, boy?' His voice was thin and croaking. He hadn't bothered to turn around. 'I suppose a full game of Jackernapes is far beyond your capabilities.'

'I'm feeling quite well, thank you,' I replied. 'Just a little bored.'

Asphodel kept his eyes fixed on the purple sky beyond the rooftops. That was such a Richardish remark he didn't suspect who I was.

'Bored, eh? Always bored when it suits you. Oh Richard – even on your presentation day you still don't want to grow up. One day, my Prince, this nursery behaviour will have to end.'

'And what will happen to you then, Asphodel?'

The fairy shrugged.

'Nothing, of course. Asphodel is an institution, as royal as sponge cake and trumpet fanfares. Asphodel will be amusing the heirs to the throne with his clever impressions and wonderful stories long after you've shuffled off your mortal coil, my Prince. Don't worry yourself over what will become of old Asphodel. Asphodel is quite capable of looking after himself.'

The fairy still hadn't turned around. On off went his lamp. On off. On off. I glanced out of the window. There were little lights everywhere, flashing like fireflies… I dared to walk closer.

'Do you know someone called Abel Goodnight?'

The fairy stopped flashing his lamp a moment. He paused to think.

'Abel Goodnight? Upon my life I've never heard such a name. Are you sure you don't mean Abel Good Morning, or Abel Good Afternoon?' he smirked. 'How came you upon this fellow?'

'I met him this morning. He was standing outside Buckingham Palace. I think he was rather disappointed he hadn't been able to kill me.'

Asphodel turned around at that. There was a mixture of spite and suspicion in his horrid little face.

'What strange magic are you practising, child? Where are you?'

'Sitting in the chair right in front of you,' I replied. 'Perhaps you can't see me, Asphodel, because your eyes are very bad, aren't they?'

The fairy squinted into the darkness.

'Jack Joliffe told me he tried to kill her too. Strange that, isn't it? I suppose Abel Goodnight does all your dirty work. Did he also kill Stephen at his presentation? Is that what happened, Asphodel?'

'I'll hear no more of this!' he rasped, wagging a thin finger in my direction. 'If you know not of what you speak, young Prince, speak not of what you know!'

'What I know is that you're lying, Asphodel. And you've probably been lying to everyone all along.'

The fairy flung down his lamp and approached the bars of his cage, his expression furious.

'You have a waspish tongue, lambykin; it shall lead you into dark corners! Why I'd rather live with cheese and garlic in a windmill than listen to such—'

There was a splash as a vase of dirty water hit Asphodel square in the face. I'm pleased to say that the fairy's shock was utter and complete. He stood there, drenched.

'You will never, *ever* be forgiven for that,' he said hoarsely, blowing water from his mouth. 'Oh flesh, flesh, thou art fishified! Never, since Adam first stepped on Eden's fair soil, has so great a wrong been—'

'OH SHUT UP WITH YOUR POETRY!' I shouted, pulling off my cape. Asphodel stared at me, his wizened face brimming with fury and hate.

'You… it's you… GUARDS!' he screamed. 'GUARDS, I'M

BEING ATTACKED! HELP! HELP!'

I grabbed the milk jug and emptied it all over him. Then I did the same with the cold tea from the teapot, the sugar, the salt – I'm not ashamed to say that I enjoyed tormenting this small defenceless creature. I wanted to provoke him. I wanted him to go crazy. I wanted to hear from his own lips what terrible things he'd done.

'No one can hear you, Asphodel, so you'd better start telling me the truth!'

'AAHHH!'

Asphodel shook himself like a dog and launched himself up to the roof of his cage. For a second he was out of sight with a pin between his teeth, then he wriggled through a tiny hole he'd opened and darted straight at my face.

'Thou lowest and most dejected thing of fortune, thou are not worth the dust which the rude wind blows in your face! Out vile jelly!'

Squirming through my fingers his fangs lunged for my eyes, trying to rip them out. I screamed and twisted, trying to beat him off.

'You will not survive this night, Jack Joliffe! Unwanted bastard you were and always will be! If not blind then wounded – yes! I shall open a vein, prepare the feast...'

I screamed again as Asphodel tried to sink his fangs into my wrist.

'GET OFF!' I shouted, and with all my strength grabbed his slender body and flung him across the room. Asphodel bounced off the tapestry, then he flew straight back again, fast.

'TELL ME THE TRUTH!' I shouted.

'Thou knowest the truth, Jack Joliffe! All that thou suspects, thou art! All of it! I know not how, or why, but who am I, pauper? Who am I!' he screeched.

'What are you talking about?' I said, trying to follow him as he whizzed about the room like a bat.

'THAT!' he howled, hovering suddenly and pointing to the window. 'See! The curtain is up, the play has begun! Look to your battlements, human child! What chance have you against such brutes? Such savages! Such dread majesty!'

I dared to approach the window and look out. Across the rooftops dark shapes were sliding like a moving mountain range… Dragons! They were everywhere! I stared at the fairy in terror. The lamp… he was guiding them in, and Tom Bootle…

'Asphodel, what have you done?'

'The wheel has come full circle! Asphodel's no longer a clown for clumsy fingers to play with! When the sun rises you shall call me Noble Asphodel! Duke Asphodel! Your Grace!'

I stared at the fairy, his black eyes gleaming. Now I really didn't understand.

'But why are you helping Wellenstorm?'

'Helping? *Helping*? HA!' Asphodel exploded with laughter. 'That great scaly oaf may lay ancient claim to the throne of Albion, but he is a mere *worm* before the once and future Queen! See how he is my dancing bear and I've led him a merry dance! Get thee to the Jackernapes, child! Away, thou art required!'

'Required for what?'

'Thine is not to reason why! The altar awaits! GET THEE TO THE JACKERNAPES!'

Asphodel had clearly gone mad. With a scream he rushed at me and I raced for the door, slamming it in his shrieking little face. There was a thud as the fairy hit the heavy oak at full tilt, then another as he hit the floor. I sincerely hoped he'd knocked himself out. If he'd broken his neck that would have been even better…

༄ 68 ༄
Near Miss

DOWN THROUGH THE courtyards I ran. Actually
it was more of a dart and skid as I dashed from one
column to another, trying to stay out of sight. When I
dared to peek up at the rooftops they seemed to be made entirely
of scales, and they were all moving... So Wellenstorm's dragons
were being guided in through some secret entrance; that much I
could believe... only somehow Asphodel had tricked them... Was
that another of the fairy's boasts? I didn't know what was true any
more – except for that one fundamental thing...

All that thou suspects, thou art...

If I'd had more time I might have sat down and thought hard

about that. How I'd just met the ghost of my mother. How she'd given me away for my own safety. How she'd never known I'd survived that terrible inferno. If she had, would she still have done what she did? And had Asphodel a hand in that too? All of these were big, important questions, tragic questions, yet Asphodel was right; the curtain was up, the great events of that night in motion, there was barely even enough time to describe what happened next. All I can remember is racing around cloisters, hugging the shadows, till somehow I reached the Keepers' Courtyard. There the Isabella tree stood, stunted and blackened in its cage... The once and future Queen... What did Asphodel mean?

'Oh. Dear. Me.'

I looked up, dazed. I barely knew who I'd collided with until Archie Queach's surprise twisted into a sneer.

'Still skipping around the palace, Joliffe? I thought you'd have more sense.'

'I thought you'd be watching the Jackernapes.'

Archie made a face like he'd smelt something terrible.

'Per-lease. Watch a load of snotty-nosed toffs chase a funny-looking ball around?'

Well yes, I sort of sympathised, only now was not the time. He grabbed me by the collar and hauled me to my feet.

'Now why do I think you're supposed to be in jail, Joliffe? Oh yes, it's because you are.'

'Archie, listen to me—'

He pinched my ear and twisted hard.

'Ow!'

'Don't think you can talk your way out of it this time, Joliffe.'

'Let me go!'

'You'll be joining all your special friends in the special cell.

Father Flog and Mother Flog, and maybe Auld Scratty as well–'

'STOP IT!' I shouted, elbowing him as hard as I could in the stomach. Archie doubled up, winded. Wow, I thought, I've really hurt him.

'You're dead now, Joliffe,' he gasped. 'You're seriously dead–'

He lunged at me clumsily and I dodged out the way.

'Archie you've got to go down to the dungeon and release all the Dragon Keepers, and find Sam Yuell, and anyone else who can fight–'

'I don't take orders from you, Joliffe!' he screamed. 'You're nothing but a nasty, evil little witch! You're going straight back to the gutter where you belong!'

'OH SHUT UP CAN'T YOU! LOOK UP THERE!'

And then Archie did look. He stared at the dark shapes slithering over the roofs and chimneys. I was pleased to see that sneer freeze on his face...

'But the palace is dragonproof–'

'Not any more. Asphodel's guided them to some secret tunnel. I saw Tom Bootle go to open it. They're coming in, Archie, *in.* Do you understand?'

At last Archie Queach did understand. And then he did exactly what I expected he would.

'AHH!' he screamed. 'AHHH!'

And for the first time in my life I was grateful to a dragon, for just as Archie fled in terror a huge scaly head dropped down from the archway in front of him and cut off his escape. The dragon's yellow eyes narrowed and Archie stood transfixed, trembling like a leaf.

'Nice Mr Dragon, lovely Mr Dragon... hello! I'm Archie, Archie Fibbler Queach, and I'm just a thin bony person, and I'm sure I taste disgusting, in fact I *know* I taste disgusting, and my feet smell, and my armpits smell, and I've got the most terrible wind, *and* a ticklish cough, and oh *no... please... no...*'

Archie continued his pathetic protests as the dragon silently opened its dripping mouth and picked him up between its jaws. Now don't misunderstand me, Archie Queach had done some terrible things and I didn't like him one little bit, but that didn't mean I wanted to see him crunched to bits – okay, mainly because he still had the keys to the jail hanging from his belt. Slowly and quietly the dragon began dragging Archie away.

'No Mr Dragon, no no, take her! Take *her*,' he pleaded as I approached, picking up Archie's staff that was lying on the ground. 'She's much tastier, no nasty long hair to get stuck in your teeth, oh *please*, Mr Dragon, *please*, why don't you eat *her*!'

The dragon growled at me like a cat guarding its mouse.

'Eat *her*! Eat *her*!' he shrieked.

Wow he was making this difficult.

'Spit him out this instant!' I commanded, trying my best to sound heroic. The dragon shook its great head and growled again, louder than before.

'PUT HIM DOWN!' I shouted, and without warning rammed Archie's staff as hard as I could up the dragon's nostril. The huge creature instantly jerked its head back and screamed in pain. The next second Archie was blasted out across the cobblestones along with several bucketfuls of green snot.

'RUN!'

The dragon roared and spat angry streams of flame after us as we raced around the cloister. Luckily its shoulders were so wide it couldn't get through the archway, otherwise I'm certain we would have been incinerated. It screamed with frustration as we slammed the door to the Keepers' Courtyard behind us.

'Now d'you believe me?' I said breathlessly.

Archie hung off the wall, panting hard. I knew an apology was out of the question, but at least he seemed completely terrified.

'Just go and release all the Dragon Keepers from the jail, Archie. Do it now. Please.'

'Where are you going?' he gasped.

'To the Jackernapes arena. I've got to warn them, haven't I?'

'But they're in the middle of the final. You can't stop it. Can you?'

~~ 69 ~~
Winner Takes All

GOOD QUESTION. I had no idea. I opened the door to the auditorium and raced up the steps towards a roar of noise. No one had any idea about what was happening outside; they were all caught up in the drama of the final, which had obviously just ended with the scoreboard tied at seventeen points each. Lily stood at the base of the Lancaster castle wall, arms linked with the rest of her team, and George Hartswood's Plantagenets stood opposite, arms thrown across each other's shoulders. They all looked sweaty, battered and nervous as Richard and Tim Iddunshy waited on that rickety little platform at the end of the Greensleeves pole. It was up to them now to decide who would win… What could I do?

Neither Onion Runyon nor Miss Squirrel spotted me as I quietly made my way round the back to where Lily stood. I noticed her armour was covered in dents and she had a long cut on her forehead. I tapped her on the shoulder and she turned around in amazement.

'Jack? What are you doing here?'

'We've got to stop the game,' I whispered.

'Okay,' she said, her eyes drifting back to the platform above. 'Why's that?'

The gong went for silence and the nasal rat-at-at-at of Sir Mouse Dipp-Diddle filled the room.

'And it's going to be Tim Iddunshy of Plantagenet who'll go first. Can he improve on the eleven steps he set?'

'Wellenstorm's come back. Lily, this is really important. His dragons are crawling across the roof. Right now.'

She wasn't listening.

'Lily, I'm serious. Asphodel's been signalling to them. I'm sure they've found some secret entrance—'

Suddenly George Hartswood appeared on the platform, pushing little Tim out of the way.

'George?!' gasped Lily. 'You can't do that!'

Boos and whistles echoed around the auditorium.

'Come on, Onion! That's not in the rules!' shouted a slightly scary-looking, red-faced girl to Lily's left. That was Blossom Cossage. 'That's cheating, ref!'

'Cheat! Cheat! Cheat!'

The Lancaster team were *not* happy.

'On the contrary, it's perfectly legal,' squeaked Sir Mouse Dipp-Diddle through the microphone. 'A team captain may take over any position, at any time, whenever he or she feels like it. An obscure rule, but a rule nevertheless, set out by that great player of Jackernapes and *inventor* of Greensleeves, Henry VIII himself.'

Tucker-Smith and Spiggins grinned hugely and jeered from the other side.

'Typical George, putting personal glory before his team,' muttered Lily primly.

'Lily?' Blossom Cossage leant forward and pointed to the platform. 'Go on, you must!'

Lily shook her head.

'No. I can't. That wouldn't be fair. This is Richard's day.'

'Oh stop being so blinking noble, Lily!' hissed Blossom Cossage. 'If George does this we're toast!'

Which was probably true. Definitely true.

'Lily, this is really, really important—'

'Sorry, Jack, I have to watch this.'

Another gong sounded and the arena hushed to silence. George steadied himself on the edge of the pole. I didn't know what to do. I looked up around the auditorium in panic. Everyone was concentrating on George up there on that lonely platform – *almost* everyone that is: the Queen was staring straight at me. I suppose my sudden appearance amongst the Lancaster team must have surprised her. I don't know any sign language, so I just pointed at the ceiling and mouthed 'dragons'. She didn't understand. 'Dragons,' I repeated. 'There-are-dragons-up-on-the-roof. Wel-len-storm.'

The Queen tugged quietly at the King's arm and whispered in his ear. He reacted as if it was some nonsense and batted her away. I pointed up again. 'Dragons...'

'One! Two... three, four, five.'

George had begun his walk. It was a point a step and he was

on his way.

'Six seven eight... nine ten... eleven... twelve...'

George was concentrating so hard he was grinning. The Plantagenets below were starting to get excited.

'Thirteen fourteen fifteen–'

George Hartswood was out in space, staring at the Greensleeve rag at the far end, stealing himself for something big. And then–

'Sixteen-seventeen... eighteen nineteen... twenty... one-two-thri-fur-fiv-six-sev-ei-ni-thirty-one-two-three-four–'

Clever George, he knew he'd lost it, and dipping and flapping he danced along the pole taking tiny steps till he finally slipped and plummeted down into the net. The auditorium erupted. Thirty-*seven* steps. Well over halfway. Amazing.

'That's got to be the school record!' shouted Jake Tiptree. George Hartswood was enveloped by his teammates in a massive pile. Smiles, screams, wild applause.

'Well done, George,' said Lily, clapping reluctantly. 'Well done.'

'Creep,' growled Blossom Cossage, thumping the wall behind her in frustration. 'That's it, we're doomed.'

The microphone blurted to life.

'And after that outstanding performance from George Hartswood, it all comes down to this, the last play of the game. Lancaster need thirty-eight points to win it, a distance never achieved in the modern era, and who better to attempt it than their specialist funambuler, it's number fourteen, His Royal Highness, Richard Lancaster!'

Screams erupted from Richard's fan club. The King cheered. The Queen clapped politely and glanced at me. I pointed up at the roof again and shrugged helplessly. I was now convinced she knew something was wrong...

'Lily, the dragons—'

'Can't you shut up?' she hissed. 'This is Richard's big moment. The palace is dragonproof!'

'But supposing it isn't?'

'So what are you expecting me to do about it?'

Lily bit her nails and ignored me. She was right. If I'd had any sense I'd have gone straight up to the commentary box, grabbed the microphone from Sir Mouse Dipp-Diddle and told everyone what was about to happen… which sort of explains what happened next. I was only trying to help…

'Excuse me! Hello everyone! I'm sorry to interrupt the game—'

'Silence for the funambulers, please!' squealed Sir Mouse Dipp-Diddle through the microphone. He peered down at me angrily as I stood on the edge of the Jackernapes arena facing the packed auditorium. What could I do? Ignore him…

'There are dragons, I mean lots of dragons, crawling across the roofs right now, and I think they've found a secret way in, so maybe it would be a good idea if—'

'SILENCE DOWN THERE!' roared Sir Mouse Dipp-Diddle in fury.

'But they've found a way in—'

'Who is this? Get out of it!' called the audience, impatiently waving me away.

'I'm serious! You have to believe me!' I cried, as the jeering and whistling got louder. Shouts of 'Come on Richard!' filled the hall and a slow handclap began.

'Off-off-off-off!'

'KINDLY LEAVE THE ARENA!'

I stared at the rows of angry faces, all booing and waving me away. I looked up at the Queen. I think she believed me, but I wasn't sure.

'RICHARD LANCASTER!'

Richard shuffled up to the end of the pole. I had no choice but to return to the side of the net. Lily gave me a very cold stare.

'What are you *doing*?' she muttered.

'Lily, I'm telling the truth—'

'I can't believe you're so stupid! Don't you realise how hard this is for him already? He doesn't need any more distractions—'

'But—'

'Shut. Your. Face! NOW!' growled Blossom Cossage, poking me hard in the chest.

Fine, I would. This was a disaster. Biting my lip, I looked up at Richard preparing himself. Compared to George Hartswood, he was so thin and puny. Taking deep breaths, he stared across at the Greensleeve, his dark features knotted in concentration. The gong rang for silence once more. Silence came, and this time it held.

'Come on, Cuz, you can do it,' whispered Lily.

Richard stretched out his arms and bent his knees.

'One.'

The first step.

'Two.'

He'd left the platform and was out in space.

'Three. Four. Five.'

Richard paused. Breathed deeply. Just a twig-like silhouette against the great dome of the Jackernapes arena. This was hard to watch.

'Seven would be amazing, eight to ten totally brilliant, anything beyond that completely incredible,' whispered Lily. 'Come on, Cuz.'

Richard held a sort of crouching position, his fingers strangely curled in the air.

'Six, seven, eight, nine... ten.'

'That's his record!' Lily gasped.

Down below a few dared to clap. I noticed George Hartswood start to bite his nails. The King was on the edge of his seat. Suddenly Richard went again, fast, scurrying like an insect. Ten to twenty in quick little steps! But how – how could he do that? Lily was holding her mouth in shock.

'This is insane,' she whispered, peering up at the tiny silhouette. 'Come on, Cuz. You can do this.'

Richard stood up there in the middle of the wooden pole, his knees bending a little as it bounced, his fingers gripping at nothing.

'Come on my boy!' shouted the King, on his feet now.

And off he went again in that strange little scurry.

'Twenty-one, twenty-two, twenty-three, twenty-four...'

Wobble. *Big* wobble. Screams from below. Richard almost smiled. Steadying himself, he concentrated hard on that dusty green rag hanging from the wooden target at the end. Then off he went again... *another* ten steps... thirty-four! By now the noise in the auditorium was deafening. Everyone was on their feet and screaming for him to do it. The great wave of sound seemed to be holding him up there like a bubble.

'Come on, Richard!' I shouted, forgetting everything else now. Win the game and break the record, and prove to them all you're not so useless after all...

Richard's brow knitted in concentration, his arms held wide as the ancient wooden pole bounced up and down. Four more steps were all he needed. He was going for it now, everyone knew it; this was it...

Taking a deep breath, Richard began to lift his foot...

Chaos Unleashed

A**ND THEN EVERYTHING** happened at once. How predictable! Just when something amazing was about to happen, something terrible happened instead! Why did it have to be then, exactly at *that* moment? Honestly, I have no idea. Things just happened when they happened; I couldn't control them. I'm only writing it down as I remember it.

Anyway, so when I say 'everything happened at once', what I mean is not *everything,* exactly, just lots of things that I've tried to put into some kind of order, otherwise it would be too confusing. It went something like this. The moment Richard began his final scurry the head of a large dragon burst through the floor of the Jackernapes arena beneath the net. It spat up a huge plume of flame, then with a roar struggled out of the hole. Then came another, then another, then another, all thrashing and wriggling and tearing at the net with their talons...

Screams filled the auditorium. Things began to catch fire. Lily turned to me in panic. What could I say? Told you so? That wouldn't have been very helpful. Everyone immediately began racing for the exits, the King and Queen going one way, Byron Chitt and his government the other, crawling fast on all fours like a herd of pigs. Only Thomas and Victoria were left standing on their seats, giggling and clapping as the flames sprayed all around.

'Kill them all! Kill them all!' they chanted gleefully. 'Kill everyone!'

'And him!' Thomas shouted, pointing to Richard up on the pole.

'*Especially* him!' screamed Victoria, suddenly very excited. 'Kill him first! He's up there!'

'KILL HIM! KILL HIM! KILL HIM!'

Solomon Knock grimaced as he bundled the pair of shrieking blonde monsters over his shoulders and carried them away to safety.

'Good Lord, he's going to do it!' shouted the King, suddenly looking up from behind a chair. 'He's going to jolly well do it!'

For a second everyone forgot to escape and looked up.

'Richard?' Lily gasped.

Through the clouds of smoke, I saw his thin silhouette, arms outstretched, now even closer to the Greensleeve... somehow he'd carried on, oblivious...

'Get back to yer microphone!' roared the King, spotting Sir Mouse Dipp-Diddle attempting to slip out the door. Hastily he returned to his seat.

'Richard Lancaster, what an absolutely marvellous achievement, quite exceptional, who would've thought it–'

'STOP BLITHERING, MAN!' fumed the King. 'SAY SOMETHING IMPORTANT!'

Sir Mouse Dipp-Diddle ducked as dragon fire blasted straight over his head.

'Right. Something important. A-hem. Ladies and gentlemen, this is history in the making! Not since the invention of Greensleeves has a prince been so fearlessly fearless, so daringly daring–'

Another blast. The table caught fire. Sir Mouse Dipp-Diddle pretended to ignore it.

'Can this sickly second son, who's never shown much enthusiasm or aptitude for the gentle art of funambling, really make it to the very end?'

'OF COURSE HE CAN!' roared the King.

'Of course he can, of course he can,' Sir Mouse Dipp-Diddle hastily agreed.

'Steady and sure as a mountain goat, his twiggy little legs are taking him further than Henry VIII, Elizabeth I, James II, George III, Queen Vic–'

The microphone popped, then exploded. Now even Sir Mouse Dipp-Diddle's bow tie was on fire, and so were his notes. He stared helplessly at the King.

'Go on, Richard!' shouted the King. 'Go on my boy!'

At last two dragons managed to rip a hole in the net and began squirming through it. Amazingly, Richard didn't flinch, didn't take his eyes off the Greensleeve for one second. If he fell now…

'I can't watch,' said Lily, peeping through her fingers.

Suddenly Richard began his final scurry. With neat little feet, he carefully stepped over the lace handkerchief left at the end of the pole by Charles II, took three more steps, then with a shout leapt up onto the narrow platform.

'HE'S DONE IT!' roared the King, punching the air. 'HOT DIGGEDY DOG – THE BOY'S DONE IT!'

Richard grabbed the ancient green sleeve from the centre of the target and turned around in triumph – only to see the pair of dragons hurtling up towards him... Richard's smile turned to terror and he pressed himself back towards the target... back and back, flattening himself against it...

'RICHARD!' screamed Lily, and so did I.

The dragons grinned and opened their mouths to strike...

WHOOSH!

The streams of fire cannoned into the wall.

And when the smoke cleared...

The target was empty. Richard had gone.

Disappeared.

Gone.

Fire and Fog

SILENCE. **LILY AND I** stared at the empty target, open-mouthed.

'It must have flipped over, like a door–'

'Like a door? To where?'

It was a silly question. How could Lily know? How could anyone know? The last person to touch the Greensleeve was Henry VIII himself over five hundred years ago…

The King thought he knew.

'He's outside, hanging off the wall!'

'That sounds very dangerous, sire,' smiled Onion Runyon in his oily way. 'Surely it's more likely that he's standing safely on the roof–'

'But there are dragons on the roof!' cried the Queen in a panic.

'I suspect that's a wild rumour, Your Majesty–'

No one paid any attention to what Professor Runyon suspected. Panic gripped the auditorium once more as the King led the race for the exit. Lily thumped the wall in fury.

'Can you believe it? How *could* he be more annoying? You just know he's going to do something ridiculous, and then, he goes and does it!'

We stared up at that empty target.

'Why don't we follow him?' I said.

'*Follow him*? Up there? How, Jack? No one's ever done that before.'

'We could crawl along the pole.'

'You can't crawl along the pole.'

'Why not?'

'Because…' Lily shook her head in frustration. 'Because that's cheating!'

'Come on, Lily! It's hardly a game of Jackernapes any more, is it?'

Lily seemed outraged by the suggestion, not that it mattered anyway. The next second one of the dragons slammed straight into the wooden pole, smashing it to pieces. Now there were at least six of them flying around, spitting fire in all directions, and more were appearing every moment.

'I suppose we *could* cheat,' said Lily, still staring up at the target. 'Do a sort of Rupert Manoeuvre in reverse. Swing across and jump sideways onto it. It might be a bit dangerous, but…' Lily suddenly turned to me with a glint in her eye. 'Hal's Defence! They won't see us!'

Up the castle wall she went like a monkey on a mission. Up

I went after her, trying to keep up and not exactly succeeding. Even in her armour, Lily's speed was amazing. We'd just reached the battlements and slithered over the top when there was a hail of shouts from below.

'Good evening, my lords, ladies and gents! If we might trouble you for a little bit of room?'

Amazingly Archie Queach had been as good as his word. Into the auditorium below burst a dozen blue-coated Dragon Keepers with all sorts of leather contraptions strung about their shoulders. At the head of this piratey gang was Ray Sunlight.

'Mind your manners, you daft beastie!' he shouted, casually disentangling a bridle as a dragon spat fire at him. Pulling down his goggles he waited till the next one flew close then flung out a leather lasso, snagging it on the spikes of its back, then he swung out into the air. Others followed his lead and soon it turned into a proper air battle, the Dragon Keepers swinging themselves aboard the dragons and attempting to bring these terrifying creatures under control.

'Hello, Mardock, haven't seen you in while!'

'Is that you, Hilda? How are the toenails? Still giving you jip?'

'Lady Gabbareen, well, well! And that smelly brother of yours—'

Of course the Dragon Keepers knew every dragon by name, and there was something about their we'll-have-this-sorted attitude that inspired an infectious confidence, even though half the auditorium was ablaze and every minute more and more dragons squirmed up through that hole in the floor...

'Let's get rid of all of these first,' panted Lily, as we climbed up onto the weatherworkers' balcony. Round we went, throwing levers and emptying whatever was left of the water, mud and goo bombs down onto the battle below. A few angry dragons spat in our direction as we ran down to the large white barrel at the end, labelled *'Hal's Defence'*.

'You remember how to open it?'

Sort of. Actually, not really.

'Turn the handle really fast, then throw that lever forward. I'll grab the ropes.'

I did as I was told. There was a rumbling hiss and then poof! The huge fog canister burst its lid.

'Point it down!' shouted Lily, quickly removing the remains of her armour.

I flipped the barrel over and aimed the billowing clouds downward... It didn't take long before the chaos below disappeared in the white cloud. I could hear the Dragon Keepers complaining but there was nothing I could do to stop it now.

'Keep aiming it down. I'll be back,' said Lily, grabbing a rope and leaping off into the fog.

Now I suppose if you were as good at Jackernapes as Lily was, you wouldn't think twice about doing something as crazy as that. You would know exactly which rope was which – even if you couldn't see anything. Still, this seemed incredibly dangerous. Lily might have swung straight into a dragon, or worse. I half-wondered if she was blaming herself for Richard's disappearance and trying to make up for it with some act of mad bravery...

A minute went by. Then another. I stared into that thick white cloud, beginning to fear the worst...

'Jack!'

Suddenly there she was, hanging off the edge of the balcony, holding onto a pair of ropes. I ran round and hauled her up out of the fog. Puffing and panting, Lily flopped down on the floor.

'Okay,' she gasped. 'This rope takes you straight to the target, this one pulls it back again. There's a wooden post in the middle that the Greensleeve was nailed to. I think if we lean on it, like Richard did, it'll be like opening the latch of a door.'

Typical Lily. She made it sound so simple.

'You remember those tips for cheating at Jackernapes I found in the Sable Tower? This was drawn on it, Jack. I remember now. I couldn't work out what it was.'

'Did it say where the door led to?'

Lily shook her head.

'Some secret part of the palace, I guess, which no one's been in for five hundred years. So who's going first, you or me?'

I'm ashamed to say I wasn't exactly enthusiastic. I could plainly see flashes of dragon fire lighting up that cloud below.

'Can't we go together?'

'The rope won't hold us both, Jack. Right, I'll lead, you follow,' she said, climbing up on the balcony and grasping the rope. 'Wish me luck.'

'Good luck,' I said, trying to be as brave as she was. 'See you on the other side.'

'Yup. Wherever that is.'

With a smile she leapt off the balcony and disappeared. I listened. Still the battle was raging below. No screams at least.

'Lily?' I called.

Nothing.

I gave it another ten seconds and then pulled in the other rope. After an age, it brought the swinging rope back, empty. Had Lily gone through? She must have done. So it was my turn. Taking a deep breath, I climbed up onto the parapet. Now someone like Onion Runyon would probably say that in moments like this you find out what you're really made of. Well I stared down into the white cloud, alive with flashes and shouts, and I don't mind admitting it; I was terrified. Totally and utterly terrified. But I couldn't stop now, and it wasn't only because I didn't want to let Lily down. The truth was, I was feeling guilty too. If I hadn't taken Richard's place, on what should have been the biggest day of his life, if I hadn't walked further than him on the Greensleeves pole, would he have tried so hard to prove himself?

I gripped the rope tightly, trying to ignore my racing heart. Oh well. If Lily Lancaster could do it, then I suppose I was just about stupid enough to follow…

~~ 72 ~~
The Enchanted Forest

THE PROPER NAME FOR IT, Richard told me later, is an 'oubliette'. It's a French word meaning 'forgotten dungeon' which you can only get into from a trapdoor in the ceiling. In certain old castles this was hidden under a carpet, and when you stepped on it, it instantly flipped over and down you went. That's kind of what happened. The second I grabbed hold of the post on which the Greensleeve had been nailed, the whole target suddenly tilted back and I fell headfirst into a narrow pipe that wound round and round in a steep spiral... There was no way of stopping or slowing down; I went faster and faster and faster until I cannoned out the end, somersaulted through some bushes, straight into a heap of moss… Breathless, I sat up and looked around. This wasn't a dungeon, far from it. It was a dreamy, ghostly wood. Soft golden light sparkled through the trees stretching away in all directions.

'Lily?' I called.

Silence.

'Lily!' I called again.

'Over here,' she replied faintly.

Lily was lying beside a mossy bank and she didn't look good. There was a nasty cut running down her leg and she was holding her arm in pain.

'What happened?'

'I hit that pointed rock. I was going so fast I couldn't stop myself… Oww.'

Poor Lily. She was blinking back the tears.

'Which pointed rock?'

'It was right at the bottom of the pipe. It looked like it'd been put there deliberately. I managed to roll it out the way for you.'

Typical Lily. Being a hero yet again. Now I really was beginning to wonder if it was possible to be too brave.

'Lily, this isn't your fault, you know.'

'I know, Jack, but we've got to find him, haven't we? You know how sick he is.'

Yes, I did. All too well. We sat in silence, looking at the ancient oak trees, the flowers, the cobwebs and the sparkling streams.

'So beautiful, isn't it?' said Lily. 'Like being in a dream. Is this a vault or something?'

I didn't reply because I didn't want to believe it. Somehow we seemed to have fallen into the most dangerous place in the entire palace…

'Can you walk?' I whispered.

'Sort of,' she said, trying to get to her feet and falling back in pain. 'You might have to help me.' I pulled her up and she leant on my shoulder. 'So what is this place?'

'I think it's the Enchanted Forest. It's part of the Fairy Vault.'

Lily noticed I was still whispering. She smiled.

'But that's okay, isn't it? Fairies are just colourful little things. They're not all as bad as Asphodel, are they?'

Lily was such a positive and practical person, I didn't want to frighten her.

'Let's just find Richard and get out of here.'

We started forward, and the second we moved something changed. Suddenly we were surrounded by a pond that hadn't been there before. We gazed at the oily black water in amazement.

'What happened?'

'Maybe we touched something.'

'But what *is* it?' said Lily, gripping my shoulder tightly. As we stared at the water a familiar figure appeared through the trees on the far side.

'I swear we've been walking round in circles for hours, Asphodel. We'll never find it.'

'You must stop being so lazy, my Prince. It's not far now.'

The fairy darted in and out of the sunlight as Richard dragged along behind, hands in his pockets.

'I bet you've forgotten where the entrance is. You haven't been down here for years.'

'Why are you always complaining when Asphodel tries to help! Come along, child, hoppity-hop, hoppity-hop–'

'Richard!' Lily called.

'Richard, come back!'

Away they went, into the trees.

'Why couldn't they hear us?' said Lily in frustration.

I stared at the black water stretching all around. Nothing made sense, including this pond...

'Supposing it's an enchantment?' I said suddenly.

'You mean it's not real? How could that be?'

I remembered the packet of revealing dust in my pocket. I took out a pinch and saying the words, blew a small handful out over the water... We watched the dust float down and settle, revealing a round patch of grass in the middle.

'Was that there before?'

I couldn't remember.

'Jack stop, wait, *wait*–'

I jumped, and held on. The grass *was* real. But I didn't know about anything else. I clambered to my feet.

'Perhaps that's why it's here. It's protecting this entrance somehow.'

Lily looked warily at the black water between us. She kicked it with her foot. The water splashed just like any other water.

'I don't trust it,' she said.

Yet a minute later the revealing dust had settled on rocks and patches of grass like stepping stones across the pond. The water was there, only somehow it wasn't. Carefully I helped Lily hobble from one to the next and we made it across to the other side.

'This place is scary,' she whispered. 'D'you think it's all like this?'

'Clue's in the name, I suppose,' I replied, trying to sound braver than I felt. We stared at the great trees stretching away in all directions. Which way had they gone? It all looked the same.

'Richard was limping. They can't have got that far,' said Lily. 'Perhaps they really are looking for the way out.'

That was a very big perhaps. Off we went into the wood,

Lily leaning on my shoulder and hobbling as fast as she could manage. We hadn't been going long before something bright buzzed into a patch of sunlight straight ahead.

'Wow,' Lily gasped.

I drew her back behind a tree. The fairy's wings were brilliant red and purple, and it was hopping from flower to flower, singing to itself.

'Where the bee sucks, there suck I:

In a cowslip's bell I lie;

There I crouch when owls do cry.

On the bat's back I do fly...

Merrily, merrily shall I live now,

Under the blossom that hangs—'

Suddenly it turned towards us and we leaned in against the tree trunk. The whirr of wings approached.

'More strangers,' said the fairy. 'Eglantine is curious.' It fluttered closer, then settled on a twig beside Lily's face. 'Ahh. What pale blue eyes, what fair skin. What long, golden hair... Beautiful child, why comest thou here?'

Lily turned and stared at the creature. It had a pinched white fairy face and long silver hair tied up in an elaborate knot. Its fine silk clothes were a dazzle of amber and green.

'We're looking for Richard, the Prince. Have you seen him?'

Eglantine smiled most charmingly, revealing a row of sharp little teeth.

'Ah, the sick one. I have seen him, child. He is with Asphodel.'

'Yes we know,' Lily smiled politely. 'I'm his cousin, actually. We've come to take him out of here.'

'Out of the forest?' Eglantine tittered.

Lily and I looked at each other.

'Why is that so funny?'

'This wood is full of noises. Secrets ways. False paths. You could walk a thousand years and never step on the same stone twice. Methinks you shall never find this prince you seek.'

'But we saw him just now—'

'Not without help.'

There was something in the way the fairy relished these words that annoyed me.

'Perhaps you can help us then,' I suggested.

Eglantine buzzed about us, her tiny face screwed up in thought.

'I could help… *one* of you.'

'Why not both?' I asked, suspecting some sort of trap.

'The way is hard. You will need to be quick. No good for the maimed and infirm.'

Lily looked at me.

'You go on then, Jack. I'll be fine. You'll catch him up much quicker without me.'

I was reluctant. I didn't trust this Eglantine for a second.

'Time is short,' said the fairy, glancing at the cut on Lily's leg. 'Stay behind with me, beautiful child. I'll lead you to a nice soft place to rest that leg of yours.'

'Would you really? That would be awfully sweet of you—'

'No Lily, we stick together.'

'But Jack, supposing I hold you back? Is the way very hard, Eglantine?'

'Asphodel has summoned the old magic of the woods,' said the fairy. 'Who knows what manner of enchantments might happen?'

Lily turned to me earnestly.

'Jack, seriously, you must go on without me. I'll be fine. I'll just sit down here and wait.'

'No Lily, you can't do that. I won't let you.'

'Why not?'

'Because...' I glanced at the brilliantly coloured fairy, smirking as she perched on a twig. 'Because you just can't, that's all.'

Lily didn't understand and I didn't want to explain.

'Very well then,' cried Eglantine, clapping her hands together. 'Both shall come. But one shall perish.'

'What?'

'Quick quick! Let us make haste.'

We followed the fairy as it skittered ahead through the trees. In seconds we were totally lost.

'Do you know what it meant?' Lily whispered.

I shook my head. Snowdrop Scott had said nothing about any ancient forest magic. But Asphodel was so full of devious plans... and now I had a terrible feeling we were part of them...

'Where's Asphodel taking him?' I asked.

Eglantine smiled as she danced through the sunbeams.

'A secret bank whereon the wild thyme blows,

Where oxlips and the nodding violet grows,

Quite over-canopied with luscious woodbine,

With sweet musk ro–'

'Is it far?' I interrupted.

The fairy flew down and examined a bent leaf.

'The Prince has a limp, has he not?'

'Yes he does.'

'See there? Now he is wounded also.'

I bent down. There was fresh blood on the surface. Eglantine tasted it and grinned.

'That is prince's blood. Oh a sick prince indeed! But hark! I am summoned. The feast is about to begin. Eglantine cannot be late. Adieu! Adieu!'

'I thought you were going to take us to him?' said Lily crossly.

Eglantine giggled merrily and flew away into the trees.

'You said you were going to help us!'

'Follow this trail, children, and if you lose it, follow the voices. They will lead you there.'

'But you can't just leave us!'

The fairy laughed and disappeared into the light. Lily gripped my hand.

'Jack I really, really don't like this.'

For the first time I knew she was truly scared, and so was I. Not only for us, lost in this enchanted place, but for Richard. I didn't like the sound of Asphodel's forest magic one little bit.

'At least we have something to follow,' I said grimly.

On we went, deeper and deeper into the trees, following the trail of blood through the bushes and ferns. I was beginning to wonder where all the fairies were...

'Master Richard is so lazy and weak. You must keep going.'

'I just want to stop. I'm so tired.'

'That's them!' said Lily. We hurried on towards the voices that seemed just ahead...

'Hoppity-hop, hoppity-hop, always complaining, aren't you, boy?'

'Richard!' we called.

They seemed very close now, just around the corner... A wind began swirling through the branches, bringing with it more voices.

'Beautiful child, why comest thou here?'

'We're looking for Richard, the Prince. Have you seen him?'

'Oh, the sick one...'

We stopped dead. To the left, on a mossy bank beside a stream was Eglantine... and two shadows behind a tree...

'But that's us!' gasped Lily.

How could it be?

'Where's Asphodel taken him?' I heard myself say. I spun around and saw another Lily and me, walking away through the trees in the opposite direction, the fairy darting ahead...

'A secret bank whereon the wild thyme blows,

Where oxlips and the nodding violet grows...'

'Jack? What's happening?' whispered Lily, clutching my arm tighter.

'See there?'

Suddenly another voice, very close. I looked down. Eglantine was at my feet again, tasting the spot of blood on a leaf...

'That is prince's blood. Oh a sick prince indeed!'

The fairy darted away into the shimmering trees.

'Eglantine, wait!'

'Wait! Wait!' my echo returned... The wood was swirling with whispers and laughter now, the great oaks rustling and bending in the little gusts of wind that blew from one direction, then another... Lily and I clung to each other in terror.

'Where the bee sucks, there suck I...'

'I could help... *one* of you.'

'The way is hard. You will need to be quick!'

'I just want to sleep, Asphodel.'

'Sickly child, what's to be done with you? Have you given up?'

'I've had enough.'

Was that him?

'Then so be it. Your little life shall be rounded with a sleep.'

'Richard!'

Lily and I stumbled on through the bushes towards the voices…
Suddenly we reached a clearing in the forest. A circle of golden
grass lay before us, swaying back and forth in the wind.

'Cuz!' Lily gasped.

There he lay, fast asleep on a bed of flowers in the middle.
Hundreds of fairies swirled down through the branches and
fastened themselves onto him, their brilliant wings covering him
like a quilt.

'What are they doing?' said Lily. 'What…'

Eglantine looked up from where she was perched on his chest,
her little white face drenched in blood. She smiled.

'Where the bee sucks, there suck I,

Under a bat's wing I do fly—'

'NO!' screamed Lily. 'NO!'

Lily seemed to forget her leg, her arm, everything. Tearing
herself away from me, she ran across the circle of golden grass
towards him… and the moment she touched it, the grass became
a slippery sucking mass, winding itself around her and binding
her tight.

'Jack!'

I ran forward and tried to pull her out, but Asphodel's forest
magic was sucking her down into it, swallowing her up…

'Only one can cross, only one can survive,' giggled Eglantine.
'That was your choice, child.'

'What's happening to me?' she said, seeing her arms forming
roots, her skin turning to mud…

'Lily–'

She looked up at me in terror.

'You have to save him!' she cried. 'Save him, Jack! Promise me you'll save him! Save Richard!'

I pulled at her, pulled at her... but even as I did, she sank away into that melting ground, her hair turning to grass, her eyes closing...

'LILY!'

There aren't any words to describe how I felt at the moment. To see Lily slip down into the earth like that, somehow becoming part of it, and to see Richard being feasted on by hundreds of bloody-faced fairies... my only two friends in mortal danger... I felt like my whole world was collapsing right in front of me. Dragging myself away, I crawled back to the edge of the clearing and stood up.

'ASPHODEL!' I screamed. 'ASPHODEL STOP THIS! STOP IT NOW!'

There he was, his mean little face red and shining. He laughed as he buzzed above Richard's body, and began to sing.

'When the hurly burly's done,

When the battle's lost and won,

When will you come, Jack? When will you come?'

There was nothing for it. With a scream of rage, I ran straight towards him, and somehow, I don't know how, the swaying grass held firm beneath my feet, like a path, and the moment I reached that island of flowers... something flashed, brilliant white—

ᜮᜮ 73 ᜮᜮ
Blood for Blood

I **T WAS LIKE I'D FALLEN** through a mirror. That's the only
way I can describe it – except the mirror wasn't there, and
nothing had broken or shattered. It must have been some kind
of magical illusion, a terrible dream, like everything else in that
enchanted place...

But now I was somewhere real again. I felt cold stones under my
hands. I could see jars of strange plants glinting in the candlelight,
smell peculiar smells... This was a vault. I looked back at where
I'd come from. It was a great arched window, full of leaves.

'So you were lost in zer forest as well, rosbif? Vat is going on
in zere?'

On the bench was Fleur de Lys. Over the fireplace in the corner, a cauldron steamed. And on the far side—

'Richard?'

He was lying on a table, unharmed. He saw me and tried to sit up but grabbing creepers pulled him back down, strapping him tight.

'Jack it's a trick, they wanted—'

'Hold your tongue!'

The voice shocked me. I turned around and there was Asphodel, standing on a shelf, staring at me with a mocking smile. Beside him stood Patrick Pettifog… Of course, Patrick, the Keeper of Extraordinary Plants. This was his vault…

'What did I tell you, Pettifog? There is one who can break the spell. Turn ice to water. I knew the moment she arrived she was the one. Foxglass thought he could hide her from me, but nothing slips past old Asphodel.'

Patrick Pettifog smiled at me in his nervous way.

'I never meant to doubt, Asphodel, I just didn't think—'

'Enough of your prattling, boy! We are ready. To work.'

Patrick obediently scurried to the back of the vault and returned with an axe.

'Patrick?' I gasped. 'What are you doing? What's that for?'

'Yes vat are you doing, rosbif?' echoed Fleur. 'Is someone going to tell me vat is going on?'

Asphodel smiled menacingly.

'Sweet flower of France, send my compliments to your King.'

'Vat?'

Fleur never noticed Patrick's shadow move behind her. The next second his axe flashed through the air, smashing her pot to pieces. She rolled down onto the floor and lay trembling, staring up at Patrick in terror.

'For mercy, Pettifog! You cannot kill Fleur de Lys! Do you forget who I am?'

They were the last words she ever spoke. With a great swing, Patrick Pettifog hacked her in two.

'I've been looking forward to doing that for a long time,' he breathed.

'Now be very careful, young Pettifog,' commanded Asphodel. 'Wisely and slowly.'

Patrick obediently put down the axe and dropped to his knees. Pushing the earth aside, he reached into the tangle of roots and carefully withdrew something dirty and black hidden within. It squirmed in his hands, shaking and shuddering for breath...

'What is that?' I whispered in horror. 'Patrick? Asphodel?'

In an instant I thought I knew. It had something to do with Richard. That's why Asphodel had lured him here using ancient magic. That's why he lay strapped to the table. This was some strange ritual I'd interrupted somehow—

I was wrong.

A pair of strong arms grabbed me from behind then held out my hand. I screamed and struggled, bit and fought, but it was no good. I was caught. Then Asphodel fluttered down with a tiny knife in his hand and before I knew it, he'd opened a cut across my wrist...

'Let me go!' I shouted.

'Blood will have blood,' Asphodel grinned. 'Gently now, Pettifog, many a slip 'twixt cup and lip.'

Patrick Pettifog came forward and despite my struggling pushed the squirming thing towards the cut. It was like some kind of oily root, with black, glittering eyes.

'Patrick, please!'

'It's the only way, Jack,' he said, watching it in wonder.

'Don't let them do it!' Richard cried out.

I didn't need any telling. I fought as hard as I could as the creature clamped on, its tiny claws pinching my skin. Asphodel grinned.

'How now, Jack? Don't panic. You gave me blood once. Offered it freely, generously.'

I felt its teeth begin to nibble at the cut and I thought I was going to faint. A cold fire began flooding up my arm, pulsing and numbing...

'What's it doing?' I whispered.

Asphodel danced in the air with glee.

'You are keen to know the true secrets of this palace, Jack, so let me tell you. When Isabella Royle died, her body and soul may have been separated, but her soul could not die. It fled to the nearest living thing in that patch of bloody ground, the grub of a death's-head hawkmoth. Clever Miss Scott understood this danger and secretly dug it up, hiding it in a jar of earth, which she gave to the oliphant for safekeeping. She hoped that would keep Isabella separated forever, but Asphodel spied out her scheme, Asphodel knew...' The fairy chittered to himself. 'Oh the oliphant had it well hidden, but eventually I discovered it and moved it into another bottle, which that leathery old numbskull foolishly gave away to the Queen as a present! It was young Pettifog's idea to bury the creature inside Fleur de Lys, and see how it has sucked life out of the ancient flower, gnawing on those brittle roots, ruining her from within! But Fleur has proved a feeble host. Now my mistress requires proper sustenance. To change into something rich and strange, she deserves the rarest blood of all – blood of the most ancient line of Albion! An earthy stew of mud and fire, oak and apple, peasant and king, a bloodline I thought forever lost – until I met you, Jack, the young pretender. How could such nobility exist in an ill-tamed, uncouth orphan? How the stars did mock me!'

'What are you wittering on about, Asphodel? What ancient bloodline is this?' said the voice behind me.

The fairy watched the creature suckling on my wrist with crazy excitement.

'Soon it will be time to sing,

Glory to the one true Queen–'

'Answer me, Asphodel!'

'Check thy green-eyed jealousy, popinjay! Thou art a dunderhead and always shall be! To business, Pettifog, this night's work is not yet done!'

I was dimly aware that Patrick had opened a large cupboard and removed a panel at the back, revealing a hole in the wall. His fingers reached through the bricks, deep into the earth beyond, and carefully drew out a long squirming tangle of roots.

'What's that?' I gasped.

Asphodel's wizened little face cracked into a smile.

'Have you forgotten where we are? Is not the corner of the Keepers' Courtyard directly above us?'

'It's the Isabella tree,' gasped Richard. 'Jack, you must stop them–'

'Silence, sick rose! See? Her body still lives, does it not?'

Patrick Pettifog hacked off a handful of black roots and approached the steaming cauldron. Lifting the lid, he squeezed them tight and spots of blood pattered down. There was a hiss and the surface turned white, then swirled red as he dropped them in. Asphodel was beside himself with excitement.

'Black spirits and white,

Red spirits and grey,

Mingle, mingle, mingle, you that mingle may... 'Tis time, Pettifog, methinks she's supped long enough.'

Patrick Pettifog placed his fingers over the muddy creature and carefully prised it away from my wrist.

'Patrick,' I whispered, 'I don't know what you're doing, but please, don't...'

He looked at me with that strange smile on his face.

'Don't you want to see this place abolished, Jack? Don't you want to see wild Albion return? We talked about it, remember?'

I didn't understand.

'It's time to go back. Back to the old ways, the true ways... freedom for all, liberty from the tyranny of kings and governments. Why don't you join us? Help us build the brave new world—'

'Silence, Pettifog! Her purpose here has ended!'

The thumping in my head had reached such a crescendo that everything in the room was pulsing, swimming, alive... What had that creature done to me? I didn't know then and I still don't know now. The only thing I could be certain of was its tiny shrivelled face, shining black with blood, staring at me as Patrick Pettifog held it over the foaming cauldron... He let it go, there was a splash, and the water began to boil.

'Two halves of the same

Be born again,

Two halves become one,

Queen of the Moon, King of the Sun,

Live in the blood of the Phoenix Child...'

Asphodel's chant ended, and something began to rise from the surface of the water. It seemed to be a moth, an enormous, beautiful, glittering moth, the size of a person, with a golden skull for a head.

It spread its huge pink and black wings and turned around – and there was a young woman standing before me. She had white skin, golden hair and a pinched, narrow fairy face… a face that was cruel and cold and clever… She was wearing fine clothes that seemed to be made entirely of flowers. Isabella Royle. This was her, at last. She looked at herself, examining her new form. She seemed… pleased.

'Behold the once and future Queen of Albion!' shouted Asphodel. 'On your knees!'

The arms behind me let me go and I fell to the ground. Gasping for breath, I turned around…

'You too, Jack Joliffe,' said Thad Lancaster, his eyes hard as bullets. Thad Lancaster… somehow I wasn't surprised to see him here.

Isabella Royle looked around the room before fixing her black eyes on me. Asphodel was hopping about in excitement.

'How now, Mistress? How shall it begin? Shall you away to the Sable Tower, or kill them first? I say vengeance, bold and bloody! All three are here!'

All three? Ignoring my throbbing wrist, I looked back – there was Richard, strapped to the table by gripping tendrils, and in a glass cabinet on the far wall… Lily! Somehow she was inside it, her limp body lying asleep in the earth… So she was alive too—

'But you can't kill us!' I gasped. 'What have we done?'

'You have existed,' said a voice.

Out of the shadows stepped a ghostly figure. It was Valentine Oak, his face as grim as a statue.

'I say kill them all,' he whispered. 'Now.'

My head was spinning. So they were all involved in it, *all* of them, plotting to bring her back…

'Do it now, Thad!' shouted Asphodel. 'Draw thy weapon and

demonstrate thy allegiance!'

Thad Lancaster turned to Isabella Royle.

'Is that what you want?' he asked.

'Thad, you can't–' pleaded Richard.

'SILENCE!' screamed Asphodel. 'Loyalty to your new Mistress, Thad. *Loyalty*. Begin with this one, the child whose trickery has made you a laughing stock. How she has mocked you with her lies and impersonations! Does she not deserve to die first?'

Thad Lancaster drew his long dagger from its scabbard. I flinched when I saw that glinting blade. Was he really going to kill me?

'Please,' I whispered. 'Don't.'

Thad stared down at me coldly, the blade turning in his hand. He glanced across at Valentine Oak, as if waiting for a sign…

'Shall I?' he asked again.

'Handy-dandy he's a cowardly dog!' hissed Asphodel. 'Yet another fool upon this stage, I should've known it.'

'I'll do it, Your Majesty,' said Patrick Pettifog suddenly. 'I am not afraid.'

'Hush young whipster!'

Asphodel perched on Isabella Royle's shoulder and began whispering in her ear. 'I say put out the lights yourself, Mistress, and I shall put out the rest. First I shall poison that other pair of kittens, then only this perfumed peacock remains. He and his imbecile brother, cabbages both–'

'Enough, Asphodel!' said Isabella Royle sharply, her voice high and strange. She stared at us all with cold curiosity. 'Which of you is it?'

Asphodel's mean little face froze.

'Your Majesty? Which of which is which?'

'There is a traitor here; one who would dare to kill me. Who is it?'

Isabella Royle stared at Thad Lancaster, Valentine Oak and Patrick Pettifog in turn. They stayed silent.

'Pribbles and prabbles, Thad, screw your courage to the sticking place, or else give Pettifog the dagger! He dares do all that may become a man, who dares do more is none!'

'WILL YOU BE SILENT!'

Isabella Royle raised her hand and suddenly a thorn bush shot up out of the floorboards and captured Asphodel within it.

'Who do you serve, Asphodel? Is it me, or just yourself?'

'Mistress! Asphodel has always been a good and loyal servant! You cannot think that I–'

She closed her fist and the needle-sharp thorns began pressing into his thin body.

'How much do you love me, Asphodel?'

'Mistress, for pity! I cannot count the ways… Mistress I love thee more than life itself… AHH!' he screamed, writhing and squirming as the thorns closed in from all sides.

Isabella Royle opened her hand. The fairy fell twitching to the floor. For a second I thought she was going to crush him beneath her shoe.

'You're a bad actor, Asphodel,' she said. 'But I believe you.' She turned back to face us. 'Well? Which of you is it?'

I glanced back at Patrick Pettifog, the Master and Thad Lancaster. Patrick immediately dropped to one knee and bowed his head.

'Your Majesty, I too would gladly die for the revolution, for the promise of a free and wild Albion to come. It's all I've ever dreamed of.'

Isabella Royle smiled.

'Brave young soldier, I know you would,' she said, touching him softly on the shoulder. Patrick dared to look up in wonder.

'So that leaves two.'

The Master and Thad stole a glance at each other. Was there something in that glance? Thad seemed very nervous. Was it *him*? Isabella Royle's expression hardened.

'Has your courage deserted you?'

'Isabella, no one here is about to kill you,' said Valentine Oak, walking forward from the shadows. 'Which of us would ever dare do that?'

The old man stood before her, leaning on his staff. Isabella Royle watched him like a snake. He went on.

'I remember the first time I saw you, Isabella. You were eight years old, sitting alone in the meadow behind that dreadful boarding school. You were asking the spiders to write your name, and I watched them weave their webs for you, spelling each letter in turn. When they'd finished, you asked my name, and made them write that too. The grass was full of daisy cottages and dandelion castles the insects had woven for you. Even then, your powers were extraordinary. The spirit of Albion runs through you like water, Isabella. In five hundred years, there's never been anyone like you.'

Isabella Royle looked at him, and for the first time I could see something else in her strange pale face. She seemed sad, lost almost... but only for a second.

'A fine speech, Valentine. What's your point?'

The Master smiled and held up his hands.

'Isabella, you have every right to doubt us. But let our actions be our judge. We have brought you back because we believe in you. Trust us. We will serve you well. Come now, Isabella.'

Valentine Oak stepped forward, and stooping down put his arms around her. Isabella Royle stood completely still, awkward in the old man's embrace. He held her for a moment, apparently lost in his memories.

'You always were so suspicious,' he said.

'For good reason.'

The Master smiled and shook his head. He stole a glance at Thad Lancaster. Thad seemed frozen with fear. The axe lay on the table behind her.

'Well, Valentine? Am I wrong?'

The next second the Master grabbed the axe and swung it hard. In the same instant Isabella Royle somehow slipped out of his grasp and Valentine Oak shot back, slamming against the wall, the axe still raised above his head. His feeble arms tried to move but thick coils of ivy burst out between the stones, holding him fast. Isabella Royle stared at him with a cruel smile.

'So you'd kill me *twice*?'

'Isabella, you might've been the greatest keeper that ever lived, but to be truly powerful you must exercise restraint!'

'How dare you lecture me, Valentine Oak!'

'I brought you here, Isabella! I gave you everything you had!'

'And you took it away. Did you think I'd ever forget? Did you honestly believe that by joining me this time you could *control* me?'

Isabella Royle drew her fists together, whispering strange words, and the ivy squirmed tighter around his neck. Valentine Oak closed his eyes.

'You can't win, Isabella,' he croaked.

'Can't I? You are the past, Valentine Oak. I am the future.'

'NO!' shouted Thad. 'DON'T!'

Isabella Royle screamed. A terrifying, animal scream, the like of which I had never heard before and never want to hear again. When I turned back all that was left of Valentine Oak was a vague outline on the wall. I stared at it, open-mouthed. Thad Lancaster looked terrified. Isabella Royle seemed rather pleased.

'Now do you understand who I am? Stand up, Jack.'

I scrabbled to my feet, still feeling dizzy. She looked down at the cut on my wrist.

'That will not do,' she whispered. I flinched as her cold hand brushed it. The wound disappeared, but I knew it was still there, I could feel it... She then walked over to where Richard lay.

'An intelligent king. That would have been a novelty.'

'Please,' Richard whispered, 'take everything, I don't want it, honestly I don't.'

'I know you don't. Hush now, sick Prince.' Isabella Royle bent forward and kissed his forehead. Richard instantly closed his eyes and lay still, his face as grey as stone.

'What have you done to him?' I gasped.

'He's still alive. But there can only be one Richard Lancaster now. One who will do as I say.' She took the breath from her mouth then opened her hand and blew. Somehow Richard's clothes were on me and I was him again, exactly, and yet I knew the clothes weren't really there at all...

'And this,' she said, handing me the wig. 'We are going to see an old friend of yours in the Sable Tower.'

'Captain, my captain, thou art cunning indeed!' squealed Asphodel, seeing how the tables had turned. Once again he began to dance and sing.

'Oh noble queen of darkest night,
White as the driven snow,
How you shall trick the oliphant,
And steal–'

Suddenly Isabella Royle snatched him from the air.

'Don't you ever shut up?'

Asphodel opened his mouth to speak.

'No. No. *No*,' she said, putting a finger to his lips. 'Try to stay like that, understand? Now go ahead and see that the way is clear. And take this sorry pair with you.'

She released him. Patrick Pettifog scrabbled to his feet. Thad Lancaster glanced nervously at Richard, then Lily.

'There's no point in killing them now, is there?'

Isabella Royle's eyes narrowed.

'Are you a greater fool than you seem?'

Thad smiled in terror.

'I was only thinking that perhaps... now you've, maybe we should—'

'GO!' she screamed.

Thad Lancaster bowed hastily, then with a cowardly glance at me and Richard followed Patrick Pettifog out of the door.

'Umballoo will realise it's me,' I said when they'd gone.

'Of course he will,' said Isabella Royle. 'Which is why he'll give you what I want.'

'Why couldn't Asphodel get it for you?'

'Because that fairy doesn't know it's there. It's an object of great importance, which its previous owner entrusted to the oliphant to keep hidden. But what it is, or isn't, does not concern you...'

Her voice trailed away and she stared at me. My heart began to thump. Why was she looking at me like that? Did she know I'd seen it? *Had* I seen it? Or even touched it... I glanced at the cut on my wrist where that horrible little creature had sucked my blood... I was beginning to feel sick...

'Supposing Umballoo won't give it to me?'

'You will have to persuade him.'

'Supposing I can't?'

Isabella Royle walked forward and I stepped back and back until I was pressed against the shelves. She stood before me like a wild animal, her eyes so black they glittered.

'Don't presume to threaten me, child.'

'You can't control me,' I whispered. 'I'm not your puppet.'

Isabella Royle's lips tightened into a smirk.

'What's this, a rebellious spirit? How sweet. Your mother would be proud of you, Jack. Because she was a rebel too, wasn't she, in her own little way?'

I stared into her wild fairy face, my heart racing.

'You knew my mother?'

Isabella Royle nodded.

'Marina had an interest in fairies. I was summoned to tell her all about them. She said she felt connected to the ancient spirits of Albion. She could see things, hear things, in the palace.' Another mocking smile crossed her lips. 'Such a shame. But I suppose she could never forgive herself for abandoning you. Because that is what she did, Jack. Abandoned you to be burned alive. Did she ever love you? I doubt it—'

'DON'T SAY THAT!'

You might be thinking *I* didn't actually say that. After all, there was the outline of Valentine Oak on the wall. But I did, because even though Isabella Royle was the most dangerous and frightening person I'd ever met (and I'm not even sure she *was* a person), something in the way she mocked my poor mother's death gave me courage I didn't possess. I didn't care what happened to me now, and she knew it. Which annoyed her even more.

'You will do exactly as I say, Jack. If you don't...' Isabella Royle glanced across at Lily and Richard lying in the gloom, '...they will die. That *is* a promise. Understand?'

⚘ 74 ⚘
Albion's Fate

WE LEFT THE VAULT of Extraordinary Plants and walked along the corridor to the Keepers' Courtyard. Everything was dark, silent. I suppose everyone was hiding, though I could still hear the mayhem inside the Jackernapes arena. Each step I took away from Richard and Lily felt like a betrayal, but what could I do? At this moment, I put all my faith in the one noble and trustworthy creature that I knew wouldn't be fooled by Isabella Royle's magic. Surely Umballoo would realise what was really happening, even if no one else did. Somehow he would stop her...

But we didn't meet the oliphant. That is, not immediately.

We met something else.

We were about to open the door to the Keepers' Courtyard when there was a growl from the far side.

'Wait,' hissed Isabella Royle, holding me back.

We listened. Footsteps walked out across the flagstones. Then they stopped.

'They're still here, I can smell it.'

I thought I recognised that gruff voice. I looked at Isabella Royle. She shook her head.

'Come out, witch!'

Now I definitely recognised it. That was Abel Goodnight, I was certain. And so was Isabella Royle.

'Let the werewolf pass, then we go on,' she whispered.

I half-wondered what would happen if I didn't. But I wasn't too keen on meeting Abel Goodnight again.

'I can smell you, witch!' shouted Goodnight again. 'And that girl who would be King. Hiding in the Plant Vault. Well well.'

I glanced at Isabella Royle, wondering what she was waiting for. Surely Abel Goodnight was no match for her...

'Show yourself,' she hissed. 'Tell him you're alone.'

I looked at her.

'Talk to the werewolf, or else they die. Now.'

I opened the door and stepped out into the Keepers' Courtyard. It was dark and empty. In the centre, beside the fountain, stood a familiar silhouette. Abel Goodnight saw me and grinned.

'Still playing the prince, Jack. What fairy trick is this?'

I was about to answer, when the whole far side of the courtyard seemed to move. I froze. There was Wellenstorm up on the rooftop, looking down at me. He seemed even bigger and more terrifying than before. Huge iron screws stuck out of his head and his mouth was a dripping forest of teeth.

'Speak up!'

'I... I'm alone,' I said, unable to take my eyes off the great bull dragon. And then I remembered what Ray Sunlight had said. That old story about battles between dragons and fairies long ago, their ancient fight for Albion...

'Isabella Royle is using me to get into the Sable Tower! She's going to steal something from it and then–'

The next second, ivy swirled away from the wall and clamped around my mouth, gagging me. I tried to run but another branch shot out of the door and curled around my ankle.

'Don't be tempted to make your life shorter than it already is,' muttered Isabella Royle, angrily barging past me into the courtyard. And then suddenly she stopped. She hadn't seen the dragon either.

'Weren't expecting that, were you,' grinned Abel Goodnight.

Isabella Royle stared up at Wellenstorm on the rooftop. The great dragon growled, a growl so low it seemed to crack the air and shake the windows. For the first time, she seemed afraid.

'Let us pass,' she said. 'I have no quarrel with you, Mr Goodnight.'

Abel Goodnight laughed.

'So says a keeper who fancies herself as the Fairy Queen of Albion! That old oliphant's not daft, you know. He'll spot your fairy tricks a mile off. And so will Wellenstorm here.'

Isabella Royle didn't reply. Careful to keep a safe distance from the dragon, she began to edge around the far side of the courtyard, speaking in that strange fairy language again.

'This is some fairy stratagem, I smell it,' muttered Abel Goodnight, watching her carefully. 'What are you looking for, witch?'

Isabella Royle ignored him. On she went, passed the tree that bore her name, talking all the time... She seemed to be asking for something, searching for something…

'Don't let her play games with you, Wellenstorm! This is fairy magic – I smell it!'

Suddenly Wellenstorm spat a huge ball of fire straight at her. In the same second she spun around and raised her hands to the flames… and they became a blizzard! The snowflakes lifted and swirled around the courtyard… even now, I can hardly believe it. I think Wellenstorm was as amazed as I was. In a flash Abel Goodnight dashed for the safety of the cloister.

'Fairy magic! What did I tell you!' he shouted.

The great dragon let out a terrifying scream and spat again and again, till the snow began piling up in drifts.

'Stolen tricks won't save you, witch!' taunted Abel Goodnight from an archway.

Through the snowstorm I saw Isabella Royle smile… I think she thought they might. With sudden boldness she strode out into the centre.

'What are you waiting for, you stupid old brute? Come down and kill me if you dare! Here I am!'

Wellenstorm didn't need any encouragement. With a roar, he opened his wings and thundered down into the courtyard. Marching forward he towered over her, poised to strike… I could barely watch as Isabella Royle crouched before him, still speaking fast in that strange fairy language of hers, her fingers pressed against the stones…

'Come on, you great oaf! What are you waiting for?'

Wellenstorm struck like a snake, his nose smashing into the cobblestones. A hollow clang rang out around the Keepers' Courtyard.

'You'll have to be quicker than that, old dragon!' shrieked Isabella Royle, somehow now directly behind him. 'Try again!'

Wellenstorm whipped around in a fury and struck hard.

'Too slow, old fool!'

Already she'd darted back through his legs.

'What's the matter with you? Here I am!'

Like some clumsy bird the dragon spun round and round after her, smashing his head into the cobblestones as Isabella Royle darted just out of reach... Wellenstorm screamed with frustration, and on the fifth strike his head plunged straight through the ground and disappeared... There was silence, then a muffled roar and a huge tower of flame shot out from the hole he'd made. Wellenstorm suddenly began heaving and straining, frantically trying to drag himself up out of the hole... Seconds later I could see why... Something massive – far, far bigger than him – had got hold of the dragon by the throat. As Wellenstorm heaved and pulled, its head emerged – a tangle of long fiery belts followed by a huge grey eye, milky and glistening... What *was* that? Wellenstorm screamed and twisted, hauling the vast creature up out of its hole, but it was too big, too strong... its oily flaming tentacles coiled around him and began to drag him back down, down... In a writhing mass of scales and flames Wellenstorm struggled and fought, then he tripped and fell headfirst into the chasm. Somewhere far below there was a deep boom...

I looked across at Isabella Royle in shock. I could barely believe what I'd just witnessed.

'You didn't know the behemoth was there, did you, Jack?' she grinned, walking towards the edge of the chasm. 'The last behemoth of Albion, hidden in its vault directly beneath this courtyard. Wellenstorm woke it up with his pecking. Always a mistake, to wake a behemoth.'

Taking a small knife from her pocket, Isabella Royle ran it across the palm of her hand then held it out over the chasm.

'Come stones, do thy work. Hide this hideous beast forever.'

She stood there, arm outstretched, the blood from her fist dripping down into the darkness. Nothing happened.

'COME STONES!' she shrieked again. 'I am mistress of the palace now and you shall obey!'

There was a great rumbling as Isabella's magic pulled at the cobblestones, the towers, the cloisters… Gutters buckled and gargoyles came smashing down… The whole courtyard seemed to be shaking and protesting…

'YOU SHALL OBEY!' she screamed.

And then I screamed too. Abel Goodnight! He grabbed me round the waist and ripped me away from the ivy. Before I knew it, he was dragging me towards the edge of the chasm.

'Let me go!' I shouted, twisting and kicking, but he was so strong…

'Enough fairy tricks, witch!' he roared, dangling me over the rim. 'Close that vault and she goes too!'

'Leave her, creature!' comanded Isabella Royle.

'I will do it!' threatened Abel Goodnight, and I gasped as he held me out over the chasm still further. 'What's this miserable orphan to you, anyway?'

Isabella Royle hurled something at us, a white flash that sent us both tumbling back away from the edge. I came to a halt in a snowdrift, and when I looked up, Abel Goodnight was already back on his feet.

'Your stolen magic can't close it, witch!' he taunted. 'The palace has found you out!'

'LIES!' screamed Isabella Royle.

'You're just a jumped-up little keeper! A fraud!'

The next second the branches of the Isabella tree squirmed out through the bars of the cage and grabbed him. Abel Goodnight jeered as they hauled him backwards towards the cage, for now his eyes were on the moon that was just beginning to emerge from behind a cloud... How exactly it happened I don't know, but as the moonlight fell upon the courtyard, Abel Goodnights' smile froze and he began shaking uncontrollably... He trembled and groaned, and then with a terrifying howl he became his other self. The huge grey wolf burst out from the branches and bounded straight towards Isabella Royle... With one leap it flew over the chasm, fangs bared... I was certain that was the end of her...

'That's what comes of switching allegiances, Goodnight,' she said, her dainty shoe pinning the panting wolf to the ground by its neck. 'I think your new master needs your help.' With a kick she sent him tumbling down into the darkness. Isabella Royle stared across the chasm at me in triumph.

'Did that oaf really think that in my new world I'd tolerate his existence?' she said.

Climbing to my feet, I dared to approach the lip and looked down. Far below, Wellenstorm and the behemoth struggled on, coiling round and round each other like a pair of enormous fiery serpents. Abel Goodnight was a mere grey speck beside them. Once again Isabella Royle held out her hand, squeezing her fist till spots of blood began to patter down into the vault.

'Come stones,' she hissed, 'now will you obey me?' Again she whispered those strange fairy words, and this time something began to happen... There was a groan, then slowly the walls of the chasm began to move...

'HA!' she screamed in delight. 'You see? It's true! I knew it!'

I didn't understand why this meant so much to her, but I watched in amazement as the walls of the chasm began turning like a whirlpool, and as it spun, it narrowed, and the dragon and the behemoth began to disappear from view... It was such an extraordinary sight that I didn't notice my wrist throbbing with pain. I looked down and gasped; the cut had opened up again – Abel Goodnight must have ripped it. There was blood running freely down my fingers, forming red dots in the snow at my feet...

'Right. There's no time to lose,' barked Isabella Royle, already marching away towards the cloister.

I shouldn't have hesitated. I shouldn't have tried to hide my bleeding hand, but I couldn't help it. And neither could she.

'What are you doing?' she demanded, spinning around. 'Come here this instant!'

And then she saw me holding my wrist; saw the blood dripping...

'What's that? What's *that*?'

There are no words to describe Isabella Royle at that moment; she stared at me in disbelief, then her lips froze into a strange, terrifying smile. Instantly I knew everything had changed. I wasn't going to help her anymore. I was going to die–

The next few seconds are hazy. I remember Isabella Royle's pinched white fairy face, her animal eyes wild with rage, screaming, 'ALBION IS MINE! ALBION IS MINE!' over and over in my head... I remember the snowflakes swirling up into a blizzard, spinning around me so fast they seemed to suck away the air and tighten around my neck... I remember Isabella Royle's fingers, so cold and deathly they stung... I heard her hiss some final fairy words...

Then a shadow appeared behind her.

I recognised that shadow–

I suppose what actually happened next is I fainted. When I

opened my eyes, I found myself lying face down in the middle of the Keepers' Courtyard. The stones were cold beneath my cheek. Everything was quiet. Somehow, I was alive.

Gingerly I sat up and looked around. The moon shone brilliantly on the fountain. Everything seemed so normal, I half-wondered if I had dreamt it all... except I hadn't. There was a bruise on my ankle where something had grabbed me, and a small pool of blood on the cobblestones where my hand had rested. My wrist still throbbed painfully.

'Jack?'

Out of the doorway in the corner staggered Lily, rubbing her head. She looked at me lying there.

'Jack? What happened? Where's Richard?'

'Right behind you,' he said, limping a little as he leant on the doorway.

'Oh Cuz!'

She enveloped him in a hug so tight it nearly knocked him off his feet.

'I thought you were dead!' she cried.

'I thought I was dead too,' he said, pushing Lily away impatiently. 'What happened, Jack?'

As I said, I wasn't sure. But the enchantment was over, or it seemed to be. I tried to explain. Lily and Richard listened in growing amazement.

'So what you're saying is that this behemoth is right underneath us?'

'And Wellenstorm. And Abel Goodnight too.'

'Wow,' Lily gasped, staring suspiciously at the dark cobblestones.

'It's not that surprising,' said Richard in that vaguely bored way of his. 'There's always been a rumour about the last behemoth of

Albion being kept hidden somewhere under the palace. They had an accident in Tudor times, a fairy started a fire or something, and the palace almost burnt to the ground. In the chaos the behemoth escaped and found its way down to the river, but it was so big it got stuck in the arches of London Bridge. It took three ships and hundreds of soldiers and horses to drag the monster back. The Master then got hold of some incredibly powerful enchantment to hide the vault forever, because there's a superstition that if the behemoth ever leaves the palace again, the age of kings and queens will pass, and Albion will return to chaos. Or something like that.'

'Or something like that,' repeated Lily, smiling. 'I suppose you've read a book about it, Cuz?'

'I might've done. But Archie Queach seemed to know quite a lot about it, and he wasn't making it up. They say whoever finds the Behemoth Vault will become the next ruler of Albion, but only the blood of a true queen can seal it. The last person to do that was Elizabeth I, five hundred years ago.'

'Right,' said Lily, looking flummoxed. 'So where's she gone, then?'

'Exactly,' said Richard, looking across to the patch of bare earth where the Isabella tree had once stood. The iron cage that had held it lay bent and smashed in the corner. All traces of Isabella Royle seemed to have literally vanished into thin air...

'Someone must've driven her away. Or some thing,' he added, watching me curiously. 'Any ideas, Jack?'

I shrugged and glanced down at that mark on my ankle. Obviously I had an idea: who else could it have been? But for some reason I decided to keep this to myself.

'It was all a bit of a blur,' I said sheepishly. Which was true.

'Oh Jack, I'm so, so pleased you're safe,' smiled Lily, enveloping me in another giant hug.

Richard looked at my wrist, still black and filthy with blood. I think he was starting to guess what had really happened, and what that meant... He gave me a wry smile.

There was a scraping sound on the far side of the courtyard. A latch squeaked.

'There's no one out there, Red Tempest. I'm certain—'

'You'll still go out and check, Mr Queach,' instructed the shrill voice of Ocelot Malodure. 'I don't want to hear any more nonsense about being scared of the dark, or it being too dangerous—'

'But supposing there's another dragon out there?'

'Then you'll be able to tell me all about it, won't you?'

'But supposing it eats me?'

'Then you'll have something else to complain about.'

'But I won't be here!'

'Out you go, Archie.'

The door opened and Archie Queach peered out nervously. His torch flashed in our direction.

'Well?' demanded the Keeper of Time. 'Any sign of them?'

Archie picked me out and scowled.

'No. Nothing. Nobody there.'

'Wait a minute!' shouted Lily. 'Miss Malodure!'

And that was the final surprise. After everything that had happened, to be rescued by Archie Queach. Well, *almost* rescued. He was a little late.

～ 75 ～
Dreams and Deceptions

I T WAS MUCH LATER, sometime in the middle of the night I guessed, when I woke up. We had been taken over to the school sanatorium to be patched up, and by the light of the small lamp beside my bed I could see Richard lying with his eyes closed and head bandaged, and beyond that Lily lying fast asleep.

'How are you feeling, Jack?'

I turned over to find William Foxglass sitting in the chair beside my bed, his face hidden in the shadows. All I could see were his hazel eyes glinting, and that strange lopsided smile of his. He nodded at my bandaged wrist. Oddly enough I'd almost forgotten about it now.

'I'm fine,' I said.

'Good. Excellent.'

I wondered what William Foxglass was doing here, just watching over me. But it was nice to see him.

'You know it was Asphodel who—'

'And he's been captured, Jack. Miss Scott found him hiding inside the lining of Richard's ceremonial jacket, and she's personally supervised his removal to a special dungeon so secure that not even he will break out of it.'

'What's going to happen to him?'

William Foxglass sighed.

'If found guilty of treason, Asphodel can expect the very harshest of punishments. The King will decide, and at this moment he's in no mood to be lenient. He's very angry with that fairy. Very angry indeed.'

'And what about the others, Patrick and—'

'Patrick Pettifog is an impressionable young man. Perhaps he didn't quite realise what he was getting himself involved in. I'm hoping that will stand in his favour when he goes to trial.'

That sounded serious. But then I suppose he might have killed us if Isabella Royle had let him.

'And Thad Lancaster? He was there too, with the Master—'

'Yes I know. Mr Knock has had his suspicions about Patrick Pettifog for a while. He's been watching what goes on in that vault very closely.'

It took a moment for me to take this in. So his seeing stones did actually see something...

'So Thad's been arrested as well?'

'Of course not.'

'But he was going to kill me!'

'Was he? Really?'

I stared into that foxy face, hidden in the shadows.

'What are you saying?'

'Thad Lancaster may not like you, Jack, but he's never wanted to kill you. You're his sister's only child, and he worshipped Marina. I suspect you remind him very much of her, and maybe that's enough for him to hate you, but he's never wanted to kill you. And neither did poor old Valentine Oak either. He'd always felt guilty about bringing Isabella Royle into the palace, and thought that by joining Asphodel's secret plot this time around he might have been able to sabotage it. The trouble was, when Thad Lancaster heard of it, he insisted on being included, which placed Valentine in a very difficult position. He was well aware that when Isabella Royle returned, she'd never trust a prince. And it's sad to say that she obviously didn't trust him either.' William Foxglass paused. 'In the end, neither of them could stop her. Unlike you, Jack.'

William Foxglass smiled again. He seemed... proud. I wasn't sure that I *had* stopped her, whatever that meant. All I had done was... I don't know what I'd done, except live, perhaps, when she was convinced I'd die. And now I thought I knew the reason for that...

'Where do you think she's gone?'

William Foxglass shrugged.

'Isabella Royle still has many supporters out there. Secret societies who dream of a wild, free Albion. There are plenty of old families who are prepared to sacrifice everything to bring it back.'

'I don't understand what that means.'

'I'm not sure many of them do either. But the oldest dreams are often the most powerful. Whatever wilderness of forests and castles and fairy magic they yearn for, there'd be no freedom.

Isabella Royle would make quite sure of that.'

I nodded. That was definitely true.

'She wanted me to get something from the Sable Tower for her. Something very old and important. I think she asked me to get it because she knew I'd seen it.'

'What did you think it was?' he asked, watching me carefully.

I told him about that ancient key I'd found in Merlin's rucksack. How it felt like it was almost alive... William Foxglass listened in silence, his head cocked to one side.

'There's always been a rumour of a door somewhere, that leads back into some other Albion,' he said mysteriously.

'Some *other* Albion? What's that?'

William Foxglass shrugged.

'A dream. A myth. Who knows, Jack. Very few people have seen what's hidden inside the Sable Tower and lived to tell the tale.'

He smiled one of those odd smiles and raised an eyebrow. Oh yes. I'd conveniently forgotten about that. We sat in silence a moment. Questions were now queuing up inside my head.

'So... is it true that my father rescued me from that burning building?'

William Foxglass nodded.

'Do you know him?'

'His name is Kazeem. Captain Hari Kazeem. He's a dragon hunter. Quite a good one, as it happens.'

A dragon hunter? That sounded dangerous.

'But Caractacus Kiddy said it was like a furnace.'

'It was, Jack, I saw it. Captain Kazeem told me he waited till everyone had gone off in pursuit of Wellenstorm, then he climbed up into the attic through a back window. I don't know how he managed that, because the flames... Anyway, he told me your cot was in the corner and it was already on fire. You were lying inside it, not crying, just staring up at the fire raging all around. He said you were wearing a little pink bonnet. It was smouldering, just beginning to burn… If he'd been a minute later…' A shadow passed over William Foxglass's face. He crossed one glove over the other a little self-consciously.

'That's why you still bear the scars of that terrible night, Jack. And so does he, as it happens.'

'What do you mean?'

'In saving your life, Captain Kazeem was badly burnt himself. Which is why he tends to wear a mask these days.'

'A mask?'

'Yes.'

I searched his shadowy face for any kind of clue, and then in a flash I realised. The man who grabbed me from the burning carriage…

'*That* was Captain Kazeem?'

William Foxglass nodded again.

'He's been tracking Wellenstorm for me. I thought it might be useful to have him around today, just in case something happened.'

I was stunned. *That* was my father!

'Why hasn't he ever come to see me?'

William Foxglass shrugged.

'Hari Kazeem is a rather strange man. After everything that happened, he disappeared and I didn't hear from him for years. In the way of these things, I think Thad Lancaster has come to blame him for the death of his sister. Which is why he knows he can never return to the palace now.'

'Is he still here? Can I meet him – properly, I mean?'

'I'm sorry to say I think he's already left.'

I stared at William Foxglass. His foxy face gave nothing away.

'He's a bit odd, Jack. I'm not sure you'd like him much.'

'But he's still my father—'

'I know. But I think he'd find meeting you extremely difficult. And as I said, he knows he's not very popular around here. Certain people have taken a great dislike to him.'

We sat in silence a moment. I felt a little hurt by this. Why didn't my father want to meet me? Was he ashamed of me? Was I an embarrassment to him? I didn't understand... and that wasn't the only thing I didn't understand.

'So... if you knew that Hari Kazeem was my father, and Princess Marina was my mother, then you must have known right from the beginning that I was never related to Galahad Joliffe, and I was never supposed to be the Keeper of Ghosts either.'

Obviously these weren't questions, exactly, more statements of fact.

'Yes,' he said, looking sheepish. 'I owe you an apology for that, Jack. With hindsight, perhaps it was the wrong thing to do.'

His calmness irritated me. The wrong thing to *do*?

'You know I was sent down to the dungeon for that. I had to share a cell with the Grindylow. He nearly killed me! If it hadn't been for Lily—'

'I'm truly sorry about that, Jack, really I am.'

'Why couldn't you have just told me the truth?'

William Foxglass shook his foxy head.

'That is the one thing I could not have done, believe me.'

'Why not?'

William Foxglass sighed and pressed his gloved hands together. I sensed he was about to tell me something he'd rather not.

'When they were children, Thad, Marina and Edward – who

is now the King – used to have Asphodel up in their rooms to entertain them. One night, Marina woke up and saw the fairy crouching on Edward's neck with a silver dagger in his hand, about to kill him. Asphodel denied it of course, and managed to convince everyone that Marina was having a nightmare. Marina had nightmares often so she wasn't believed; nevertheless, Asphodel was immediately sent back down to the Fairy Vault as a precaution. And ever since, Marina was convinced that one day Asphodel would take his revenge. As she grew up, she began to see things woven into the tapestries, words appearing in blood on the walls… in dreams she heard voices warning her, taunting her… Slowly but surely, Marina was tormented into believing that Asphodel would kill her firstborn child. People thought she was nervous and highly-strung, imagining everything, but she wasn't. There's still plenty of fairy magic in this palace, Jack. I think you know that by now.'

William Foxglass watched me steadily. He was right, of course he was. I'd seen what that magic did to Tom Bootle; even felt it myself…

'So that's why I couldn't tell anyone who you really were. Sooner or later Asphodel would've heard of it. And the fact that you look exactly like Marina and your cousin probably aroused everyone's suspicions, especially Thad Lancaster's. Somehow I had to get you away from Abel Goodnight, and also come up with a convincing reason for you to be in here. I'm afraid my dear friend Galahad Joliffe knew nothing about it at all. The only part he played was to conveniently go missing.'

Well. William Foxglass. At least he'd admitted it.

'So when you showed me his photograph…'

'I was searching the country trying to find him. It was as simple as that, Jack.'

There was a knock at the door and a shadow appeared.

'Now it really is time for me to go. Get well soon. All three of you,' he added with a wink. I watched William Foxglass walk to the door, leaving it ajar.

'Wow!' whispered Lily from the darkness. 'You know, I did wonder if it might be something like that. I mean, what are the chances of two people looking identical?'

'Unless it wasn't an accident,' yawned Richard.

'What d'you mean, Cuz?'

'Think about it, Lily. Jack just so happened to be brought into the palace right before my presentation. Isn't that a massive coincidence?'

The door closed and the Queen strode quickly towards my bed. She was carrying a bag.

'Jack, darling,' she whispered, giving me a kiss and smiling such a generous, motherly smile I couldn't help smiling back. Only I was beginning to wonder if Richard was right...

'I gather Mr Foxglass has been telling you the truth,' she said, taking my hand and squeezing it.

'Sort of.'

'Yes, he's a very discreet fellow, thank goodness. We have a lot to thank him for.'

The Queen was so composed, so perfect, I didn't quite dare ask the question straight away. So I asked another.

'Did you ever meet my father?'

'Yes I did.'

'What was he like?'

'Brave. Clever. Kind.'

'Is he?'

'Yes, of course he is. Why d'you ask?'

'Did my mother love him?'

'Absolutely,' said the Queen. 'And he loved her too, very much. I'm quite sure of that.'

The Queen smiled at me in her perfect way.

'It's difficult for him, Jack, even now. There are certain people who still hold rather old-fashioned views about these things, and Captain Kazeem is erm... well, he's Captain Kazeem. Put it like that.'

I had no idea what she meant.

'It can't have been easy for her to give me away.'

'It wasn't. It broke her heart, I think. But your mother was a very strong-minded person, and when she decided to do something, that was it. There was no alternative. She did it for you, Jack. And the Sunlights were very good people.'

The Queen sat smiling at me. If only she wasn't so perfect, it might have been easier. Maybe I should just come straight out with it.

'Did you know that Richard and I looked identical before I came into the palace?'

The Queen seemed a little surprised.

'What do you mean?'

'It's just that... Mr Foxglass must've known we looked identical, and because of what happened to Stephen at his presentation, and Richard being so ill... The thing is, if *I* took his place, and I was killed, or poisoned, or something, it wouldn't have mattered really, would it? Because no one knew I even existed... The main thing was you wouldn't lose another son.'

This was a terrible accusation, I knew it. The Queen looked at me for a long while, her expression never wavering.

'Is that what you truly believe, Jack? That William Foxglass smuggled you into the palace so that you could be a double for Richard at his presentation?'

No I didn't. And yet… all those times she'd stared at me when I was being Richard, those miraculous recoveries I made… had she really not recognised that I wasn't her son?

'Listen, Jack,' she said at last, 'as I understand it, Mr Foxglass brought you here for a very simple and practical reason, and that was to save you from a werewolf. Now while it may appear to you that there was some other scheme going on, honestly, we're not as sharp as you give us credit for. If there *has* been any swapping, then you and Richard and Lily must have been extremely ingenious about it, because neither the King nor I have for one moment suspected, or encouraged you, in any way. Have we?'

Her face was golden, as smooth as soap. I wanted to believe her, I really did. The Queen stood up, bent forward and kissed me on the forehead. I smelt her perfume, felt a lock of hair brush my cheek.

'Let us be friends, Jack. It's what your mother would've wanted, and it's what I want too. More than anything.'

She smiled, and I listened to her heels clicking away to the door.

'You left your bag,' I said, pointing to the shape on the chair.

'Oh no, that's for you, darling. I gave it to Mr Foxglass some time ago for safekeeping. Then it seemed that too many people were becoming interested in finding out who you really were, so I had to take it back again. Frankly it's no one's business but yours. You should have it now.'

With a wave she quietly closed the door.

The moment she'd gone both Lily and Richard swung out of bed and hobbled over.

'Wow, that was brave,' said Lily.

'What d'you mean?'

'Accusing the Queen of plotting to bring you here as Richard's double! Not many people could've got away with that.'

'It's probably true though,' said Richard in his bored way. 'Mother always smiles like that when she's lying.'

They came and stood either side of me as I opened the bag. Inside was a slim grey photograph album.

'What did she mean "had to take it back again"?' asked Richard.

And then I remembered. *That's* who it was, watching me as I came down from William Foxglass's room. I explained.

'You mean she actually went into his room and *stole* it?'

I suppose she must have done. Even Richard seemed a little shocked.

'It probably is important then.'

At first glance it didn't seem to be. On the first page of the album was a piece of paper with a baby's handprint in blue paint.

'That must be yours, Jack, mustn't it?' said Lily.

I stared at the tiny hand and put my hand next to it. It was so small. On the next page was a photo of Marina holding me. She looked so happy, proud... What might my life have been like if she had never given me away? I felt a lump rising in my throat. I almost didn't want to look at these. The next photograph was of a young couple in old brown keepers' coats sitting on a log with a baby. Behind them lay a forest and the corner of a thatched building.

'That's your foster parents, isn't it?'

Ned Sunlight looked very like his brother, Ray – big and burly and smiling. And Molly looked nice too, with her braided dark hair and purple dungarees. Staring into their laughing faces, I instinctively knew they'd cared for me and loved me as best they could. Richard squinted at the pencil writing below.

'Jacaminta Honeymoon Sunlight, aged three months. Interesting name—'

'You can talk about names, Cuz,' said Lily, nudging him hard in the ribs. 'I like it. Very much.'

'Don't worry, Lily, I'll stick with Jack,' I said.

The next photo was interesting in a different way. There I was again, cradled in the lap of a man sitting in a pub. The white window behind had turned him into a silhouette, and there was a half-drunk glass on the table.

'D'you think that could be my dad?' I said suddenly.

'You mean, the mysterious Captain Kazeem?'

We studied the photo. The man was wearing a tatty blue polo-necked jumper, and with his wild hair and small black glasses he had the look of an explorer... yet even in silhouette there was something familiar about him...

'If that's Hari Kazeem then I can't see what's wrong with him,' Lily said. 'He looks quite handsome in a way.'

'He's obviously not nearly grand enough though, is he?' said Richard. 'You know what Father's like about that sort of thing. Marina would've had to marry an emperor at the very least.'

There were more pages of photos. Me stroking a cat, me on a swing, me asleep on a blanket on the grass, my hands above my head, wearing a little pink bonnet—

'That's probably the one that...' Lily sighed and shook her head. 'It's so shocking. So, so shocking.'

We stared at the photos a little while longer in silence. Lily threw her bandaged arm around my shoulder.

'You've had a very up-and-downy sort of life, Cuz,' she said. 'The good thing is I can definitely call you that now, can't I?'

She grinned, and I found I couldn't stop grinning back. Lily and Richard were my real actual cousins. That was sort of amazing to me. They left me to it.

'By the way, Richard,' yawned Lily as she crawled back into bed, 'I've been meaning to ask you something. You know you walked all the way to the Greensleeve.'

Richard sighed.

'Strangely enough, I haven't forgotten going further than anyone else in history, Lily.'

'I was just wondering how you actually did it?'

'What do you mean, "how I *actually* did it?"'

Lily looked at me and winked.

'Oh come on, Cuz.'

'Lily, I understand it must be hard for you to accept that I've done something in Jackernapes which is completely beyond you, but you're just going to have to get used to it.'

'Hey, Cuz, I respect your amazing achievement. I was only wondering why you were standing in such a strange way, that's all.'

'What was strange about it?'

'It's just that it looked like you might be, I dunno, holding onto something?'

'Weirdly enough, Lily, when you're in the middle of the air there's nothing to hold onto.'

'Not even the hand of a ghost, perhaps?'

Richard was outraged.

'You know something, Lily? I feel sorry for you. Seriously, I do. Your jealousy is truly pathetic.'

'Night, Cuz.' Lily closed her eyes, still grinning.

I can't remember how long I spent staring at that photo album. The first grey light of dawn was creeping through the windows when eventually I too fell asleep.

ᔰᔰ 76 ᔰᔰ
Similar but Different

WHAT HAPPENED NEXT? The next few days slipped
by almost without me realising. The Queen had
decided that Richard, Lily and I needed to be nursed
back to life after all our trials, so we stayed in the sanatorium
on the far side of St James's Palace while Dr Mazumdar patched
us up, made us eat chicken soup and generally bossed us about.
Little snippets of gossip floated our way. We heard that all the
dragons that had broken in had been captured, and all the Dragon
Keepers pardoned. Patrick Pettifog had confessed and been quietly
removed, William Foxglass had become the new Master, and
Thad Lancaster had suddenly gone abroad, nobody knew where.

The biggest news of all was that Asphodel was going to stand trial, accused of high treason.

'Which he will obviously talk his way out of,' Richard said.

'I wouldn't be so certain, Cuz,' Lily replied. 'I think everyone's finally seen through Asphodel. There's probably some horrendous medieval punishment they've got lined up for him. Is there, Jack?'

We were sitting on a sunny window seat watching Jake Tiptree and his friends smash up the last muddy remains of a snowman in the school courtyard.

'Do you really want to know?'

'Of course we really want to know,' said Richard.

So I described it. It sounded even more gruesome and disgusting the second time around.

'You see, Lily?' said Richard when I'd finished. 'Why wouldn't Asphodel have a plan to get out of that? He's not a fool.'

No he wasn't. And it was hard to imagine that the wily old fairy didn't have one final trick up his sleeve...

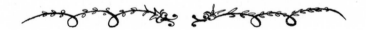

The week sped by, until one fine afternoon Dr Mazumdar decided he'd had enough of us messing around in his sanatorium and I was more than well enough to be formally presented to the King. Through the tunnel to Buckingham Palace by coach we went, and once again I found myself standing in that same long yellow drawing room before the roaring fire. Lily had lent me a dark blue velvet dress for the occasion, and we'd made a brightly coloured turban to cover up my scraggy head. I'd say I looked almost royal...

'Dearest darling Jack, how lovely to see you,' smiled the Queen, immaculate as ever in cream silk. I curtsied to her, and she kissed me. Then I curtsied before the King. He smiled in his confused way.

'You're sticking with the "Jack", are you?' he said.

'I'd like to keep it. If you don't mind,' I added.

'It's your name, darling,' smiled the Queen. 'We'll call you whatever you want to be called.'

'We will?' snorted the King. 'Anything?'

'One cannot help one's own name, Edward, can one?'

'Hmm,' the King growled. He was plainly a little mystified, though I guessed many things probably mystified him. 'Very well. Princess… Jack. You're part of the family now. Welcome aboard.' He smiled then quietly drew me aside.

'Now listen here, my spirited young bandicoot,' he whispered, 'a little birdy tells me there might have been some *swappin'* goin' on.' He looked at me knowingly and winked. At least, that's what I thought he was doing. 'Not entirely sure I know the truth, and not entirely sure I want to either. But, young Jack-a-me-jo, if that *was* you up on the balcony, swearing to serve your country and become the next King of Albion, let's pretend you got in a muddle. You said "I do" when really you meant "I don't". Slip of the tongue; said *do*, meant *don't*, do, don't, piffly little words, all in a twist, said the wrong one. Simple as that, eh? And I'll let you into a little secret.' He bent down so close, the tip of his moustache began to tickle my ear. 'I fluff me lines, all the time. And amazingly, *no one ever notices*. Not even Queenie,' he grinned, doing that winking thing again. 'But, young Geronimo, if that *wasn't* you up on the balcony saying the do-don't bit, then you probably haven't the first clue what I'm talking about, have you, hmm?'

The King's moustache twitched. He was waiting for an answer.

Did he really not know?

'Thought so. You haven't the foggiest, have you? Excellent news. So let's keep this little chat between ourselves, d'you understand?'

'Yes, Your Highness.'

'Or was that, "*No*, Your Highness"? You see? All the same!' He honked loudly, then turned around and smiled at the Queen. 'Message received, proud and near.'

The Queen looked at me and beamed.

'I'm so glad. Now, Jack, you know you'll have to join the school.' I nodded.

'And you're going to have to play rather a lot of Jackernapes – for Lancaster, of course,' added the King.

'I don't mind that.'

'But on no account are you allowed to cheat like yer cousin!'

Unfortunately Richard's brilliant achievement had been revealed. You've probably guessed how. Yes, Lily was right, Richard had been holding the hand of a ghost, and who else could it have been but helpful Dancing Dan, helpfully helping him to walk across that slippery wooden pole, further than anyone had ever managed in the entire history of Jackernapes… but of course, Dancing Dan insisted he knew nothing about that. Neither did he know that Asphodel must have overheard them discussing it while everyone was out at the presentation, which is why the fairy arranged for that secret trapdoor to be opened up behind the target, so that when Richard reached it (as Dancing Dan had promised him he would), he would grab the Greensleeve and tumble all the way down into the Enchanted Forest… *Is* that what happened? That's the only way I can make sense of it, though no one was admitting anything, especially not Dancing Dan.

Whatever the truth, Richard's howls of protest were ignored.

The final score was reversed, Plantagenet awarded victory, and George Hartswood became even more of a school hero than he was already. The tatty old Greensleeve was nailed back on the target.

'Understand, Jack?'

'Yes, Your Highness.'

The King grinned broadly.

'And you can't keep calling me that either. Feels peculiar. Obviously Father's no good, because I'm not your father. And no one's ever called me by my real name, not even my mother. So...'

'Uncle?' I ventured.

The King shook his head.

'No. Lily calls me that already. Too confusing.'

'Maybe Unc—'

'What?'

I'm not sure why I said that, I didn't mean to exactly. The King's moustache twitched.

'Unc? *Unc?* Unc. Unnnnccc.' He said the word a few more times, like a piglet practising its grunt. 'You know that's jolly good. Never thought of that before. Unc, what? Unc. Unc! Unc!'

'Marvellous,' said the Queen, her perfect smile just a tiny bit less perfect. 'Everyone's happy.'

Not quite everyone. You might have guessed that Thomas and Victoria Lancaster had quite a lot to say about my arrival, most of which I cannot repeat here because their language was too awful. But at least they knew that whatever happened, they would always become King and Queen before me, and they spent every day reminding me of that.

In the new spirit of cooperation, the Queen decided to hold a feast to celebrate Richard's presentation.

'A proper palace feast, where both sides of the palace meet and maybe even talk to each other. Because we all live here, after all,' she said.

'And so do the jabberwocks, my dear,' said the King. 'I hope you're not expecting me to talk to them as well, because I don't speak Jabber, or Wocky,' he snorted.

'You need to try and be a bit more modern, Edward.'

'Don't know about that.'

'Yes you do. We all need to try.'

At Richard's insistence, the great palace feast would be held in the Keepers' Hall. I don't remember much about it, except feeling very awkward as Lily, Richard and I followed the King and Queen in through the great door and up to the high table. They had been greeted with a politely hostile silence, but when the lines of keepers saw me, the place erupted.

'Bravo! Bravo!' they roared, stamping their feet and banging their tankards.

I was still one of them, you see. Even George Hartswood, Spiggins and Tucker-Smith looked vaguely impressed as they trooped in behind. But neither they nor the keepers knew that it was Richard they were really cheering. It was him, not me, who had proved himself to be the most gifted young keeper since Isabella Royle.

'I always said there was something about that lass,' grinned Sam Yuell, throwing me a wave.

'You never said anything of the sort,' scoffed Snowdrop Scott, sitting beside him. She smiled at me approvingly.

'But I did *think* it, Snowdrop. I thought, "Sam, that's blue blood, that is, through and through." Stinky guessed it right from the start, didn't yer, Stinky? Right from the start. She can tell. Always.' There was a growl and shower of sparks under his legs.

Next to them stood Tom Bootle, scratching his ears and smiling awkwardly.

'How nice to see you again, Mastress,' he said, bowing low. 'And you, Your Highness. That was a very fine trick. Not one, but two Jacks! Magic, eh? How about that?'

I wondered if he actually knew what had happened. Perhaps not.

'Did you really never suspect we were different, Mr Bootle?' asked Richard.

'I *might* have had an inkling, Your Highness,' he said, 'but anything goes around here, doesn't it? I mean, people can transmogrify out of all recognition, yet they's still the same person underneath. One is what one is, isn't one, with all one's faults. Can't be helped.'

Tom Bootle smiled again, and I realised that he was, of course, talking about himself. It wasn't his fault that he had fallen under Asphodel's spell, but that hadn't stopped him telling everyone different versions of every truth and lie he'd ever heard... However the King decided it would be too cruel to punish him for it.

'If boneheaded foolishness was a treasonable offence, most of my family would have been hung, drawn and quartered years ago, what?' he declared.

Nobody dared to agree with him.

And there in the far corner stood Archie Queach. Poor Archie. He saw me coming and stared hard at the floor. If a convenient hole had opened up in front of him, I'm sure he would have gladly jumped straight in.

'How was I supposed to know who you really were? I'm not psychic, am I? How was I supposed to know?'

'It doesn't matter now, Archie.'

'It's not my fault, is it?'

No it wasn't. Except he *had* locked Sam Yuell in the cheese cellar on the day of the presentation – accidentally, of course; it had just sort of 'happened'… Whatever the truth, Archie's role in all this was never discovered, and he was never punished either. Instead, Archie was given his old job back. Perhaps that was punishment enough.

The only person who wasn't at the great feast was the one I was most curious to see. Jacky Joliffe (the real one) had been sent home again, and Galahad was very keen to tell me why.

'Jellybean has returned from his great adventure – and lived to tell the tale!' he chortled, rubbing his hands with glee. 'Can't mention it in public, my dears, it's too scandalous. Why don't all three of you come to my rooms tomorrow for tea, and I'll tell you the whole story. The final piece of the puzzle, eh?' he winked.

～ 77 ～
Galahad's Tale

A ND SO IT WAS that the following day Richard and Lily and I presented ourselves at Galahad Joliffe's door. After many, *many* fine words of welcome, Galahad insisted we all sit down and explain ourselves, which wouldn't have taken so long had he not kept interrupting with so many 'that's astonishings!' and 'quite unbelievables!', hooting with laughter so loud I seriously thought he might faint.

'It's the strangest business!' he declared at last. 'To think that you, Jack, were brought here under false pretences, and that you, Your Highness, should turn out to be such a capital Keeper of Ghosts! A ghost-hunting King! Now that would be quite something!'

After all that – oh and I almost forgot 'the famous toad impression' (Galahad insisted on doing his 'famous toad impression'), followed by 'the dancing of the jig' (Tom Bootle was roped into this as well; you had to be quite patient with Galahad) – at last he collapsed into a soft armchair and mopped his brow.

'And now, my dears, it's my turn,' he gasped.

Over several pots of tea, he told his story. Predictably, it had nothing to do with being tied up in a boat, or chasing a goat, or being locked in a cellar by a man called Dave. In fact, it was very simple. Galahad had fallen in love, got married in secret, then run away.

'I knew I was breaking the cardinal rule of keepers!' he cried, nibbling his fourth macaroon. 'One is not permitted to retire without a very good reason, and only the King can approve it. But to retire for *love*? Oh my dears! Can you imagine how tongues would wag!'

How did it happen? It went like this.

Galahad Joliffe had been summoned to Liverpool by Cherry Bodkin, a grumpy old widower, who claimed his late wife Violet had come back to haunt his house.

'She sours the milk, pours sugar in my shoes, kicks the cat – that ghost wants bottling, Mr Joliffe!'

Galahad lay in wait, and encountered Violet one night in the kitchen, helping herself to some cheese crackers. Far from being the jealous and troublesome ghost he expected, Galahad found Violet to be perfectly delightful, and then he discovered that it was old Cherry Bodkin souring the milk and kicking the cat himself.

'Well one thing led to another,' said Galahad, helping himself to another excellent macaroon. Night after night he sat in the kitchen with the charming Violet, while old Cherry got crosser and crosser upstairs.

'That ghost's a thieving menace! It's spooking me out of me mind! If you don't do something, Mr Joliffe, I'm calling the fire brigade, the police, the army—'

'Quite a crowd, Mr Bodkin, do you think there will be room?'

Cherry Bodkin was not amused. When he threatened violence there was only one thing for it. Galahad charmed Violet into a bottle and off they went to a seaside town where they tied the knot. After a week of enjoying the seafront and plenty of fish dinners, Galahad and Violet were strolling down the sand one morning when who should they encounter?

'William Foxglass! That cunning old fox tracked me down! "Listen here, Jellybean," he said, rather stern, "you may've broken the cardinal rule of keepers, but worse than that, you haven't left any instructions!" Straight away he sat me down and made me write a letter of advice to my successor.' (The one I found in the drawer, remember?) 'Then he said I'd better find some suitable young Joliffe to fill the post, A-S-A-P. "Got any young relatives, Jellybean?" Well indeed I did. Plenty. There was Benjamin, Darcy, Flossie and Pete, Tabitha, Jade, and Jackson. "Jackson?" said William Foxglass. "Sometimes known as Jack?" "Not sure, never met the tadpole, but from what I've heard—". "Let's have little Jackson, Jellybean, or else there'll be dire consequences for you and Mrs V" (as Galahad liked to call Violet). What could Jellybean do, my dears, but fold before the greater wisdom? The secret would be out!'

So Galahad meekly did as he was told, and three weeks later obediently returned to the palace with the real Jackson Joliffe and his parents in tow... only to find me sleeping in his bed.

'Wowee! You could've knocked me down with a feather!'

Because he knew nothing about me, of course; no one did – except William Foxglass... Why, I wonder, had he insisted that it should be little *Jackson* Joliffe, as opposed to any of the others? Exactly. Because he knew I was already here. And he wanted everyone to think he'd made a mistake...

Galahad gobbled down another macaroon and continued his tale. So when he *did* meet 'the kid' (as he liked to call young Jacky), Galahad realised that perhaps he'd been a little too hasty after all. 'Too green about the gills for my liking,' he declared. 'Not quite ready to leap from the lily pad and grasp the nub of the thing' (whatever that meant). In other words, he hated it. So Galahad was allowed to return to his post as Keeper of Ghosts, Inspector of Badgewinkles, Phasma Argent, etc., etc., and in return William Foxglass allowed Violet to come and visit at weekends.

'Oh she's mad about the palace. Absolutely intrigued! Likes to see what old Jellybean's up to, but she's very quiet, keeps herself to herself. You wouldn't even know she was here – would you, my dear?'

⁓ 78 ⁓
The Final Performance

GALAHAD JOLIFFE settled right back into life as he knew it, which is more than I can say for Asphodel. A month after the presentation the ancient fairy was brought to trial in the palace. It was a big event. The little courtroom was packed with keepers and even Byron Chitt was there in the gallery, looking particularly disapproving and grim. Not as grim as Asphodel, though. He sat on the edge of the dock with a tiny chain around his neck, his plumage painted in thick white paint to prevent him escaping.

'All rise,' said Ocelot Malodure.

In came the King, looking more serious than I'd ever seen

him before. He sat down in the judge's chair and Asphodel made a mocking bow.

'All hail to thee, donkey King,' said the fairy.

'SILENCE!' roared the King, smashing down his gavel.

Asphodel spotted the three of us sitting in the gallery and smirked.

'See?' whispered Richard. 'He's going to give the performance of his life.'

'*For* his life, you mean,' Lily whispered back.

And did he? If it was sympathy he was after, Asphodel chose a strange way to get it. I won't bore you with all the details, because basically the fairy boasted that he was behind every bad thing that had ever happened. Asphodel even claimed he'd hidden inside the Black Bull of Clarence's ear and ordered it to sit down in the middle of The Mall.

'But you can't escape from your cage! It's a lie, it's a lie!' blurted out Snowdrop Scott.

The fairy laughed long and loud. Of course he could escape. He'd been escaping for years. Asphodel would have slit the King's throat when he was a boy, only Marina had woken up and disturbed him. (So he'd admitted it at last.) And yes, he'd been secretly poisoning Richard too. Every night he'd suckled on the Prince's neck, then hidden the bite marks so that by morning there was no trace of them. How had he done it? With a peculiar skin-healing cream he'd found in the Sable Tower. It was a gift from a Russian count, who happened to be a vampire. Lily and I looked at each other. So that was what Umballoo had been trying to tell us. I noticed Richard rubbing his neck. I think he felt a little foolish for not noticing…

'Do you have any regrets?' Ocelot Malodure asked.

Asphodel glanced at Richard, his wizened little face screwed up in spite.

'Only that my work was not finished. That boy will make a useless king.'

'Do you know where Isabella Royle has gone?'

'I do not.'

'Are you plotting to bring her back?'

'Are you afraid of what will happen to you when she does?'

'Answer the question.'

'To be or not to be. That is the question.'

Ocelot Malodure smiled thinly.

'If you think reciting Shakespeare impresses anyone, you are very much mistaken, Asphodel.'

'Reciting? *Reciting*?' The fairy was beside himself. 'Listen, Fattypuff, every word that scribbling fool, Wer-hilli-am Sher-hakes-*piddle* wrote, he stole – from *me*! Why, that thieving nipcheese, that naughty nighthawk, that, that... *actor*! *I* am who I'm reciting! I, *me*, Asphodel! Asphodel!'

Ocelot Malodure ignored his outburst and fixed him with a hard stare.

'May I remind you that you're under the King's oath to tell this court the truth,' she said.

'The King's *oath*? What ancient and fishy thing is that!' Asphodel howled with laughter. He looked around the packed courtroom and smiled. 'You want to know about Isabella Royle? Very well, let me tell you about Isabella Royle. Why, even now she's speaking the riddles of the rivers, calling long-sleeping serpents slithering from the woods, waking the ancient giants in the hills. Her name is whispered in the fields, in the hedges and in the bogs... The wild world is coming back, and when it does, *I pity you.* You fear the vorpal powers of dragons, but when Isabella Royle rides in through those palace gates she will bring much worse. For she will throw open your vaults, cast down your towers, fill your hallowed halls with cries, run your cellars slippery with blood! Blood of every handy-dandy crimson mongrel who dares to stop her! Blood for every drop you *stole* from her! Blood for blood, ten times over! Oh Isabella's kingdom is coming, and when it does, methinks it is *you* who should be pleading with *me*! For without cunning old Asphodel, clever and wise, who knows the compass of her mind and speaks the same silver tongue of fairy, who shall beg for mercy on your behalf? No one! I dread to think what will happen then. This great palace of yours will become nothing more than a... than a playground for hedgehogs! 'Tis too awful to contemplate.'

Silence. Everyone stared at the tiny figure chained to the lip of the dock.

'You rather enjoy frightening people, don't you?' said Ocelot Malodure, folding her arms. The wizened fairy turned to her and smirked.

'Frightening people? *Frightening* people? The walls a-whispering, *a-whispering*, Fattypuff, listen; did you hear that? The palace is awake, even now; the stones are talking, the tapestries are busy weaving their spells... Can your piggy ears not hear it?'

Ocelot Malodure smiled uncomfortably.

'What about you, donkey King?'

'Utter bilge,' snorted the King. 'Dream on, fruit cake.'

Asphodel screwed up his face in spite.

'Indeed I shall! And so will you fool, just as Isabella commands. Have you not seen her riding her chariot down the corridors of the night, scattering nightmares from her saddlebags? No? Never?

Isabella knows every thought, feeds every dream. Nothing escapes her. *Nothing.* See? Look, there!' he suddenly pointed, as if following a fly. 'She's here, even now, in this very room—'

'That's enough!' commanded Ocelot Malodure.

'There she goes! Behind you, Fattypuff!'

'Oh I think she's behind you, old fruit!' honked the King. 'Make way, Fairy Queen coming through!'

Asphodel stared up at him in absolute disgust.

'Mock on, donkey King. Ee-aw, ee-aw.' The fairy turned back to the courtroom. 'So be it. Believe me not. But the hellkite is a-hovering over the hen coop, and old Asphodel has done his best to warn you. All of you,' he added, glancing up to where we sat. I stared down into those little black eyes, cold and scheming... What did Asphodel know? Whatever it was, I didn't want to think about it...

'The scary thing is, I almost believe him,' whispered Lily.

'Come on, Lily, he's acting,' said Richard.

'How could you *ever* have liked him, Cuz?'

'I still do, in a way.'

Lily was flabbergasted.

'Richard, he bit your neck and sucked your blood!'

'I know. But that makes it more flattering in a way. He's so evil.'

Lily shook her head.

'You're mad, Cuz. You really are. Totally and utterly mad.'

Asphodel was removed and the King retired to consider his judgement. Snowdrop Scott was all for repeating the punishment handed out to that other fairy traitor, Pumblechook, but even the King blanched at the thought of hanging Asphodel from a gibbet then watching his eyes being pecked out by the palace rooks. Instead, he decided that Asphodel must be chained to a hamster wheel, and make five hundred revolutions a day for the next fifty years, which would be just enough to wind up the palace alarm clock. If he refused, then his blood ration would be stopped. Snowdrop Scott thought that was far too lenient: a thousand revolutions at least – but softer voices prevailed. After all, this wasn't the Middle Ages any more.

ᵔ 79 ᵔ
A New Beginning

S OMEHOW THE GREAT TRIAL of Asphodel brought
everything to an end. The summer term was almost over
and as the sun began to warm the courtyards, everyone's
thoughts turned towards their holidays. I had been feeling a
little nervous about this. The last thing I wanted was to be left in
the palace on my own with only Archie Queach and a few old
keepers for company. What was I supposed to do? I wasn't sure
where I belonged any more... which was probably the reason I
often found myself drifting away to sit and daydream in front of
a picture of my mother.

Now that it was okay to talk about Princess Marina again, a

large portrait of her had been brought up from the storerooms and hung prominently in one of the halls. There she was, aged twenty, standing beside a window in a long red ballgown, with a single pale sapphire around her neck. She looked so beautiful, radiant and happy. I wondered whether it was painted soon after she'd met my father, the mysterious Captain Kazeem. I spent hours sitting in front of that picture, imagining all sorts of things about Marina's short, tragic life, knowing that this was as close as I was ever going to get to her... unless I bumped into that sad ghost again. That was something I never, ever wanted to happen...

Lily must have noticed the change in my mood, because she immediately came to the rescue and invited me to stay for the entire holiday.

'It may sound grand, Jack, but it really isn't, it *really* isn't,' she said, not very reassuringly. 'We live in a castle in Scotland, but it's half falling down, honestly it is, and my mum breeds sheep, and my dad's an earl but he's basically a handyman who's not even very handy, and there's loads of rabbits and dogs, and we can go swimming and canoeing and bog snorkelling–'

'Anything that ends in "ing" that gets you cold and wet,' said Richard, who was sitting in the window seat reading a book about gnomes. 'I'd be very careful if I were you, Jack.'

'Well?'

'It sounds amazing,' I said.

'It's actually a nightmare,' muttered Richard, crunching on a gobstopper. 'I hope you haven't invited me.'

'What do you think, Cuz? Oh, and hopefully we'll get to ride Dolly if we can find her.'

In the forest behind Lily's castle lived the last wild unicorn left in the country. Dolly was as friendly as anything, apparently – *if* you could find her...

'Why on earth would anyone want to ride a unicorn?' asked Richard.

'Because it's fun, Cuz. What are you going to do?'

Not surprisingly, Richard had quietly been making plans of his own. Having now completely recovered, he was on such good terms with Galahad Joliffe that the Keeper of Ghosts had asked him if he wouldn't mind looking in on the Ghost Vault while he went on holiday, to the seaside, for a whole month.

'Rest assured you've nothing to worry about, Your Highness. Dancing Dan has everything well under control, and I've assured Red Tempest that there'll be no breakouts, parties or ghostly merriments of any kind,' he winked. 'Bags packed, bucket and spade ditto. Come along, Mrs V, we're going to have some fish dinners!'

Off he went round the cloisters, whistling merrily and twirling his staff.

'A whole month, eh?'

Richard looked at me slyly. I knew what he was thinking.

'Isn't that going to get you in a heap of trouble?' I asked.

'Oh I don't think so,' he smiled. 'The palace will be empty except for Ocelot Malodure. Dancing Dan has promised to show me the sewers. There's quite a few interesting ghosts down there apparently, that no one's ever seen before. Certainly not Archie Queach.'

Richard grinned. How devious he was. And how typical that he wanted to spend his summer holidays hunting around in the dark passages under the palace...

'He also said there's something called the Grindylow living in a well down there. I thought I might try and catch it.'

I looked at the fine crop of black hair sprouting on Richard's head.

'Be very, very careful, Richard.'

Richard looked at me and smiled.

'So he's dangerous? Even better.'

That afternoon I grabbed my bag, and Richard and I joined the excited procession filing down the staircases towards the great courtyard at the front of the palace. We were walking through an archway when I happened to glance back towards the Sable Tower, and through a high window I spotted a familiar shape... the silhouette of a small castle on top of a mountain... It was the first time I'd seen it since the presentation. There was something I had to do...

'Hey where are you going, Jack?' called Richard.

'I'll catch you up!' I replied, running off around the cloister. I darted up the steps then pushed open the great wooden door, and there he was at the other end of the hall, standing before the large window just as he had been that first time I met him, reading the paper and waiting for the Queen's list. I approached the great oliphant and smiled.

'Hi.'

Umballoo turned the page. His trunk absently wandered around my head, as if saying hello. I looked up into those small sad eyes, and somehow I already knew the answer to my question.

'I just wanted to say thank you,' I said quietly. 'I've been meaning to say it for ages, but... it was you, wasn't it? You saved me that night.'

The oliphant flapped his ears. That might have been yes, or no, or what kind of a daft question is that?

'I suppose you got rid of Isabella Royle too, somehow. Did

you, Umballoo?'

The oliphant turned back the page of the paper, and pointed to a headline.

'Palace Mystery Deepens. Spokesman refuses to comment.'

'Oh I haven't told anyone,' I whispered. 'I mean I didn't know, exactly.'

His long trunk ran over my head again, I'd like to think in a friendly way, then dipped into a bag and offered me a carrot.

'I'm fine. Thanks.'

Umballoo flapped his ears and ate it himself. He went back to reading his paper.

'Bye,' I said. Umballoo vaguely raised his trunk.

I closed the door quietly and walked away unable to stop smiling. Umballoo the oliphant. He'd saved my life. He'd probably saved the entire palace as well. What an amazing creature he was.

By the time I caught up with Richard the whole school was assembled in the great courtyard, waiting excitedly for their parents to arrive. There was a huge cheer as the gates opened, and one by one the procession of cars came in. Matty Wong's mother climbed out of a bright red Ferrari, Jake Tiptree disappeared into some blacked-out box the size of a small house, George Hartswood's older brother climbed out of a sleek silver Mercedes...

'Who's that?' he asked, looking disapprovingly at me standing there next to Richard. George told him.

'Oh,' he said, suddenly rather interested.

Like many other people in the school, George hadn't quite forgiven me for leapfrogging my way from the very bottom of the palace to the very top, and he probably never would. Despite that, we did have one thing in common. The night Wellenstorm had killed my foster parents, he'd also killed George's father. And that made me just about tolerable, somehow.

'Hiya, Richard!' Mrs Tucker-Smith climbed out of a Bentley and waved excitedly. Richard waved dutifully back.

'Have a good'un, man,' said Tucker-Smith, knocking past us with an unusually friendly high five.

'And don't you go walking that pole again before next term,' added Spiggins with a wink. They wandered down to their parents who looked on beaming with pride.

'Strange, isn't it, how my mother and father assumed I'd only be able to get on with rich people,' said Richard in his bored way. 'It's not like I've got anything in common with most of them.'

'Isn't that why there's a ballot?' I said.

'I suppose so.' Richard leant back against the wall, watching all the excitement. 'But I can get on with normal people. I'm not *that* weird, am I?'

Richard was wearing his Lancaster cap and a pair of baggy white dungarees he'd found in a cupboard in Patrick Pettifog's vault. There was a half-eaten banana poking out of his pocket and for some reason he wasn't wearing any shoes.

'What?'

'You might take a bit of getting used to.'

'D'you think so?'

'Definitely.'

'Ready, Jack?'

Up puffed Lily with her bags. She dumped them on the ground next to me.

'Where's all your stuff?'

'Erm… in here?' I said, pointing at the small bag at my feet.

'You're joking! You know it's going to rain. It'll probably be raining for a month!'

The bang of an engine interrupted us and we turned to see a very old and dented green van pull up in the next courtyard and judder to a halt. Out stepped the familiar figure of William Foxglass, now wearing his long white Master's coat. He looked back through the archway at all the cars and bustle and seemed surprised.

'Why d'you think he still drives that funny old van around?' asked Lily.

'Probably because he doesn't want to draw too much attention to himself,' said Richard with a wry smile. 'That's the collector's van, isn't it, Jack?'

I nodded. He stared at it with interest.

'I wonder if he'd mind if I borrowed it.'

'I'm sure he wouldn't mind at all, Cuz,' said Lily. 'Perhaps you could go and do some collecting for him.'

'I might as it happens,' he said. 'There's a couple of snarks been spotted in a wood in Kent. And there's a screaming abdab causing a lot of trouble in Newcastle—'

'Seriously, Richard, please don't.'

'Why not?'

'Because you don't know how to drive and you'll probably crash it.'

'D'you think so? Oh I suppose that wouldn't be good, would it?'

Lily was doing her best not to be wound up.

'Archie Queach really doesn't know you're staying here on your own?'

'Not yet.' Richard winked.

Poor Archie. I almost – *almost* – felt sorry for him.

'Here they are!' shouted Lily.

Into the courtyard swept a muddy old Land Rover pulling a trailer. Lily waved and ran forward. Out stepped a tall, good-looking woman with red cheeks and frizzy hair, followed by a dog, then another dog, and then another dog...

Darling, darling, kiss, kiss–

'Mum, this is Jack.'

Lily's mother was the Queen's older sister, and looked exactly how I imagine the Queen might have looked had she become a farmer instead of marrying the King.

'Jack,' she smiled. 'I've been hearing so much about you.' She gazed at me a moment, and I knew what she was thinking.

'What's the trailer for, Mum?'

Lily's mother grinned.

'Your father's been busy twisting Sam Yuell's arm. I'm hoping we have something to take away with us.'

'Like... what?'

'Well you know how lonely Dolly gets on her own.'

Lily stared at her, then her mouth fell open.

'You mean... you *don't* mean–'

'You two want to go riding together, don't you? Sam Yuell said it's okay. The company would do her good.'

Lily squealed with delight. She hugged her mother then turned to me, breathless.

'Jack – *two* unicorns! This is going to be so amazing, seriously...' On she went. I didn't understand half of what she was talking about, but Lily was so excited. She skipped and jumped after her mother as they headed down to the vaults.

'Come on, Jack!' she shouted.

I was about to follow them when I spotted William Foxglass making his way towards me across the busy courtyard. He raised a gloved hand and waved.

'I'll catch you up!' I called, as Lily disappeared through the archway.

William Foxglass took off his hat and smiled, his hazel eyes twinkling.

'Well, Jack. Look at you.'

I'd changed, I'll admit. What with all this palace food and exercise I was growing fast. And even better than that, for the first time in my life I had hair! Richard and I had shared a bottle of 'Grizzle-Up' that Umballoo had found for him in the Sable Tower. It was an unwanted present from Coatless Curly Macgregor, a Canadian explorer who used to impersonate bears, and it was working already. I'd cut my hair into a bob and parted it at the side, just like my mother's.

'Have you been enjoying yourself?'

I smiled. What could I say?

'It's been amazing. Thank you for bringing me here, Mr Foxglass.'

'This is where you belong, Jack,' he said, smiling that topsy-turvy smile of his. 'For better or worse, this is where you're meant to be.' He hesitated, and I thought he was about to say goodbye. Instead he said, 'Actually, there's someone here who'd very much like to meet you. Have you got a minute?'

'Who is it?'

'Oh, just a friend. He's round the back.'

I glanced at the archway. No sign of Lily or Sam Yuell.

'A friend? Of yours?' I said, looking into William Foxglass's foxy face.

'That's right. He'd like to introduce himself.'

Okay. William Foxglass led the way back through the courtyards across to the keepers' side, then along the passages and cloisters I knew so well till we reached the narrow cobbled alley at the very back of the palace. At one end stood the large bricked-up gateway, at the other The Black Coat Inn.

'In here,' he said, ducking inside.

Groups of keepers sat drinking in the smoky darkness. They looked up at me curiously as William Foxglass hunted amongst the tables.

'Strange, he was here only a moment ago,' he said. 'I suppose he might've gone outside. Shall we check?'

I followed him out into the tiny walled garden behind the inn. It was empty.

'I wonder where he's got to,' said William Foxglass, scratching his head.

Walking over to a narrow arched door, almost hidden in the ivy, he opened it and we went out into a little alley. On both sides were high brick walls, and there was an old street light at the end. Apart from that, this too was empty.

'I don't suppose this "friend" is Captain Kazeem, by any chance?' I asked, beginning to wonder what we were doing here.

'Captain Kazeem?'

'Yes. My father, obviously. Is it? Oh!'

I turned around and the doorway we had just come through had disappeared. Completely gone. There was no trace of it at all.

'Oh it does that,' mumbled William Foxglass. 'This is the keepers' other entrance. I'm afraid Asphodel was right; the palace is still full of Isabella Royle's spies. You can't keep any secrets in there at all. Maybe that's why he's come outside. It's safer.'

'But he's not here.'

'No. That's strange. He isn't.'

At this moment I confess I felt a twinge of fear. I wasn't certain what was going on. William Foxglass was just standing there, looking up and down the empty alley, waiting... for what?

'So... would you still like to meet him, Jack?'

I looked at him, thinking what kind of a question is that?

'Of course I want to meet my father; I've always wanted to meet him. But he doesn't want to meet me, does he?'

'That's not true.'

'Isn't it? Why does he keep running away then?'

'He doesn't.'

William Foxglass was still acting very mysteriously. He wasn't explaining anything. To be honest, this was all starting to get slightly weird.

'Maybe we should just go back inside. It doesn't matter. I don't care if—'

'No wait, wait a minute.' William Foxglass was staring at me intently now. 'The thing is, Jack, it's hard to know how to say this without sounding very foolish.'

I wasn't being deliberately stupid, I promise you, I really wasn't. But it was only at this moment that I started to have an inkling of the truth. William Foxglass was looking at me, and I was looking at him, trying to read his strange expression.

'It's... you? *You* are Captain Kazeem?'

He nodded, smiling that topsy-turvy smile.

'So, wait a minute... *you* are my dad?'

'That's right. I am. Your dad.'

My mouth fell open in shock. I couldn't speak.

'But... why should I believe you?'

'Hari Kazeem is my real name. I changed it to William Foxglass the day I stepped through the palace gates when I was seven years old. I am your dad. Your real dad.'

I didn't know what to think. I stared into those hazel eyes, that watchful face. For the first time, I looked at his thick black hair and his olive complexion in a different way…

'You're definitely not joking, are you?'

'I've never been more serious in my life. I've been wanting to tell you for a long, long time, Jack. But it was too complicated.'

And the funny thing is, at that moment, I couldn't have been happier. My heart felt like it was going to explode. *William Foxglass was my dad.* I couldn't stop smiling. I just couldn't stop smiling. I looked down at his gloved hand.

'That's why you pulled me from the flames. That's how you burnt your hand, isn't it? That's the real reason?'

'Of course it is. You're my daughter, Jack. I'd do anything for you. Anything in the whole wide world.'

That did it. I ran to him and he opened his arms and I hugged him tight — so tight. I had a dad! A real, proper, living dad! Actually I was quite tearful, to tell the truth. I realised that this was the moment I'd been longing for my entire life. I noticed that William Foxglass's eyes had gone a little misty too.

'Does anyone else know?'

'Only the Queen. Marina told her everything.'

I nodded. Somehow that didn't surprise me.

'But this has to stay a secret, understand? Nobody else knows, and they don't need to.'

I understood. Thad Lancaster, the King… not even Asphodel knew this.

'It's none of their business, is it?' I said.

'None at all. And that's how your mum would've wanted it.'

I hugged him again. Perhaps it was greedy, but now I had a father I could suddenly imagine having a mother too, and how that might've been, the three of us together as a family… a real family… I closed my eyes as I held him, and suddenly I felt very sad about that. If only she'd read his scribbled note; if only she'd known I'd survived, then maybe, maybe… There was no point going over it all again. It could never happen now. I wiped my eyes and smiled.

'Why did you change your name?'

William Foxglass grinned in that topsy-turvy way of his.

'It's a long story, Jack,' he said. 'William Foxglass suits me better now. And of course, Hari Kazeem is still around, in his way,' he winked. 'One day I'll tell you, if you like.'

I would like that. And there was something else I wanted to know.

'Tell me honestly, was I brought here to be a double for Richard at his presentation?'

'Absolutely not.'

'Even though you knew I'd taken his place?'

'I did?'

'You called me Jack when you rescued me from the burning carriage. Remember?'

William Foxglass had forgotten. He smiled sheepishly.

'No, Jack,' he said. 'You were out there that day because of who *you* are. It had nothing to do with me, or anyone else. I would much rather you weren't risking your life to save your friends. But you're very brave and special person. It's true,' he nodded, seeing my embarrassment. 'I mean you've even sworn to become the next *king* of Albion. D'you really think I could have planned all that?'

I stared into his foxy face. I suppose it didn't matter. At that moment I would have forgiven him anything at all. William Foxglass was my dad. I had to pinch myself. I didn't ever want to let him go.

'So, Jack,' he said after a bit. 'I was wondering whether you'd like to do a spot of dragon riding?'

'Dragon riding?' That sounded dangerous. 'But aren't they all bad-tempered, smelly and horrible?'

'Oh no. That's just Albion's dragons. Italian dragons are delightful. Small. Acrobatic. They eat daisies and buttercups. Sometimes the odd pizza—'

'Pizza?' I laughed.

'Of course. Couldn't be nicer.'

Dragon riding with my dad. Wow. And then I remembered. 'You mean *now*?'

'I was sort of thinking of now, it being the start of the holidays. Unless you've got something better to do. Have you?'

I told him. William Foxglass (I suppose I should call him Dad now) was silent. I could tell he was disappointed.

'I can't just miss it, can I?'

'No, I suppose you can't. Go with Lily, Jack, go and have some fun. You deserve it.'

I looked at him. That smile was so mysterious.

'You don't mind?'

'Not a bit. Go and enjoy yourself. But I will come and visit you. That's a promise.'

So that is how my summer holidays began – in the best possible way.

What happened next? 'All's well that ends well,' as Asphodel might have said. I did come to Scotland, and Lily was right, it has rained almost every day. Never mind, we've done all those crazy things that Lily promised, and yes, Richard probably would have hated it. Though I think even *he* might have enjoyed riding unicorns. There's something about galloping through the woods, not quite touching the ground... it's almost like flying.

And now it's six o'clock in the morning. The candle has burnt out, the first rays of sunshine are turning the dripping forest golden, and I think I've finished. I made a promise to myself that I'd write it all down exactly as I remembered it. I think it's done. But what shall the last words of this book be? I so want them to be something clever and funny, the sort of thing Richard might say... only my mind's gone blank. I'm so tired, all I can think of is the wildly original...

'The End'

Except it wasn't, quite. At that moment something large and silent flapped past the window and landed down on the lawn in front of the castle. A dragon! A sleek green dragon, with shining silver scales down its spine... A moment later its calf appeared – a smaller, ganglier version of itself. William Foxglass jumped off the mother and caught the young one. He stroked its nose reassuringly and led it forward, looking up at the windows.

'Da–' I shouted... and then I remembered. 'Mr Foxglass!'

He spotted me waving and pressed a finger to his lips.

'Want to take him for a ride before breakfast?' he whispered. 'His name's Rondolfo. A Venetian Silverwing. Very friendly.'

I stared down at the beautiful young dragon prancing about. How could I say no?

'Put a jumper on,' he smiled. 'It's still a bit chilly.'

I'm scribbling these words down as fast as I can, because I have a funny feeling this adventure is going to go on and on... in fact, I might even need a new notebook.

Now that's a much better ending, isn't it?

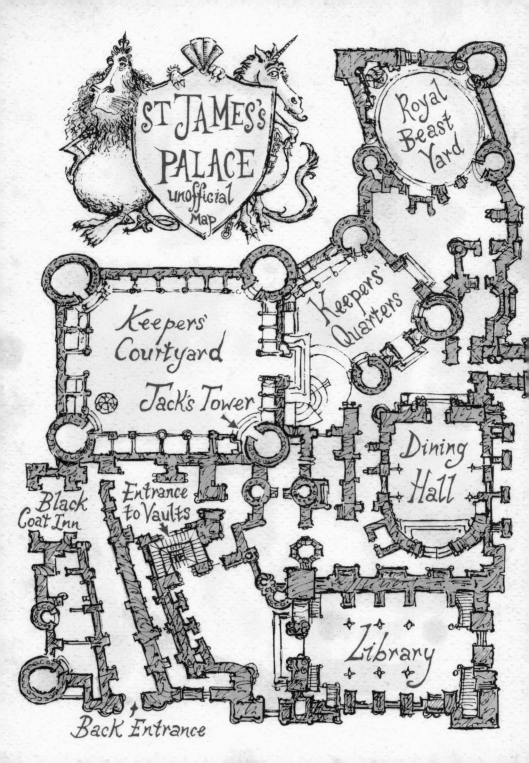